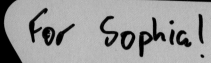

The Unfinished CORNER

For Sophia!

WRITTEN BY
DANI COLMAN

ILLUSTRATED BY
RACHEL "TUNA" PETROVICZ

COLORED BY
WHITNEY COGAR

LETTERED BY
JIM CAMPBELL

DESIGNED BY
BONES LEOPARD

EDITED BY
REBECCA TAYLOR

WONDERBOUND™

In loving memory of Rabbi Dr. Jeremy Collick.

שָׁלוֹם עָלֶיךָ אֲדוֹנֵינוּ מוֹרֵנוּ וְרַבֵּנוּ עָלֶיךָ הַשָּׁלוֹם מֵעַתָּה וְעַד עוֹלָם.

Wonderbound
Publisher Damian A. Wassel
Editor-in-Chief Adrian F. Wassel
Art Director Nathan C. Gooden
EVP Branding & Design Tim Daniel
Managing Editor Rebecca Taylor
Sales & Marketing, Direct Market David Dissanayake
Sales & Marketing, Book Trade Syndee Barwick
Production Manager Ian Baldessari
Principal Damian A. Wassel Sr.

PROLOGUE

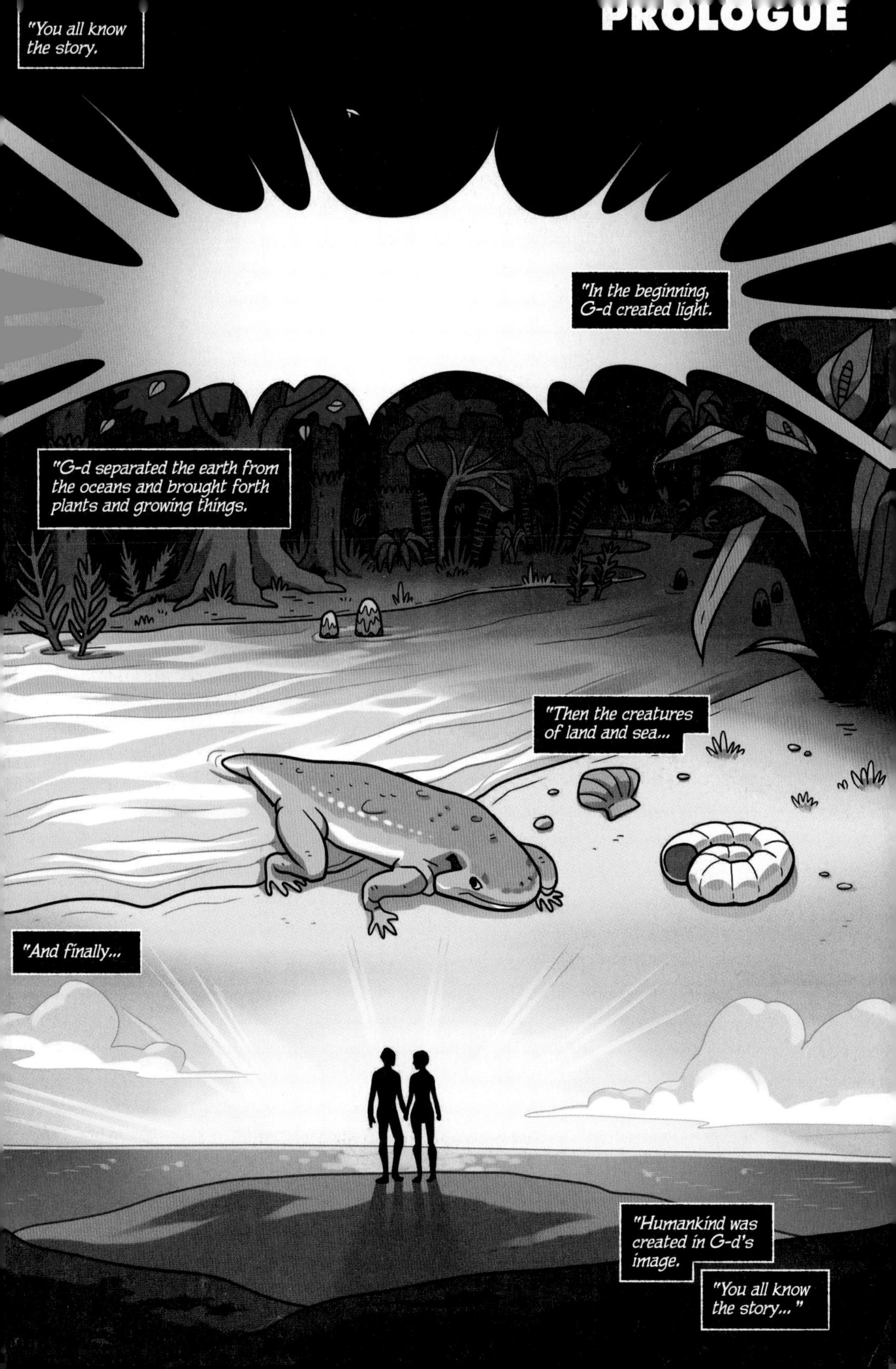
"You all know the story.
"In the beginning, G-d created light.
"G-d separated the earth from the oceans and brought forth plants and growing things.
"Then the creatures of land and sea...
"And finally...
"Humankind was created in G-d's image.
"You all know the story..."

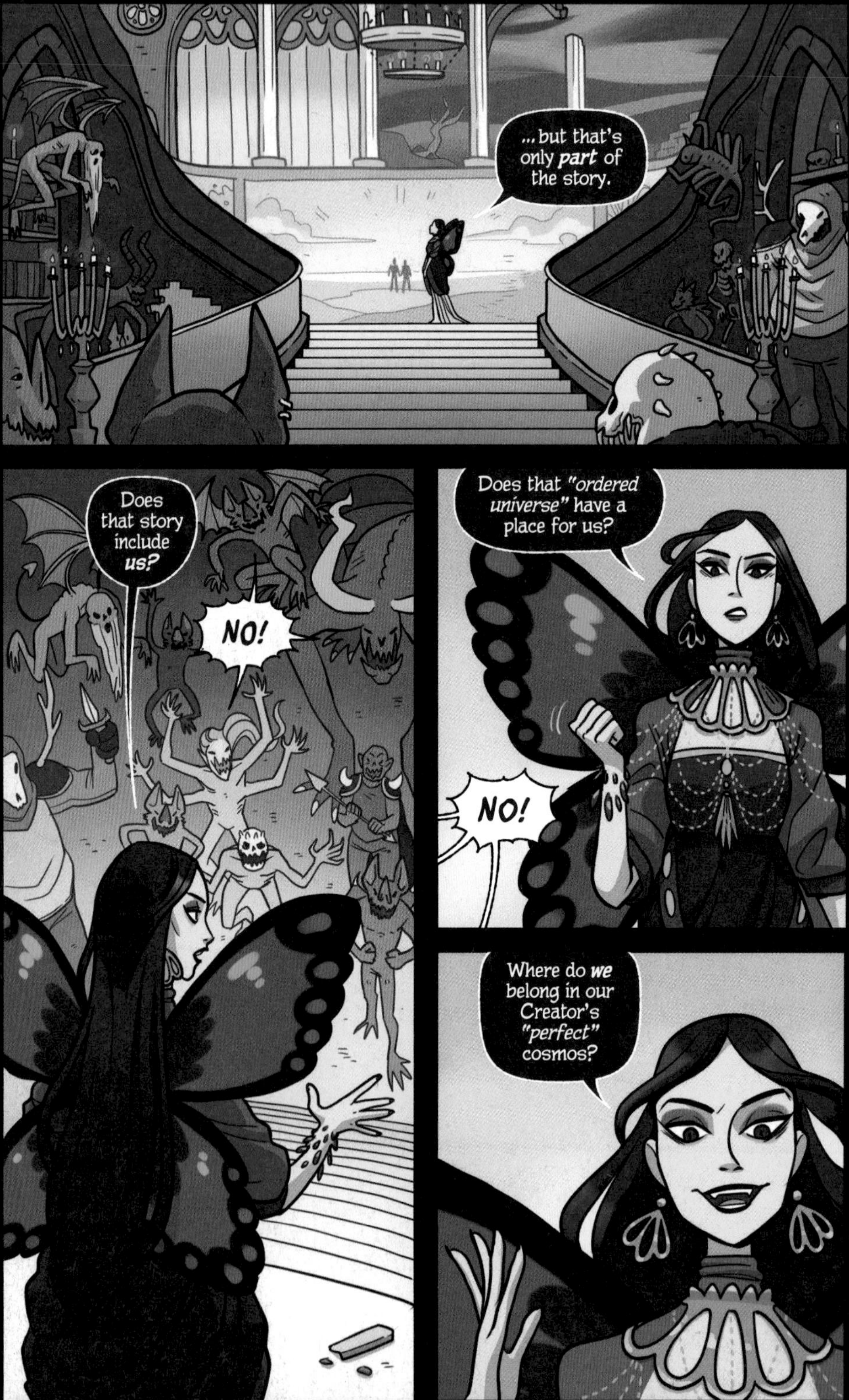
...but that's only *part* of the story.
Does that story include *us?*
NO!
Does that *"ordered universe"* have a place for us?
NO!
Where do *we* belong in our Creator's *"perfect"* cosmos?

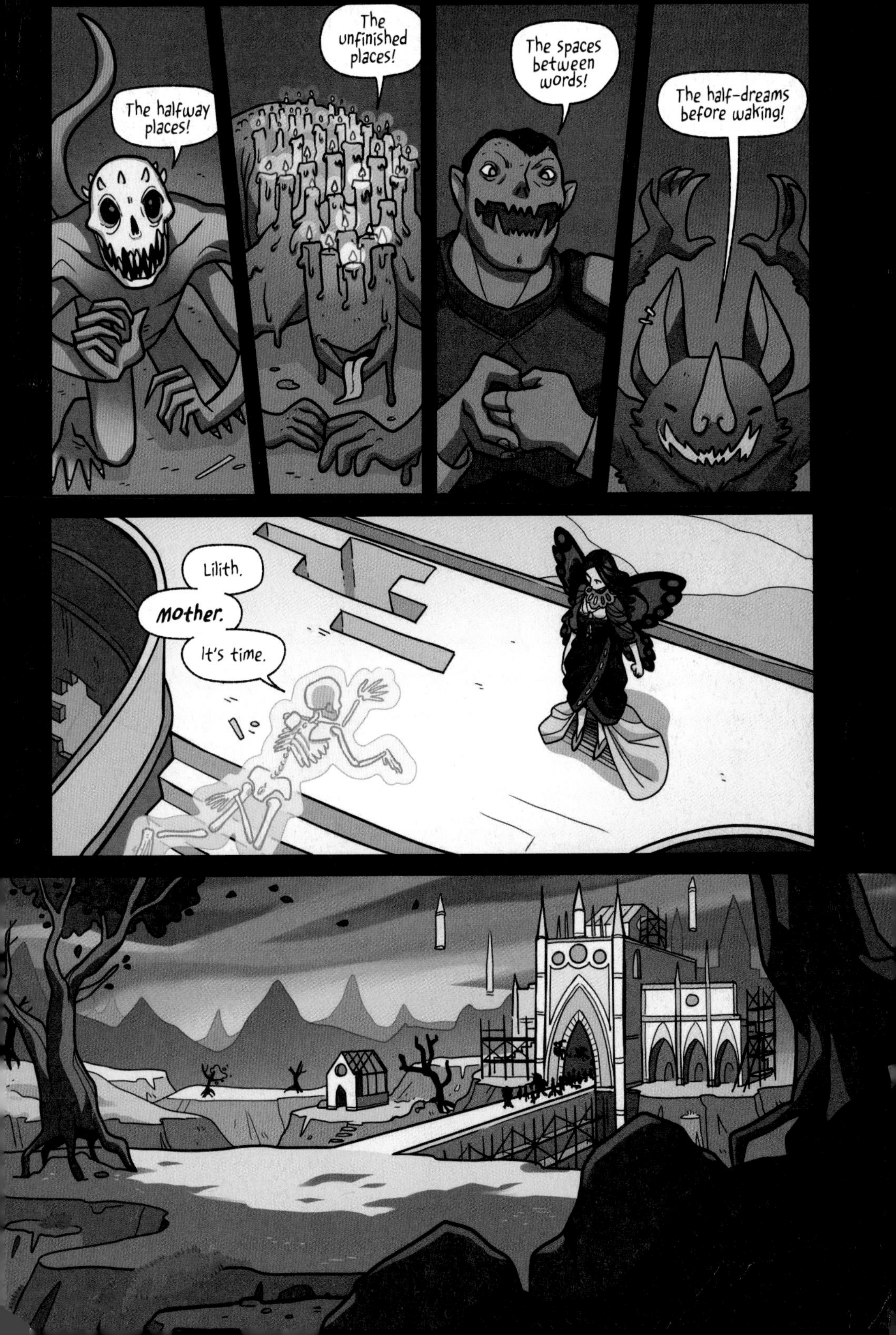
The halfway places!
The unfinished places!
The spaces between words!
The half-dreams before waking!
Lilith.
Mother.
It's time.

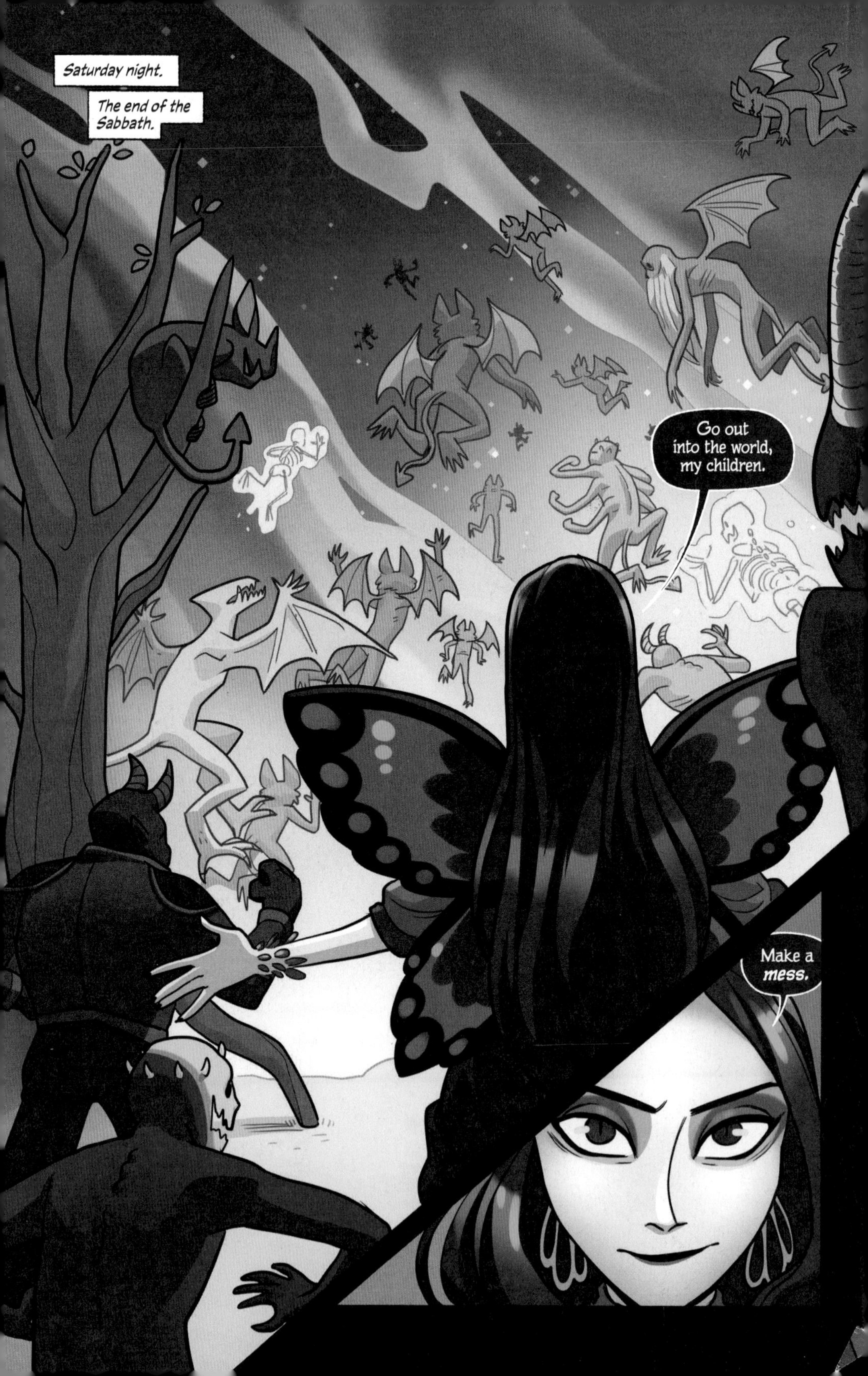
Saturday night.
The end of the Sabbath.
Go out into the world, my children.
Make a *mess.*

CHAPTER ONE

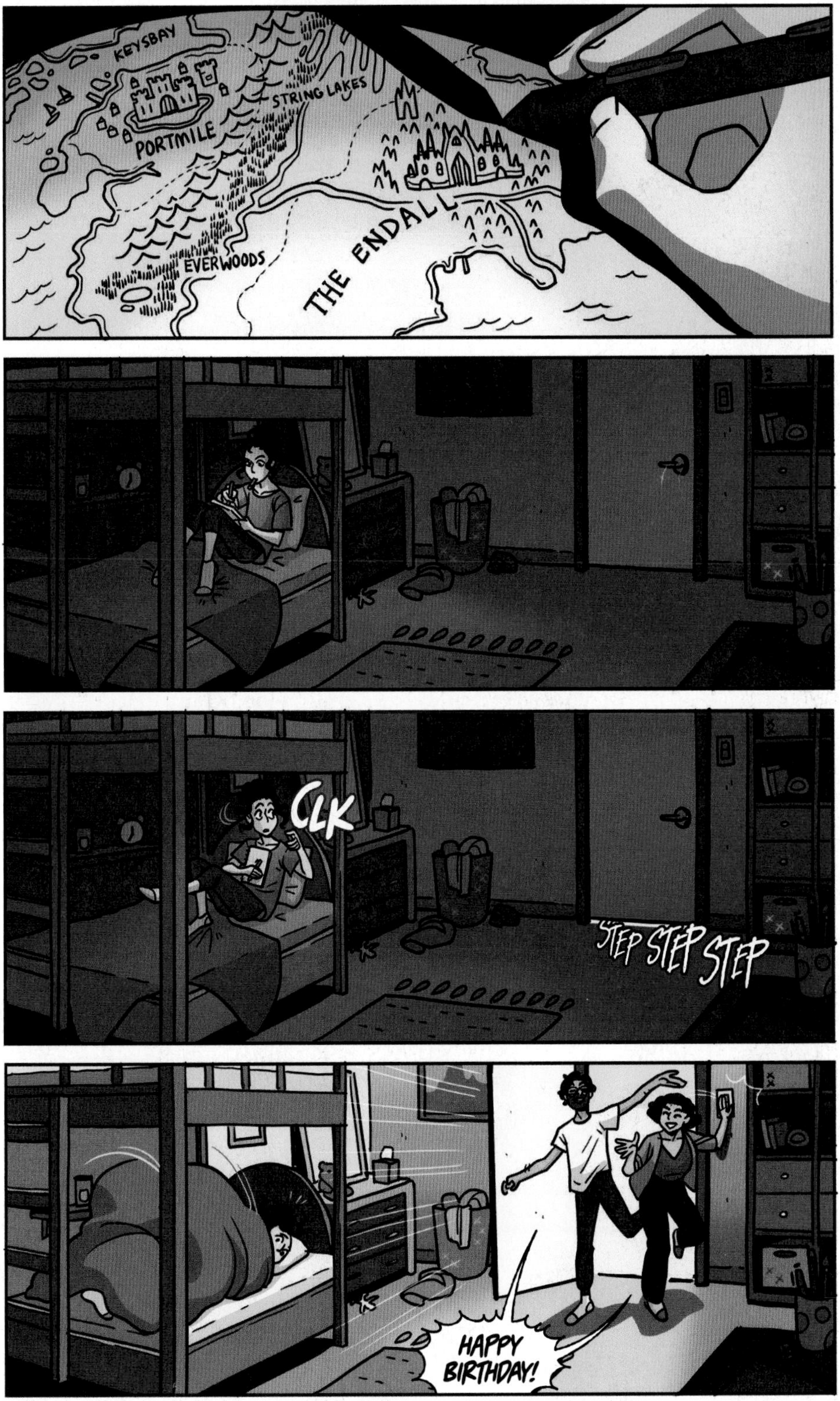

KEYSBAY
PORTMILE
STRING LAKES
EVERWOODS
THE ENDALL
CLK
STEP STEP STEP
HAPPY BIRTHDAY!

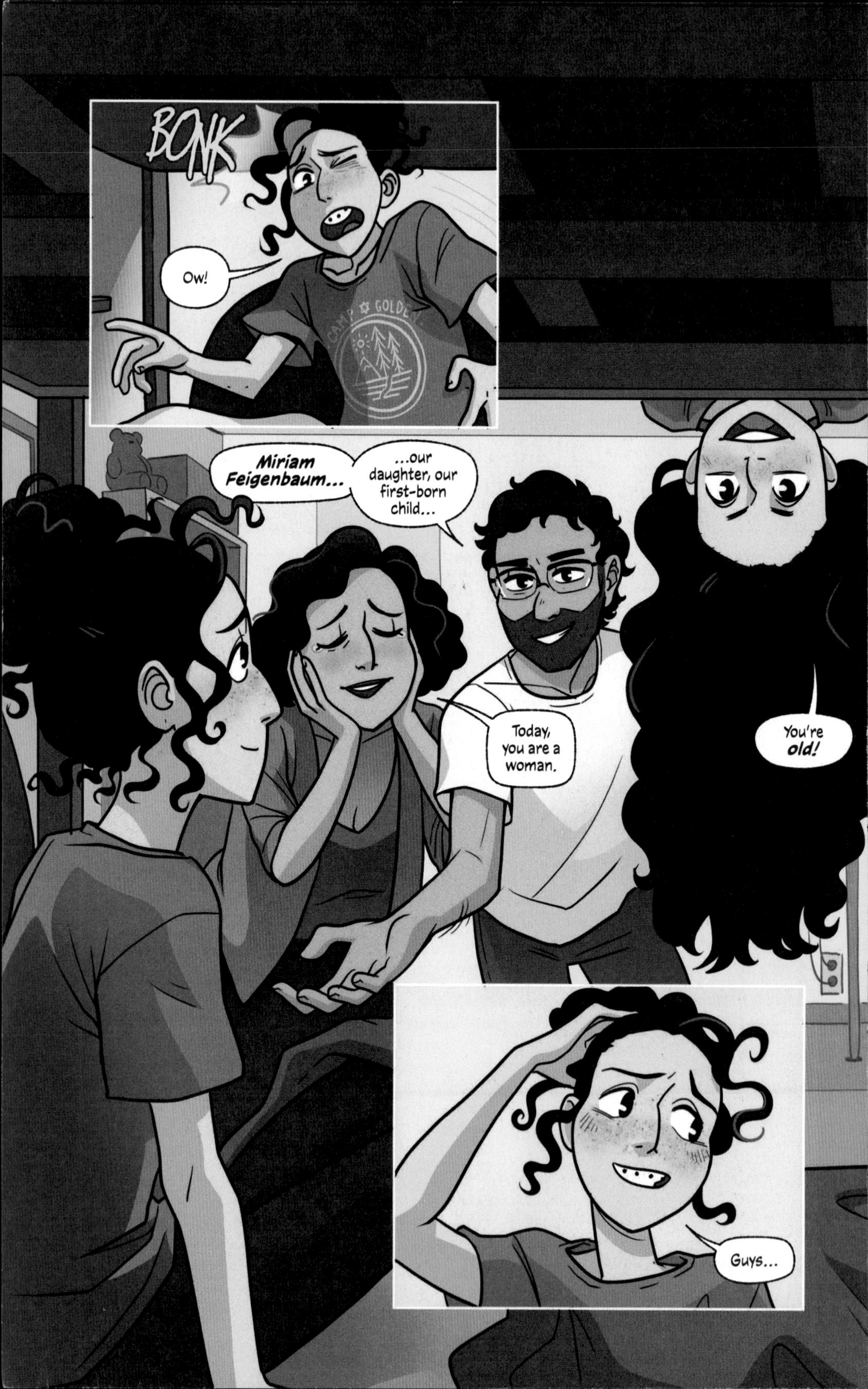
BONK
Ow!
CAMP ✡ GOLDEN
Miriam Feigenbaum...
...our daughter, our first-born child...
Today, you are a woman.
You're old!
Guys...

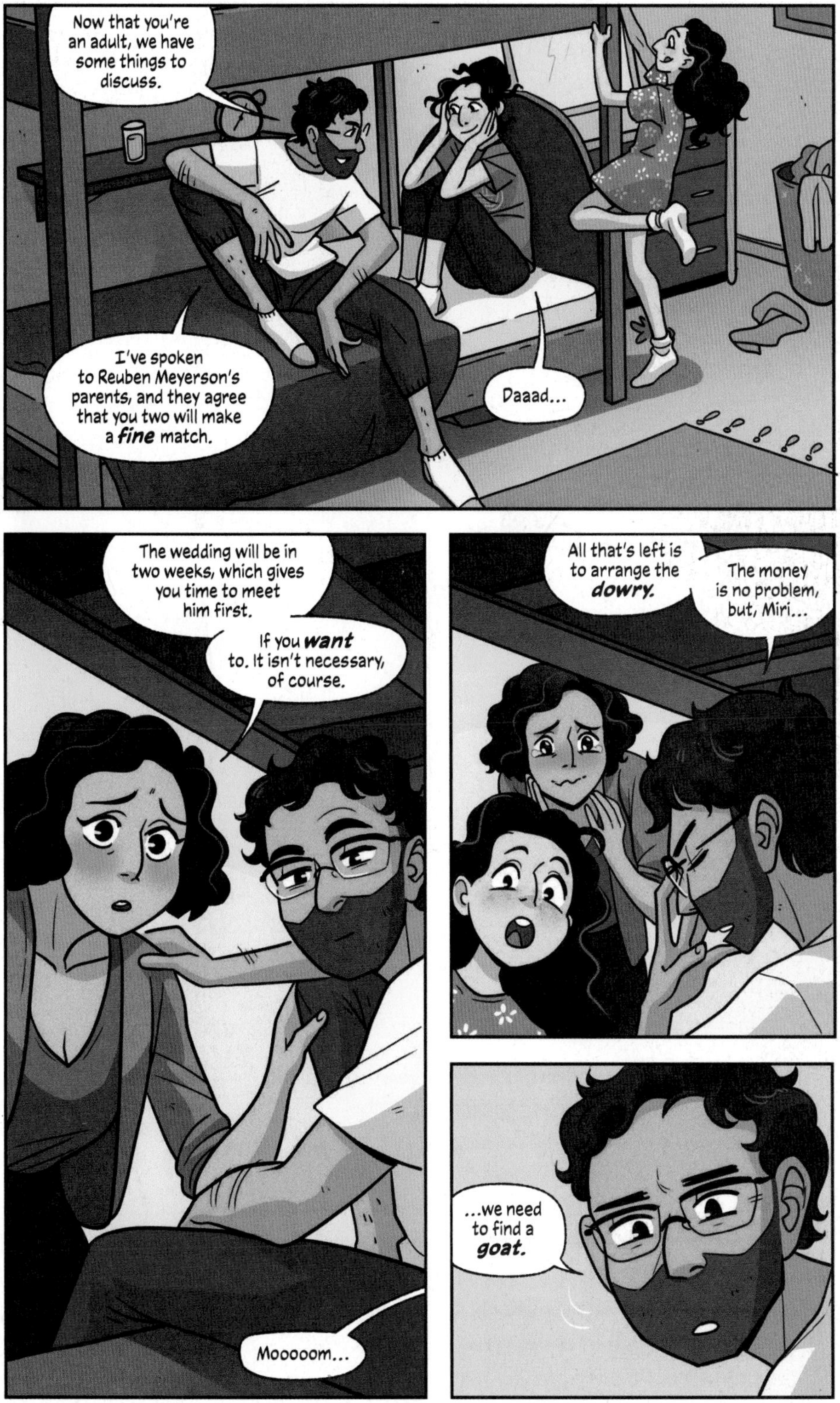
Now that you're an adult, we have some things to discuss.
I've spoken to Reuben Meyerson's parents, and they agree that you two will make a *fine* match.
Daaad...
The wedding will be in two weeks, which gives you time to meet him first.
If you *want* to. It isn't necessary, of course.
Mooooom...
All that's left is to arrange the *dowry.*
The money is no problem, but, Miri...
...we need to find a *goat.*

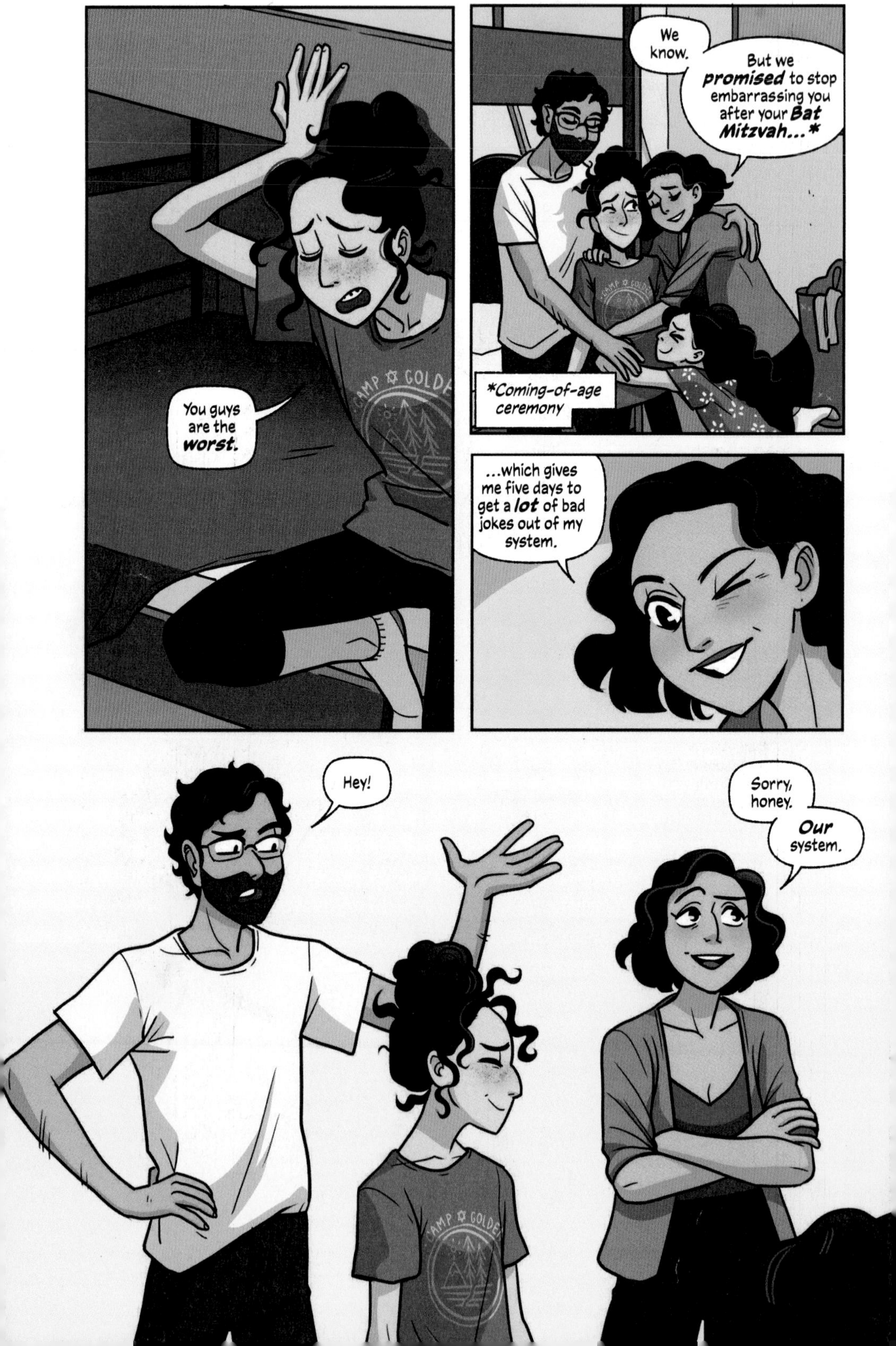
You guys are the *worst.*
We know.
But we **promised** to stop embarrassing you after your **Bat Mitzvah...***
*Coming-of-age ceremony
...which gives me five days to get a *lot* of bad jokes out of my system.
Hey!
Sorry, honey.
Our system.

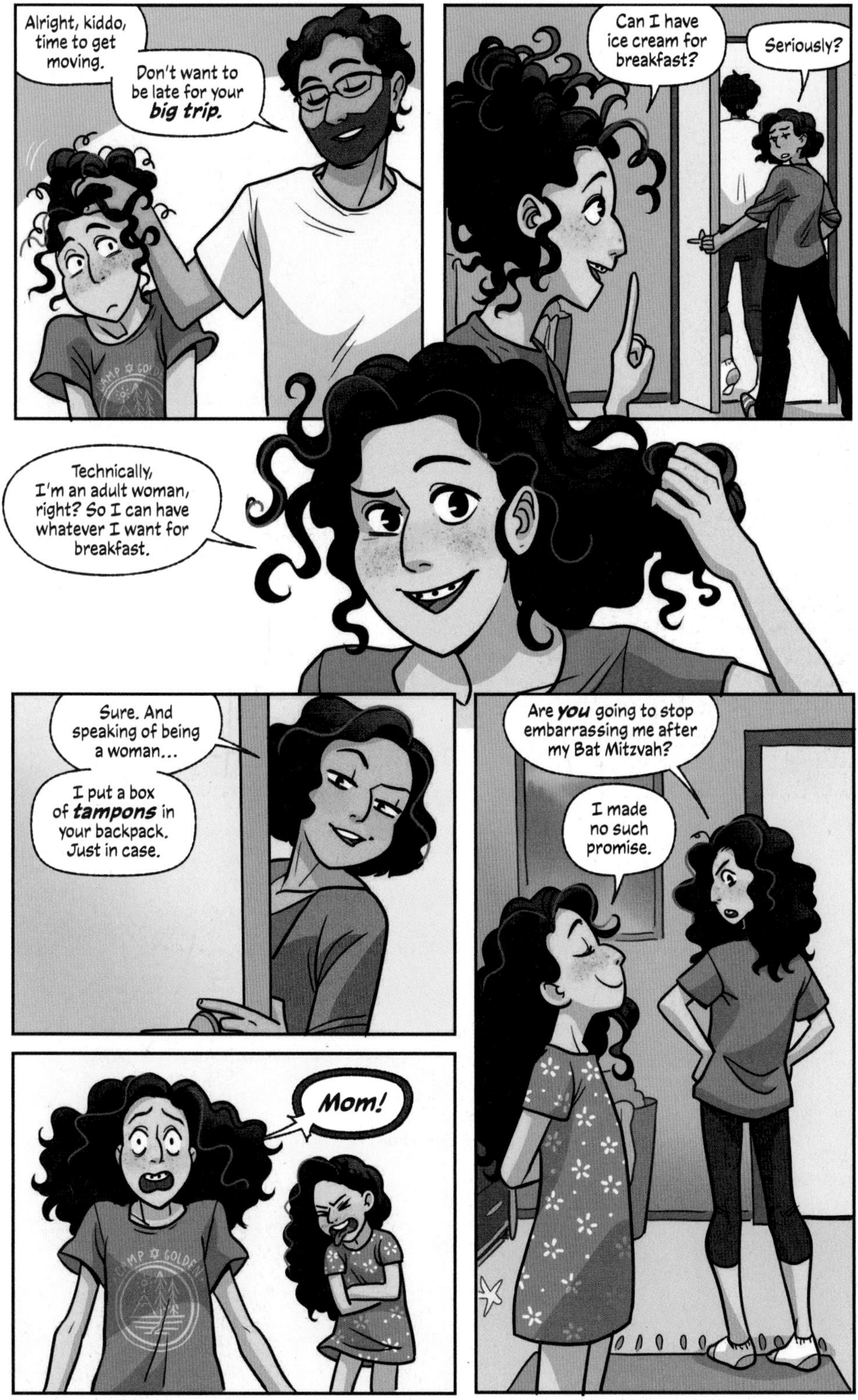

Alright, kiddo, time to get moving.
Don't want to be late for your **big trip.**
Can I have ice cream for breakfast?
Seriously?
Technically, I'm an adult woman, right? So I can have whatever I want for breakfast.
Sure. And speaking of being a woman...
I put a box of ***tampons*** in your backpack. Just in case.
Are ***you*** going to stop embarrassing me after my Bat Mitzvah?
I made no such promise.
Mom!
CAMP ✡ GOLDEN

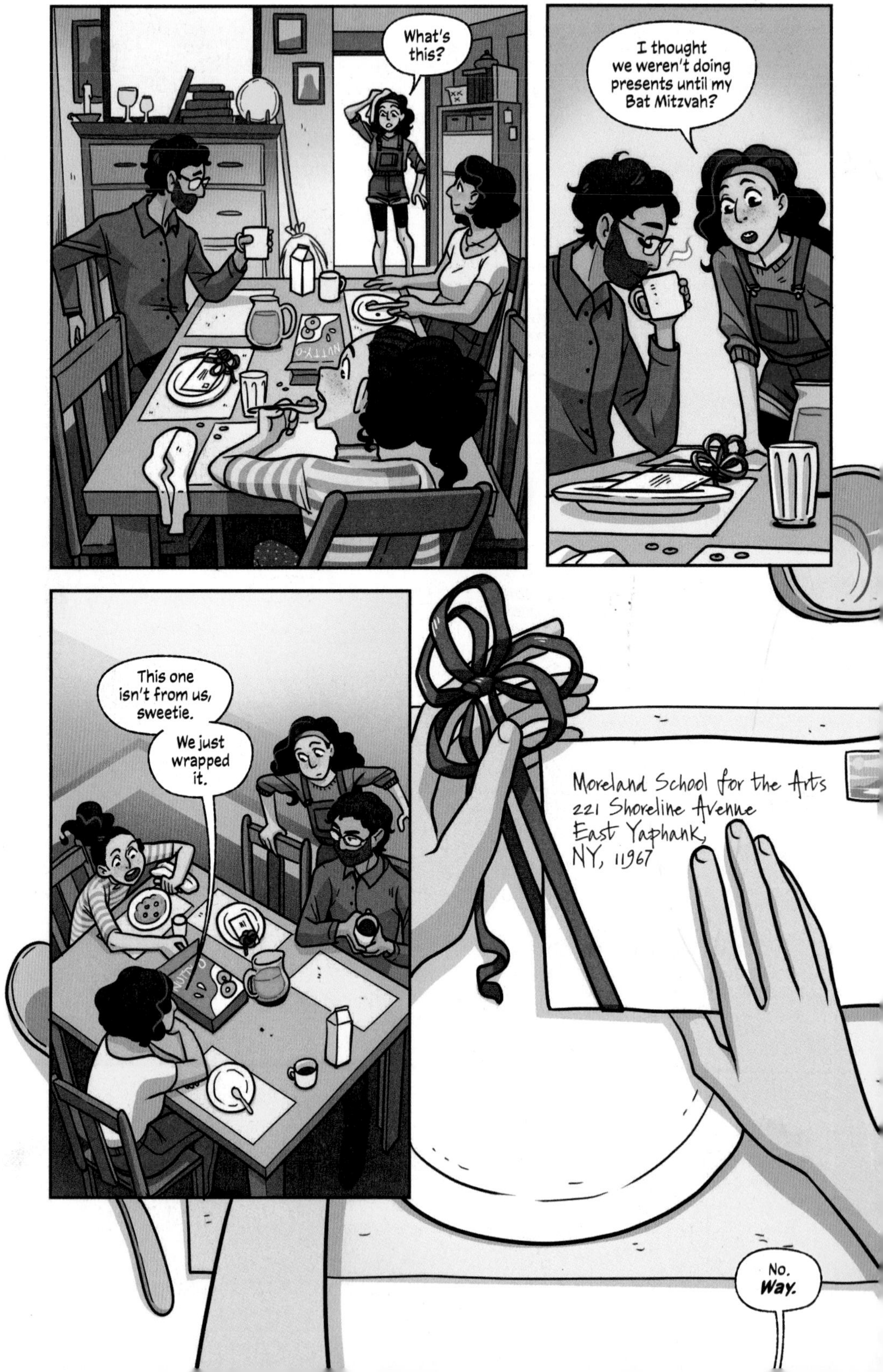
What's this?
I thought we weren't doing presents until my Bat Mitzvah?
This one isn't from us, sweetie.
We just wrapped it.
NUTTY-O
Moreland School for the Arts
221 Shoreline Avenue
East Yaphank,
NY, 11967
No. *Way.*

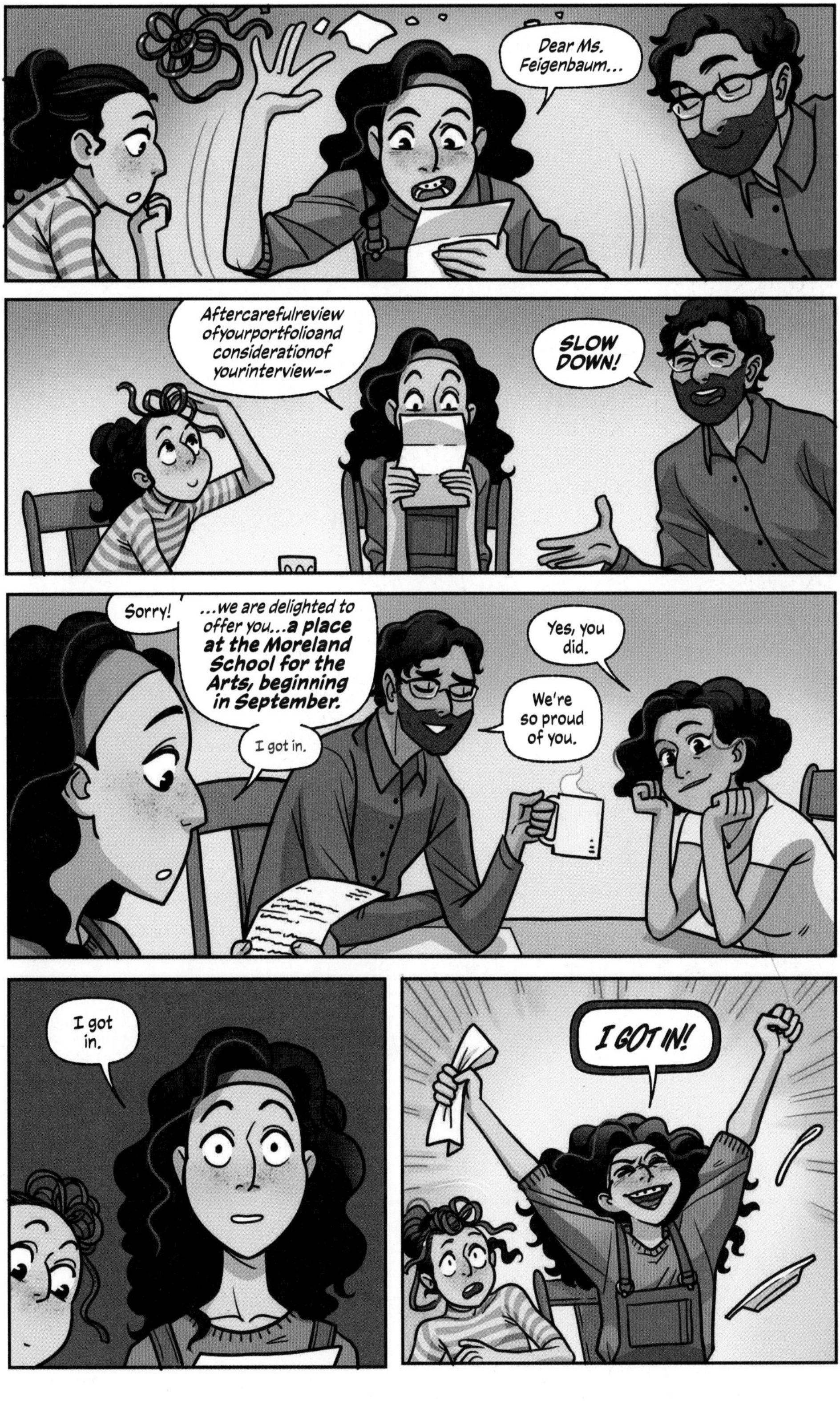
Dear Ms. Feigenbaum...
Aftercarefulreview ofyourportfolioand considerationof yourinterview--
SLOW DOWN!
Sorry!
...we are delighted to offer you...a place at the Moreland School for the Arts, beginning in September.
I got in.
We're so proud of you.
Yes, you did.
I got in.
I GOT IN!

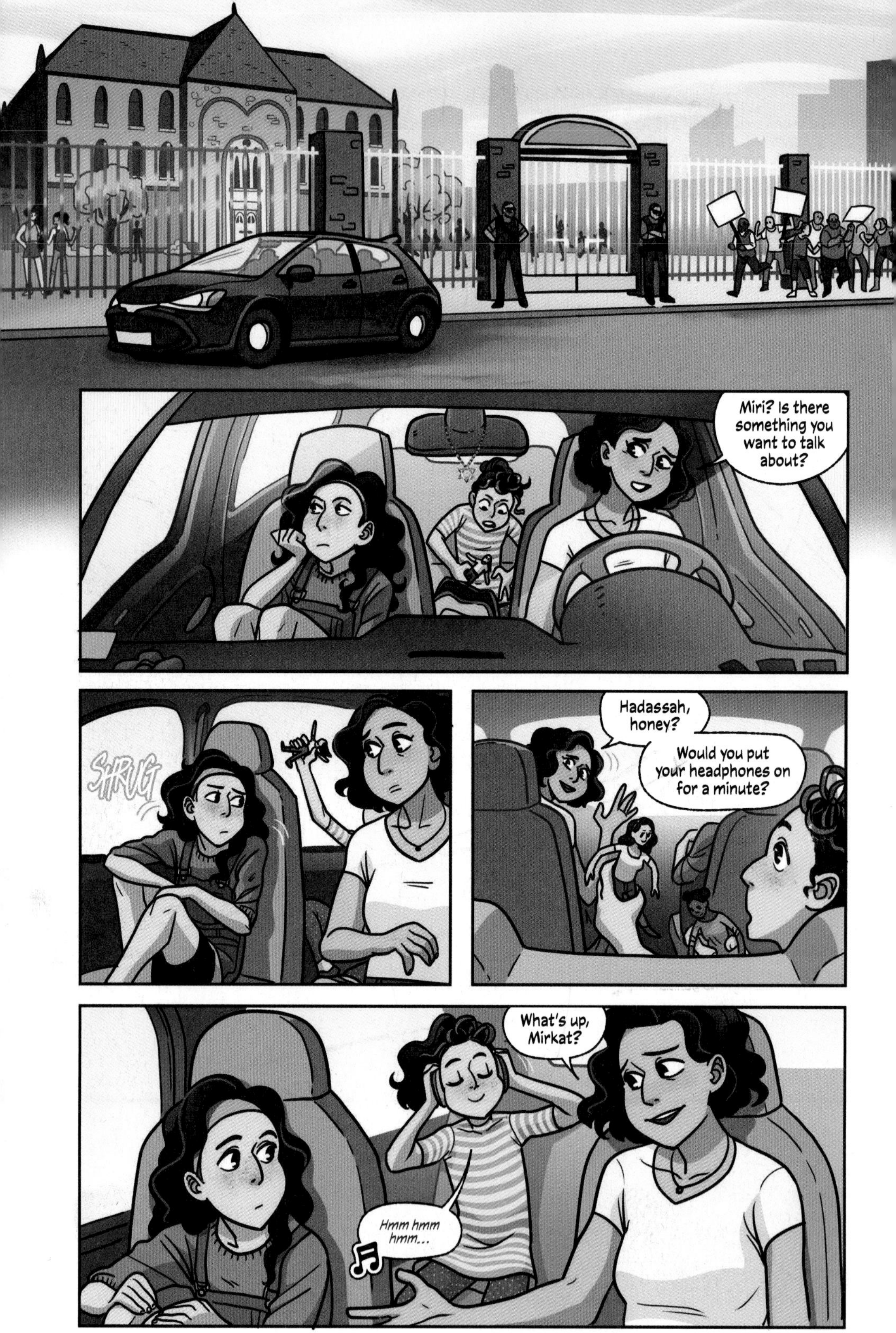
Miri? Is there something you want to talk about?
SHRUG
Hadassah, honey?
Would you put your headphones on for a minute?
What's up, Mirkat?
Hmm hmm hmm...

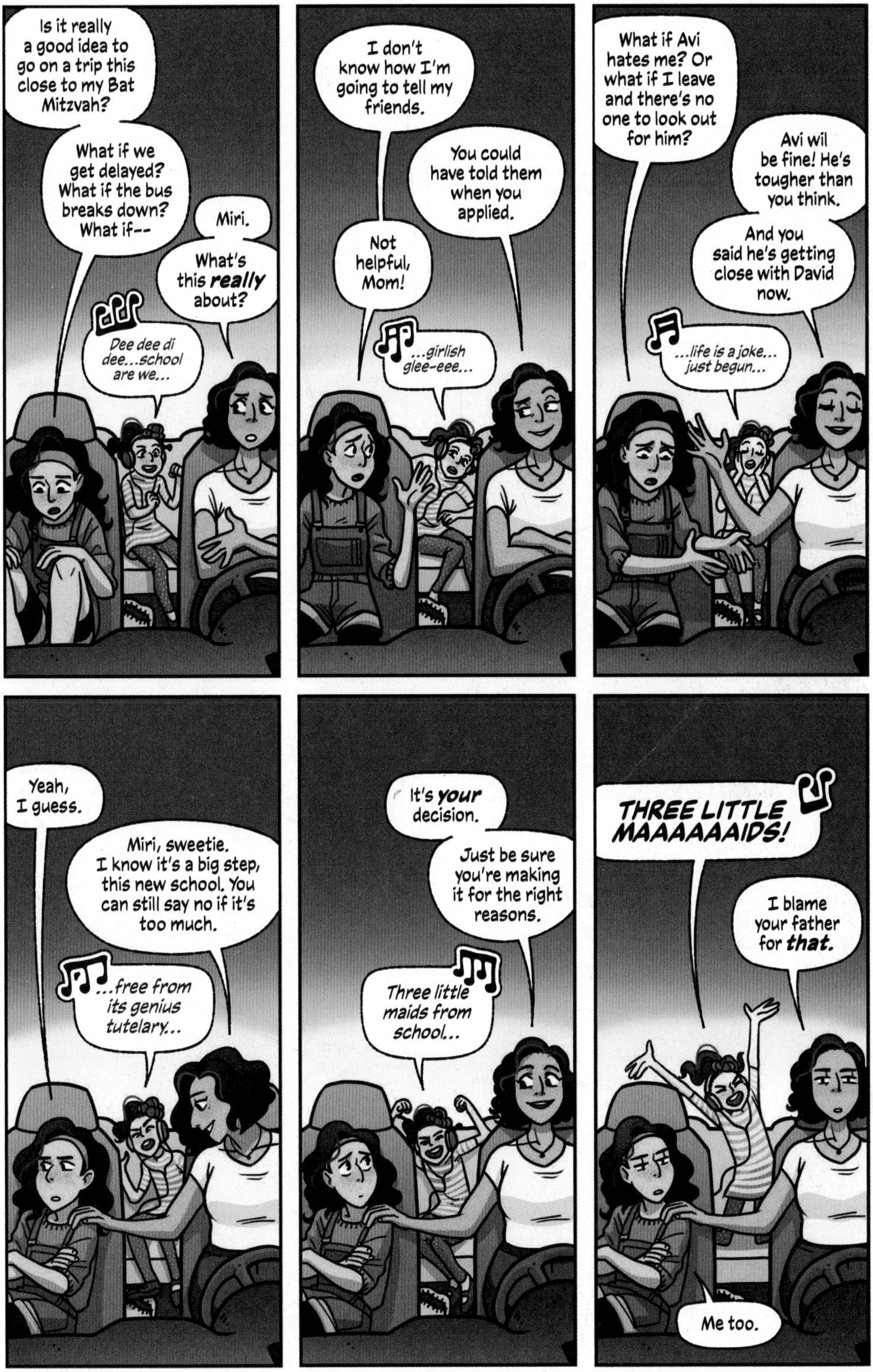
Is it really a good idea to go on a trip this close to my Bat Mitzvah?
What if we get delayed? What if the bus breaks down? What if--
Miri.
What's this *really* about?
Dee dee di dee...school are we...
I don't know how I'm going to tell my friends.
You could have told them when you applied.
Not helpful, Mom!
...girlish glee-eee...
What if Avi hates me? Or what if I leave and there's no one to look out for him?
Avi wil be fine! He's tougher than you think.
And you said he's getting close with David now.
...life is a joke... just begun...
Yeah, I guess.
Miri, sweetie. I know it's a big step, this new school. You can still say no if it's too much.
...free from its genius tutelary...
It's *your* decision.
Just be sure you're making it for the right reasons.
Three little maids from school...
THREE LITTLE MAAAAAAIDS!
I blame your father for *that*.
Me too.

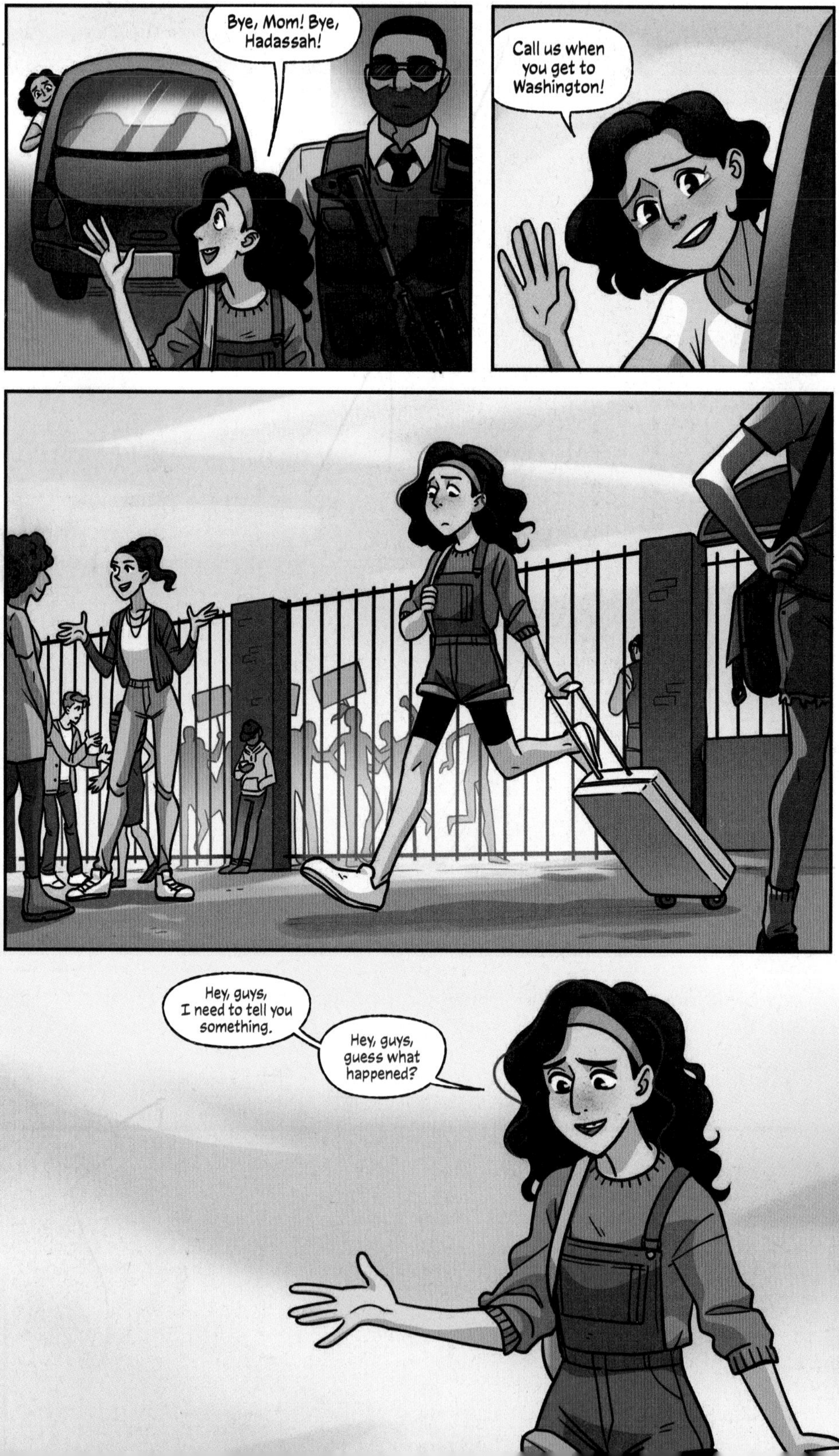
Bye, Mom! Bye, Hadassah!
Call us when you get to Washington!
Hey, guys, I need to tell you something.
Hey, guys, guess what happened?

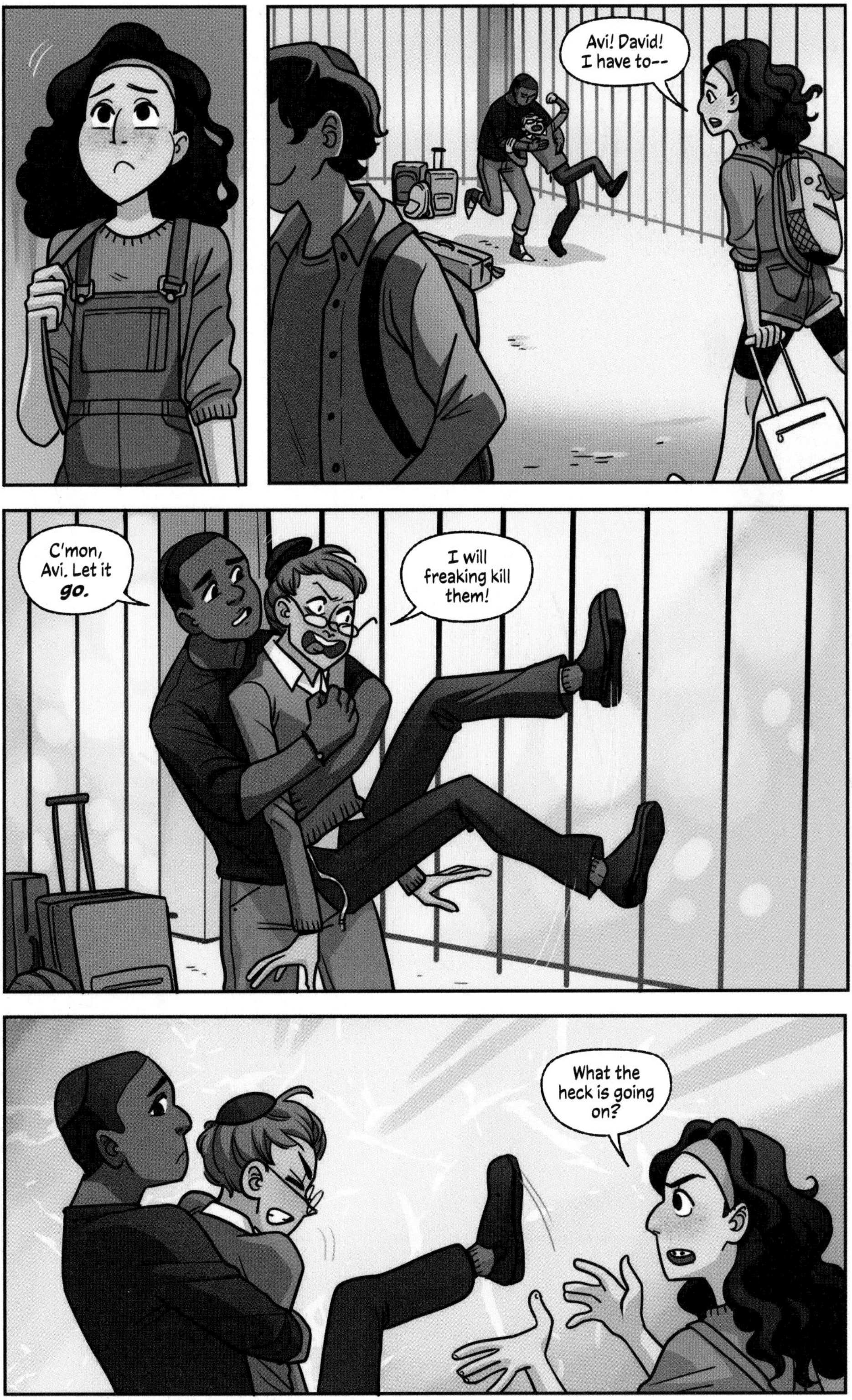
Avi! David! I have to--
C'mon, Avi. Let it *go.*
I will freaking kill them!
What the heck is going on?

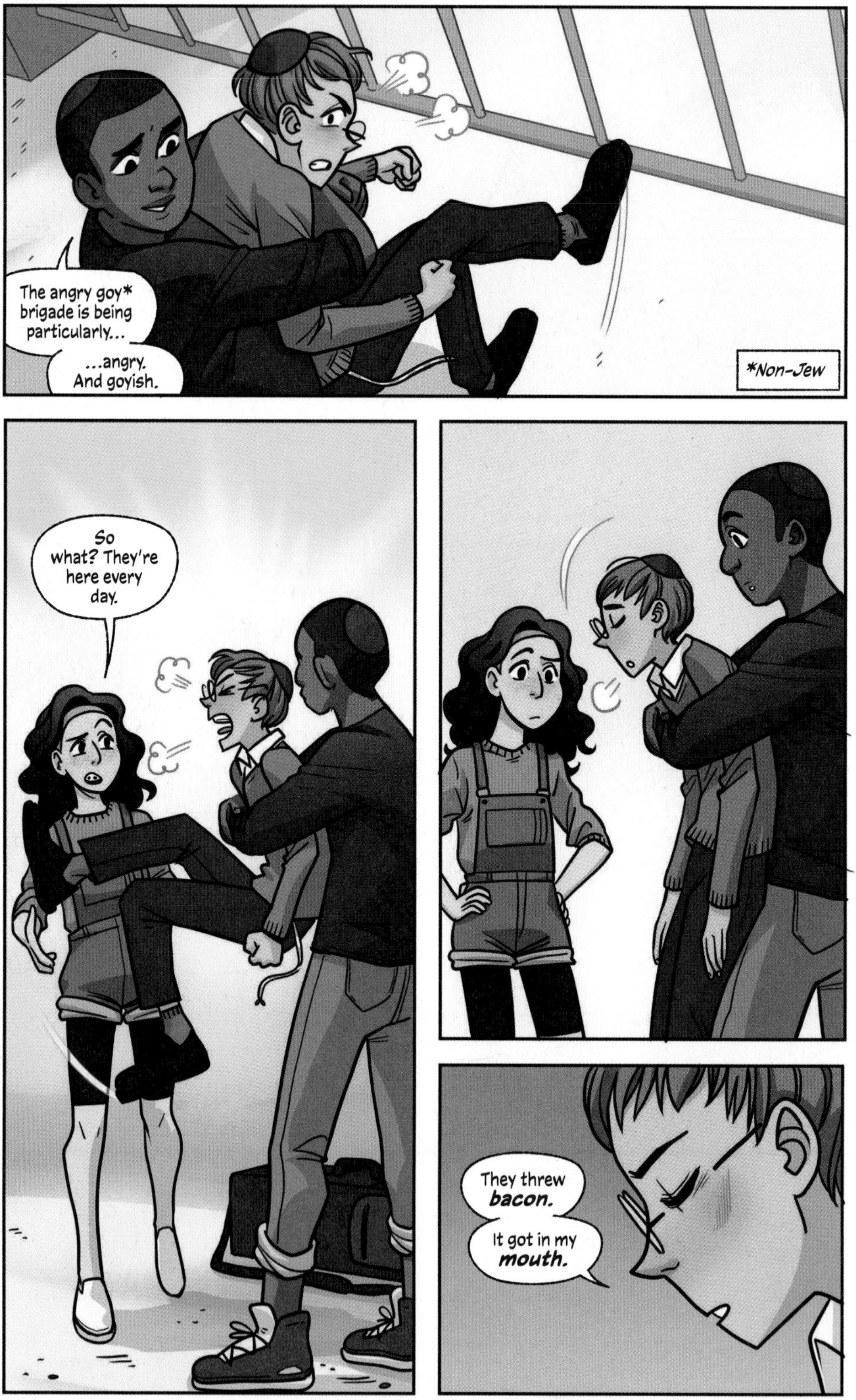
The angry goy* brigade is being particularly...
...angry. And goyish.
*Non-Jew
So what? They're here every day.
They threw **bacon.**
It got in my **mouth.**

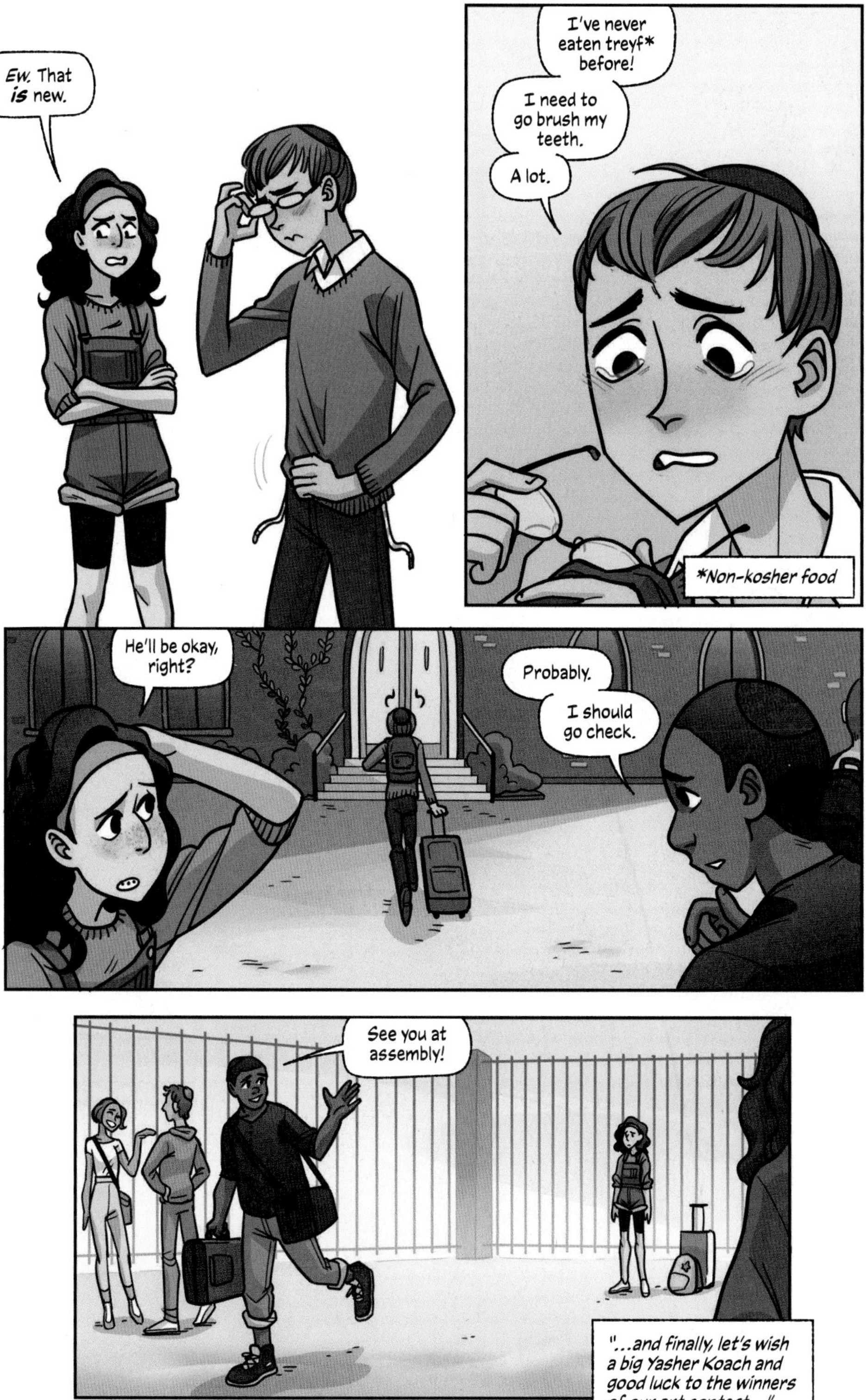

Ew. That ***is*** new.
I've never eaten treyf* before!
I need to go brush my teeth.
A lot.
*Non-kosher food
He'll be okay, right?
Probably.
I should go check.
See you at assembly!
"...and finally, let's wish a big Yasher Koach and good luck to the winners of our art contest..."

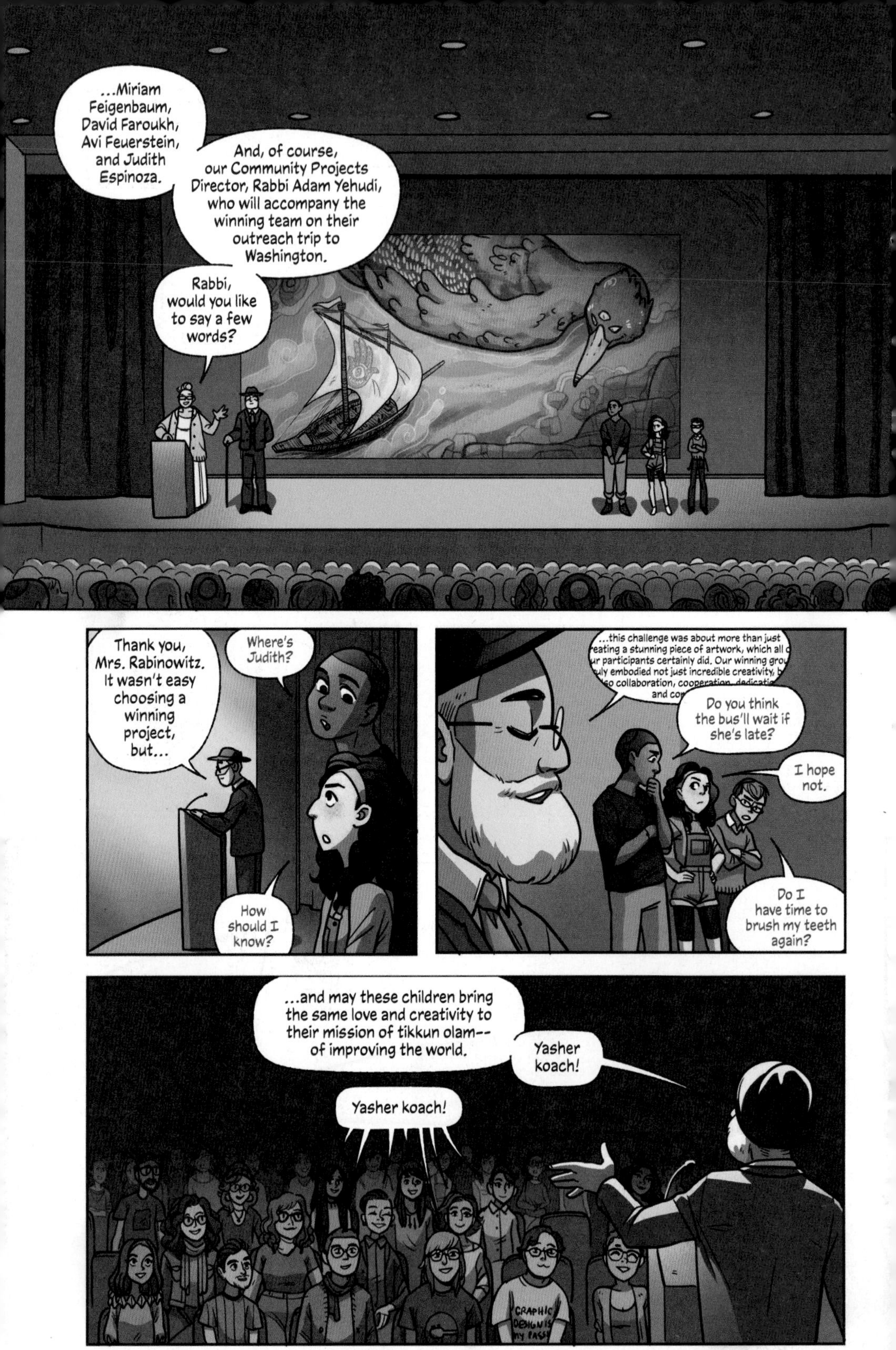
...Miriam Feigenbaum, David Faroukh, Avi Feuerstein, and Judith Espinoza.
And, of course, our Community Projects Director, Rabbi Adam Yehudi, who will accompany the winning team on their outreach trip to Washington.
Rabbi, would you like to say a few words?
Thank you, Mrs. Rabinowitz. It wasn't easy choosing a winning project, but...
Where's Judith?
How should I know?
...this challenge was about more than just eating a stunning piece of artwork, which all o ur participants certainly did. Our winning gro uly embodied not just incredible creativity, b so collaboration, cooperation, dedicatio and co
Do you think the bus'll wait if she's late?
I hope not.
Do I have time to brush my teeth again?
...and may these children bring the same love and creativity to their mission of tikkun olam-- of improving the world.
Yasher koach!
Yasher koach!
GRAPHIC DESIGN IS MY PASS

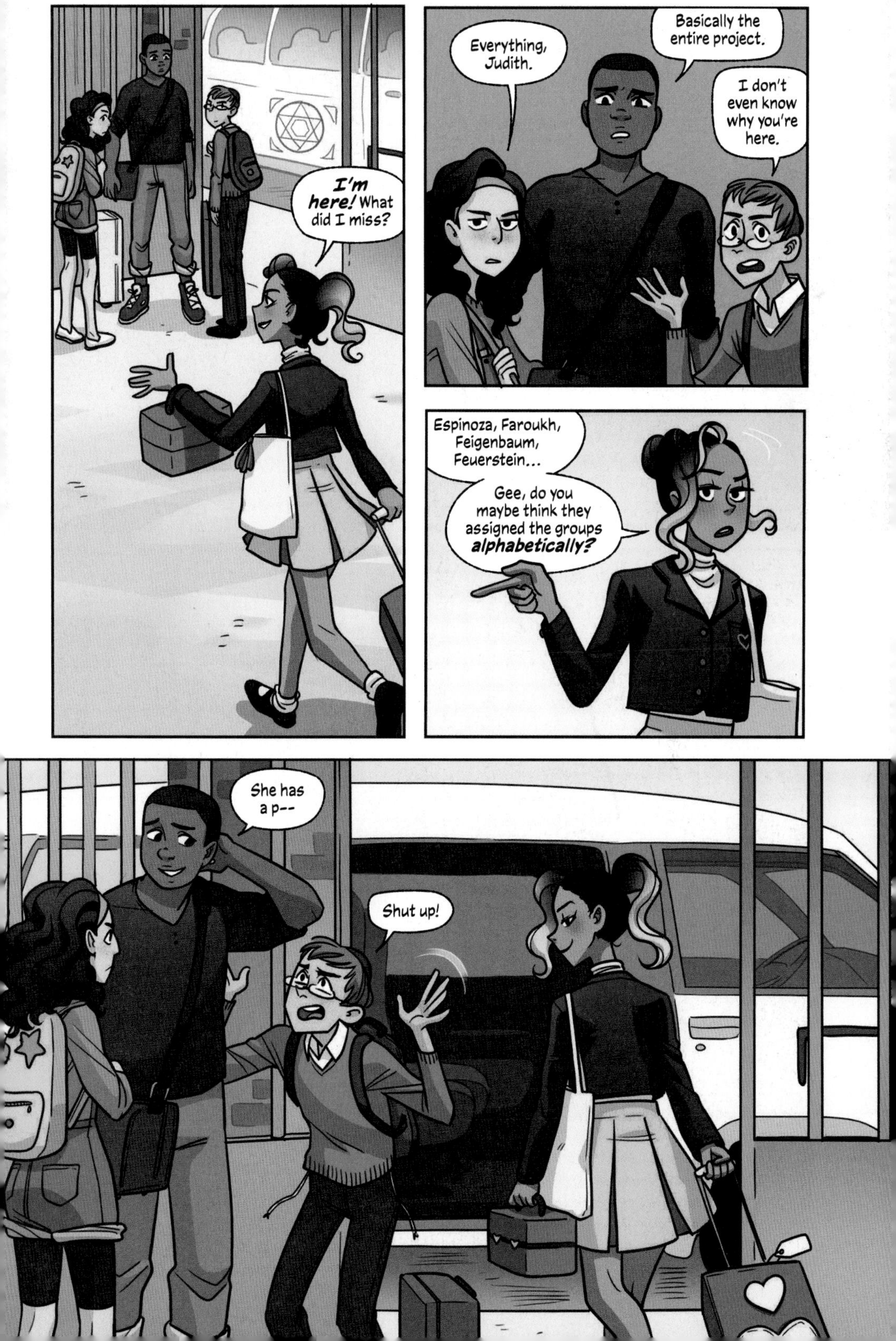
I'm here! What did I miss?
Everything, Judith.
Basically the entire project.
I don't even know why you're here.
Espinoza, Faroukh, Feigenbaum, Feuerstein...
Gee, do you maybe think they assigned the groups alphabetically?
She has a p--
Shut up!

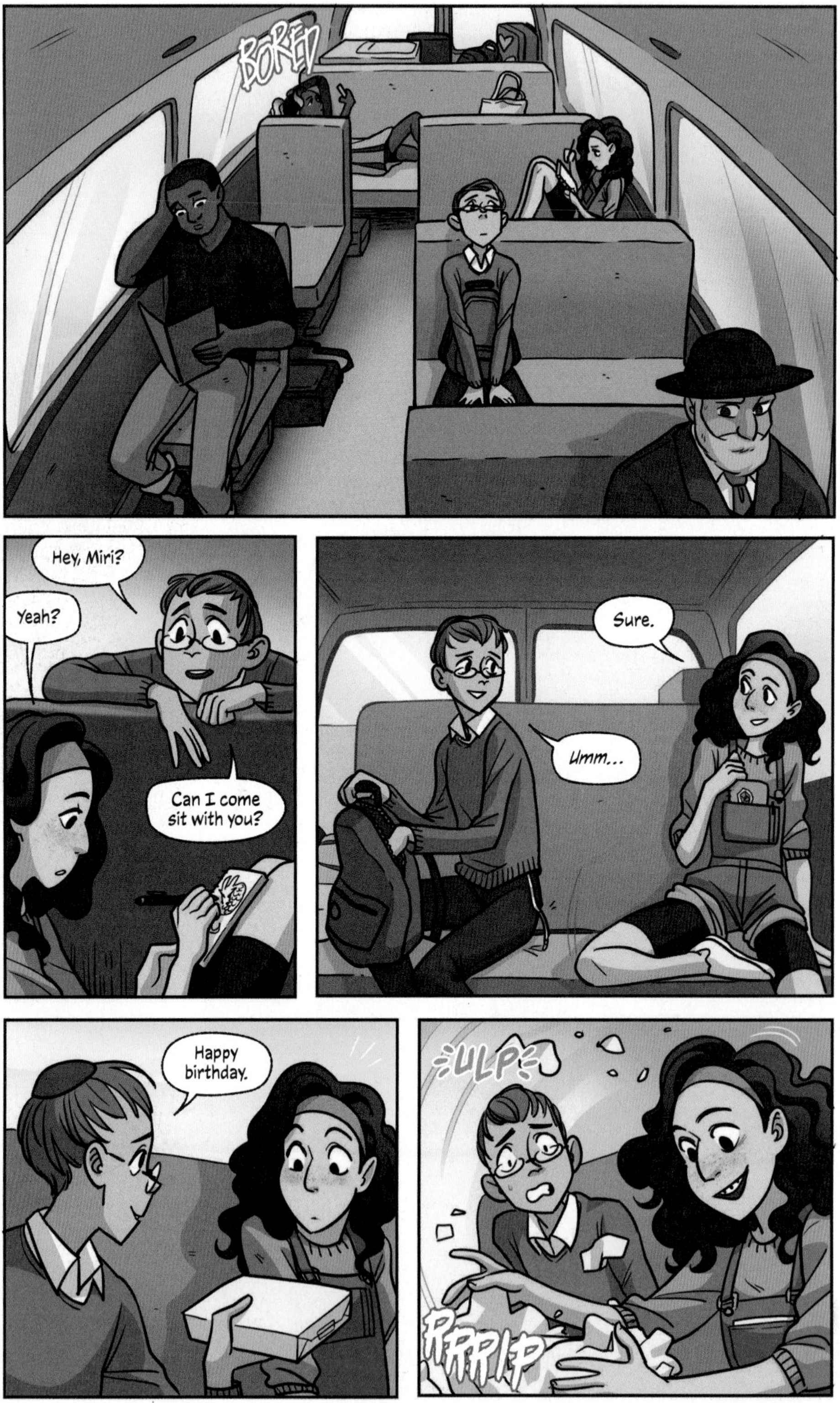
BORED
Hey, Miri?
Yeah?
Can I come sit with you?
Sure.
Umm...
Happy birthday.
ULP
RRRIP

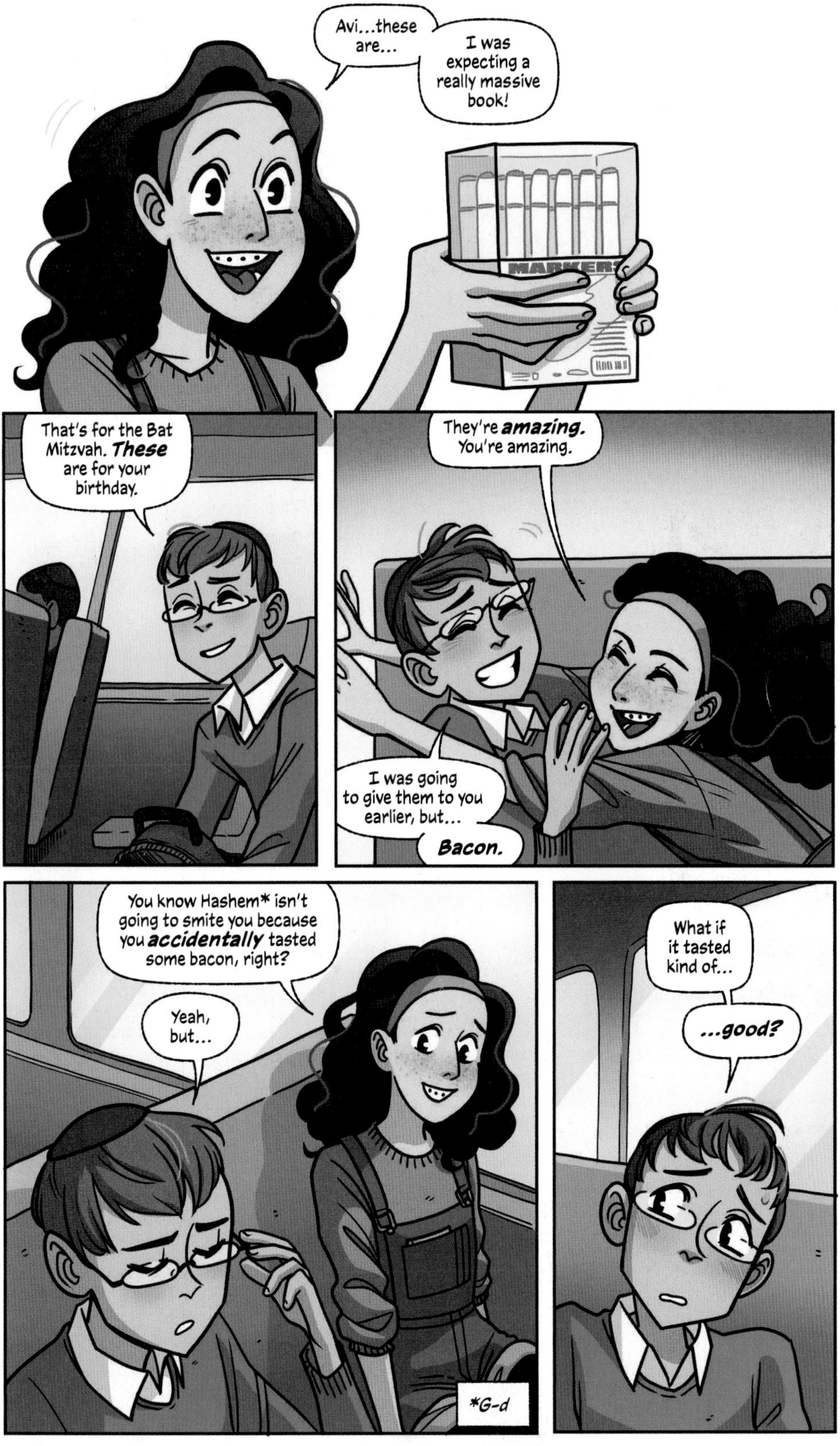
Avi...these are...
I was expecting a really massive book!
MARKERS
That's for the Bat Mitzvah. *These* are for your birthday.
They're *amazing.* You're amazing.
I was going to give them to you earlier, but...
Bacon.
You know Hashem* isn't going to smite you because you *accidentally* tasted some bacon, right?
Yeah, but...
*G-d
What if it tasted kind of...
...good?

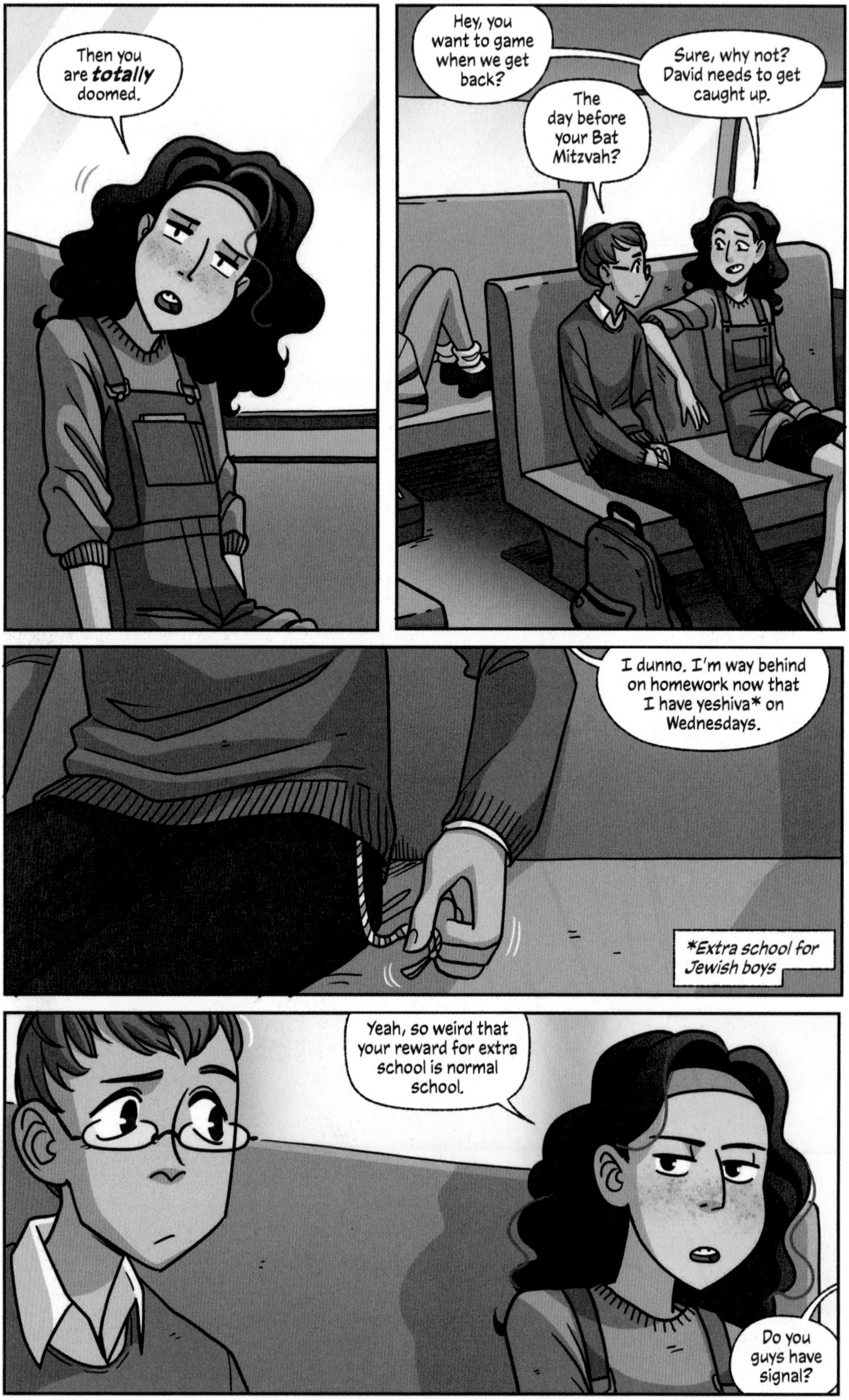
Then you are ***totally*** doomed.
Hey, you want to game when we get back?
The day before your Bat Mitzvah?
Sure, why not? David needs to get caught up.
I dunno. I'm way behind on homework now that I have yeshiva* on Wednesdays.
*Extra school for Jewish boys
Yeah, so weird that your reward for extra school is normal school.
Do you guys have signal?

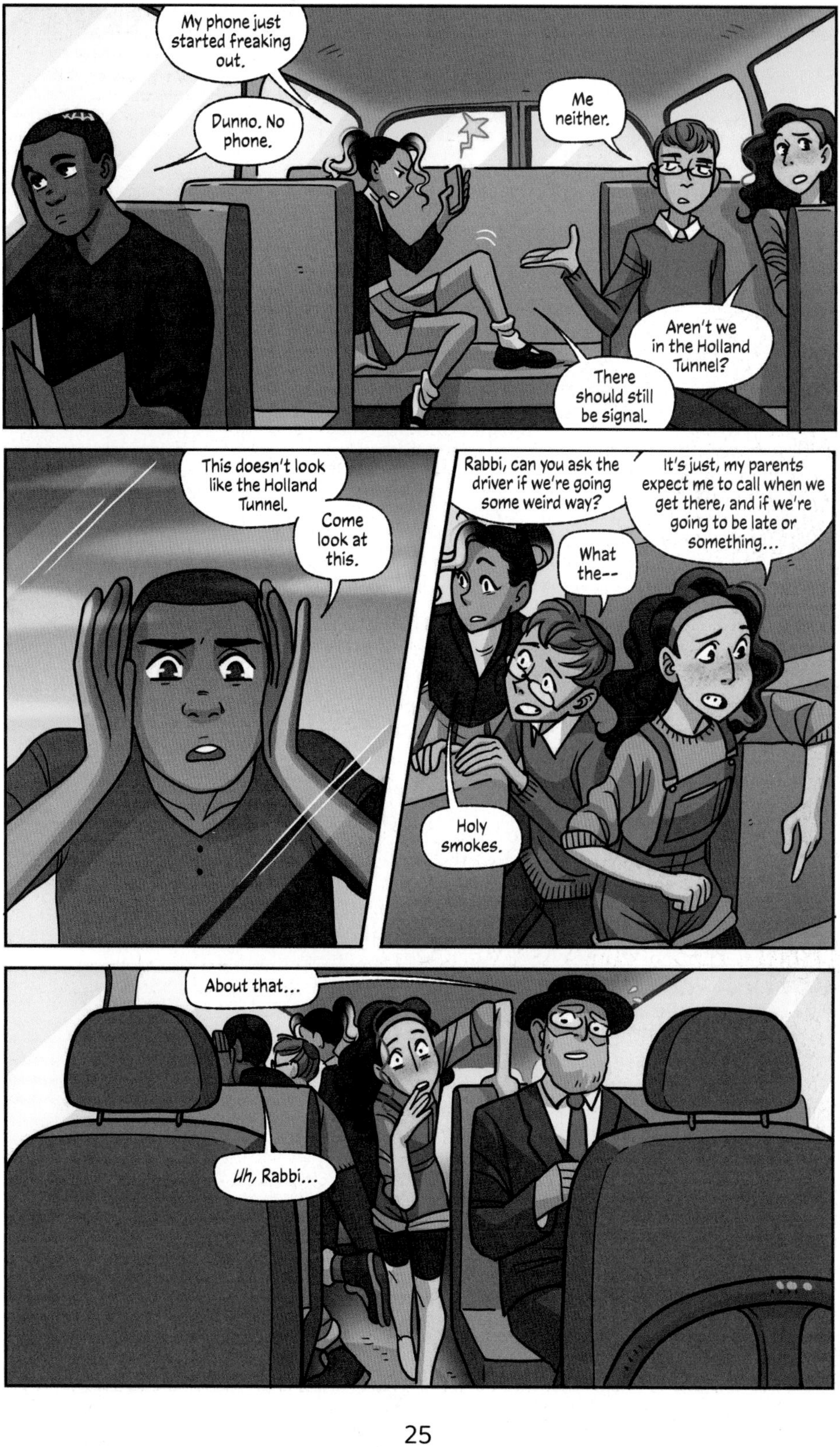
My phone just started freaking out.
Dunno. No phone.
Me neither.
Aren't we in the Holland Tunnel?
There should still be signal.
This doesn't look like the Holland Tunnel.
Come look at this.
Rabbi, can you ask the driver if we're going some weird way?
It's just, my parents expect me to call when we get there, and if we're going to be late or something...
What the--
Holy smokes.
About that...
Uh, Rabbi...

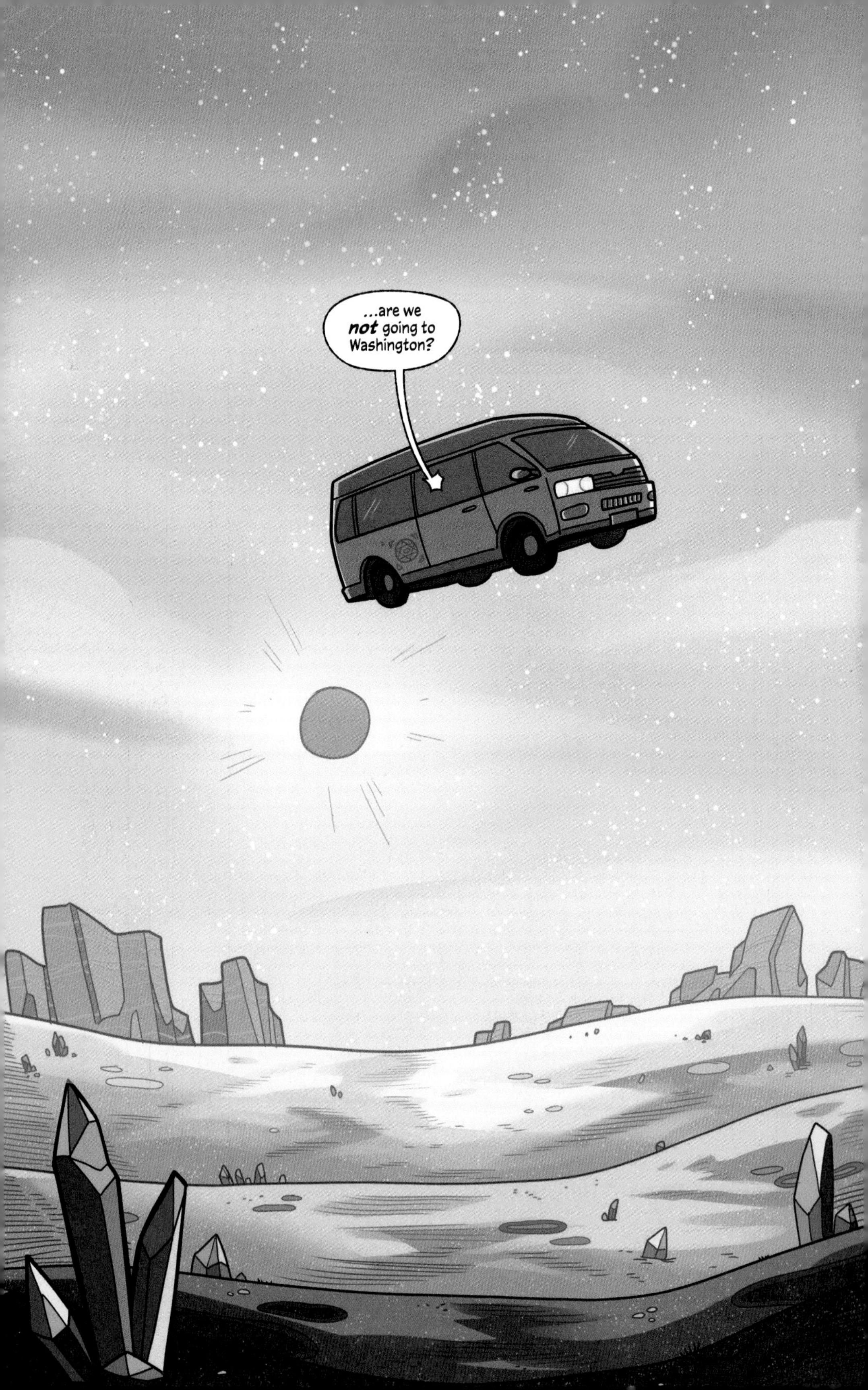
...are we **not** going to Washington?

CHAPTER TWO

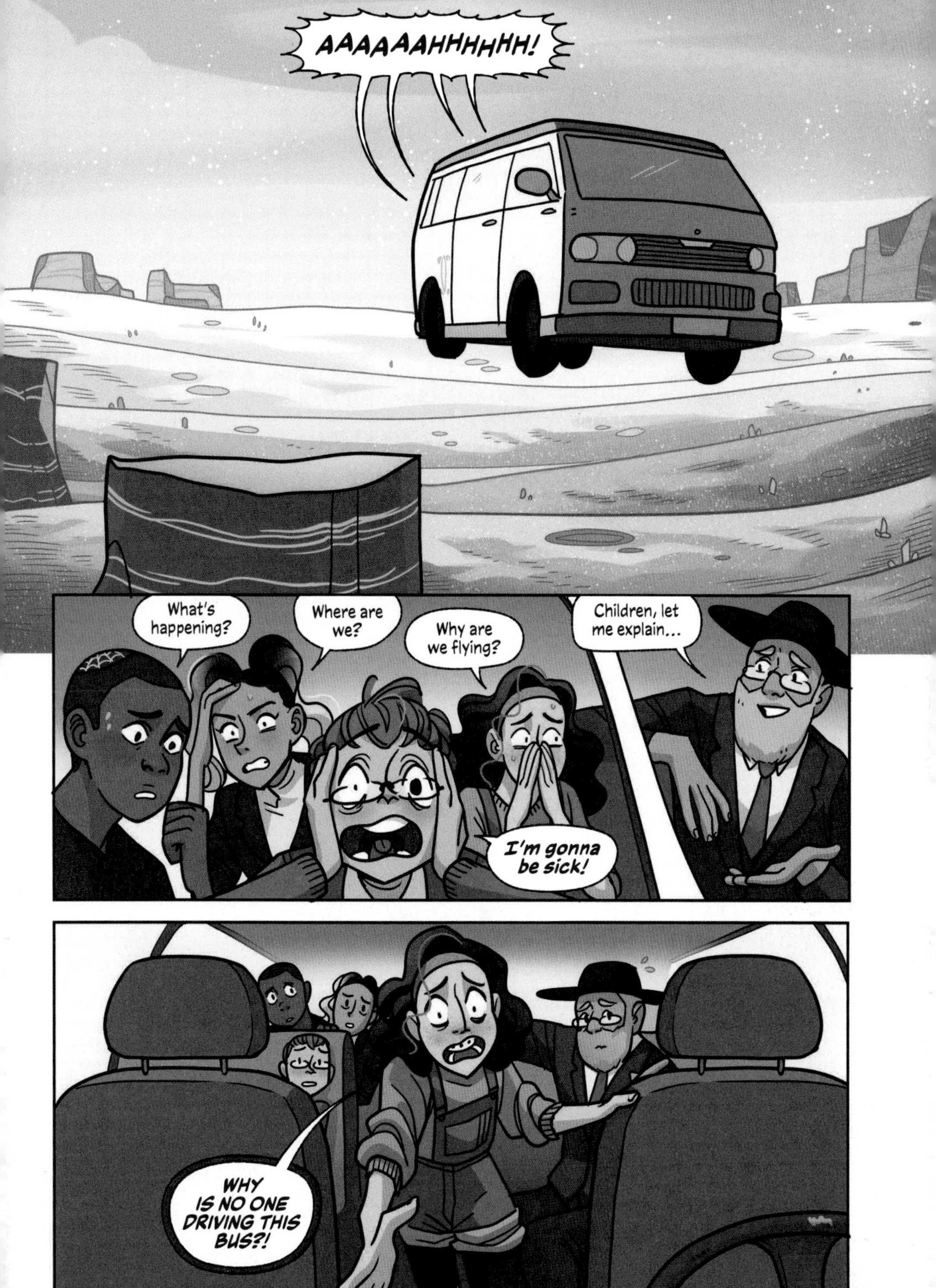

AAAAAAHHHHHH!
What's happening?
Where are we?
Why are we flying?
Children, let me explain...
I'm gonna be sick!
WHY IS NO ONE DRIVING THIS BUS?!

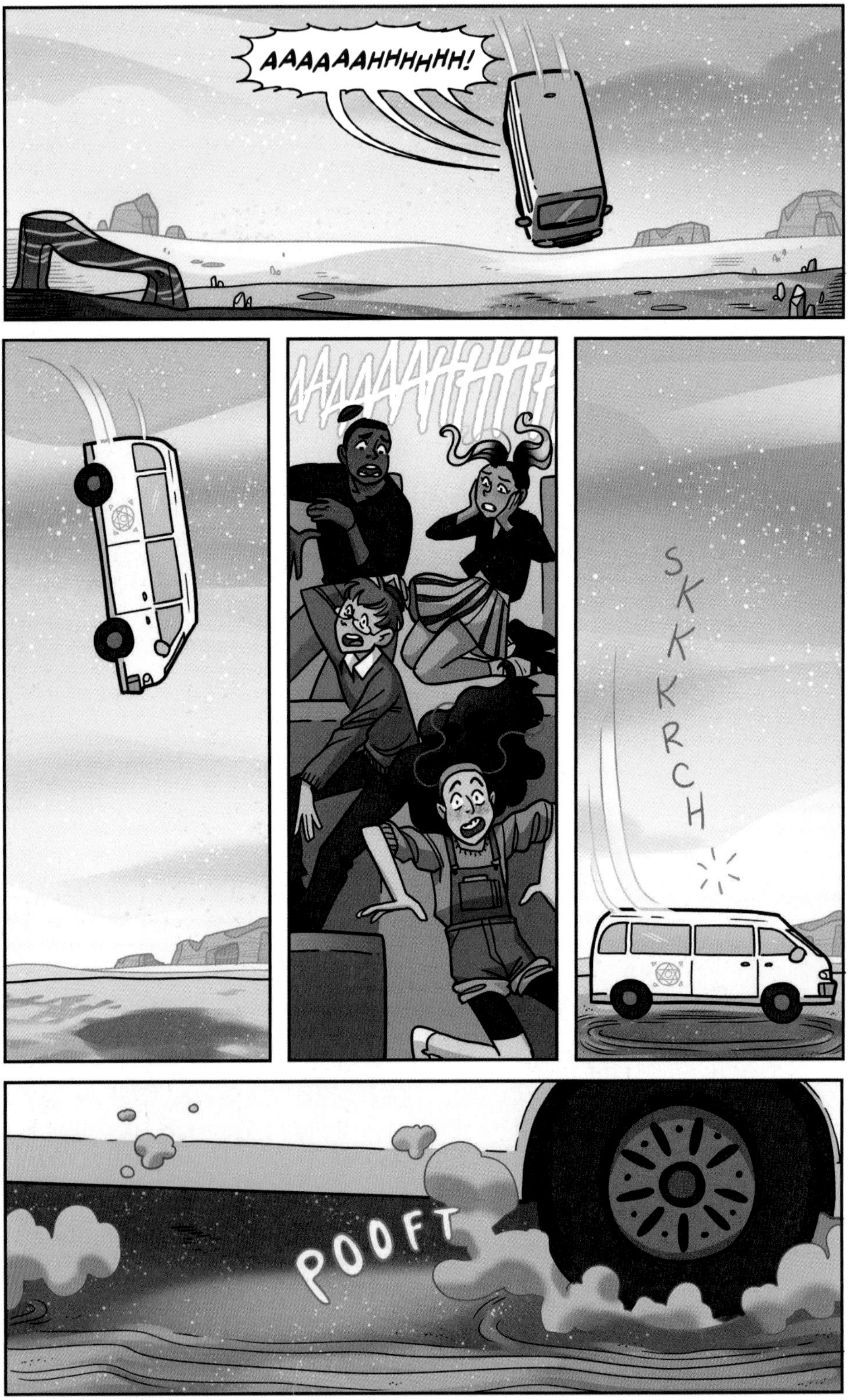
AAAAAAHHHHHH!
AAAAAAHHHHH
SKKKRCH
POOFT

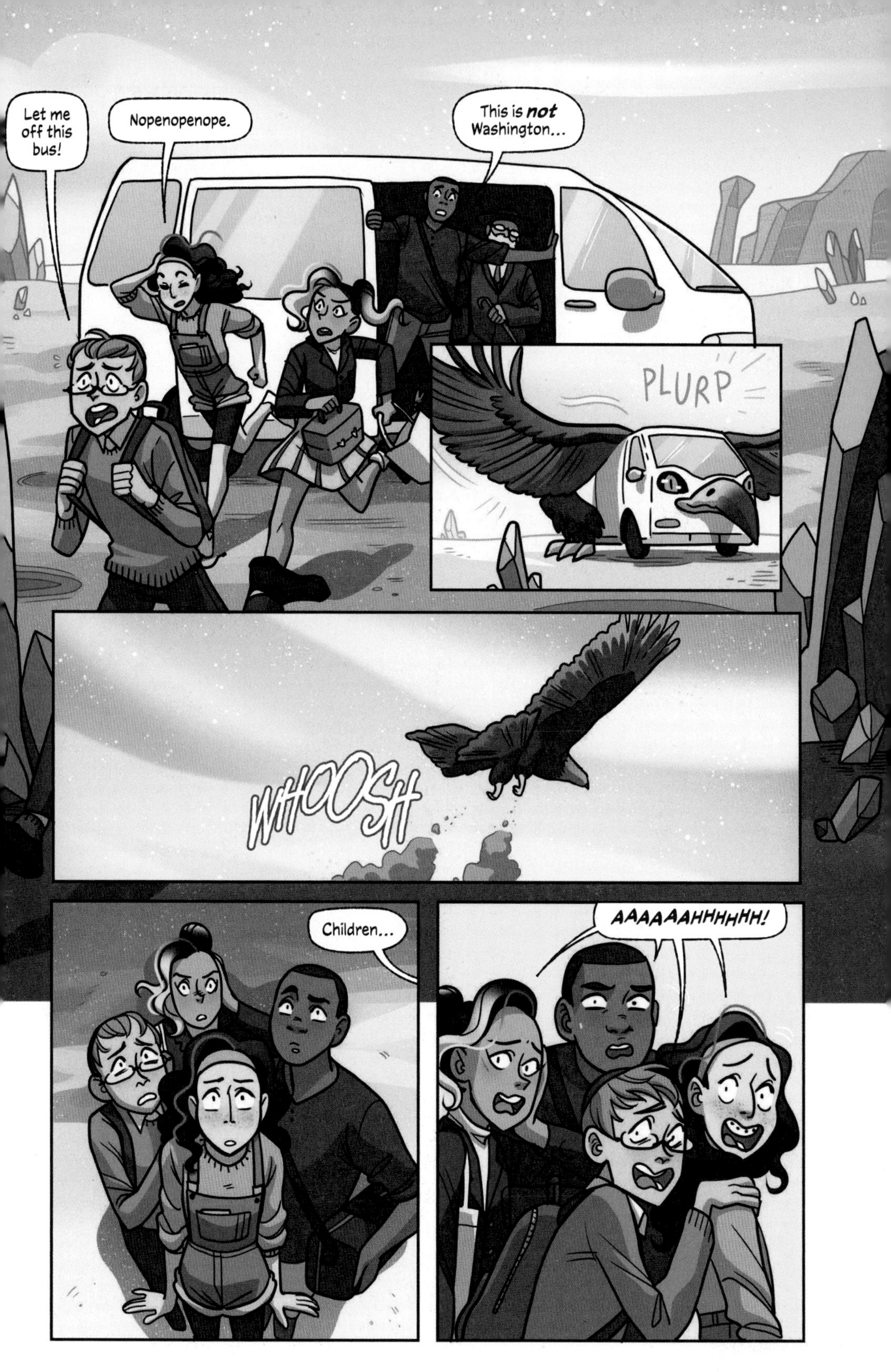
Let me off this bus!
Nopenopenope.
This is not Washington...
PLURP
WHOOSH
Children...
AAAAAAHHHHHH!

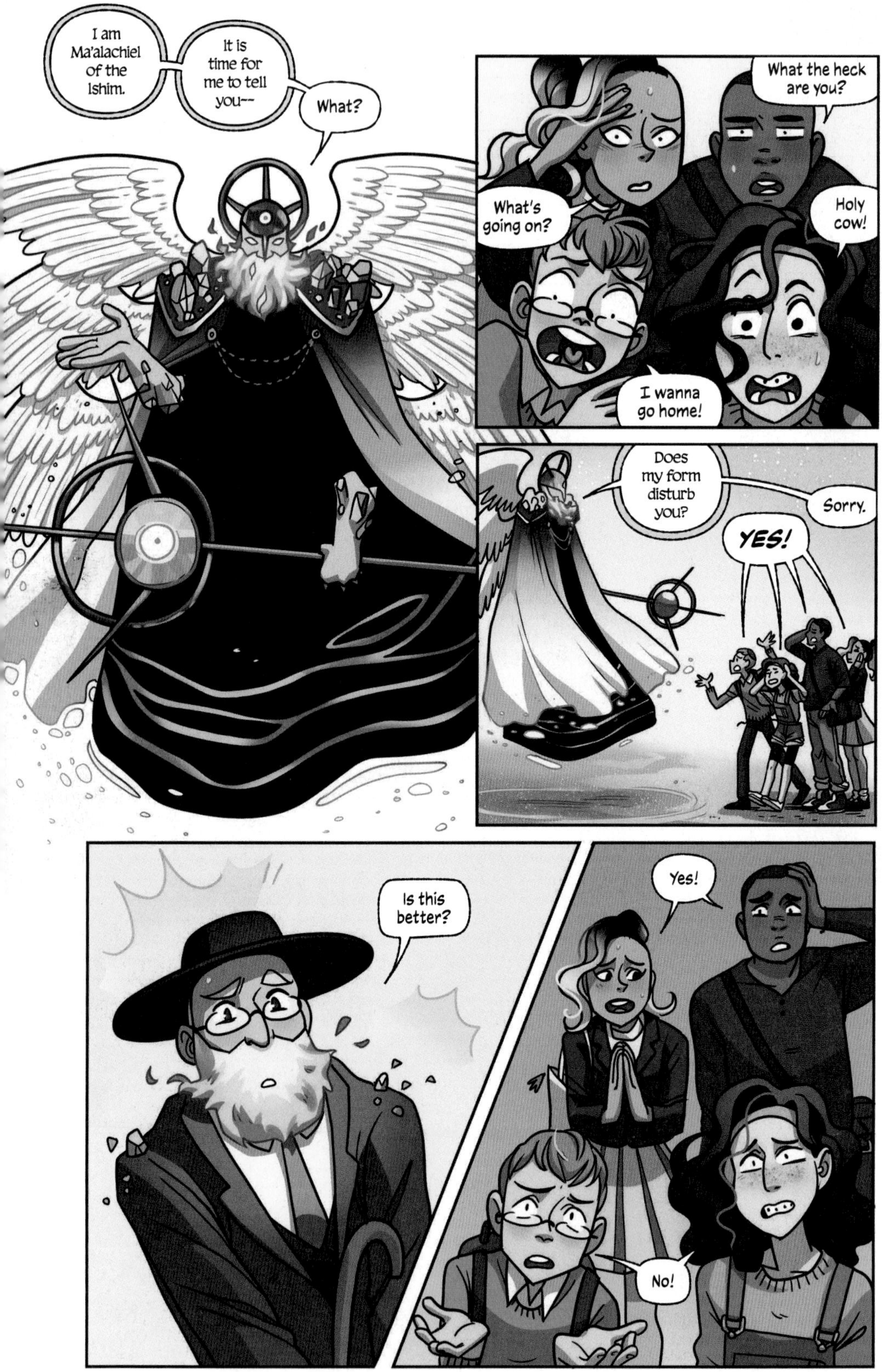
I am Ma'alachiel of the Ishim.
It is time for me to tell you--
What?
What the heck are you?
What's going on?
Holy cow!
I wanna go home!
Does my form disturb you?
Sorry.
YES!
Is this better?
Yes!
No!

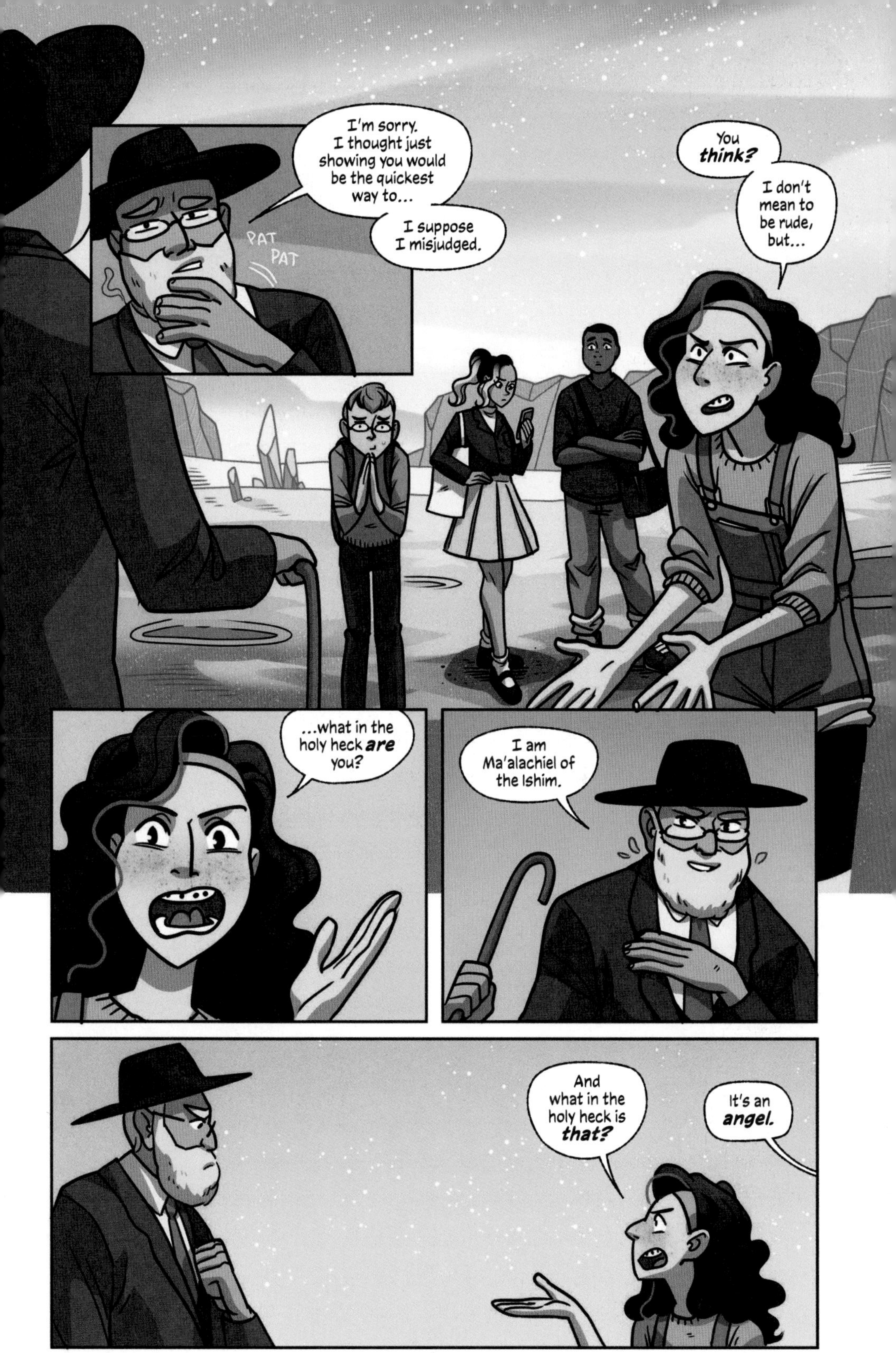

I'm sorry. I thought just showing you would be the quickest way to...
I suppose I misjudged.
PAT PAT
You *think?*
I don't mean to be rude, but...
...what in the holy heck *are* you?
I am Ma'alachiel of the Ishim.
And what in the holy heck is *that?*
It's an *angel.*

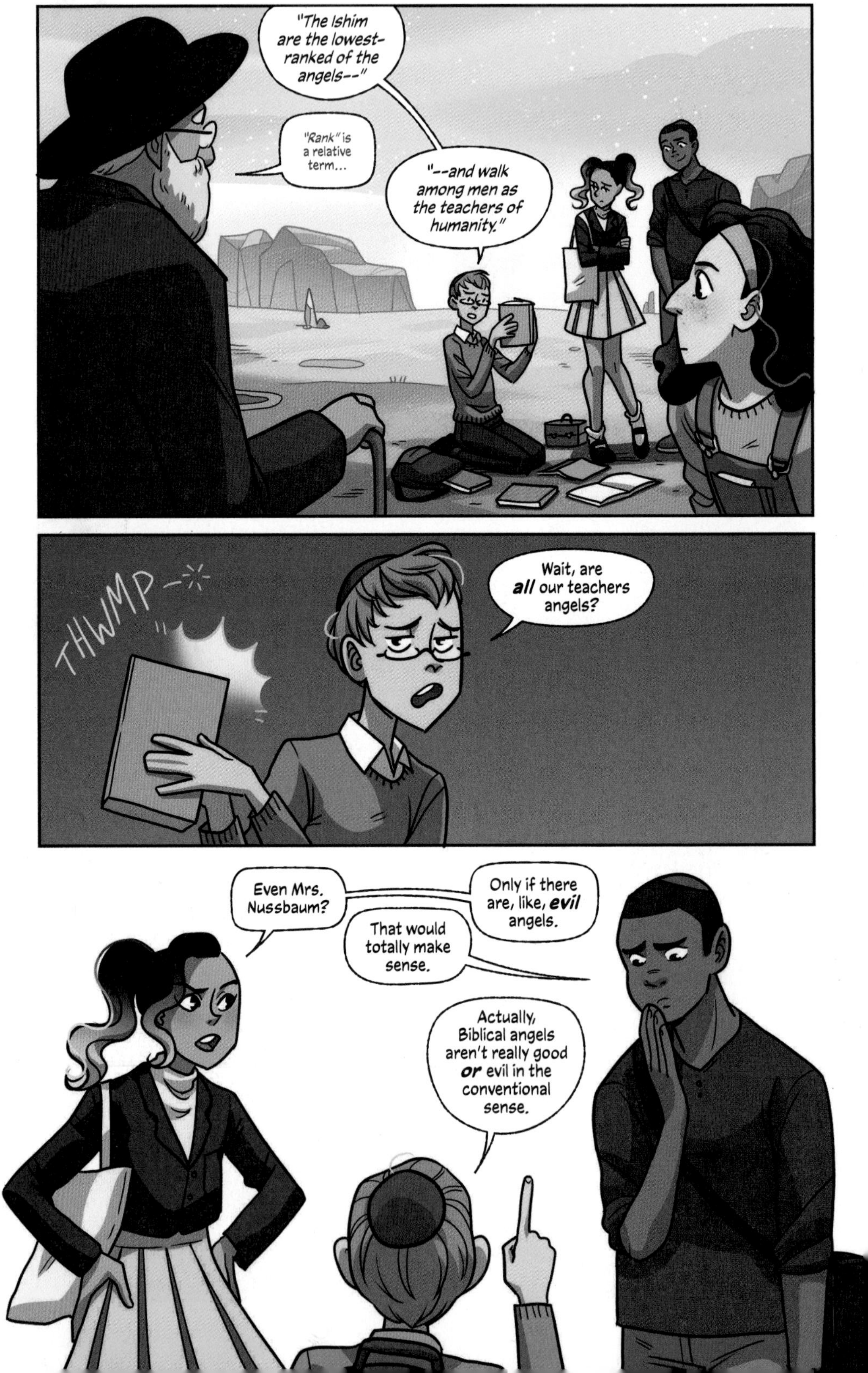
"The Ishim are the lowest-ranked of the angels--"
"Rank" is a relative term...
"--and walk among men as the teachers of humanity."
THWMP
Wait, are all our teachers angels?
Even Mrs. Nussbaum?
Only if there are, like, evil angels.
That would totally make sense.
Actually, Biblical angels aren't really good or evil in the conventional sense.

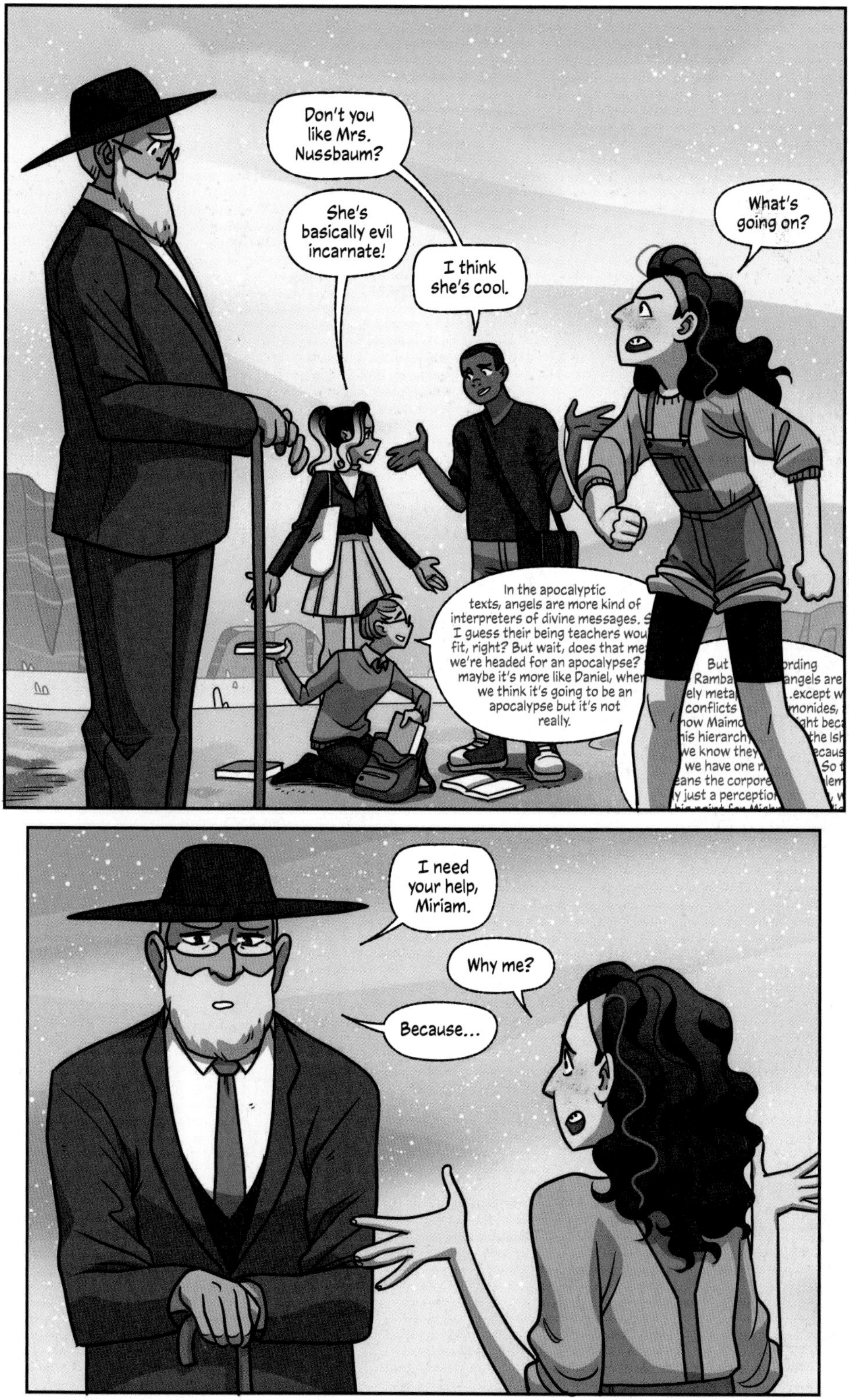
Don't you like Mrs. Nussbaum?
She's basically evil incarnate!
I think she's cool.
What's going on?
In the apocalyptic texts, angels are more kind of interpreters of divine messages. S
I guess their being teachers wou
fit, right? But wait, does that me
we're headed for an apocalypse?
maybe it's more like Daniel, when we think it's going to be an apocalypse but it's not really.
I need your help, Miriam.
Why me?
Because...

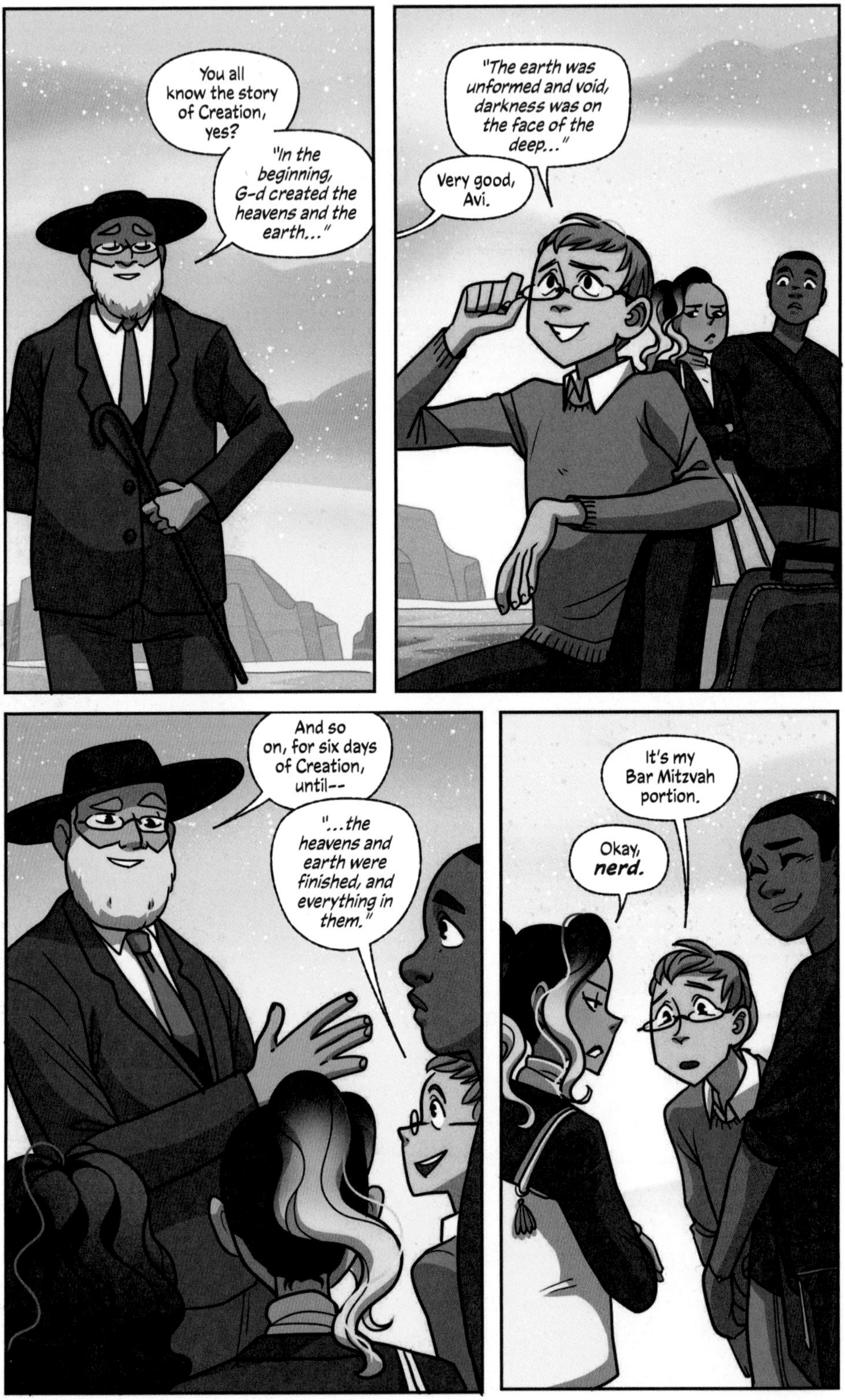
You all know the story of Creation, yes?
"In the beginning, G-d created the heavens and the earth..."
"The earth was unformed and void, darkness was on the face of the deep..."
Very good, Avi.
And so on, for six days of Creation, until--
"...the heavens and earth were finished, and everything in them."
It's my Bar Mitzvah portion.
Okay, **nerd.**

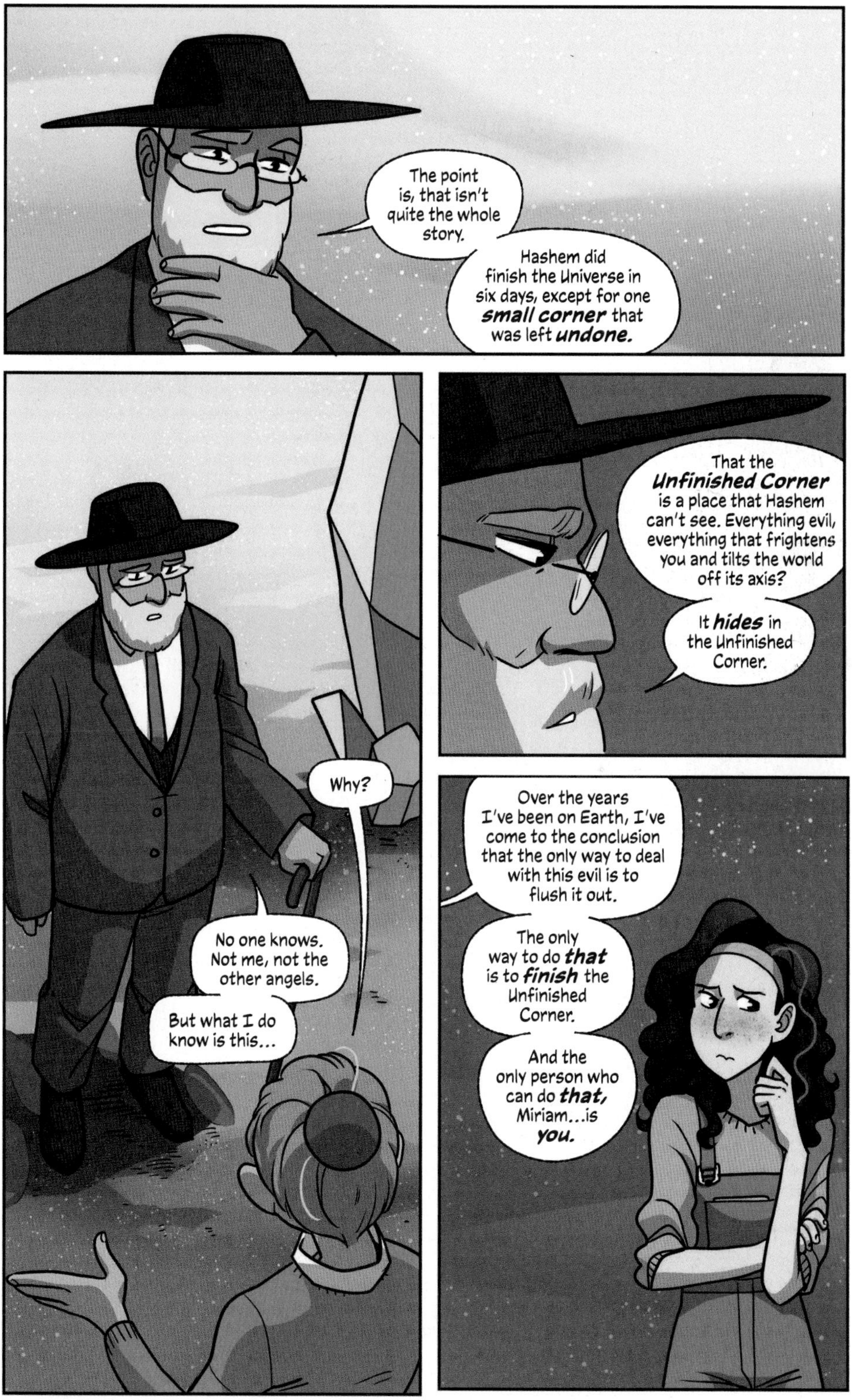
The point is, that isn't quite the whole story.
Hashem did finish the Universe in six days, except for one **small corner** that was left **undone.**
Why?
No one knows. Not me, not the other angels.
But what I do know is this...
That the **Unfinished Corner** is a place that Hashem can't see. Everything evil, everything that frightens you and tilts the world off its axis?
It **hides** in the Unfinished Corner.
Over the years I've been on Earth, I've come to the conclusion that the only way to deal with this evil is to flush it out.
The only way to do **that** is to **finish** the Unfinished Corner.
And the only person who can do **that,** Miriam...is **you.**

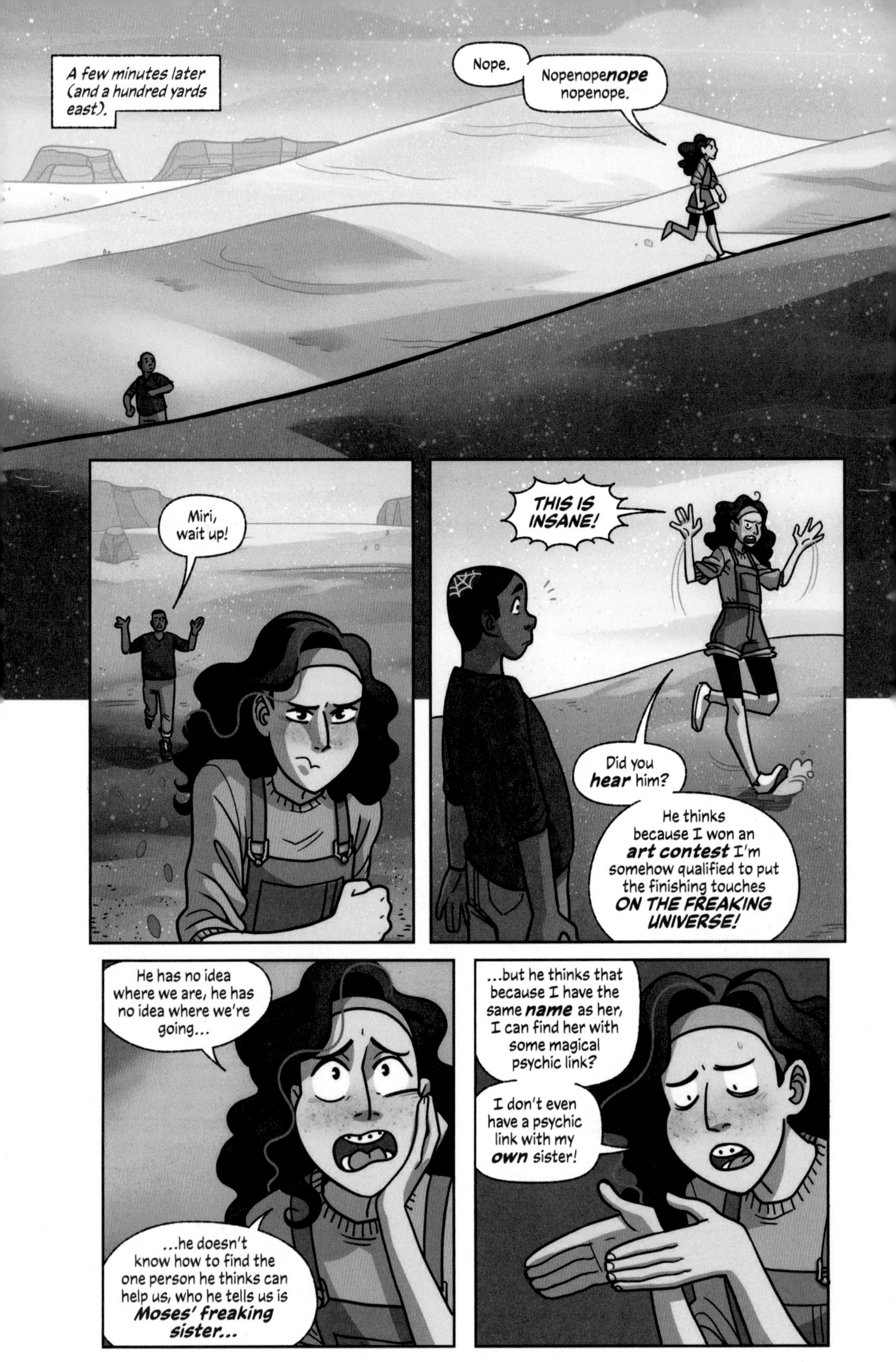
A few minutes later (and a hundred yards east).
Nope.
Nopenope**nope** nopenope.
Miri, wait up!
THIS IS INSANE!
Did you **hear** him?
He thinks because I won an **art contest** I'm somehow qualified to put the finishing touches **ON THE FREAKING UNIVERSE!**
He has no idea where we are, he has no idea where we're going...
...he doesn't know how to find the one person he thinks can help us, who he tells us is **Moses' freaking sister...**
...but he thinks that because I have the same **name** as her, I can find her with some magical psychic link?
I don't even have a psychic link with my **own** sister!

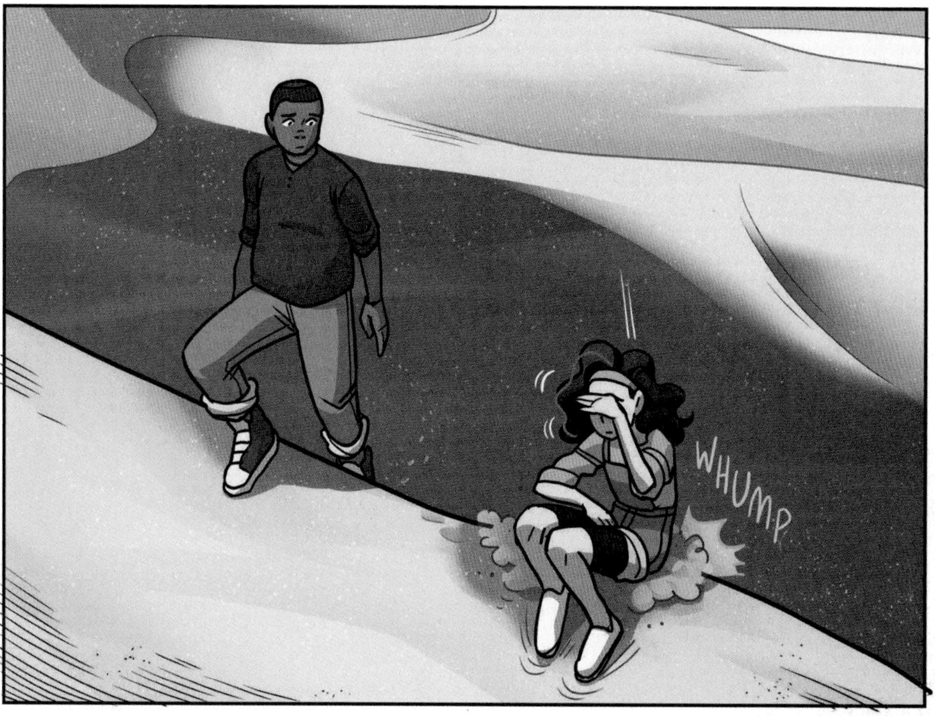
WHUMP

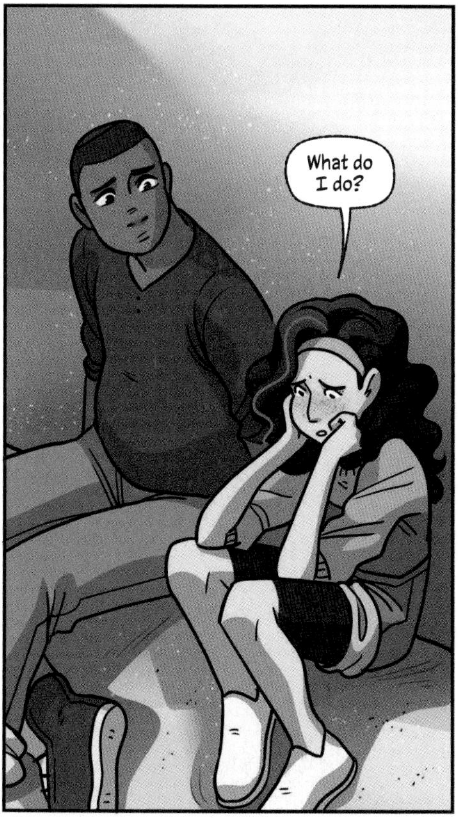
What do I do?

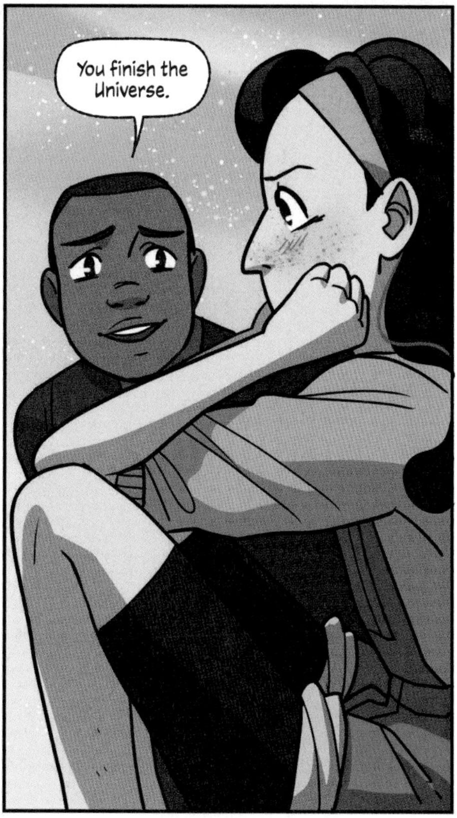
You finish the Universe.

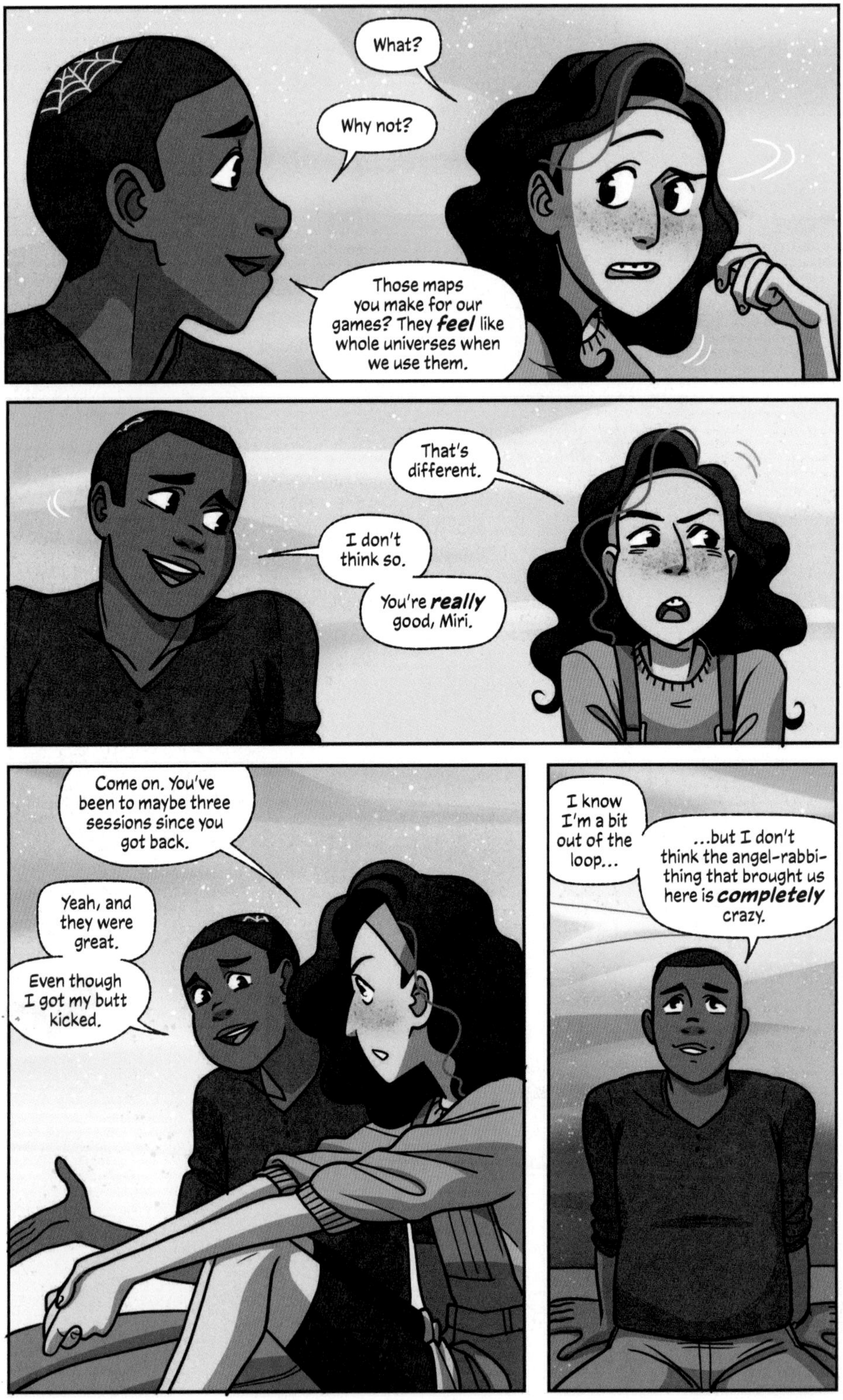
What?
Why not?
Those maps you make for our games? They *feel* like whole universes when we use them.
That's different.
I don't think so.
You're ***really*** good, Miri.
Come on. You've been to maybe three sessions since you got back.
Yeah, and they were great.
Even though I got my butt kicked.
I know I'm a bit out of the loop...
...but I don't think the angel-rabbi-thing that brought us here is ***completely*** crazy.

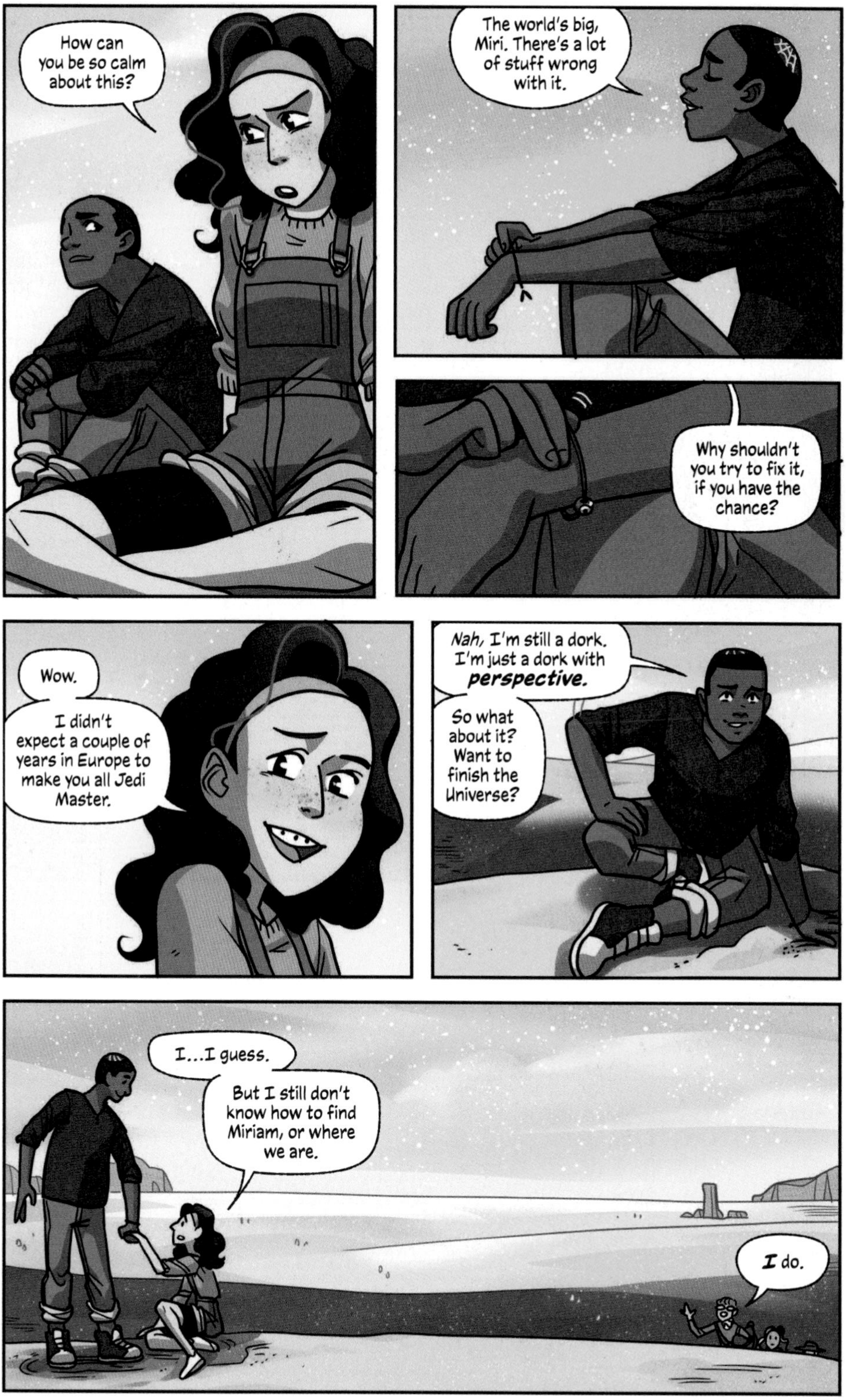
How can you be so calm about this?
The world's big, Miri. There's a lot of stuff wrong with it.
Why shouldn't you try to fix it, if you have the chance?
Wow.
I didn't expect a couple of years in Europe to make you all Jedi Master.
Nah, I'm still a dork. I'm just a dork with **perspective.**
So what about it? Want to finish the Universe?
I...I guess.
But I still don't know how to find Miriam, or where we are.
I do.

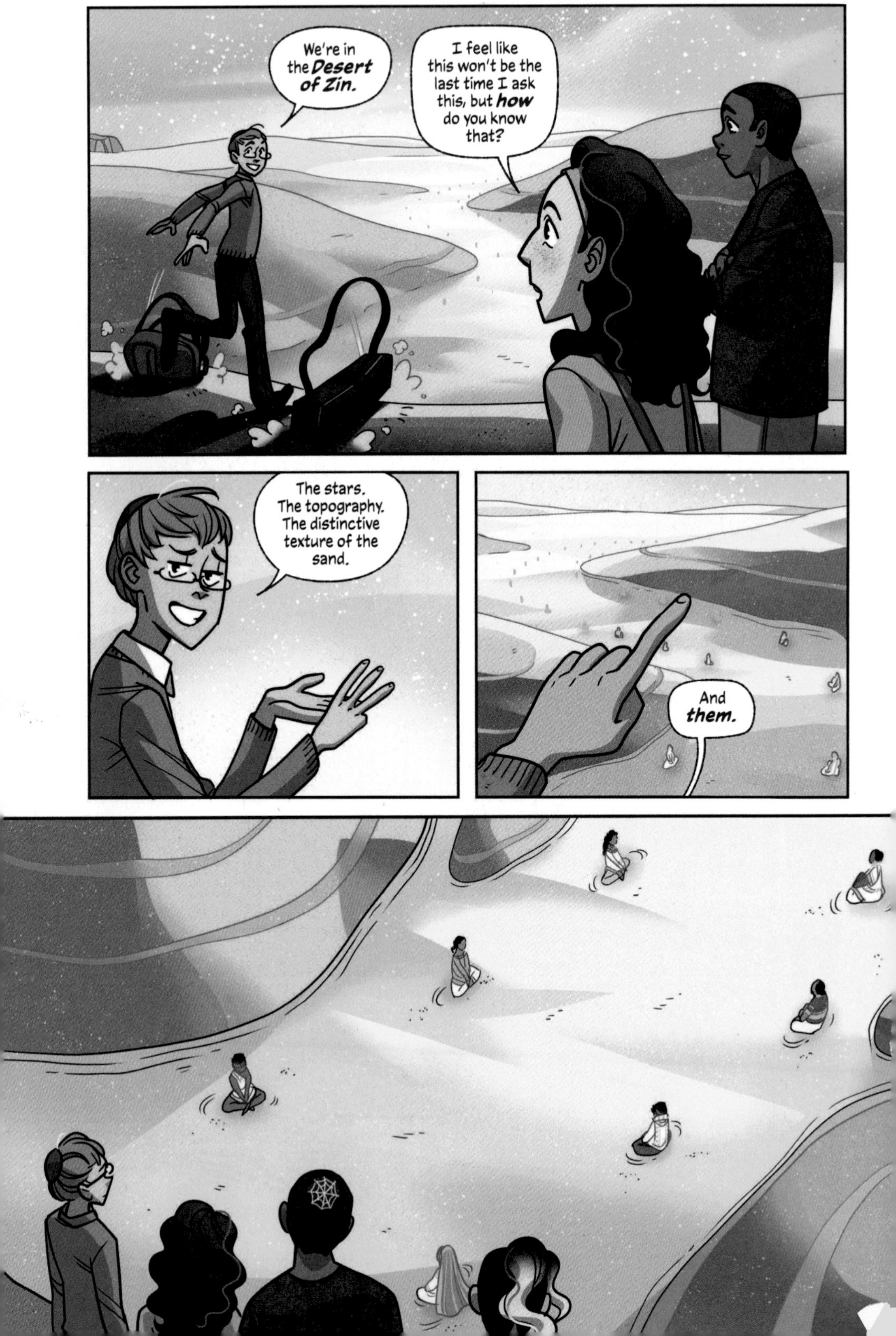
We're in the *Desert of Zin.*
I feel like this won't be the last time I ask this, but ***how*** do you know that?
The stars. The topography. The distinctive texture of the sand.
And ***them.***

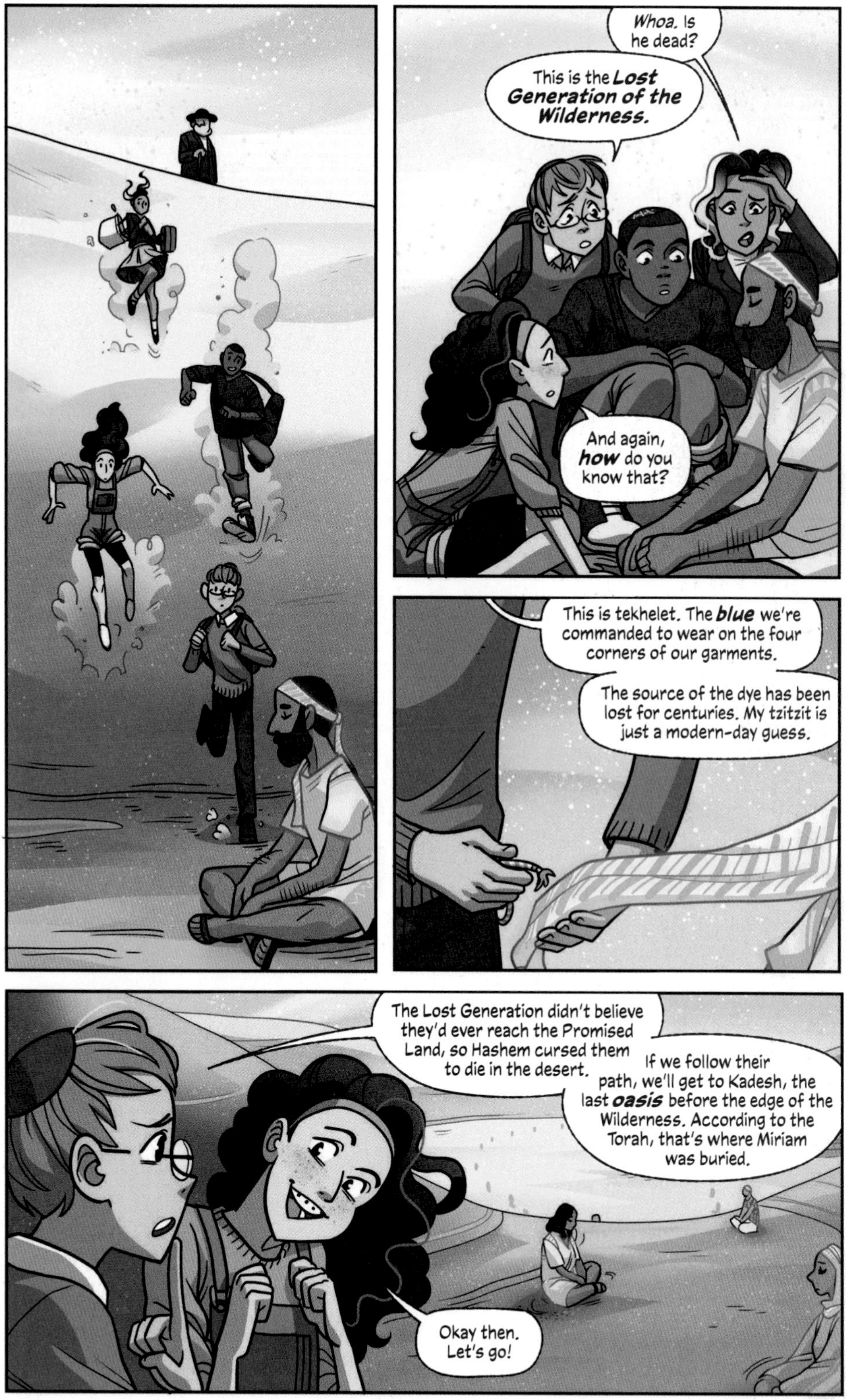
Whoa. Is he dead?
This is the *Lost Generation of the Wilderness.*
And again, **how** do you know that?
This is tekhelet. The ***blue*** we're commanded to wear on the four corners of our garments.
The source of the dye has been lost for centuries. My tzitzit is just a modern-day guess.
The Lost Generation didn't believe they'd ever reach the Promised Land, so Hashem cursed them to die in the desert.
If we follow their path, we'll get to Kadesh, the last ***oasis*** before the edge of the Wilderness. According to the Torah, that's where Miriam was buried.
Okay then. Let's go!

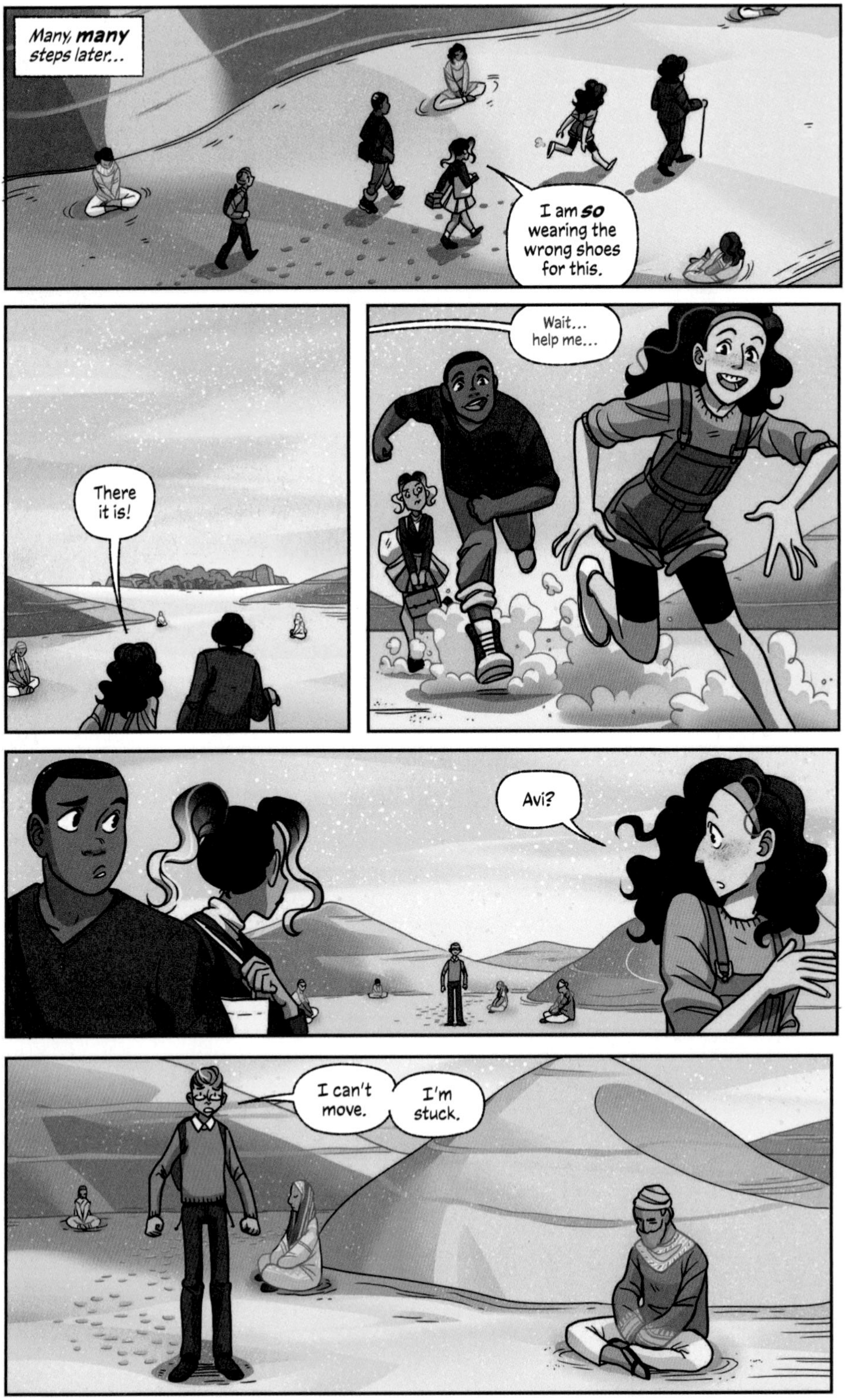

Many, **many** steps later...
I am ***so*** wearing the wrong shoes for this.
There it is!
Wait... help me...
Avi?
I can't move.
I'm stuck.

CHAPTER THREE

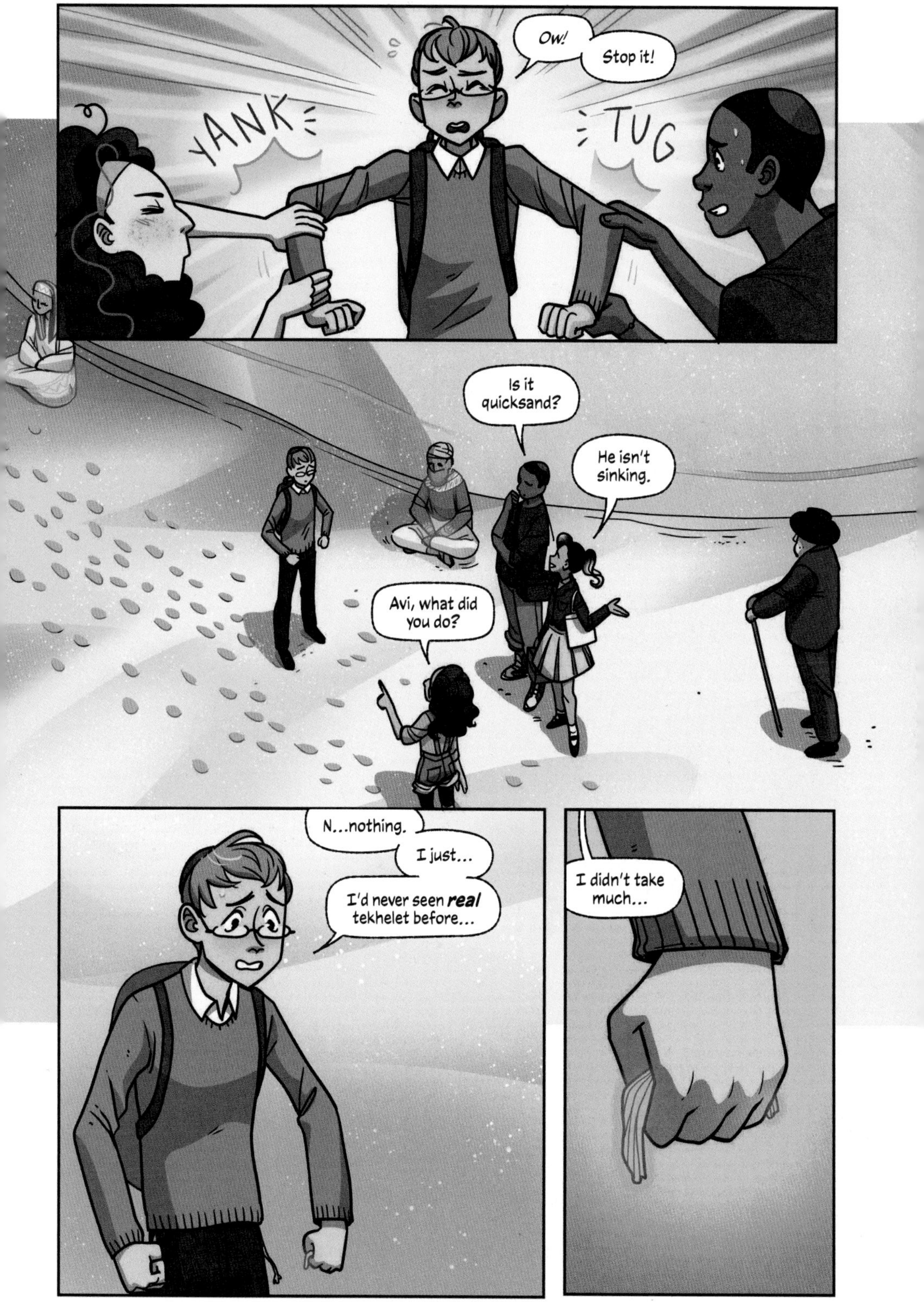

Ow!
Stop it!
YANK
TUG
Is it quicksand?
He isn't sinking.
Avi, what did you do?
N...nothing.
I just...
I'd never seen *real* tekhelet before...
I didn't take much...

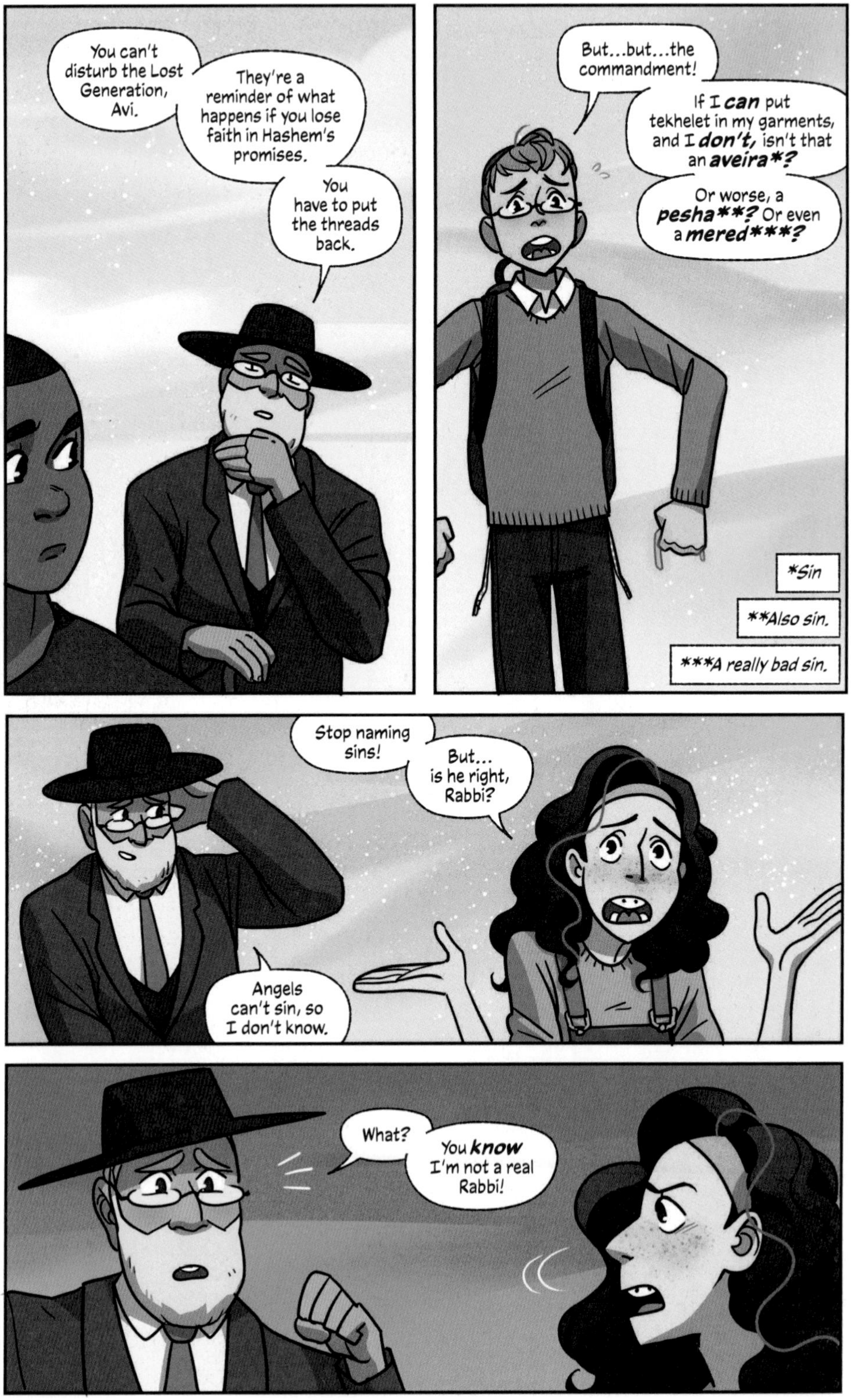
You can't disturb the Lost Generation, Avi.
They're a reminder of what happens if you lose faith in Hashem's promises.
You have to put the threads back.
But...but...the commandment!
If I **can** put tekhelet in my garments, and I **don't,** isn't that an **aveira*?**
Or worse, a **pesha**?** Or even a **mered***?**
*Sin
**Also sin.
***A really bad sin.
Stop naming sins!
But... is he right, Rabbi?
Angels can't sin, so I don't know.
What?
You **know** I'm not a real Rabbi!

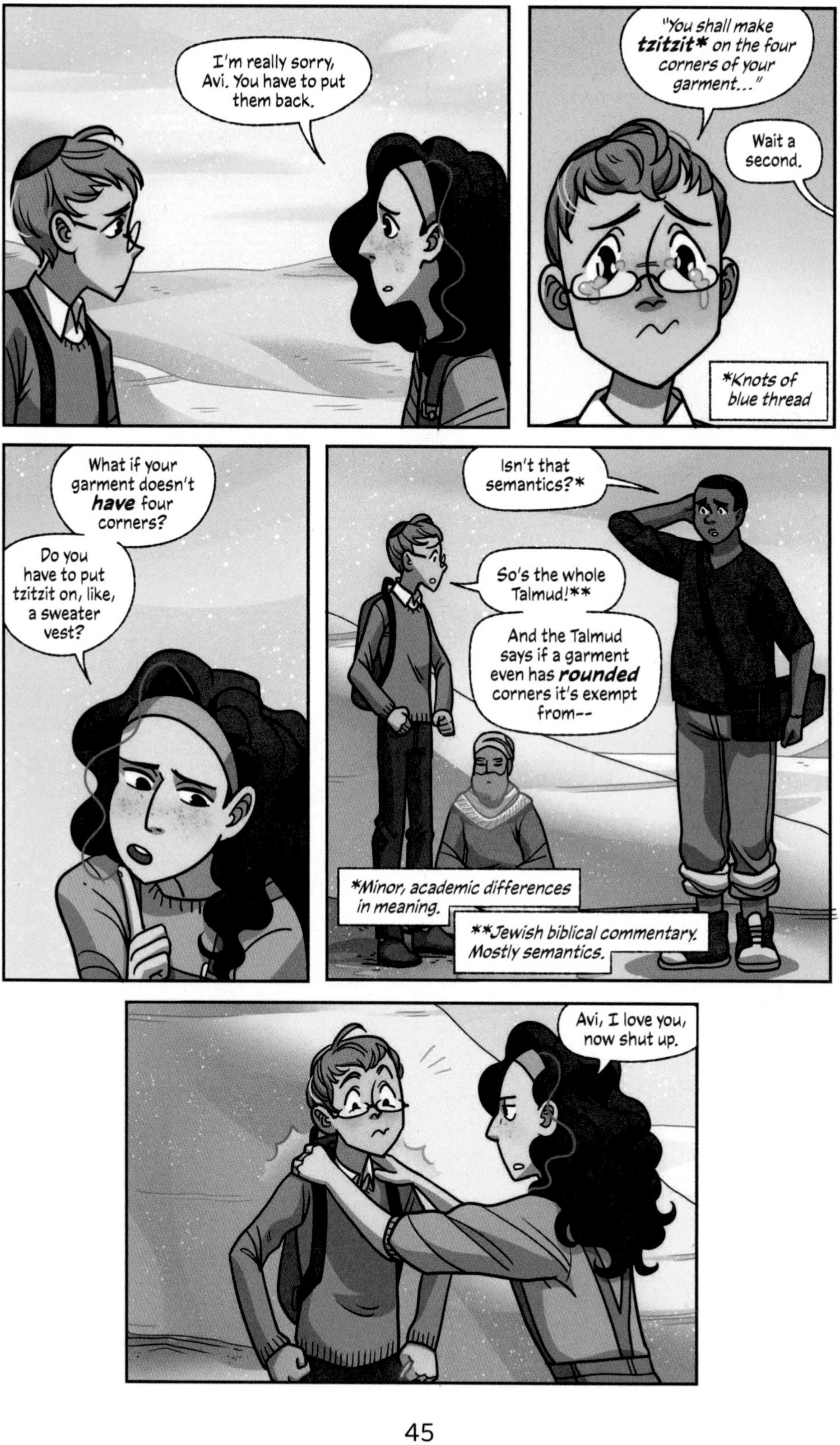
I'm really sorry, Avi. You have to put them back.
"You shall make tzitzit* on the four corners of your garment..."
Wait a second.
*Knots of blue thread
What if your garment doesn't have four corners?
Do you have to put tzitzit on, like, a sweater vest?
Isn't that semantics?*
So's the whole Talmud!**
And the Talmud says if a garment even has rounded corners it's exempt from--
*Minor, academic differences in meaning.
**Jewish biblical commentary. Mostly semantics.
Avi, I love you, now shut up.

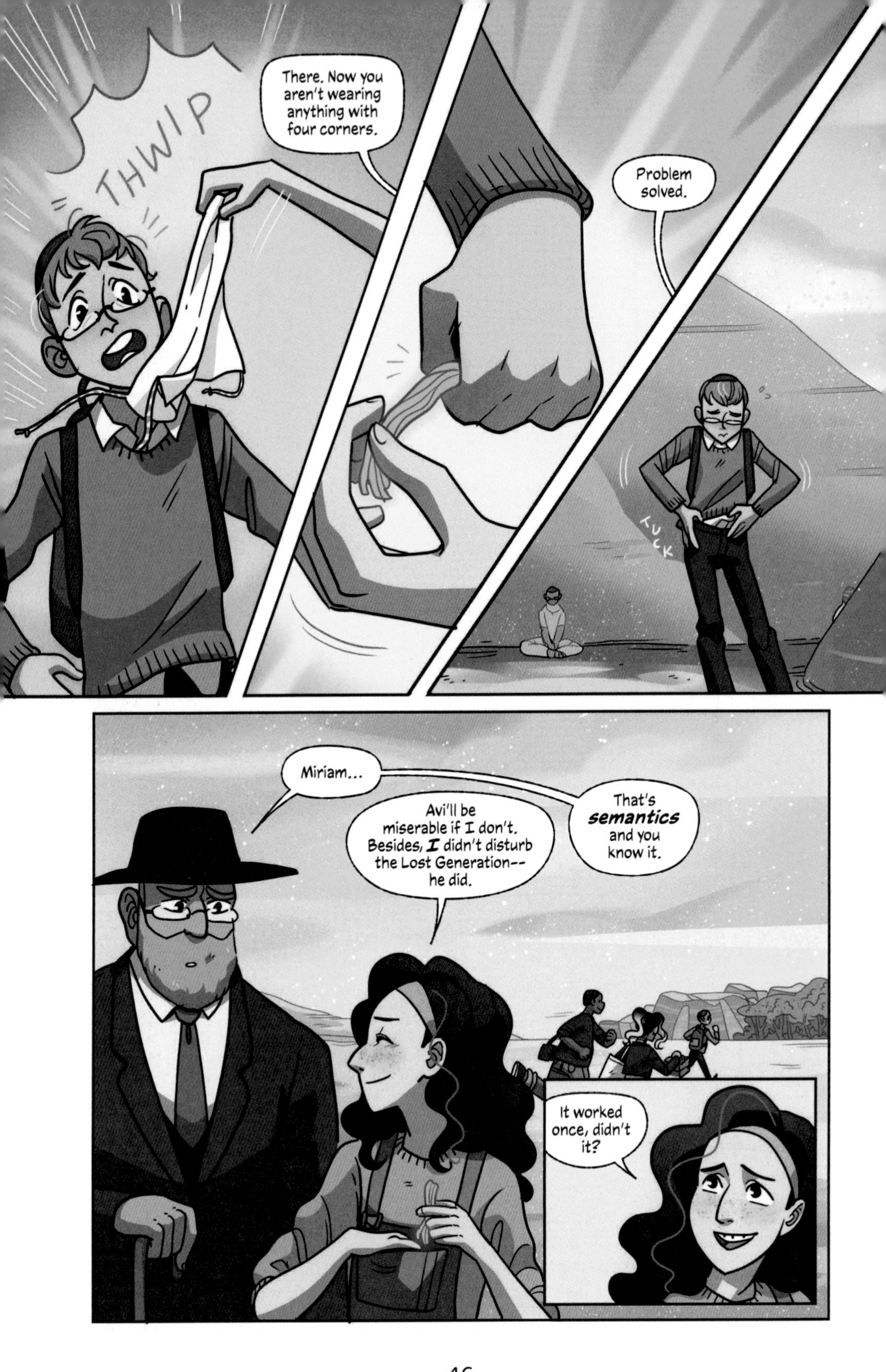
THWIP
There. Now you aren't wearing anything with four corners.
Problem solved.
TUCK
Miriam...
That's *semantics* and you know it.
Avi'll be miserable if I don't. Besides, *I* didn't disturb the Lost Generation--he did.
It worked once, didn't it?

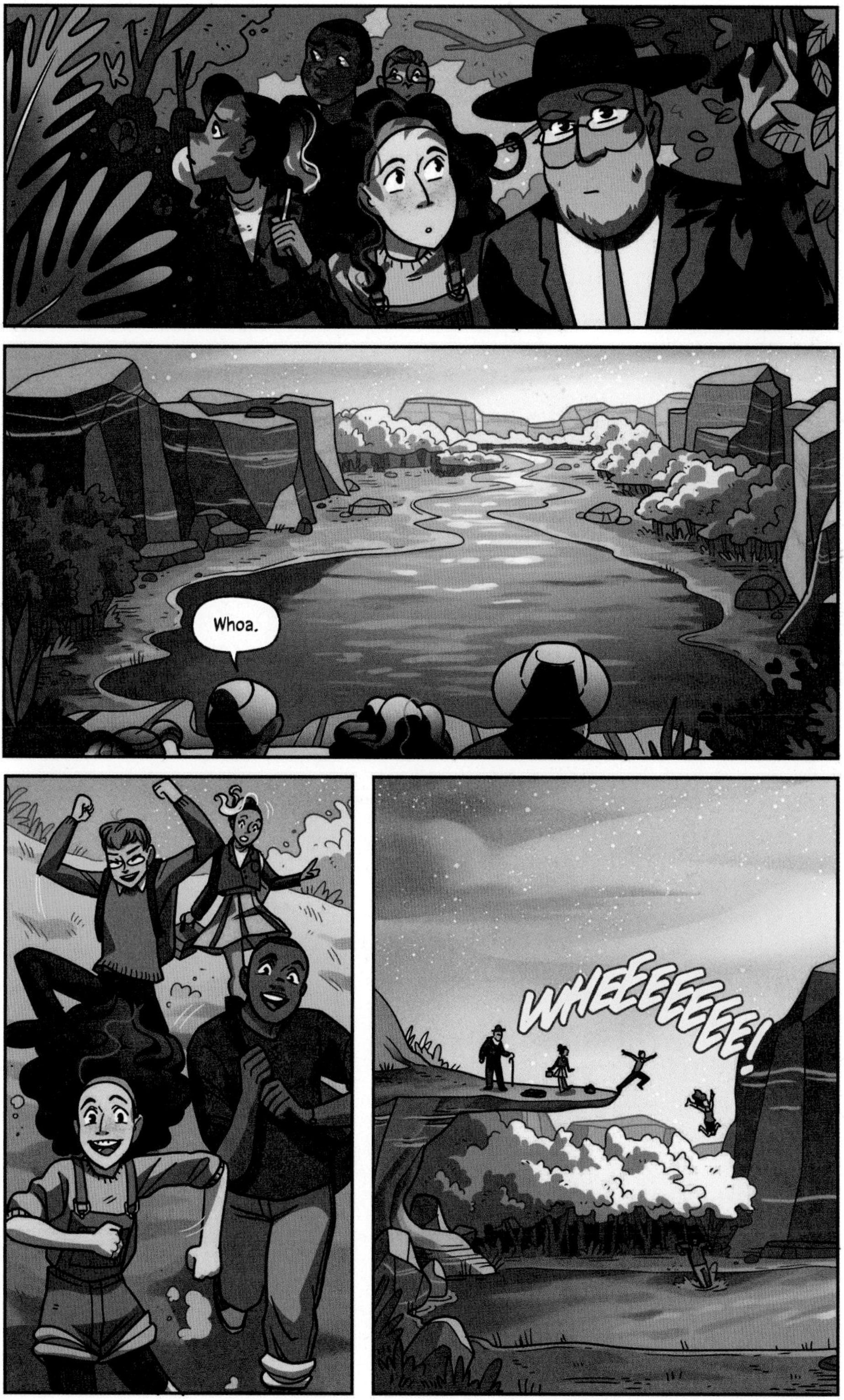
Whoa.
WHEEEEEEEE!

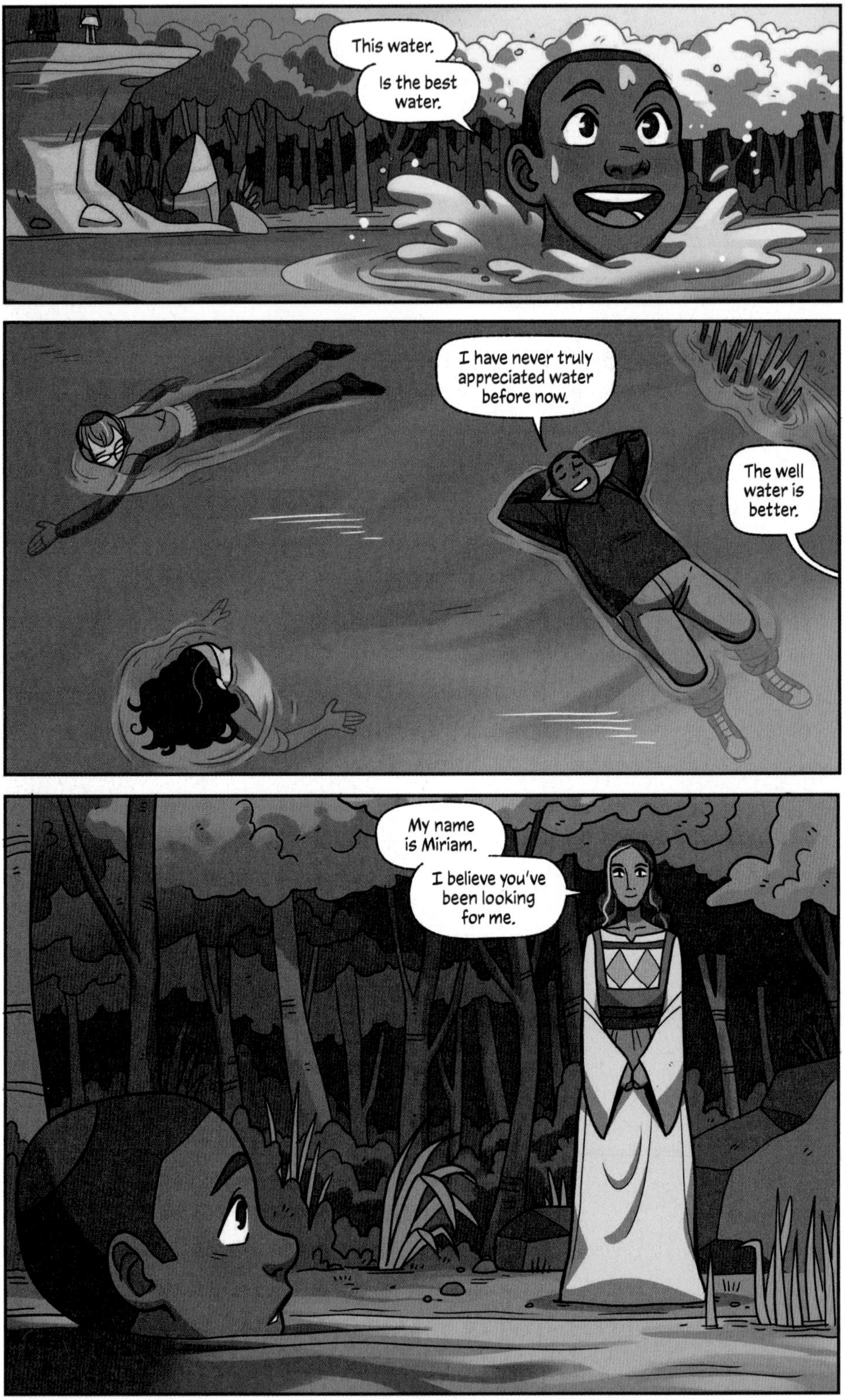
This water.
Is the best water.
I have never truly appreciated water before now.
The well water is better.
My name is Miriam.
I believe you've been looking for me.

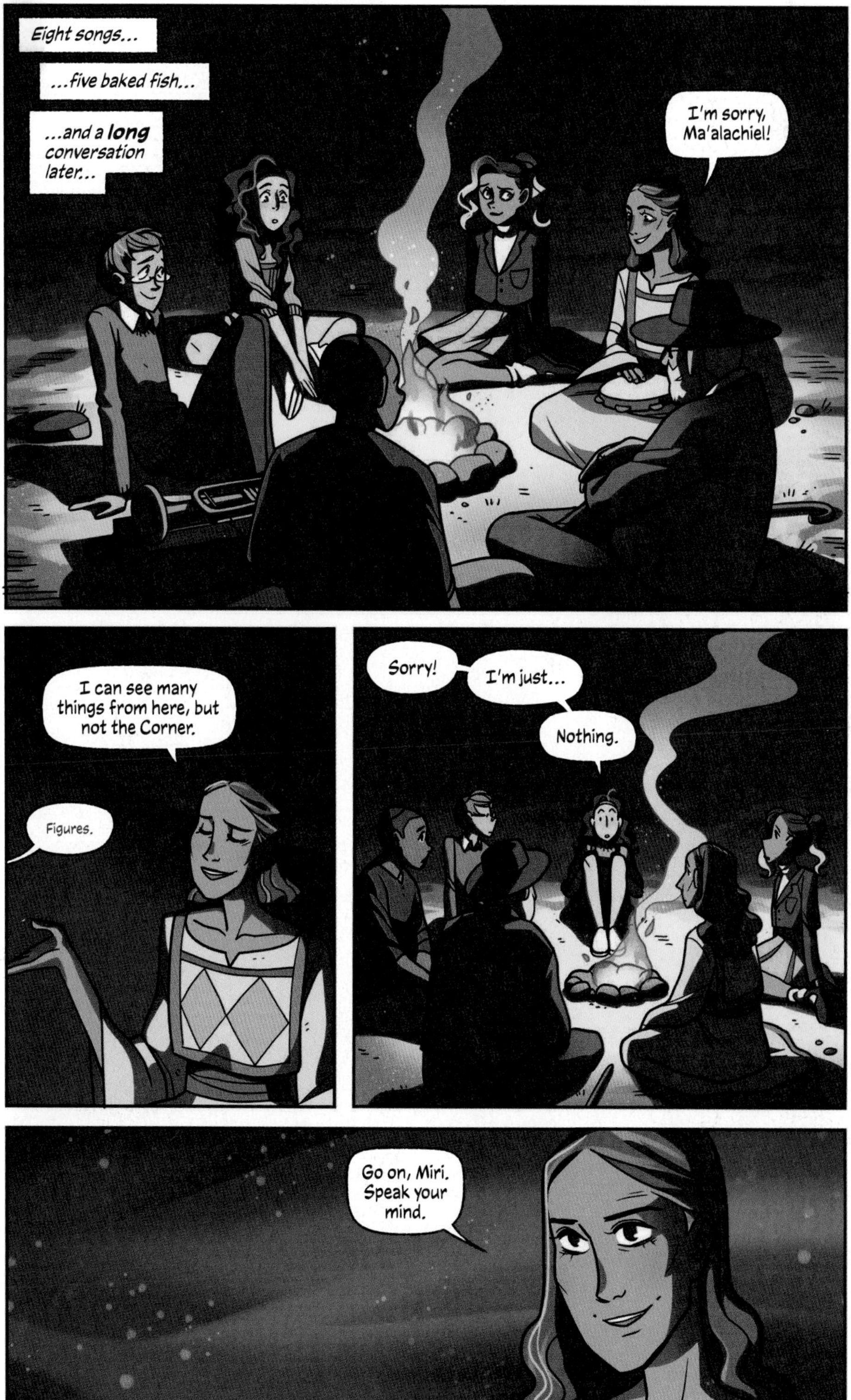
Eight songs...
...five baked fish...
...and a **long** conversation later...
I'm sorry, Ma'alachiel!
I can see many things from here, but not the Corner.
Figures.
Sorry!
I'm just...
Nothing.
Go on, Miri. Speak your mind.

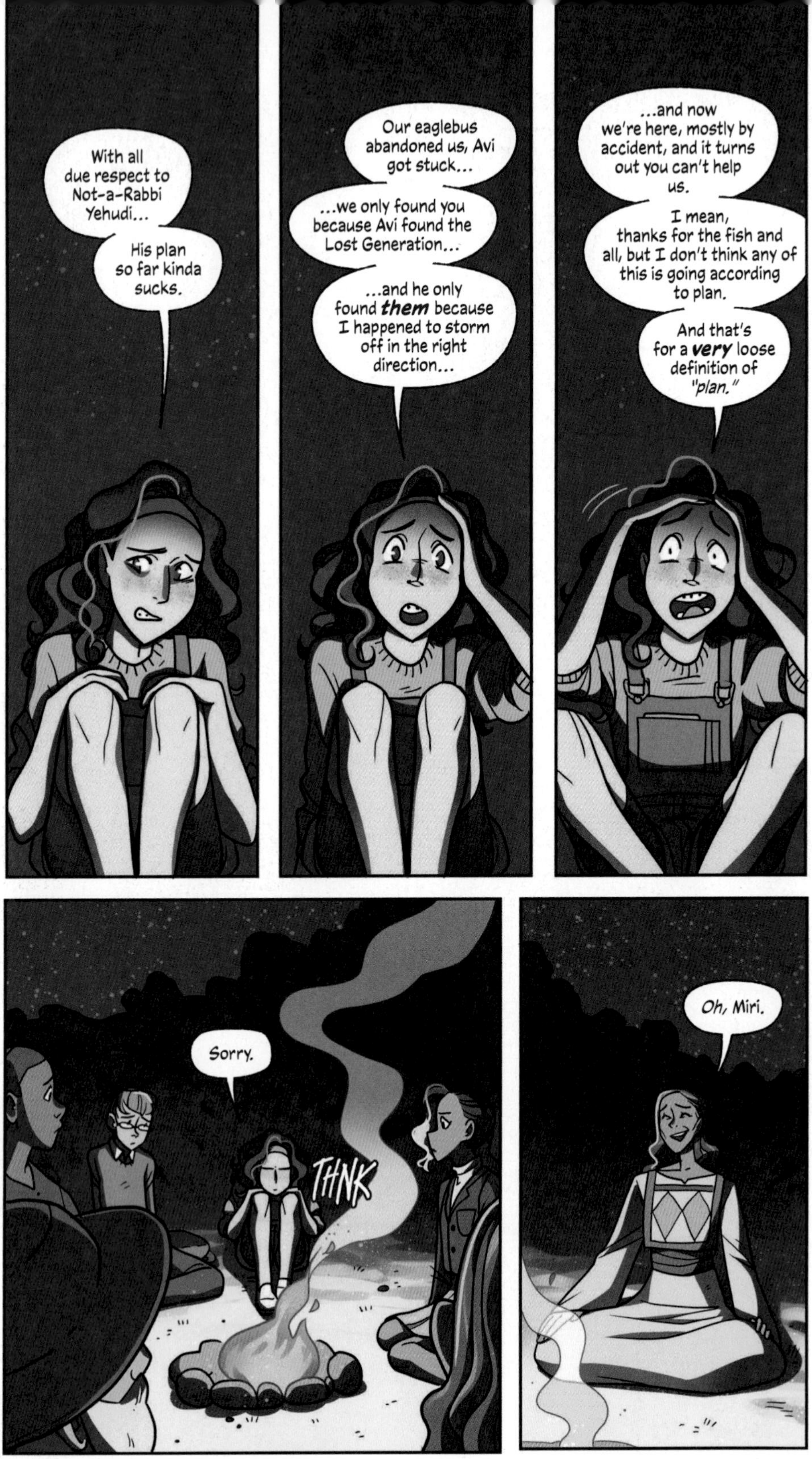
With all due respect to Not-a-Rabbi Yehudi...
His plan so far kinda sucks.
Our eaglebus abandoned us, Avi got stuck...
...we only found you because Avi found the Lost Generation...
...and he only found *them* because I happened to storm off in the right direction...
...and now we're here, mostly by accident, and it turns out you can't help us.
I mean, thanks for the fish and all, but I don't think any of this is going according to plan.
And that's for a *very* loose definition of *"plan."*
Sorry.
THNK
Oh, Miri.

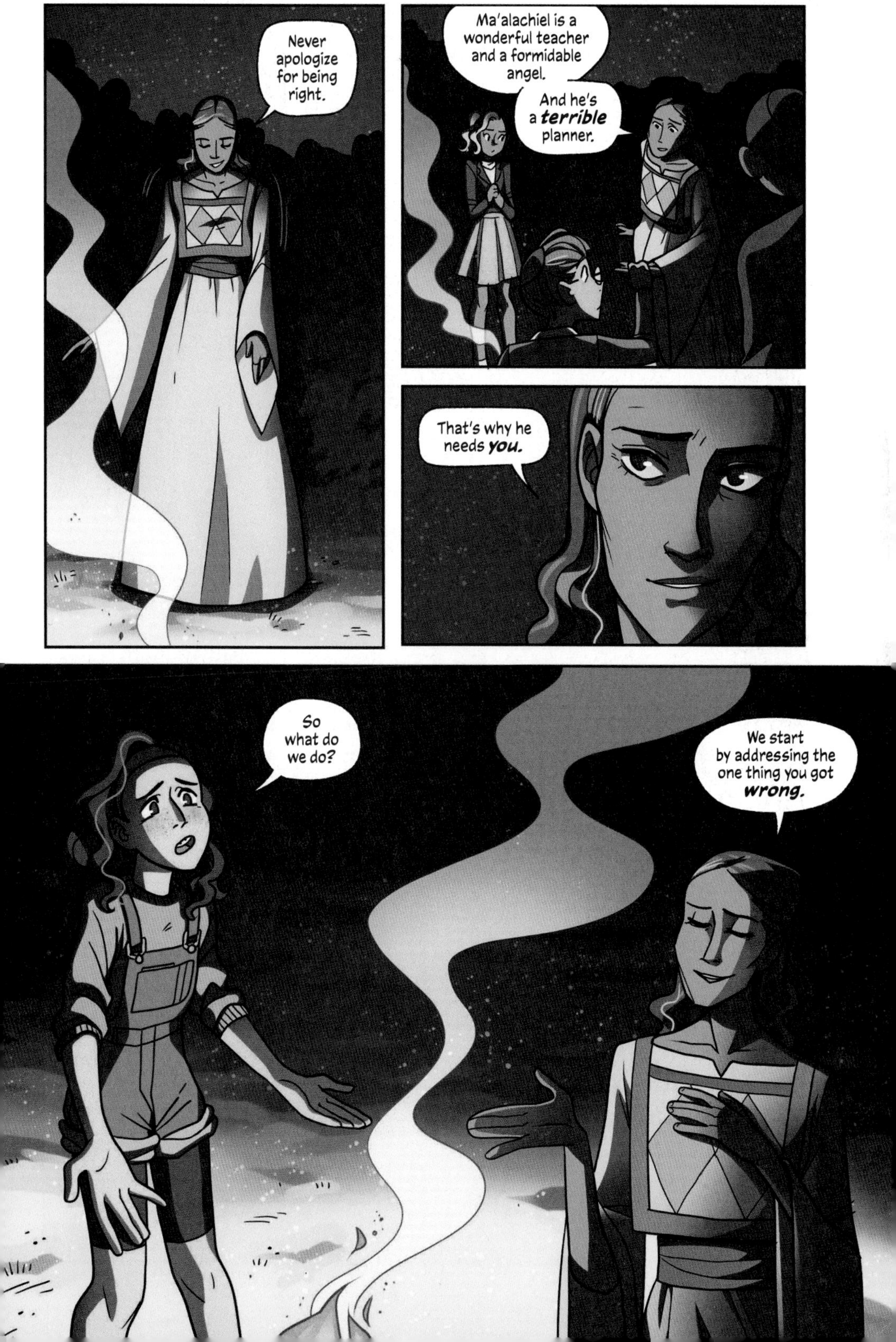
Never apologize for being right.
Ma'alachiel is a wonderful teacher and a formidable angel.
And he's a ***terrible*** planner.
That's why he needs ***you.***
So what do we do?
We start by addressing the one thing you got ***wrong.***

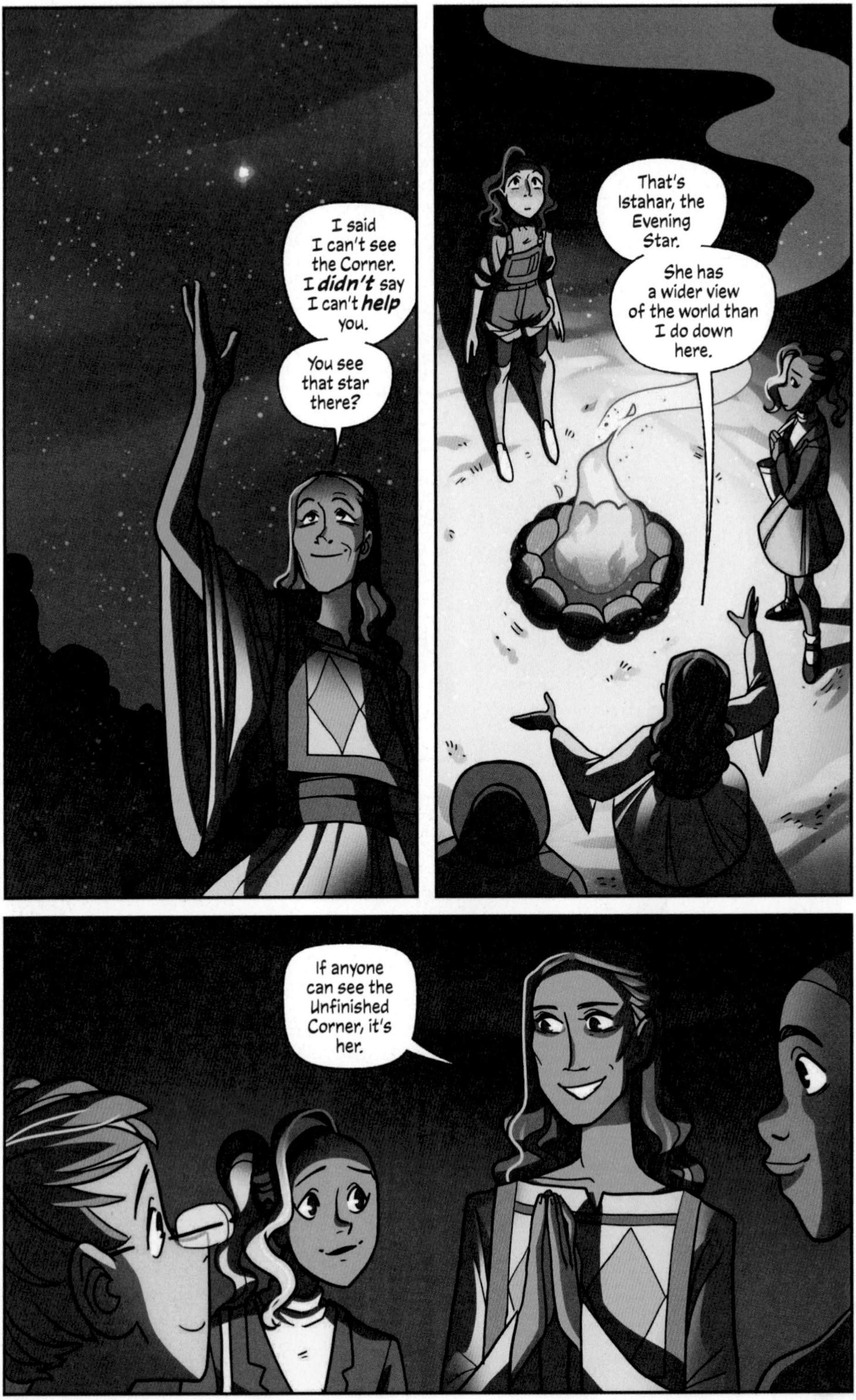
I said I can't see the Corner. I **didn't** say I can't **help** you.
You see that star there?
That's Istahar, the Evening Star.
She has a wider view of the world than I do down here.
If anyone can see the Unfinished Corner, it's her.

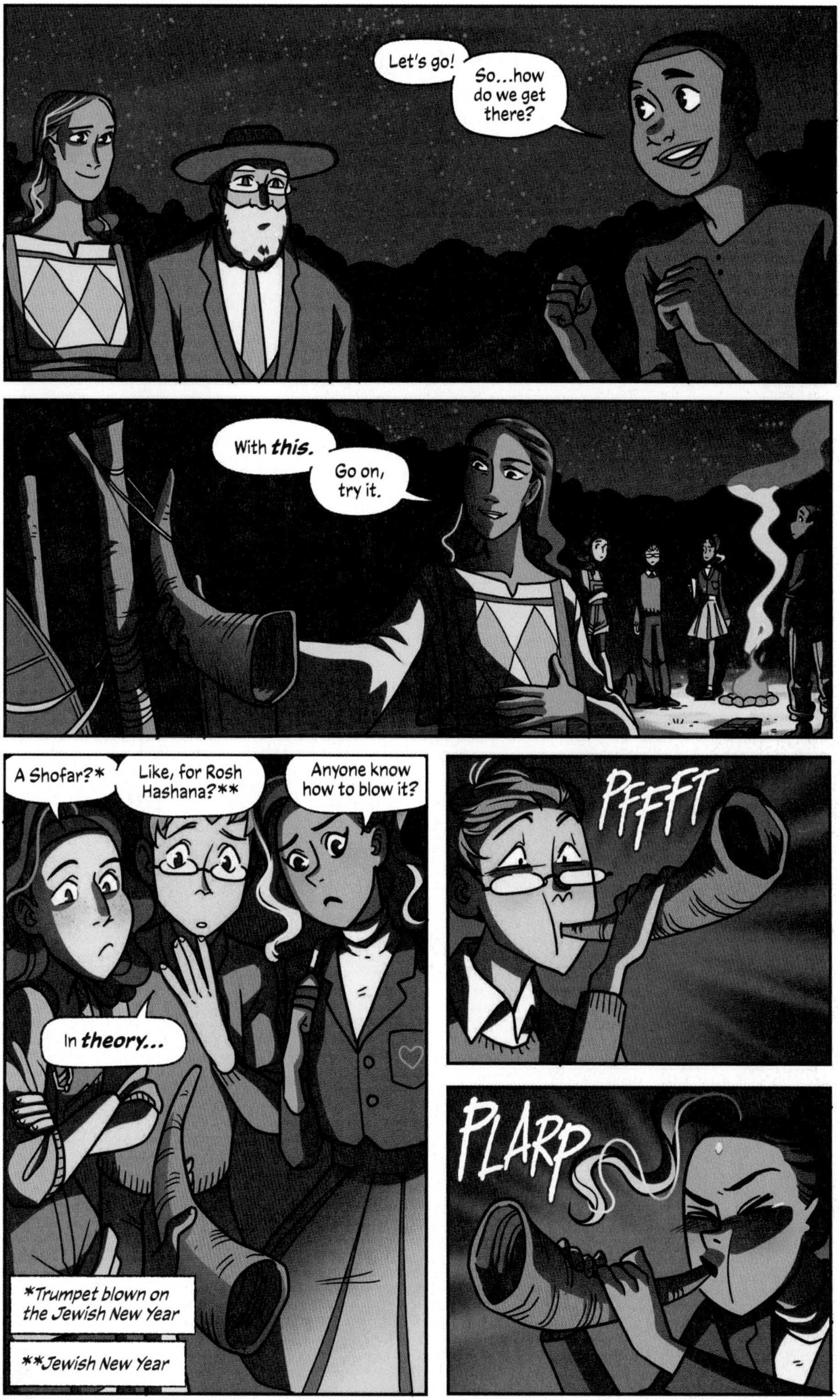
Let's go!
So...how do we get there?
With *this.*
Go on, try it.
A Shofar?*
Like, for Rosh Hashana?**
Anyone know how to blow it?
In *theory...*
*Trumpet blown on the Jewish New Year
**Jewish New Year
PFFFT
PLARP

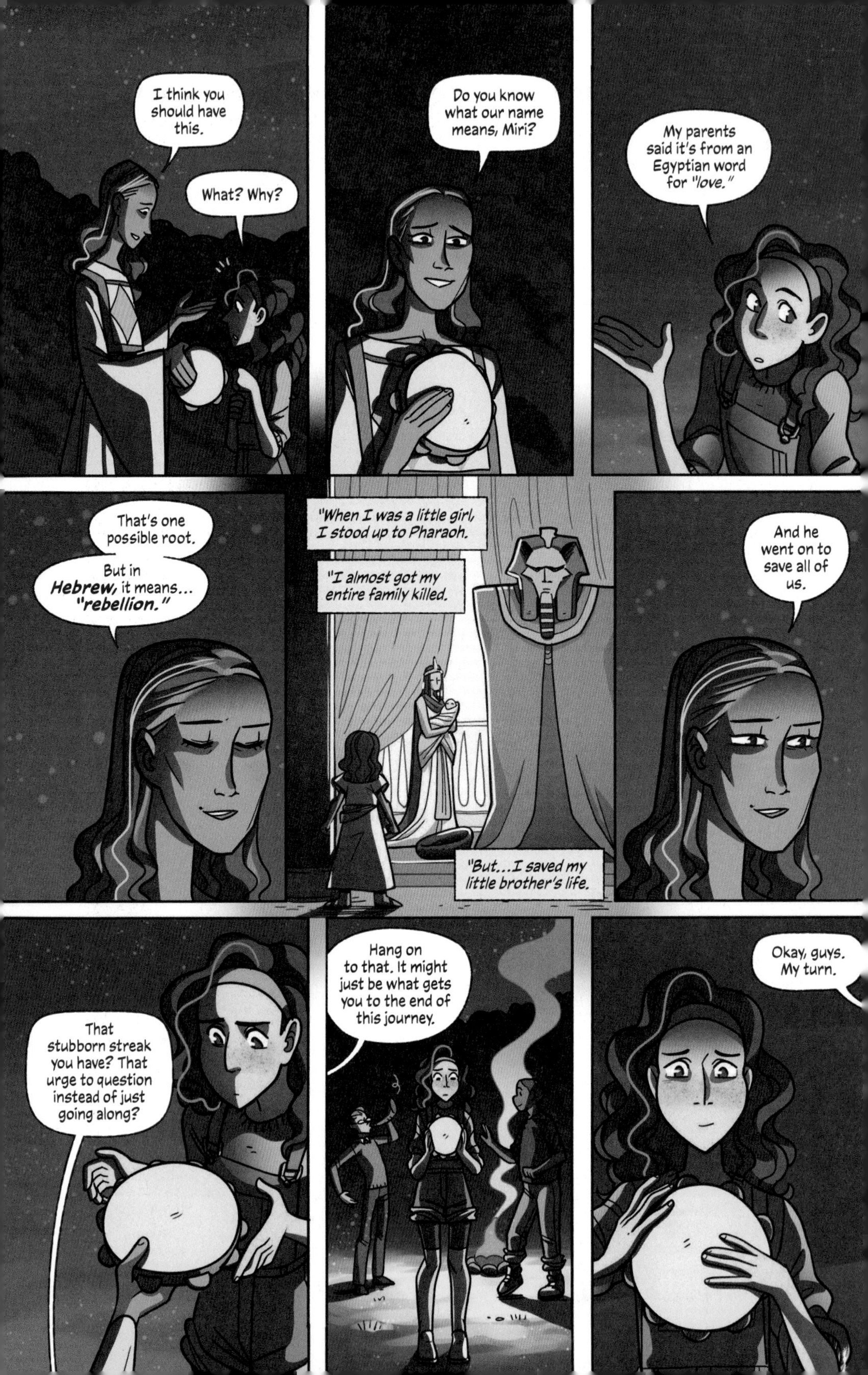

I think you should have this.
What? Why?
Do you know what our name means, Miri?
My parents said it's from an Egyptian word for "love."
That's one possible root.
But in **Hebrew,** it means... **"rebellion."**
"When I was a little girl, I stood up to Pharaoh.
"I almost got my entire family killed.
"But...I saved my little brother's life.
And he went on to save all of us.
That stubborn streak you have? That urge to question instead of just going along?
Hang on to that. It might just be what gets you to the end of this journey.
Okay, guys. My turn.

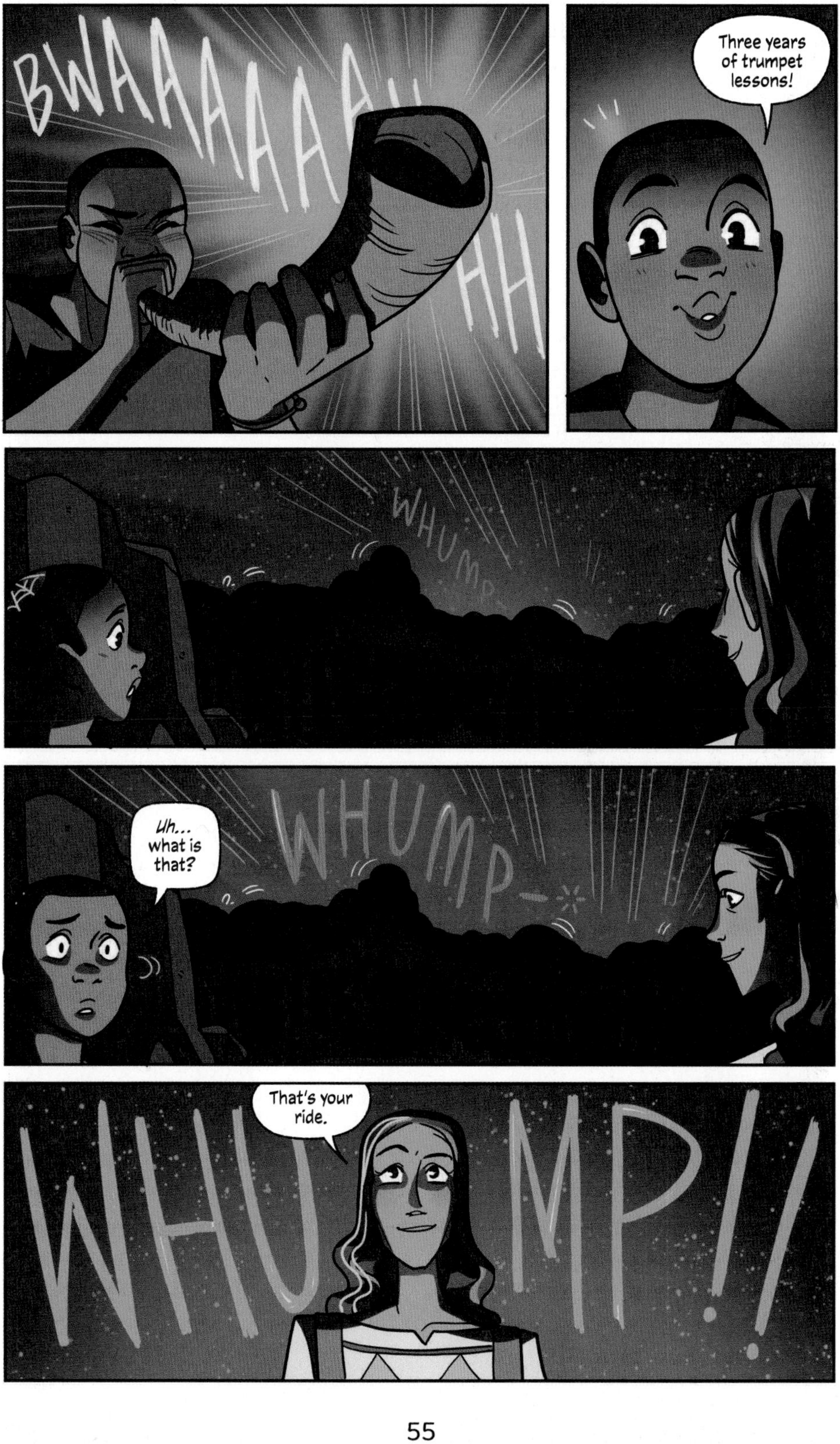
BWAAAAAAAHH
Three years of trumpet lessons!
WHUMP-
Uh... what is that?
WHUMP-
That's your ride.
WHUMP!!

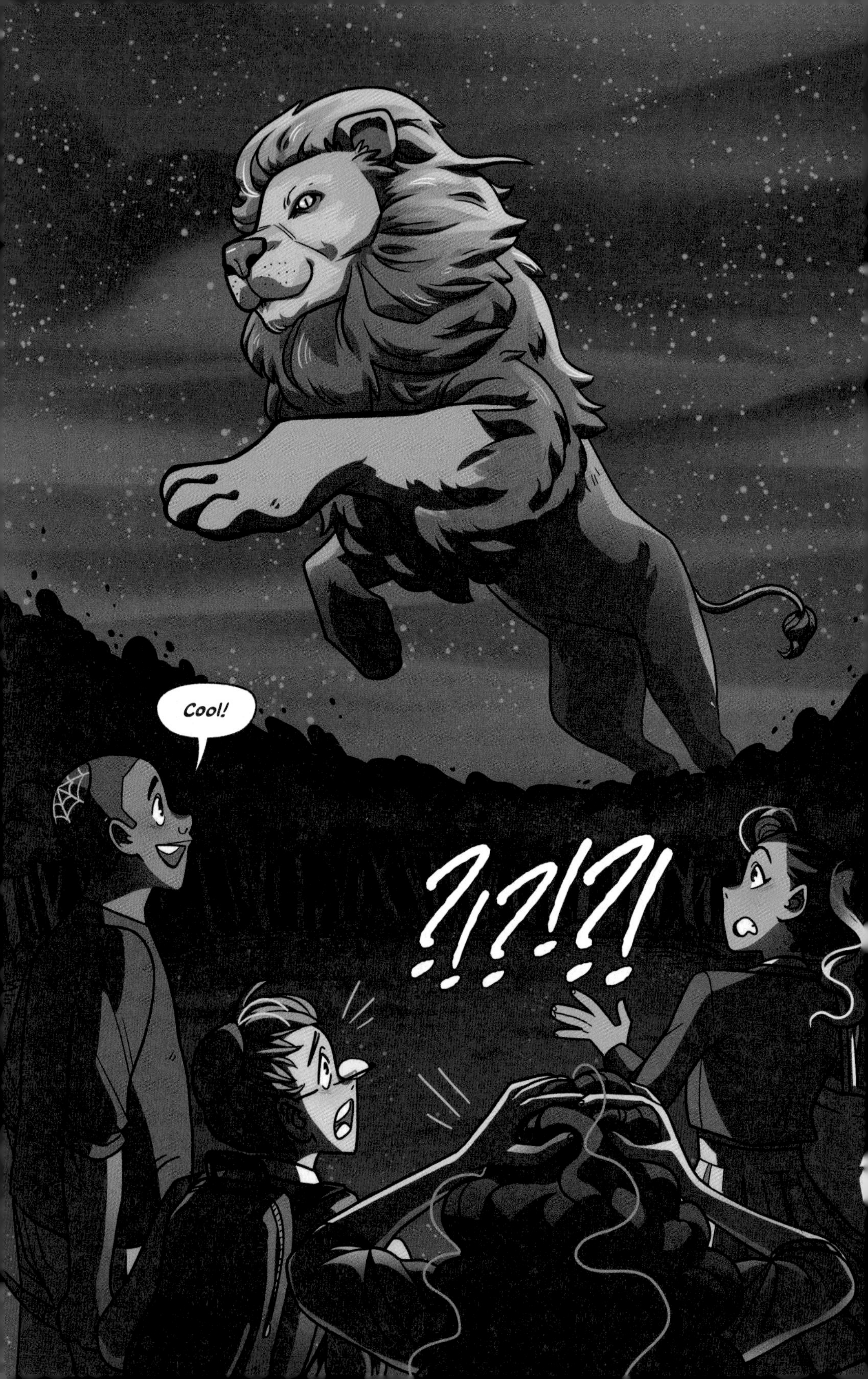
Cool!
?!?!?!

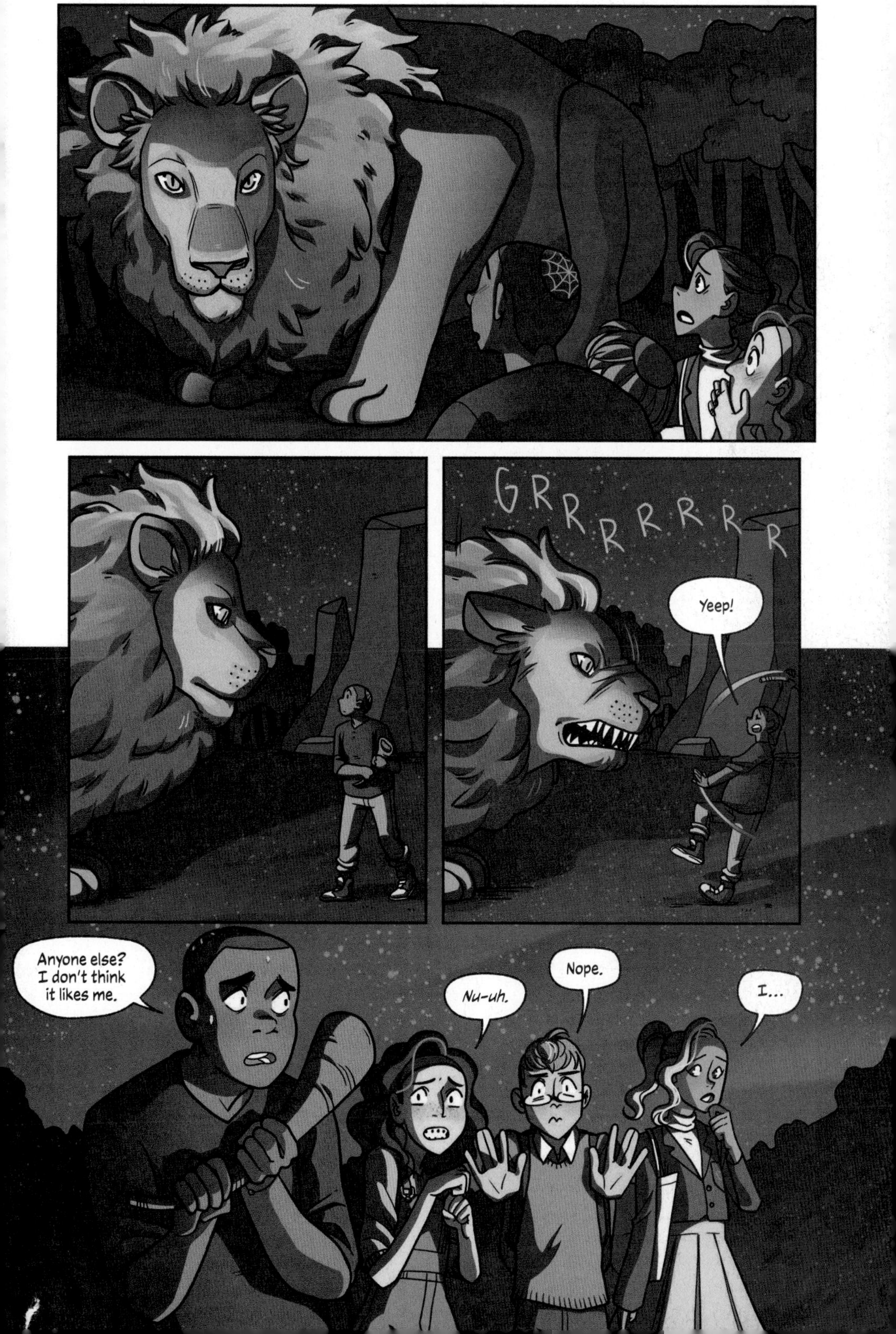
GRRRRRRRR
Yeep!
Anyone else? I don't think it likes me.
Nu-uh.
Nope.
I...

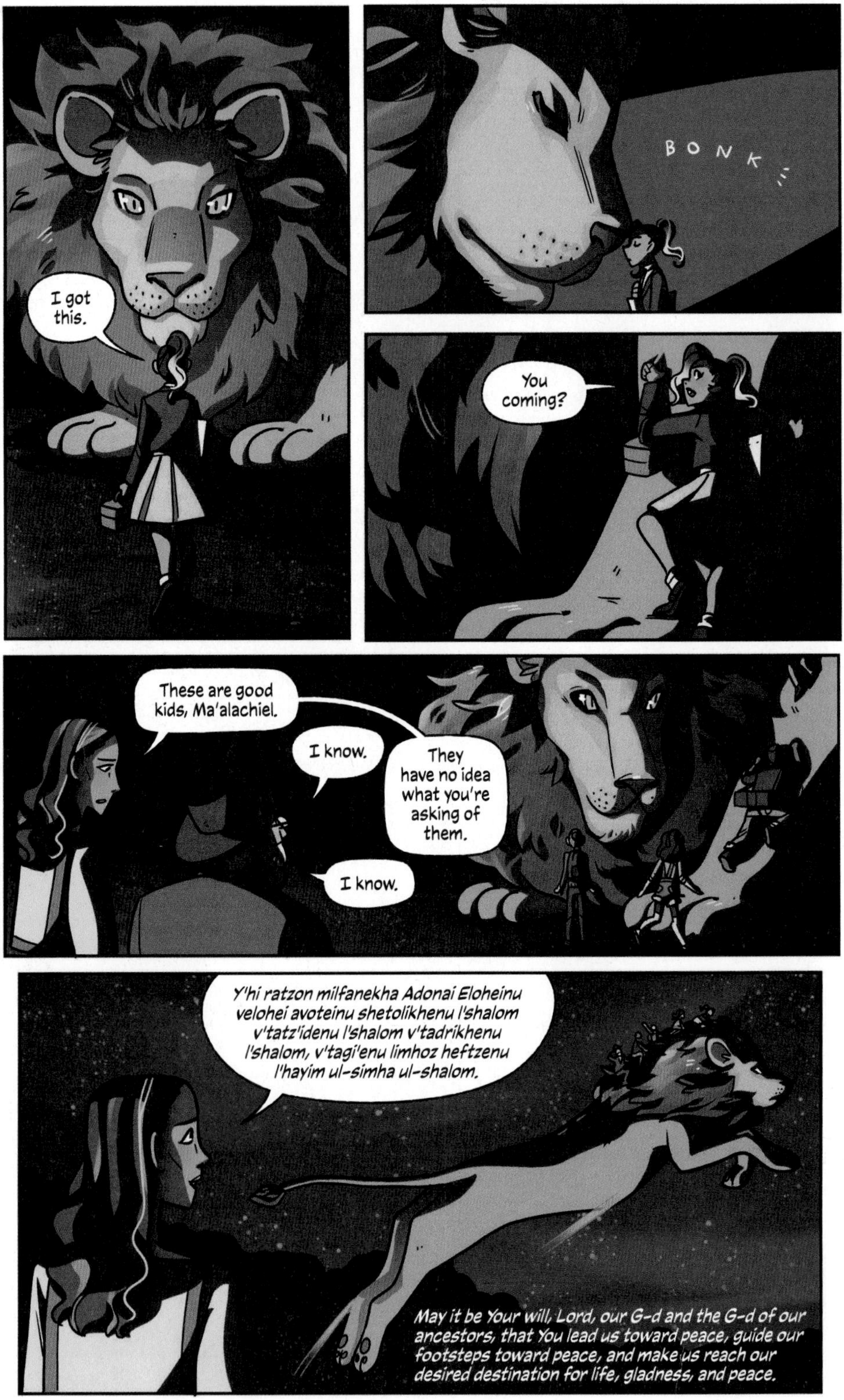
I got this.
BONK
You coming?
These are good kids, Ma'alachiel.
I know.
They have no idea what you're asking of them.
I know.
Y'hi ratzon milfanekha Adonai Eloheinu velohei avoteinu shetolikhenu l'shalom v'tatz'idenu l'shalom v'tadrikhenu l'shalom, v'tagi'enu limhoz heftzenu l'hayim ul-simha ul-shalom.
May it be Your will, Lord, our G-d and the G-d of our ancestors, that You lead us toward peace, guide our footsteps toward peace, and make us reach our desired destination for life, gladness, and peace.

CHAPTER FOUR

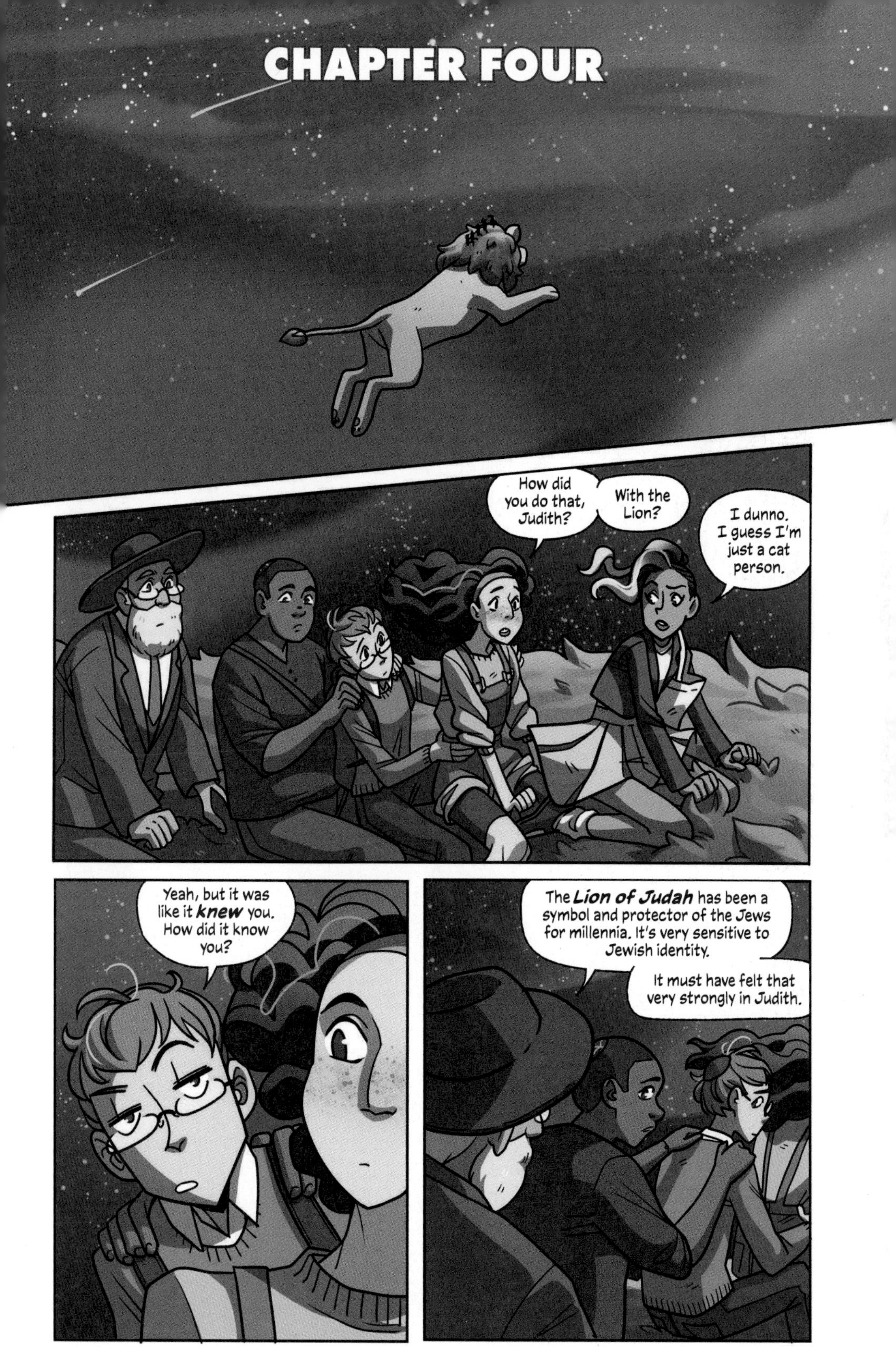
How did you do that, Judith?
With the Lion?
I dunno. I guess I'm just a cat person.
Yeah, but it was like it ***knew*** you. How did it know you?
The ***Lion of Judah*** has been a symbol and protector of the Jews for millennia. It's very sensitive to Jewish identity.
It must have felt that very strongly in Judith.

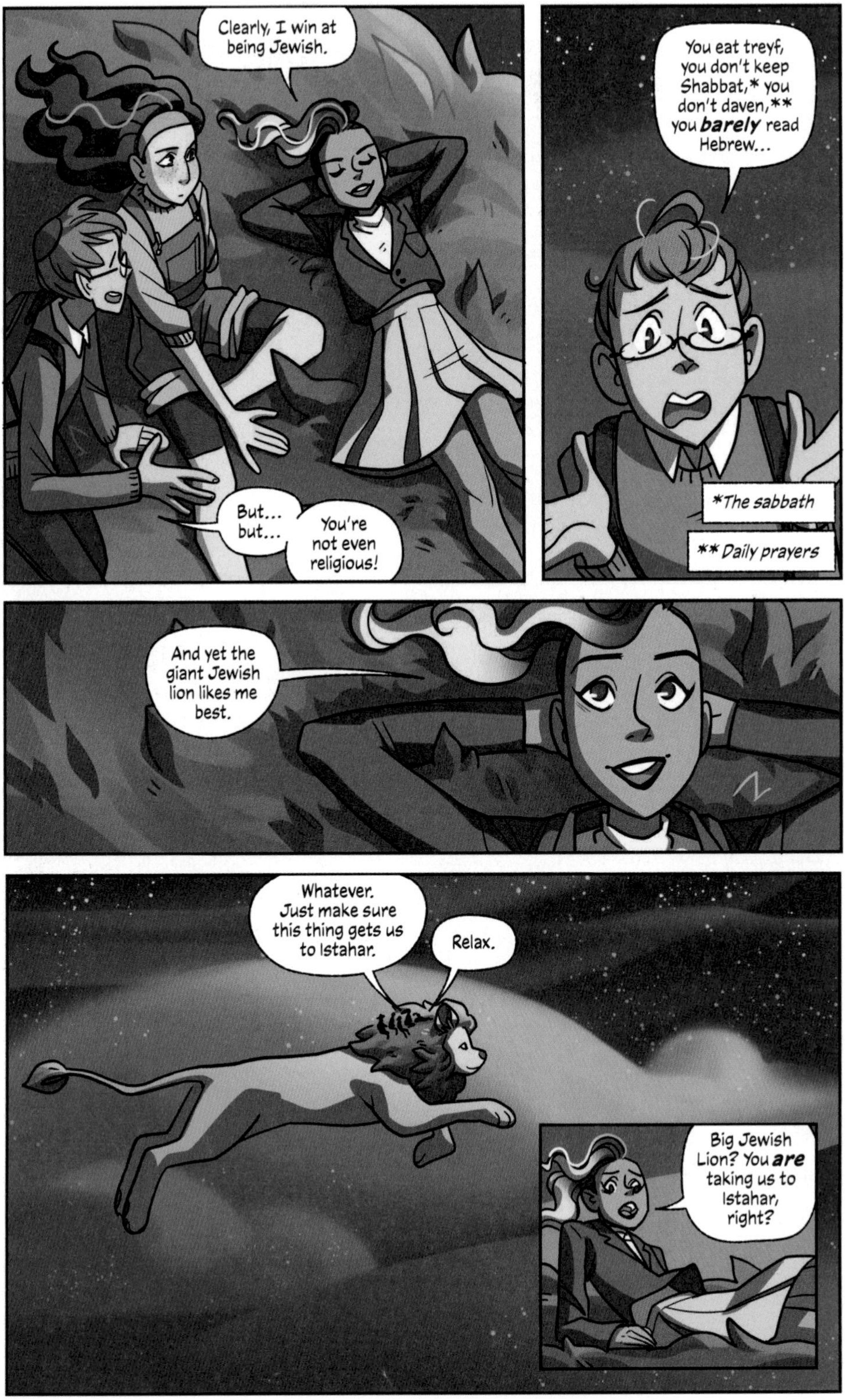
Clearly, I win at being Jewish.
But... but...
You're not even religious!
You eat treyf, you don't keep Shabbat,* you don't daven,** you **barely** read Hebrew...
*The sabbath
** Daily prayers
And yet the giant Jewish lion likes me best.
Whatever. Just make sure this thing gets us to Istahar.
Relax.
Big Jewish Lion? You **are** taking us to Istahar, right?

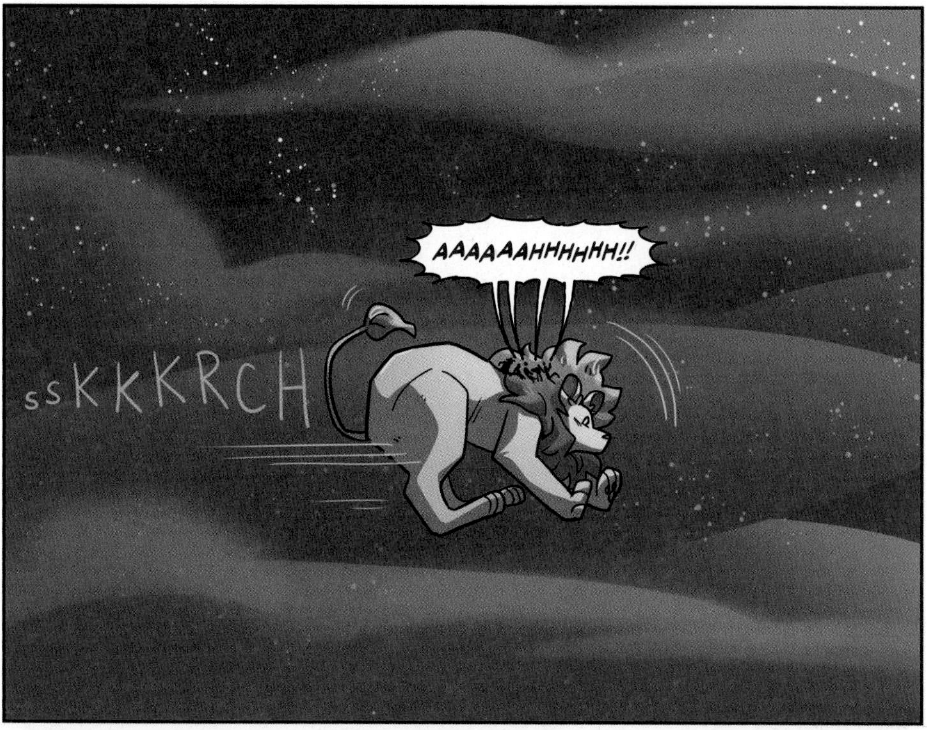
AAAAAAHHHHHH!!
sSKKKRCH

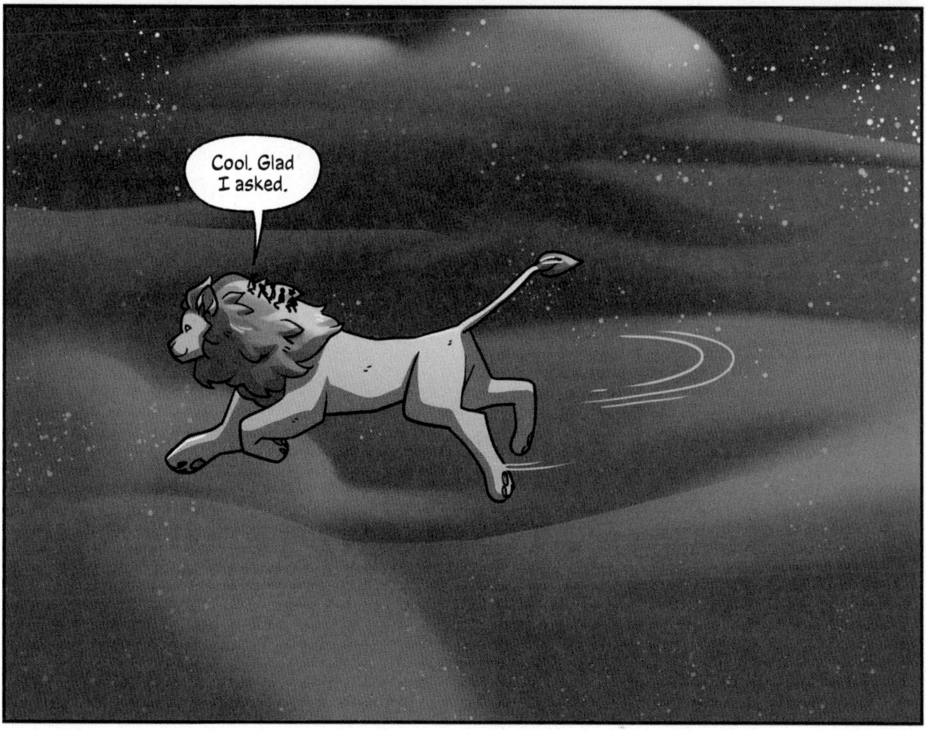
Cool. Glad I asked.

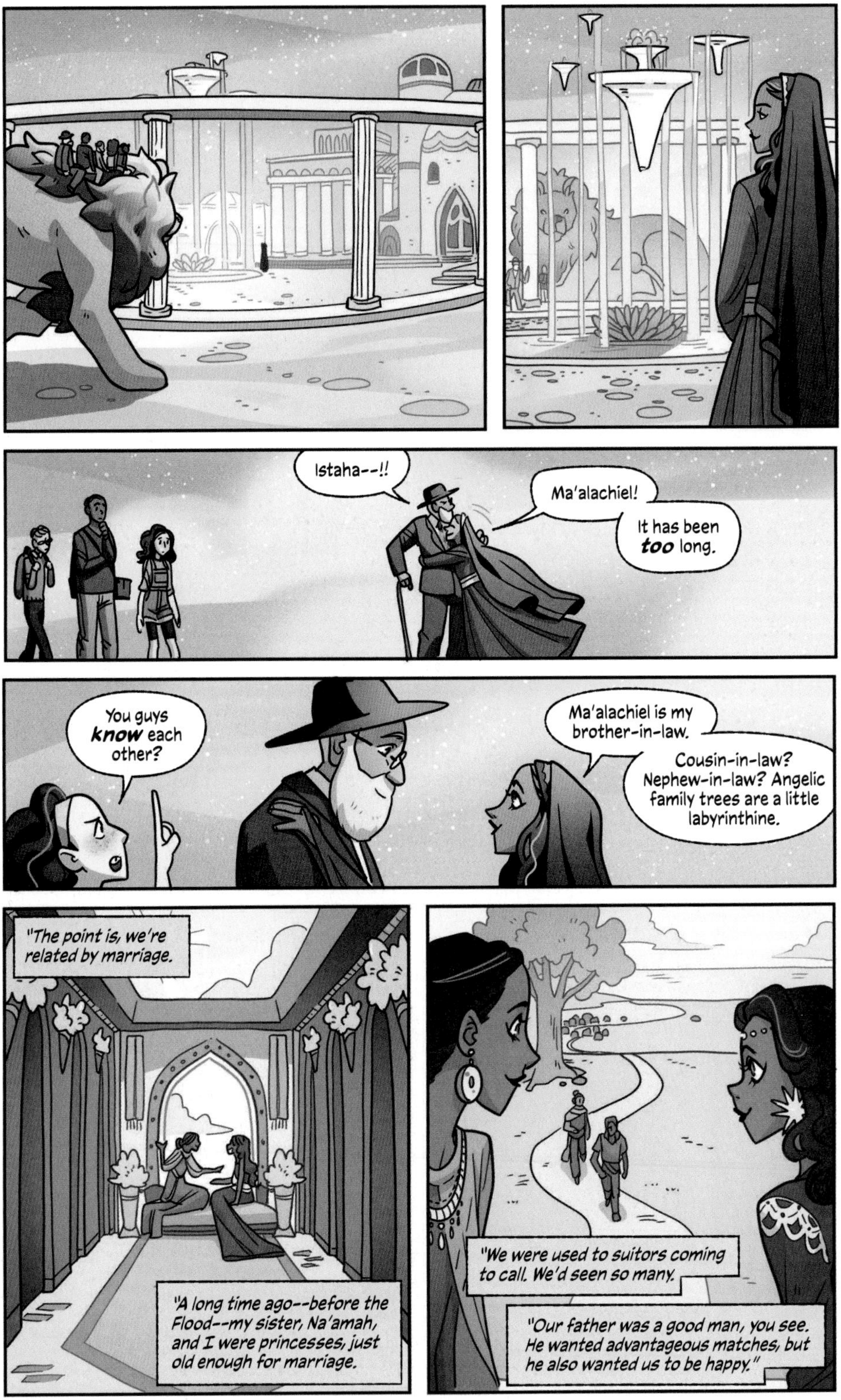
Istaha--!!
Ma'alachiel!
It has been **too** long.
You guys **know** each other?
Ma'alachiel is my brother-in-law.
Cousin-in-law? Nephew-in-law? Angelic family trees are a little labyrinthine.
"The point is, we're related by marriage.
"A long time ago--before the Flood--my sister, Na'amah, and I were princesses, just old enough for marriage.
"We were used to suitors coming to call. We'd seen so many.
"Our father was a good man, you see. He wanted advantageous matches, but he also wanted us to be happy."

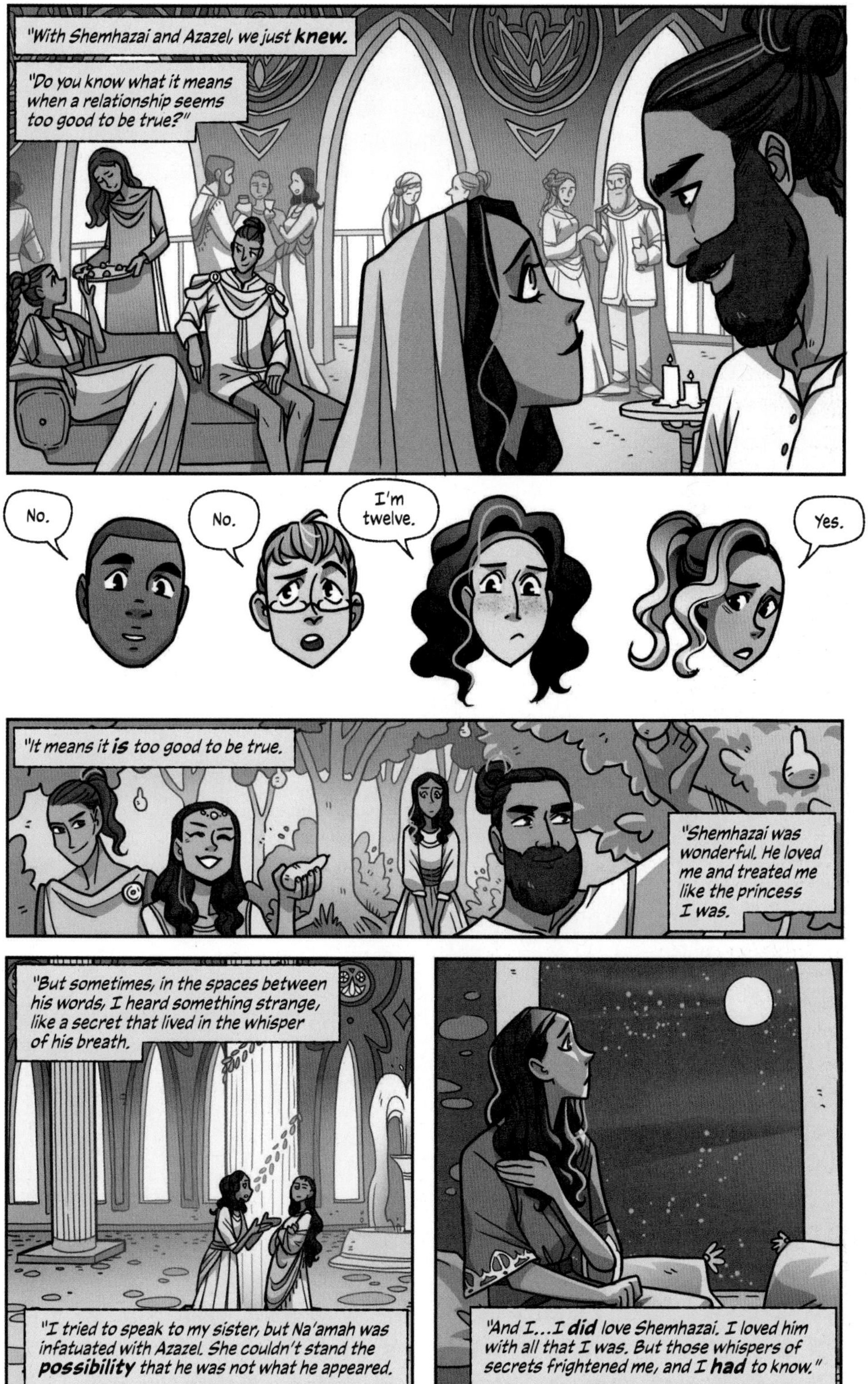
"With Shemhazai and Azazel, we just **knew.**
"Do you know what it means when a relationship seems too good to be true?"
No.
No.
I'm twelve.
Yes.
"It means it **is** too good to be true.
"Shemhazai was wonderful. He loved me and treated me like the princess I was.
"But sometimes, in the spaces between his words, I heard something strange, like a secret that lived in the whisper of his breath.
"I tried to speak to my sister, but Na'amah was infatuated with Azazel. She couldn't stand the **possibility** that he was not what he appeared.
"And I...I **did** love Shemhazai. I loved him with all that I was. But those whispers of secrets frightened me, and I **had** to know."

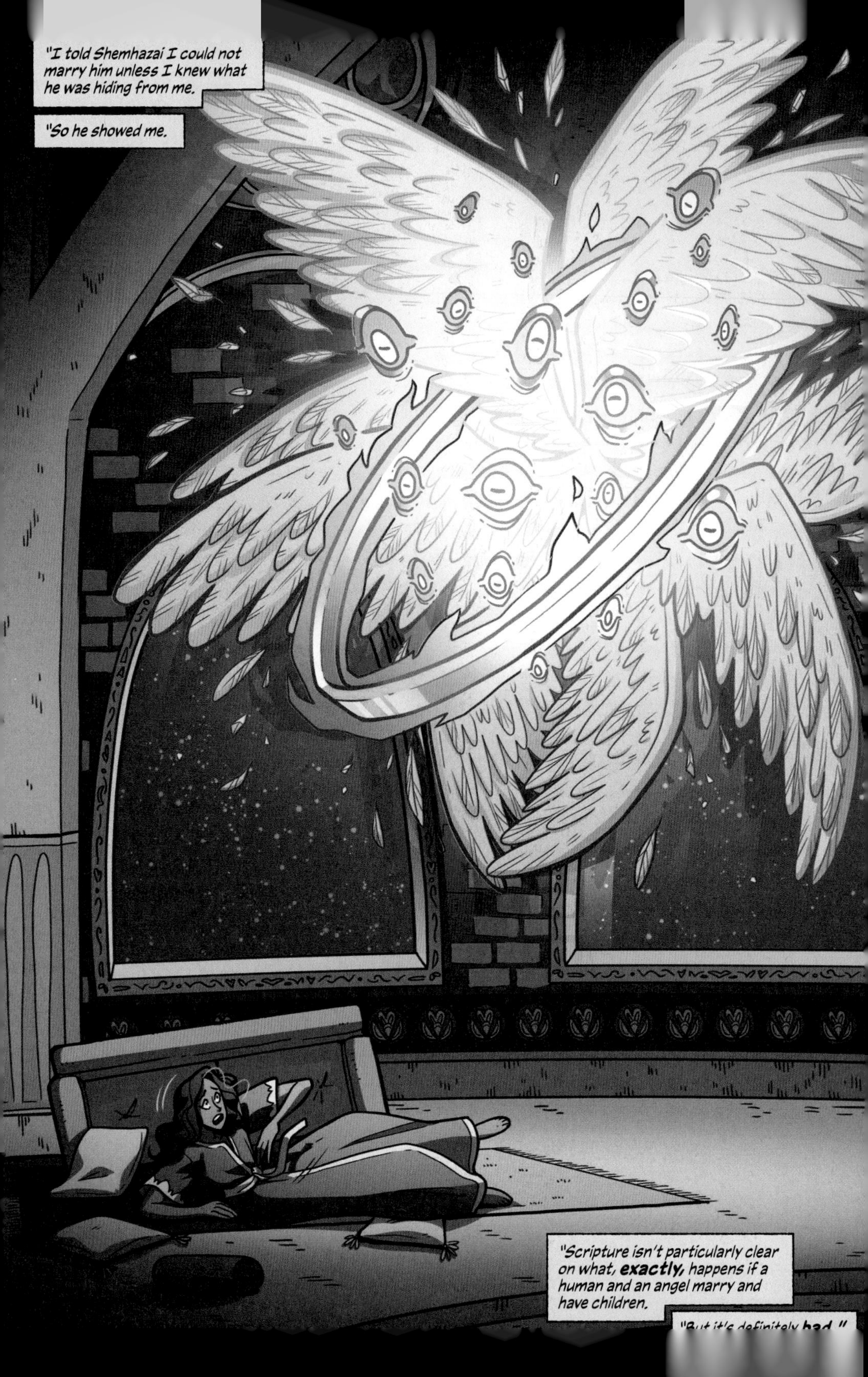
"I told Shemhazai I could not marry him unless I knew what he was hiding from me.
"So he showed me.
"Scripture isn't particularly clear on what, **exactly,** happens if a human and an angel marry and have children.
"But it's definitely **bad.**"

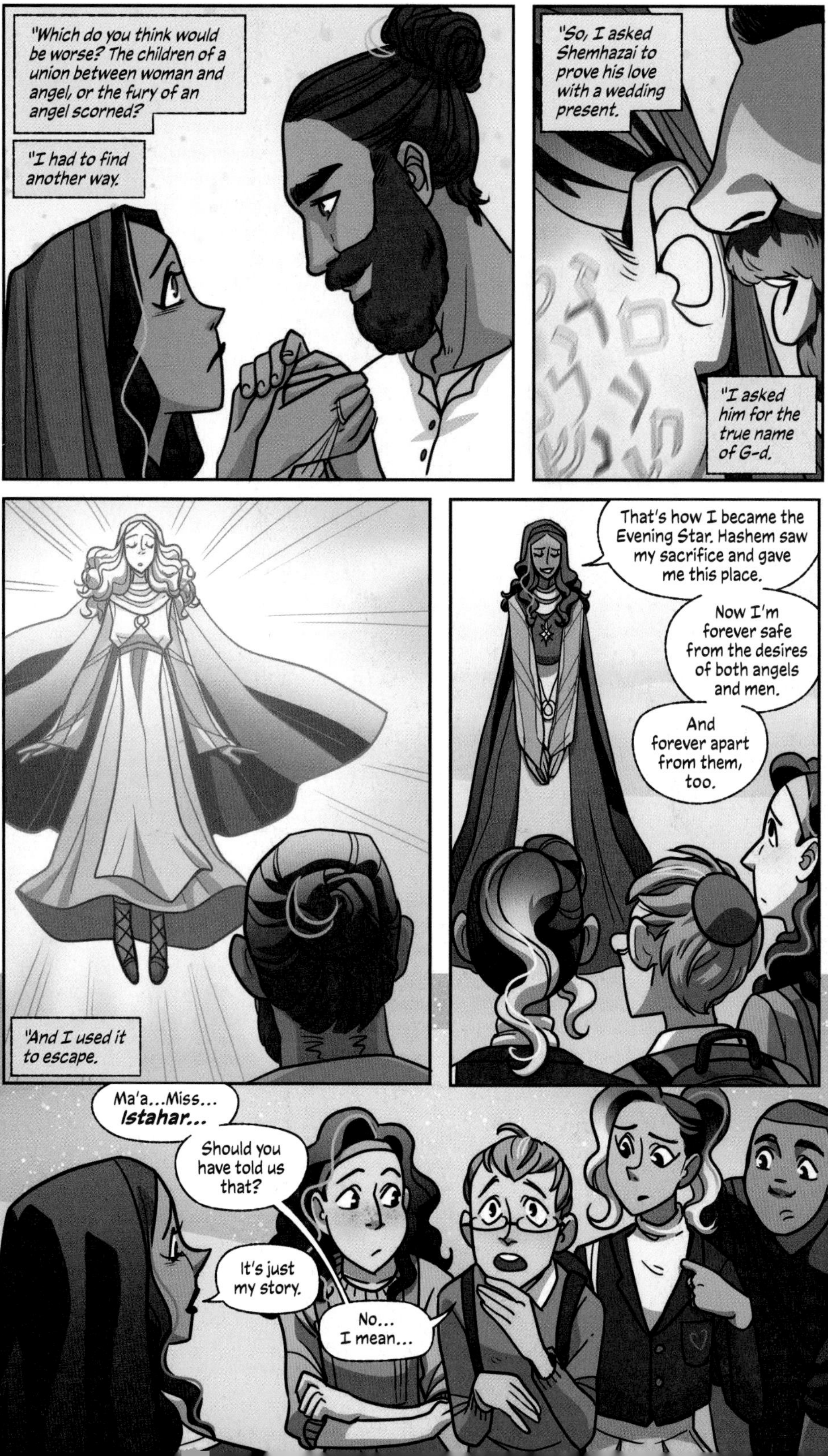
"Which do you think would be worse? The children of a union between woman and angel, or the fury of an angel scorned?
"I had to find another way.
"So, I asked Shemhazai to prove his love with a wedding present.
"I asked him for the true name of G-d.
"And I used it to escape.
That's how I became the Evening Star. Hashem saw my sacrifice and gave me this place.
Now I'm forever safe from the desires of both angels and men.
And forever apart from them, too.
Ma'a...Miss... Istahar...
Should you have told us that?
It's just my story.
No... I mean...

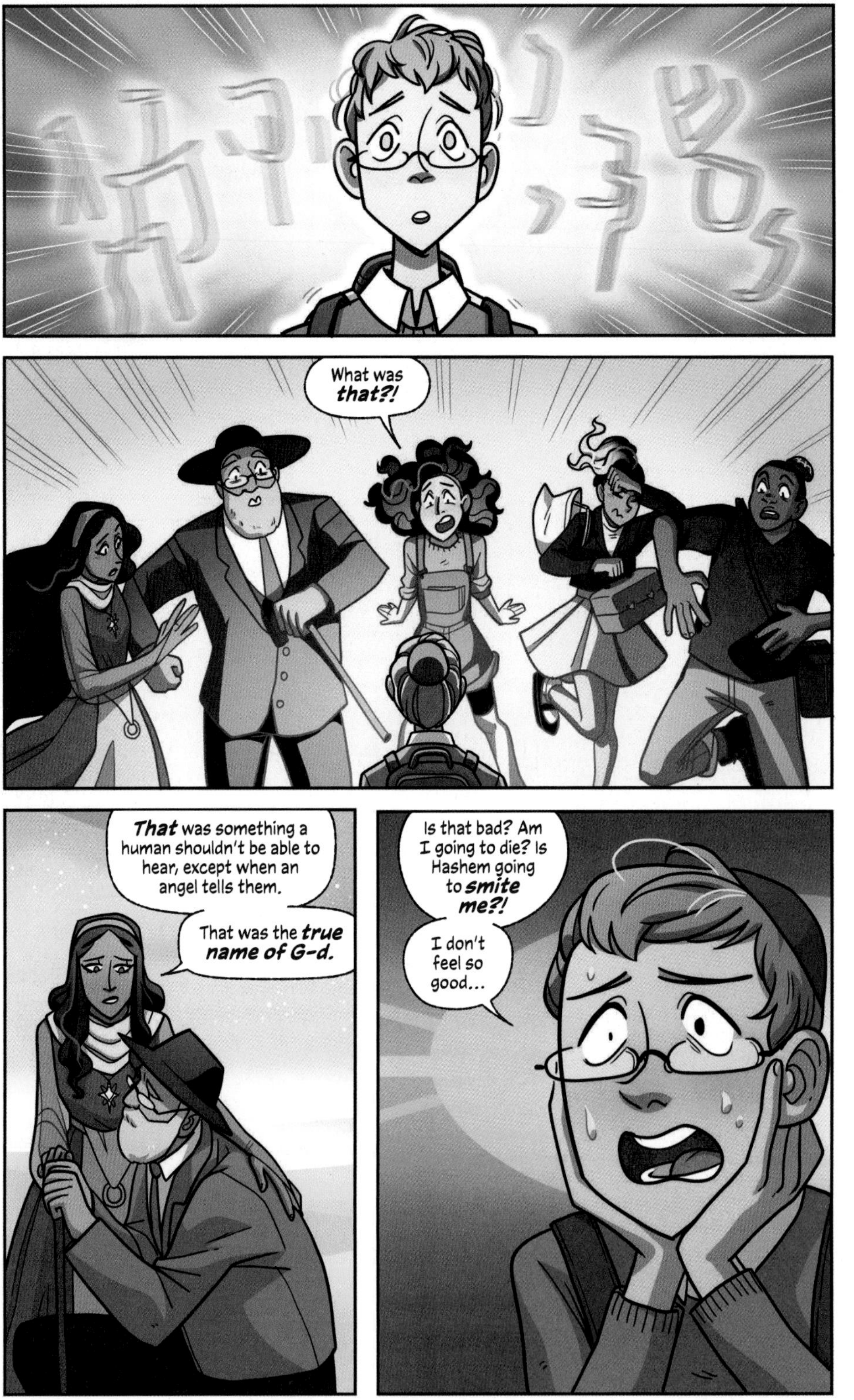

What was that?!
That was something a human shouldn't be able to hear, except when an angel tells them.
That was the true name of G-d.
Is that bad? Am I going to die? Is Hashem going to smite me?!
I don't feel so good...

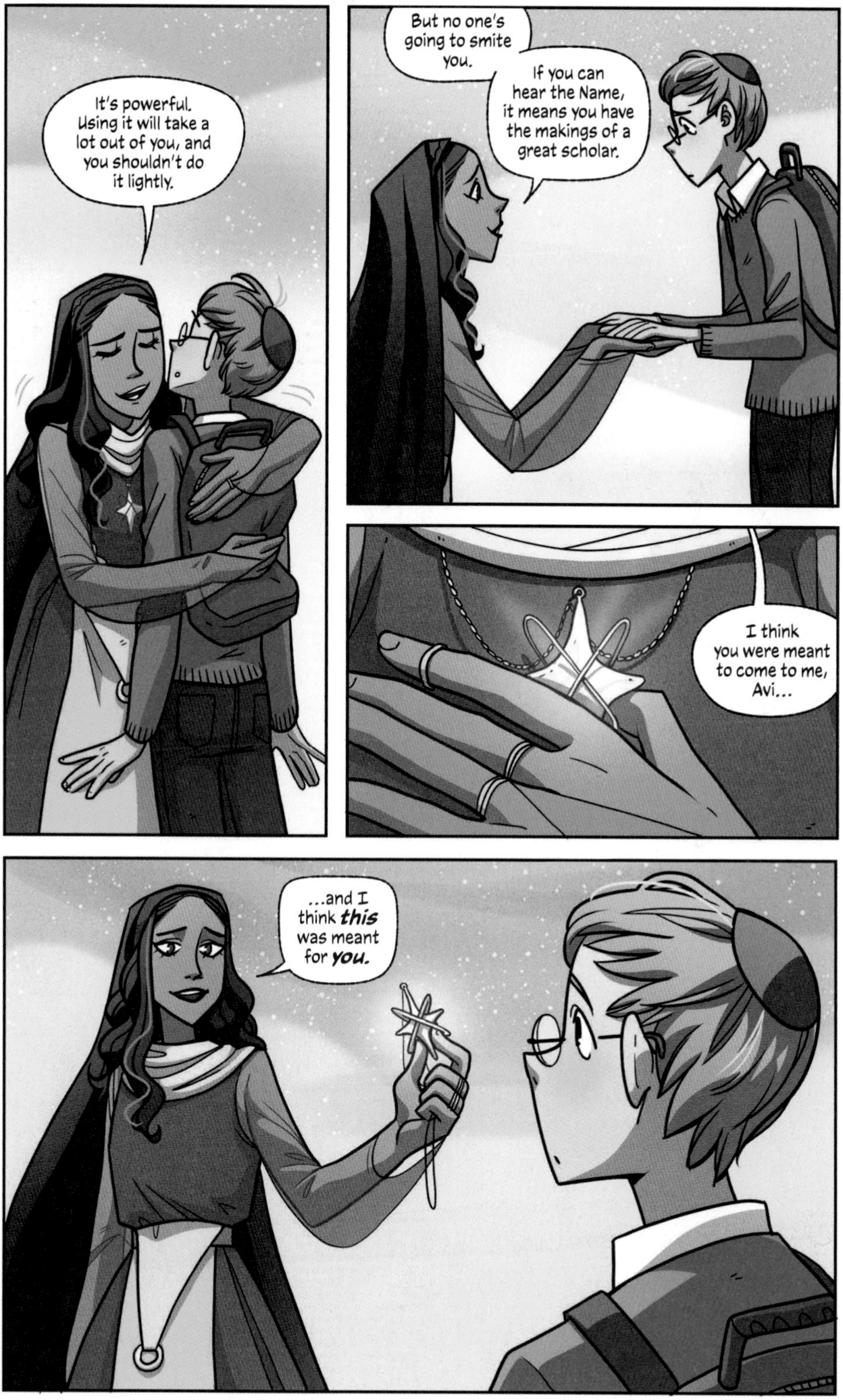
It's powerful. Using it will take a lot out of you, and you shouldn't do it lightly.
But no one's going to smite you.
If you can hear the Name, it means you have the makings of a great scholar.
I think you were meant to come to me, Avi...
...and I think this was meant for you.

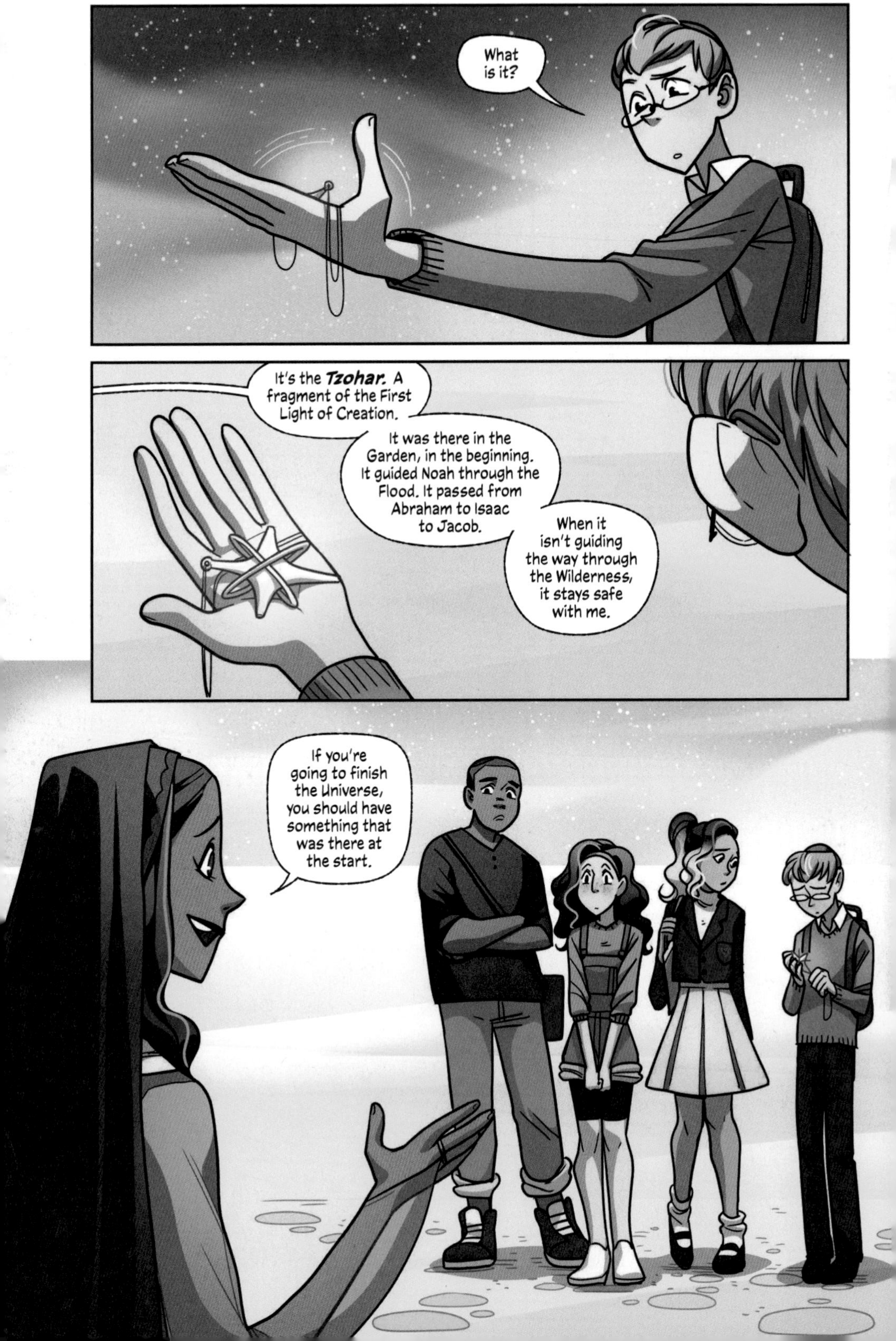
What is it?
It's the **Tzohar.** A fragment of the First Light of Creation.
It was there in the Garden, in the beginning. It guided Noah through the Flood. It passed from Abraham to Isaac to Jacob.
When it isn't guiding the way through the Wilderness, it stays safe with me.
If you're going to finish the Universe, you should have something that was there at the start.

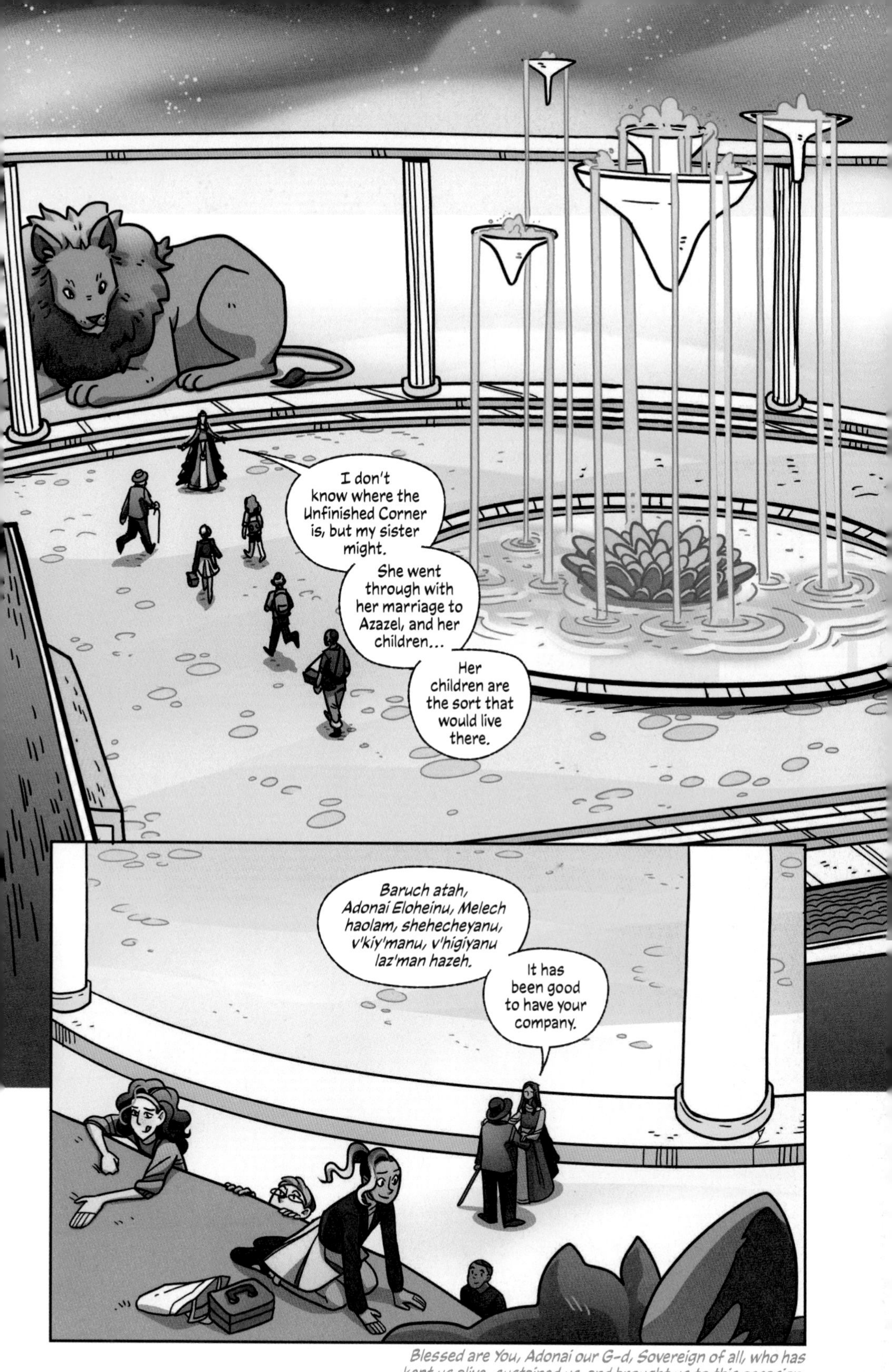
I don't know where the Unfinished Corner is, but my sister might.
She went through with her marriage to Azazel, and her children...
Her children are the sort that would live there.
Baruch atah, Adonai Eloheinu, Melech haolam, shehecheyanu, v'kiy'manu, v'higiyanu laz'man hazeh.
It has been good to have your company.

Blessed are You, Adonai our G-d, Sovereign of all, who has kept us alive, sustained us, and brought us to this occasion.

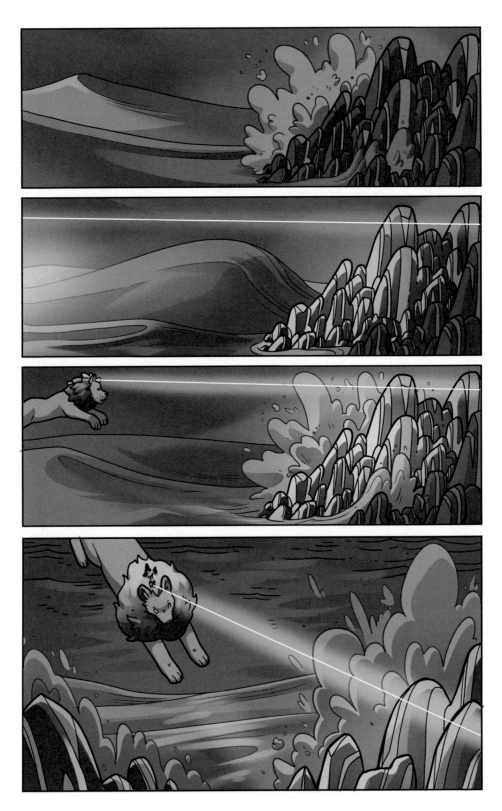

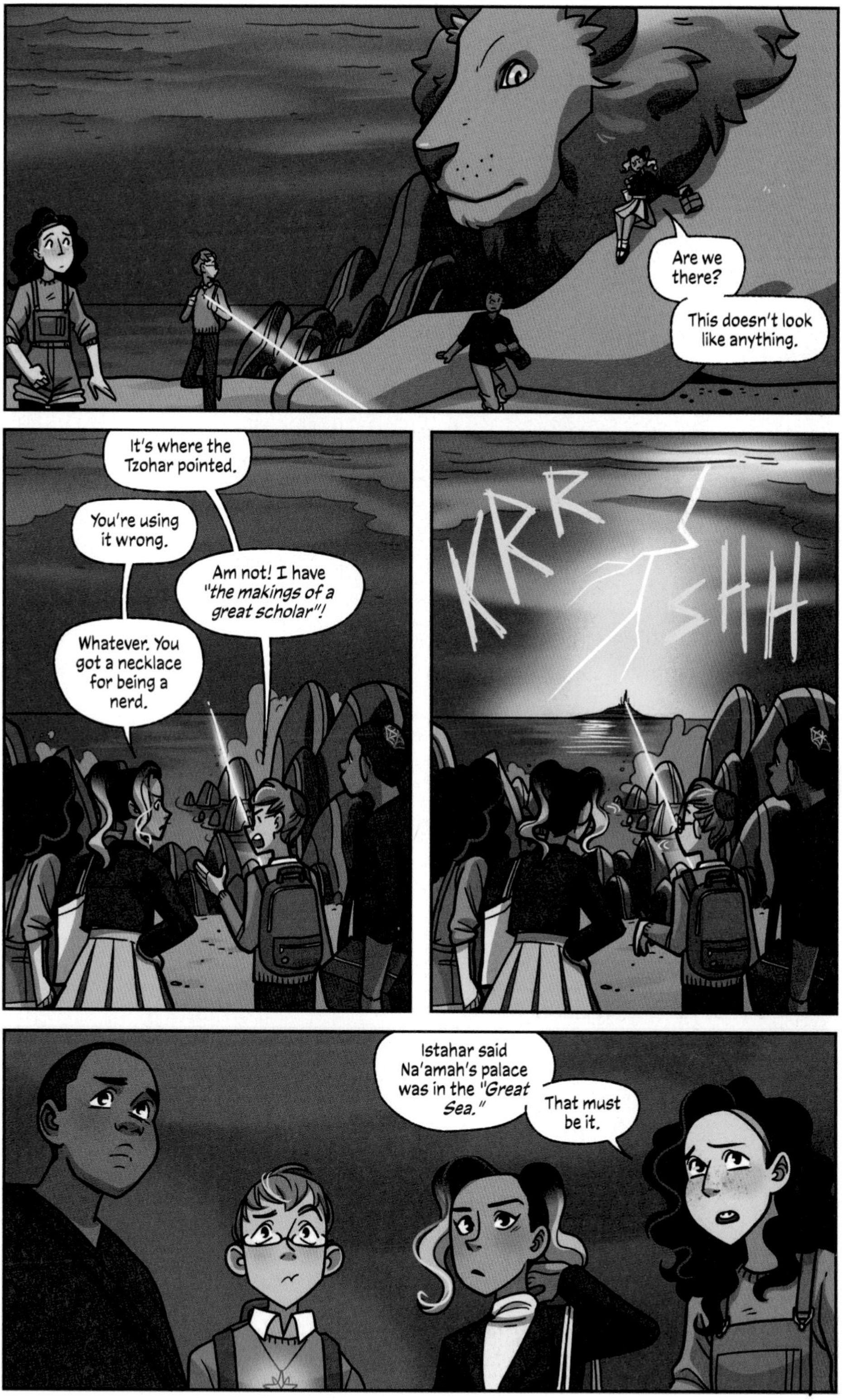

Are we there?
This doesn't look like anything.
It's where the Tzohar pointed.
You're using it wrong.
Am not! I have *"the makings of a great scholar"*!
Whatever. You got a necklace for being a nerd.
KRR SHH
Istahar said Na'amah's palace was in the *"Great Sea."*
That must be it.

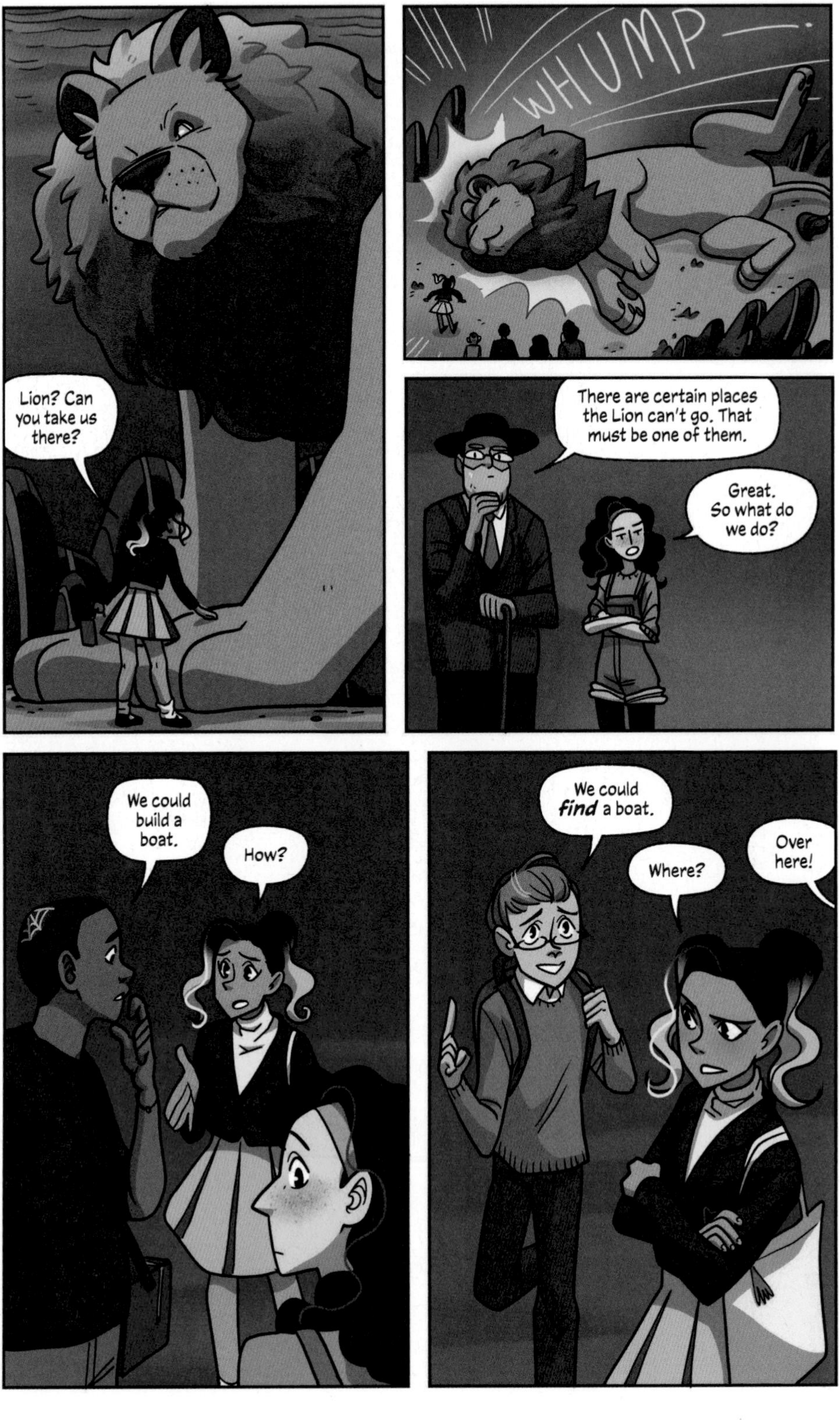

WHUMP
Lion? Can you take us there?
There are certain places the Lion can't go. That must be one of them.
Great. So what do we do?
We could build a boat.
How?
We could *find* a boat.
Where?
Over here!

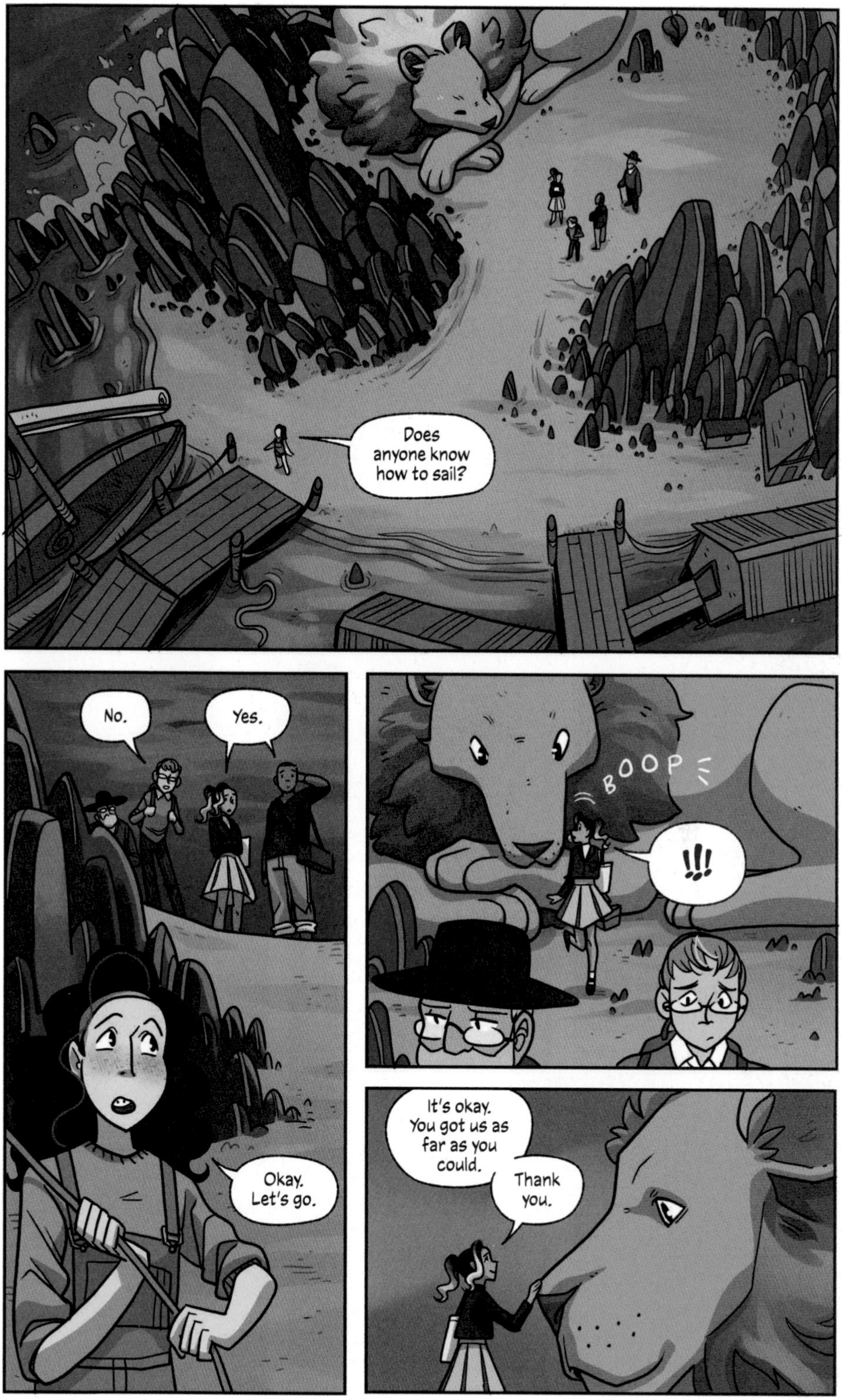
Does anyone know how to sail?
No.
Yes.
Okay. Let's go.
BOOP
!!!
It's okay. You got us as far as you could.
Thank you.

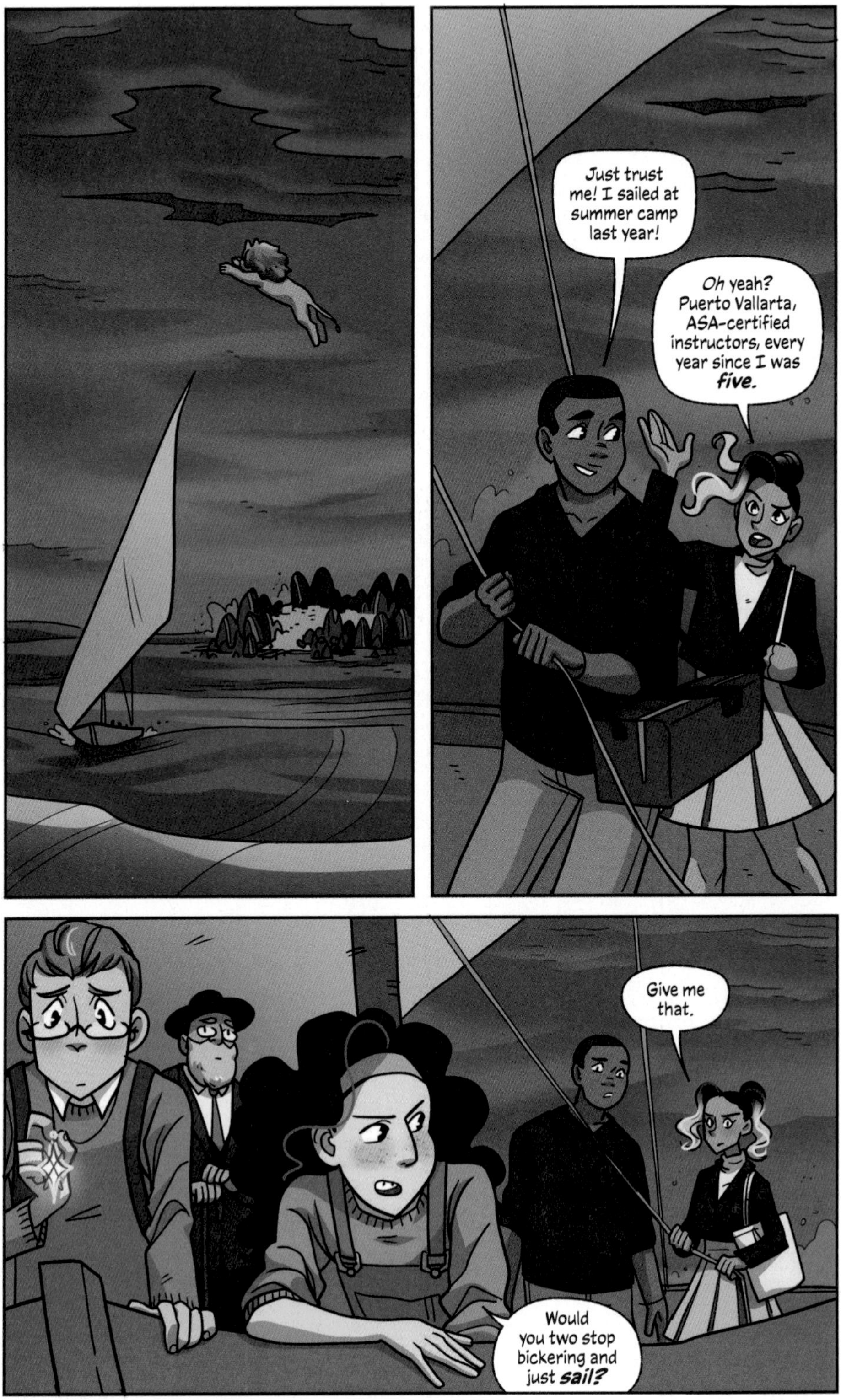
Just trust me! I sailed at summer camp last year!
Oh yeah? Puerto Vallarta, ASA-certified instructors, every year since I was ***five.***
Give me that.
Would you two stop bickering and just ***sail?***

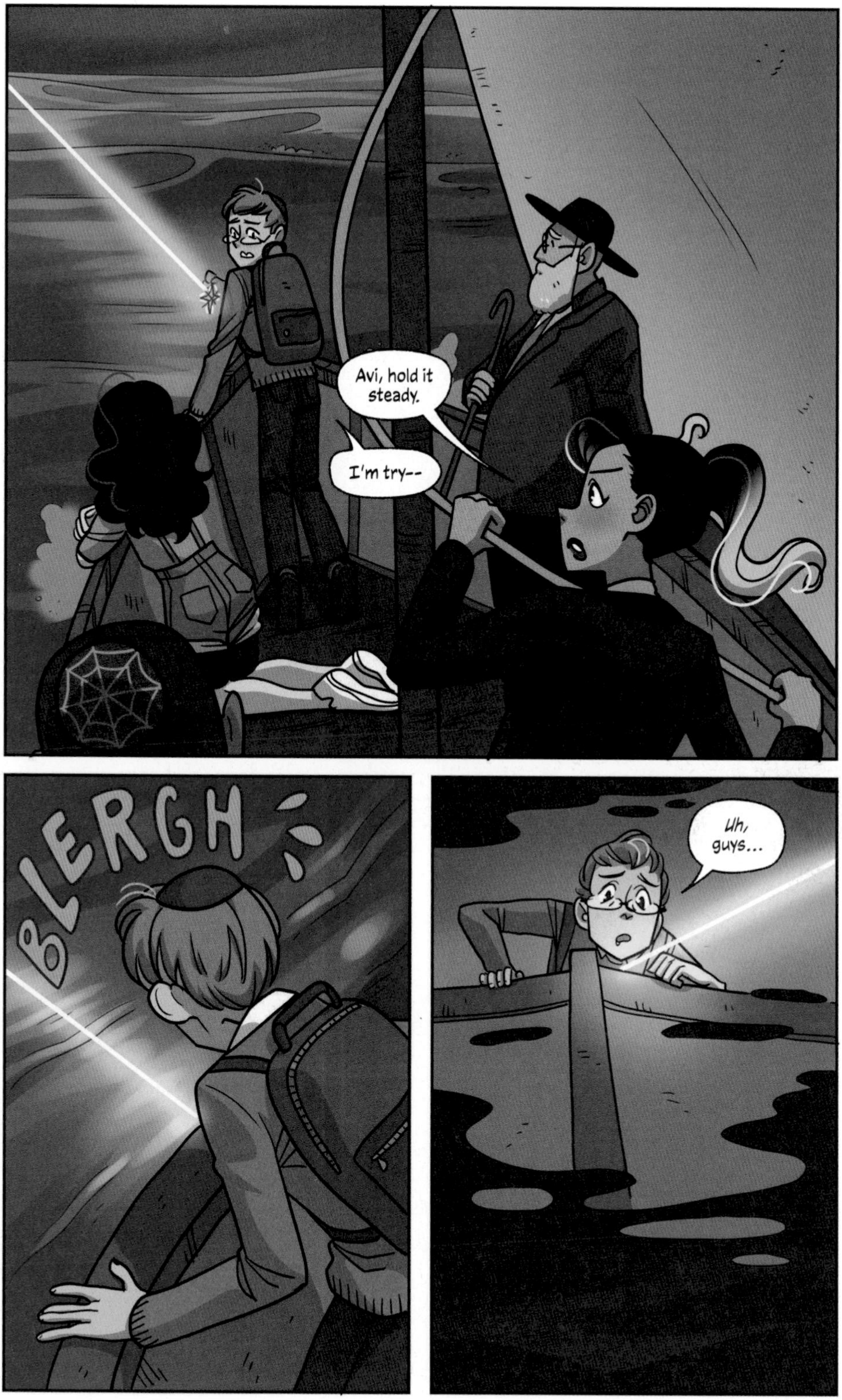
Avi, hold it steady.
I'm try--
BLERGH
Uh, guys...

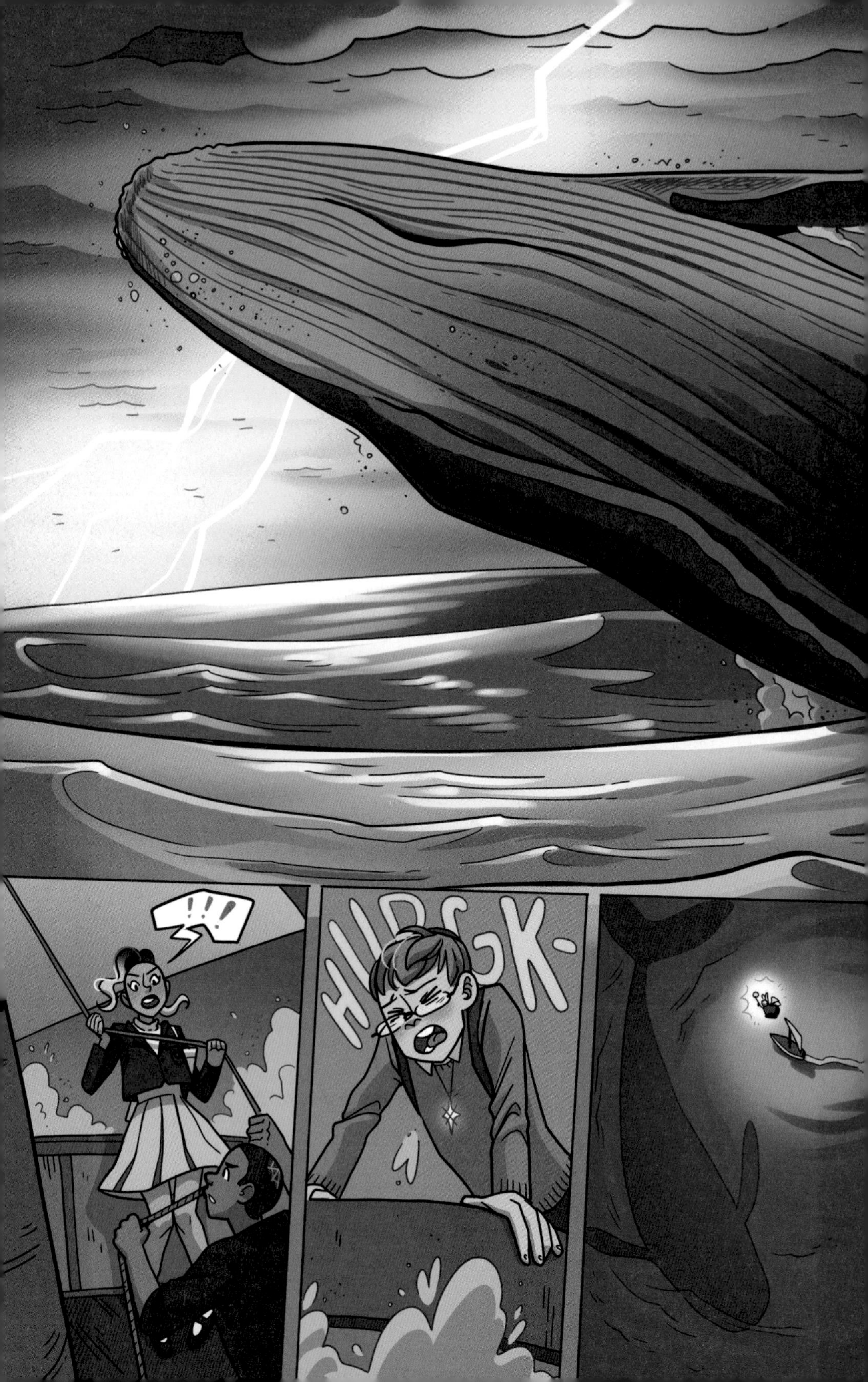
!!!
HURGK-

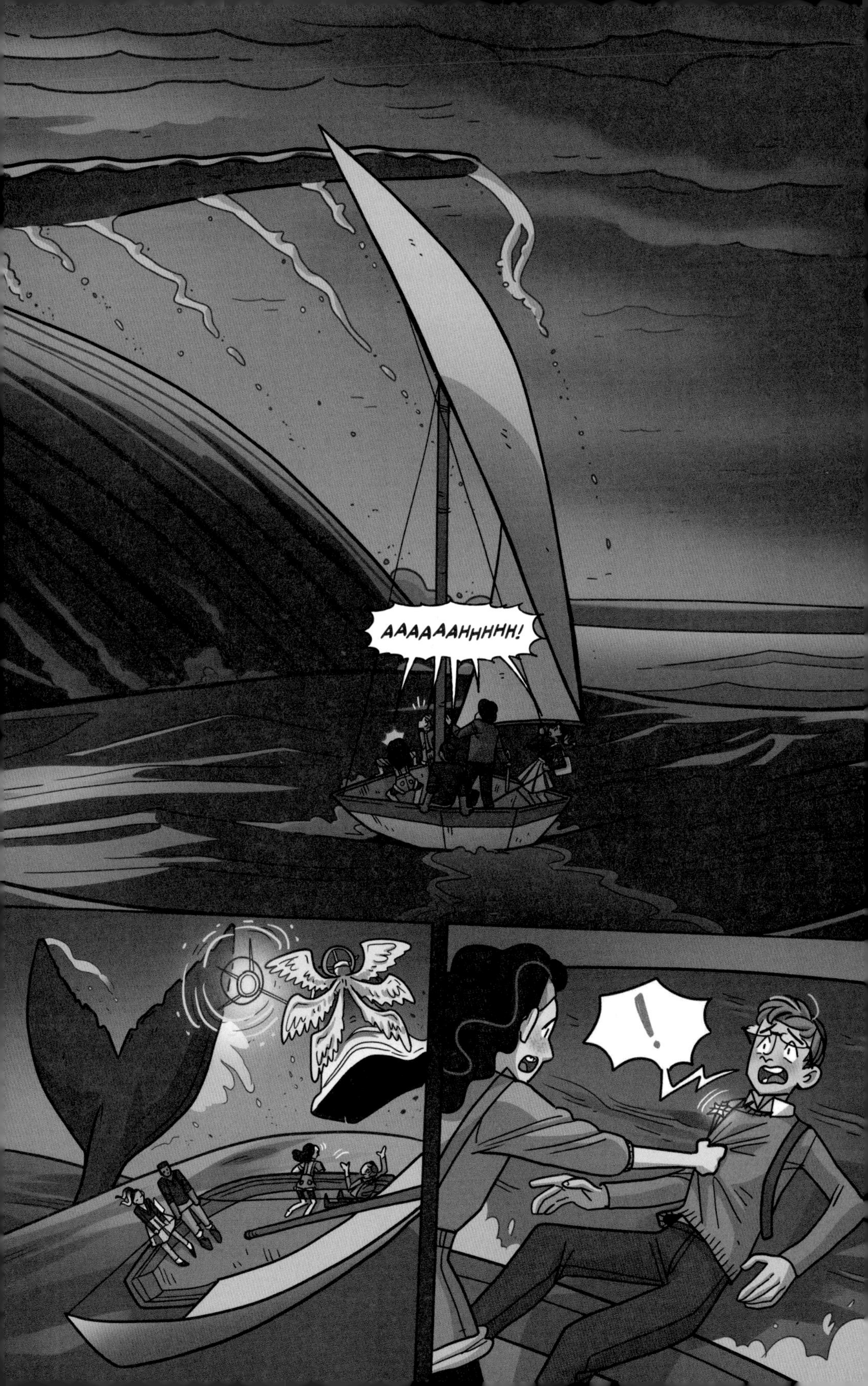
AAAAAAHHHHH!
!

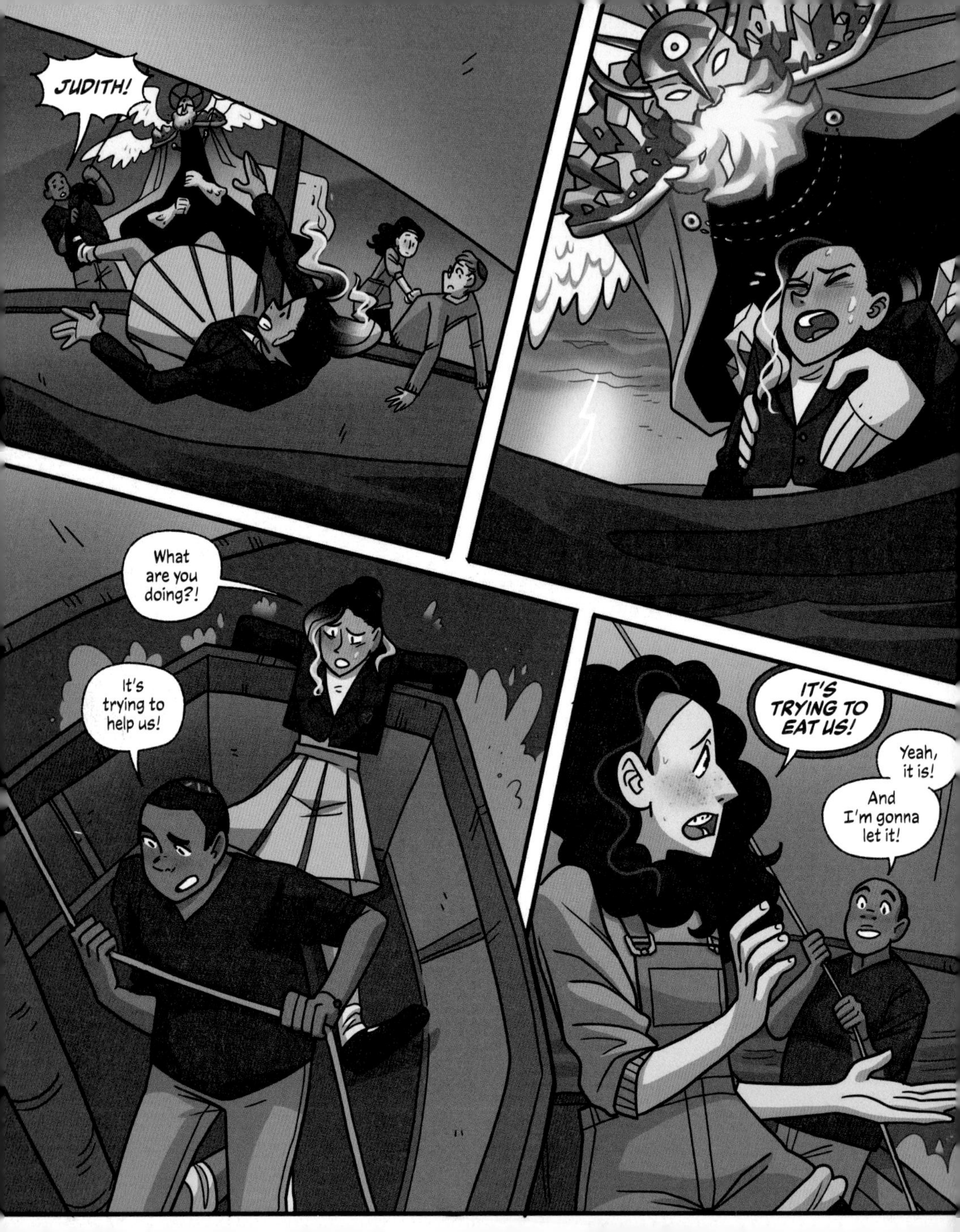
JUDITH!
What are you doing?!
It's trying to help us!
IT'S TRYING TO EAT US!
Yeah, it is!
And I'm gonna let it!

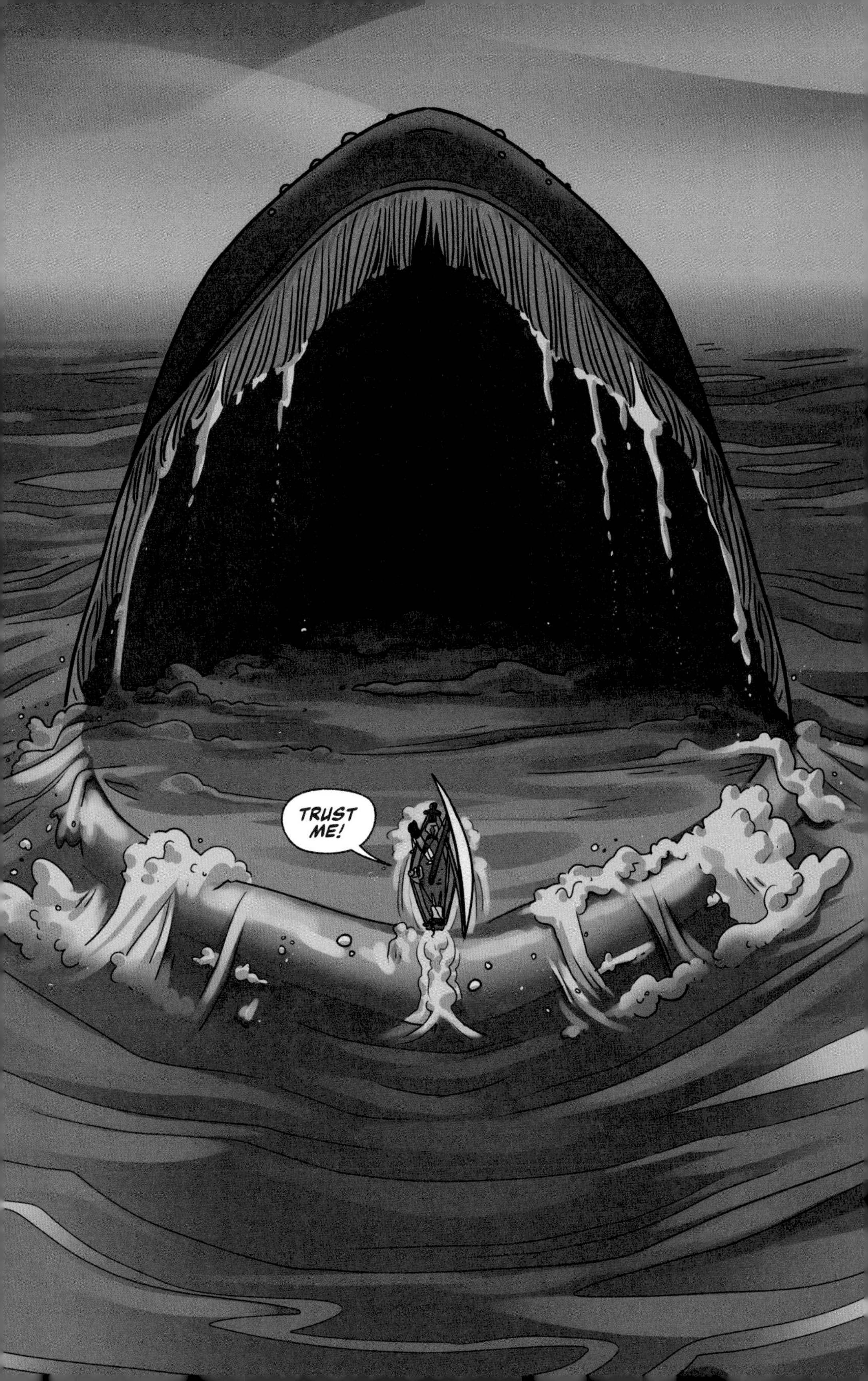
TRUST ME!

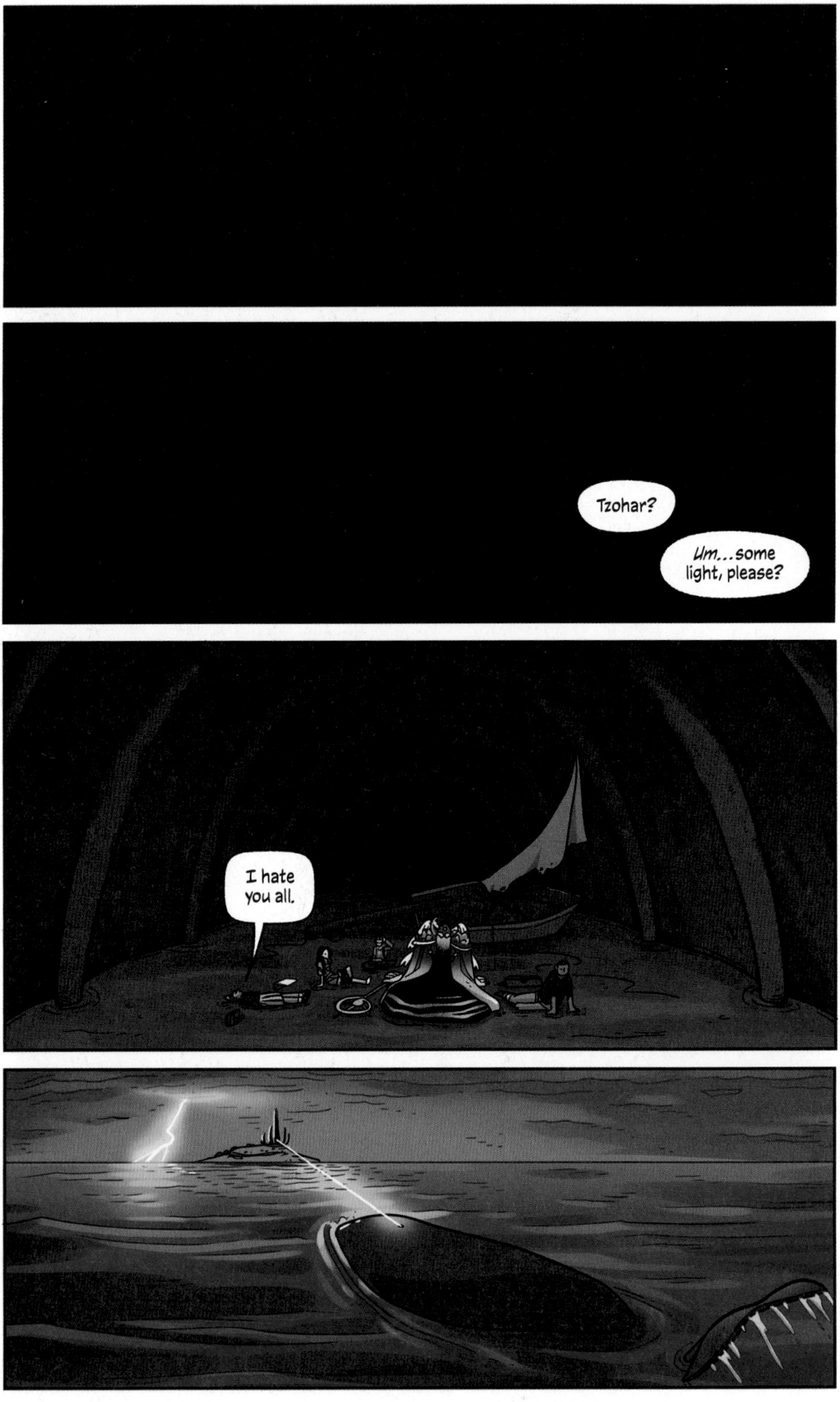
Tzohar?
Um...some light, please?
I hate you all.

CHAPTER FIVE

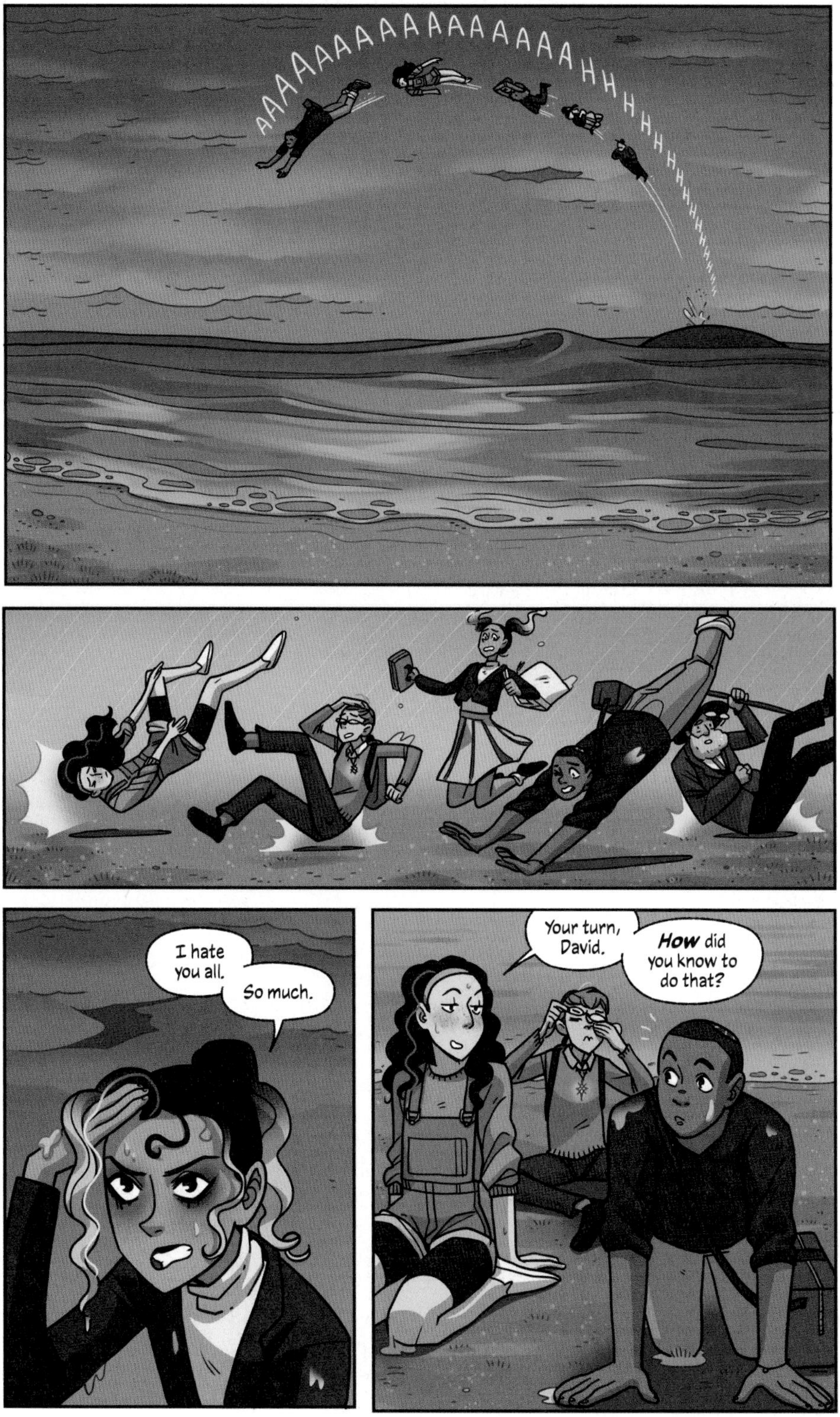
AAAAAAAAAAAAAAAAAHHHHHHHHHHHHHH
I hate you all.
So much.
Your turn, David.
How did you know to do that?

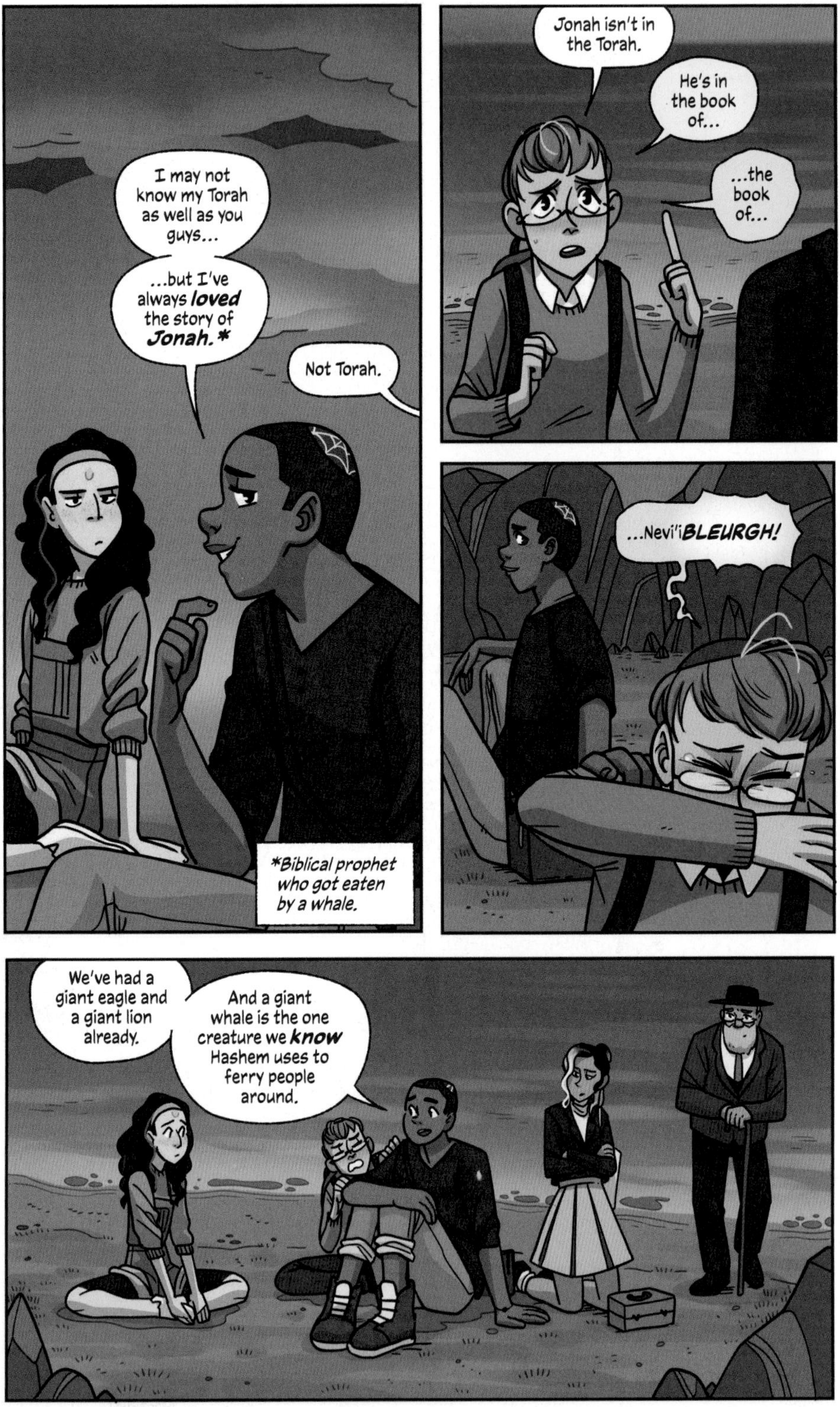
I may not know my Torah as well as you guys...
...but I've always *loved* the story of ***Jonah.****
Not Torah.
*Biblical prophet who got eaten by a whale.
Jonah isn't in the Torah.
He's in the book of...
...the book of...
...Nevi'i***BLEURGH!***
We've had a giant eagle and a giant lion already.
And a giant whale is the one creature we ***know*** Hashem uses to ferry people around.

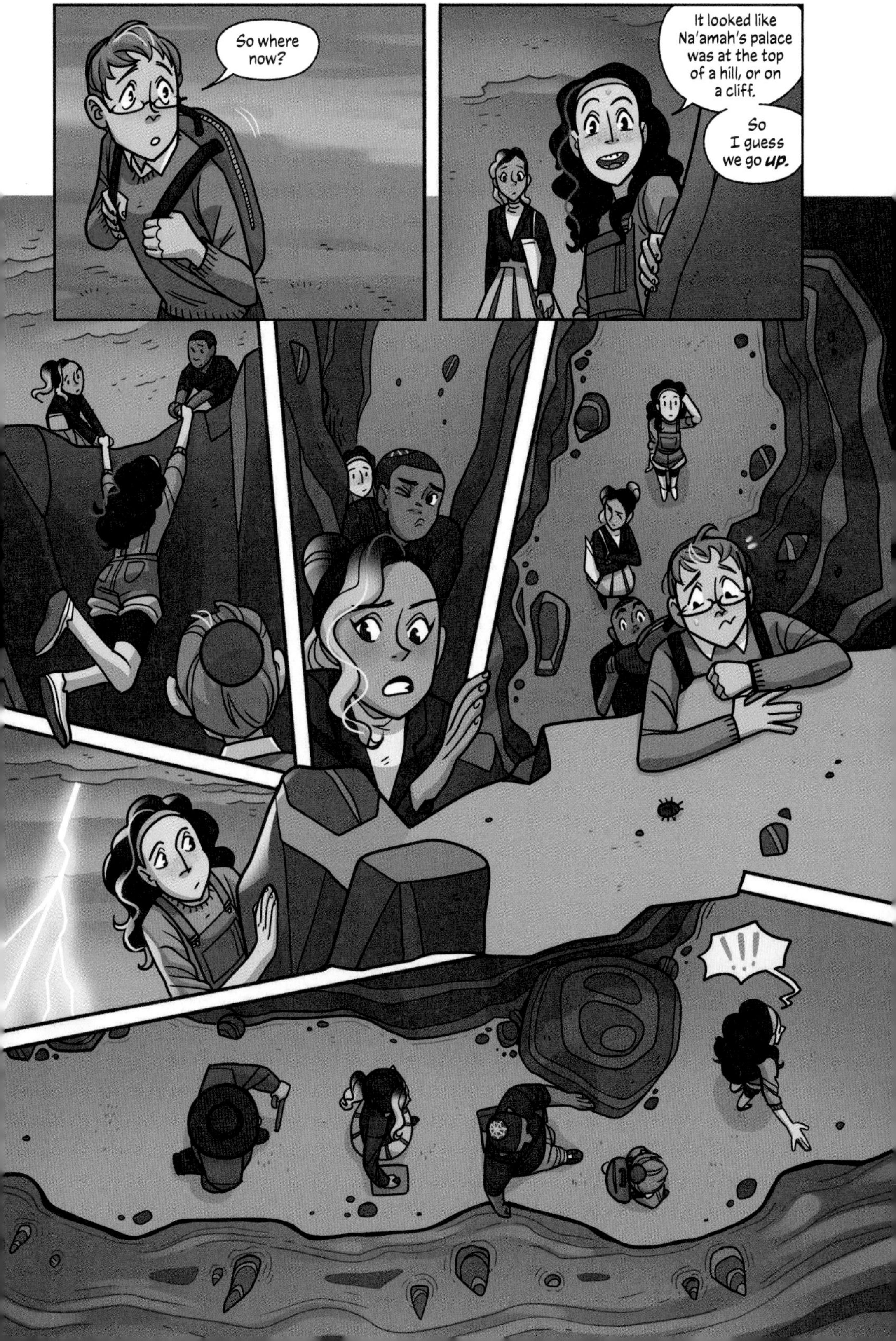
So where now?
It looked like Na'amah's palace was at the top of a hill, or on a cliff.
So I guess we go *up.*
!!!

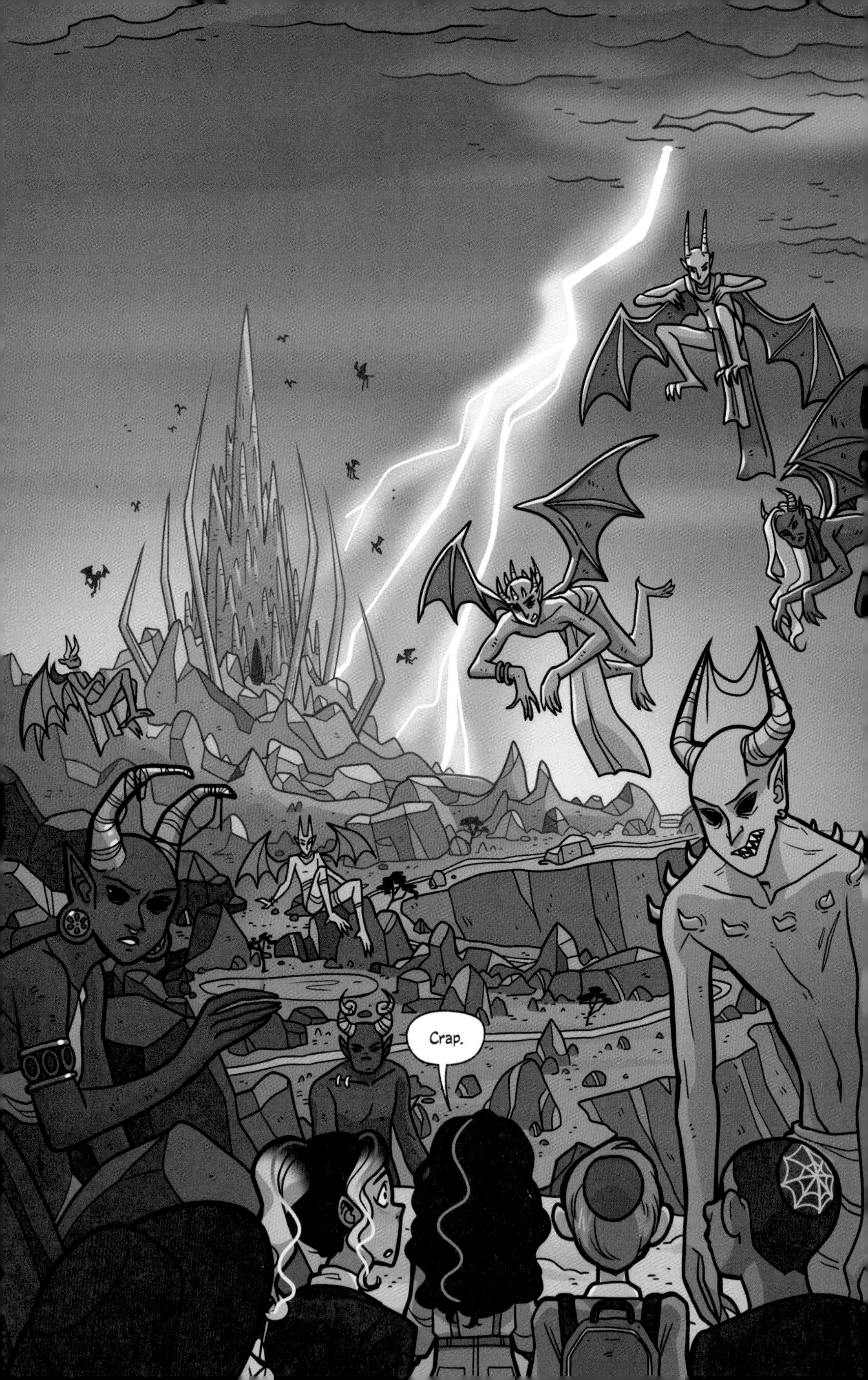
Crap.

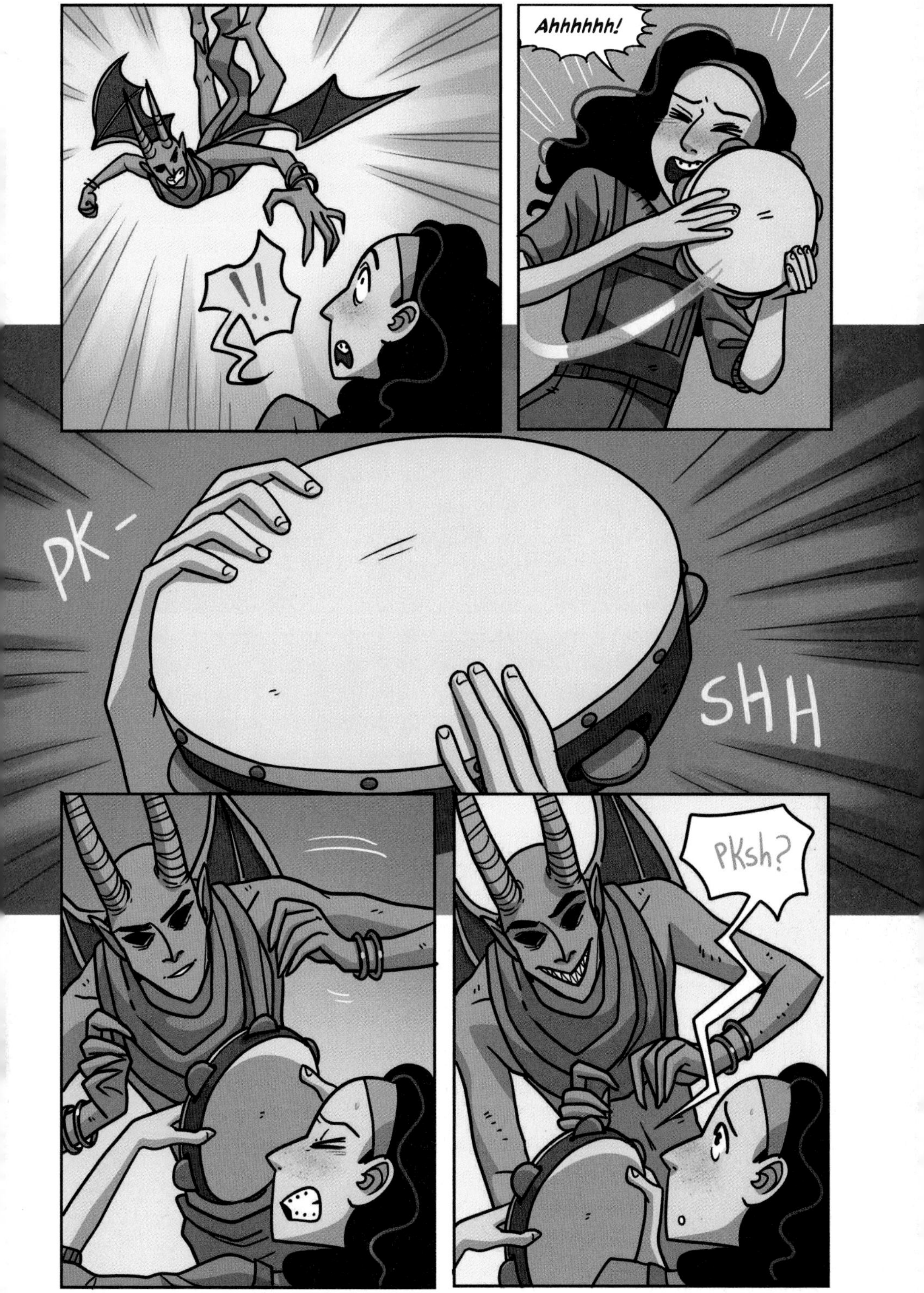
!!
Ahhhhhh!
PK-
SHH
PKsh?

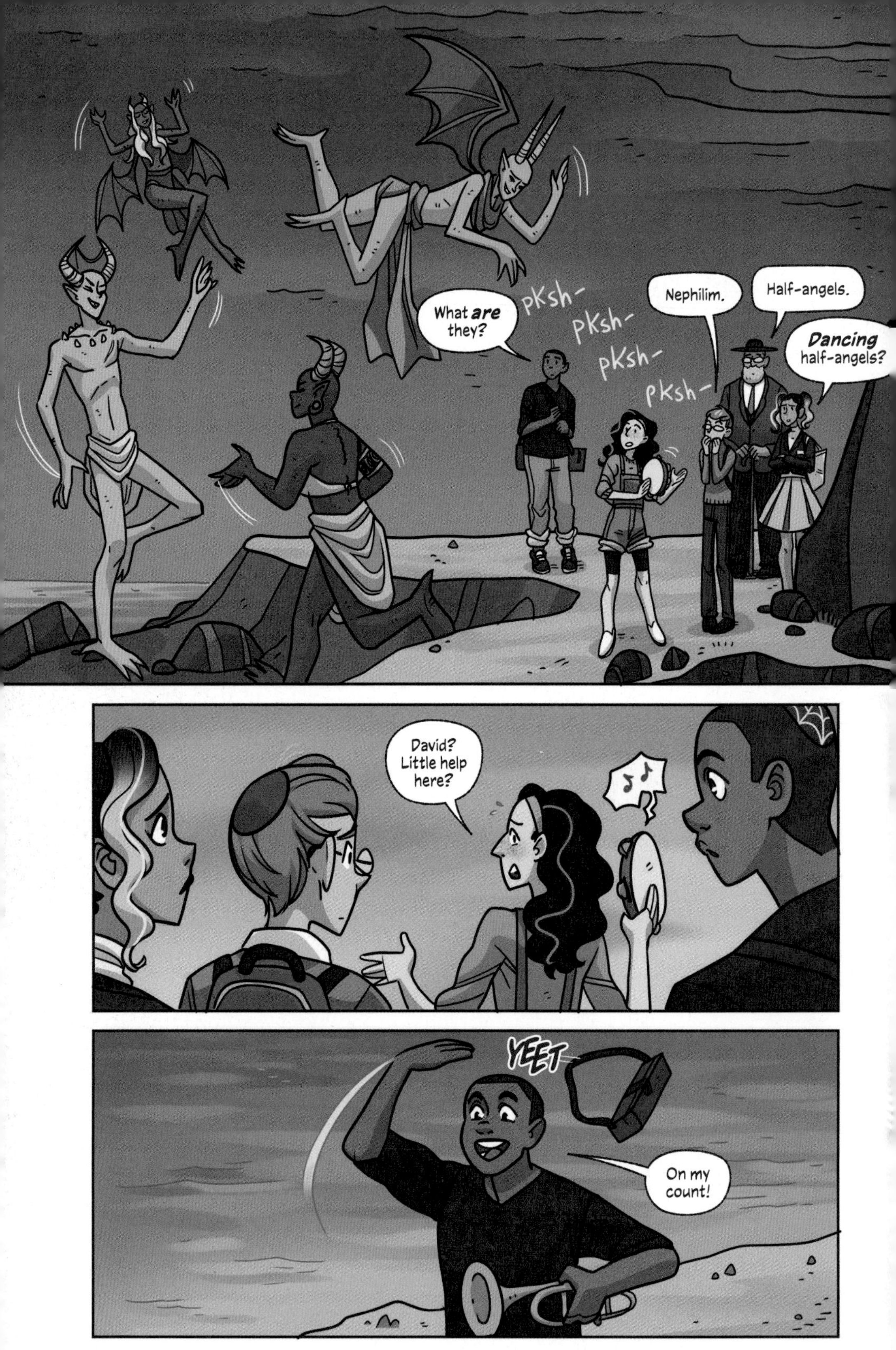
What are they?
pKsh-
pKsh-
pKsh-
pKsh-
Nephilim.
Half-angels.
Dancing half-angels?
David? Little help here?
♪♪
YEET
On my count!

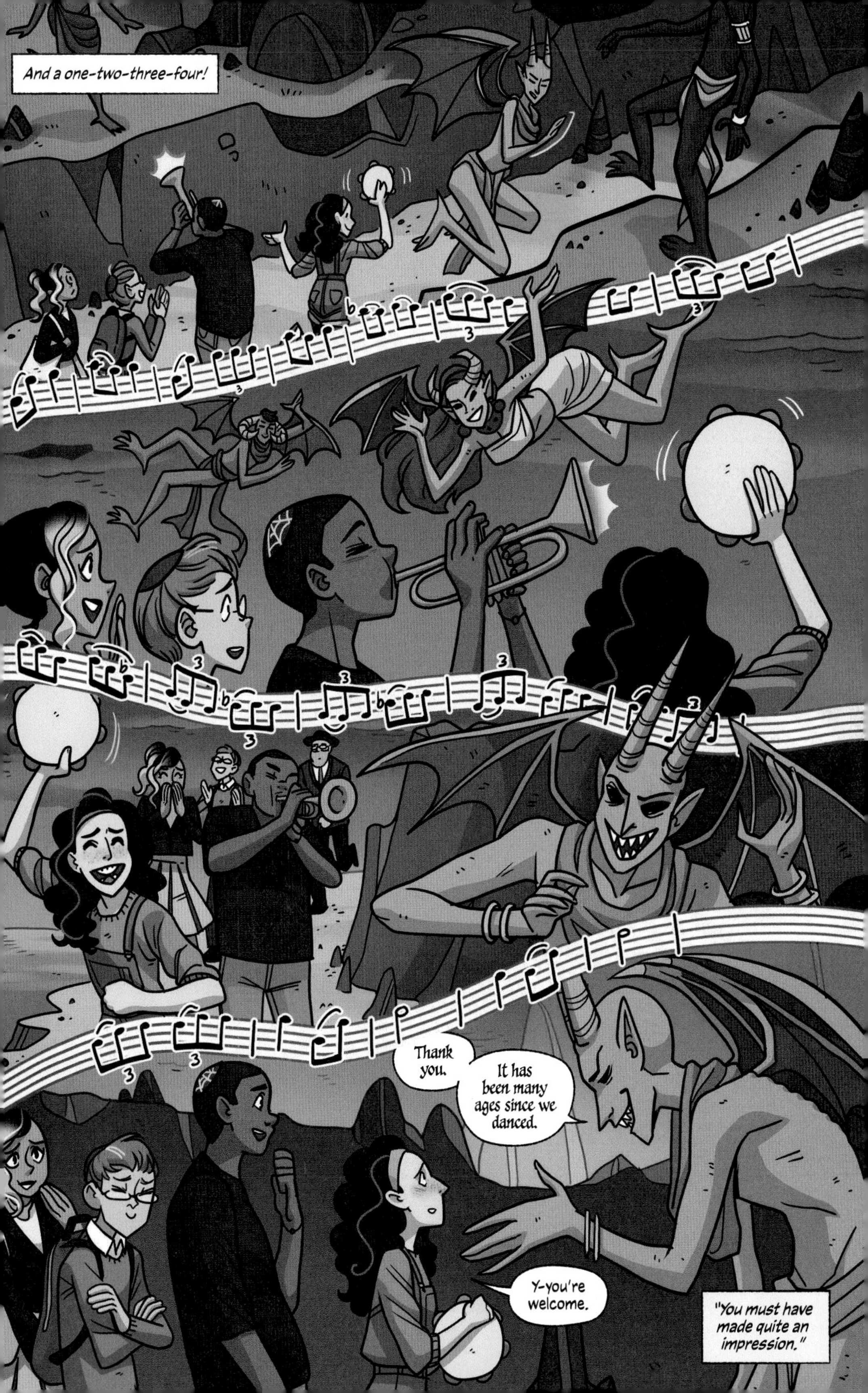
And a one-two-three-four!
Thank you.
It has been many ages since we danced.
Y-you're welcome.
"You must have made quite an impression."

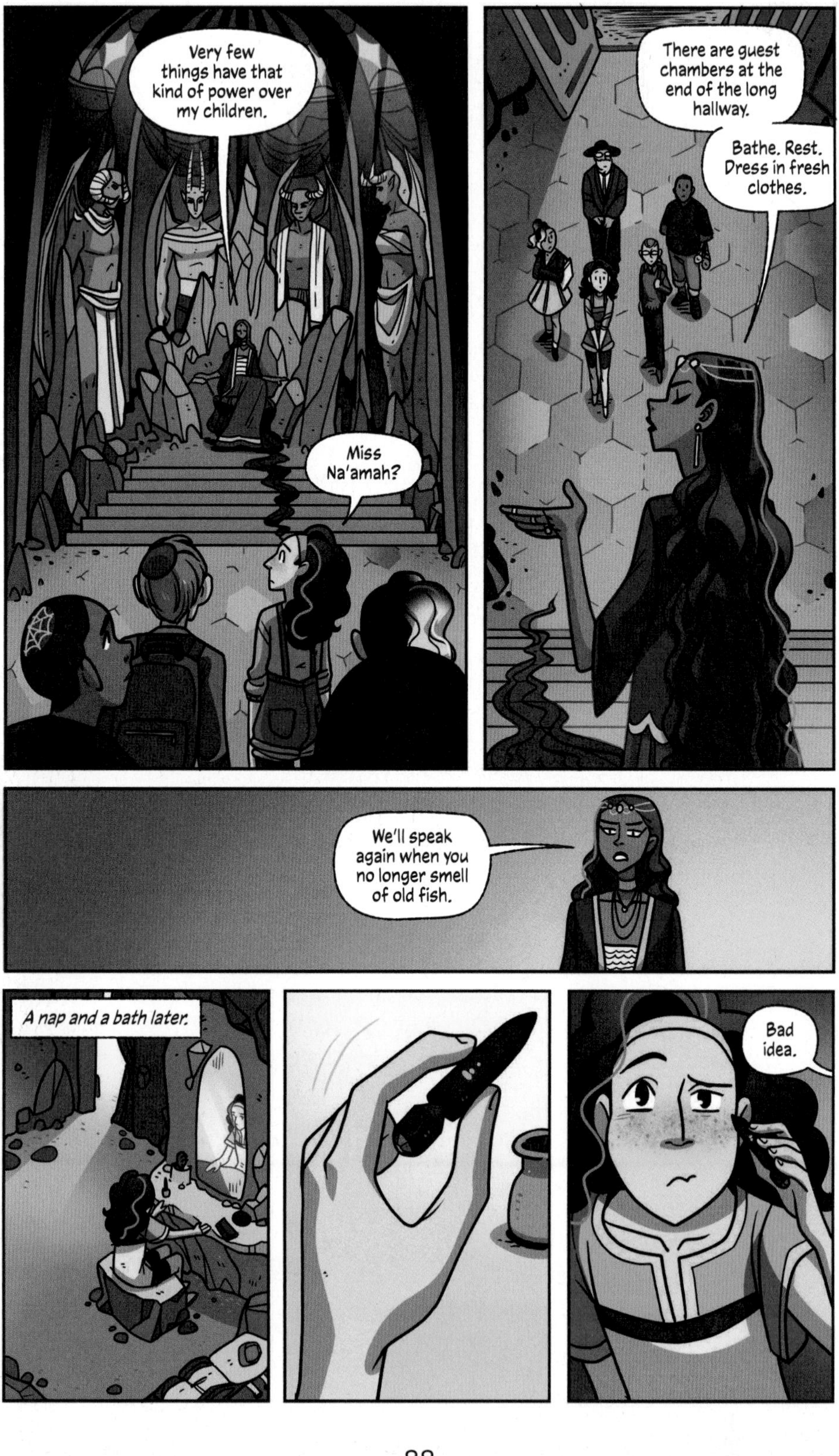
Very few things have that kind of power over my children.
Miss Na'amah?
There are guest chambers at the end of the long hallway.
Bathe. Rest. Dress in fresh clothes.
We'll speak again when you no longer smell of old fish.
A nap and a bath later.
Bad idea.

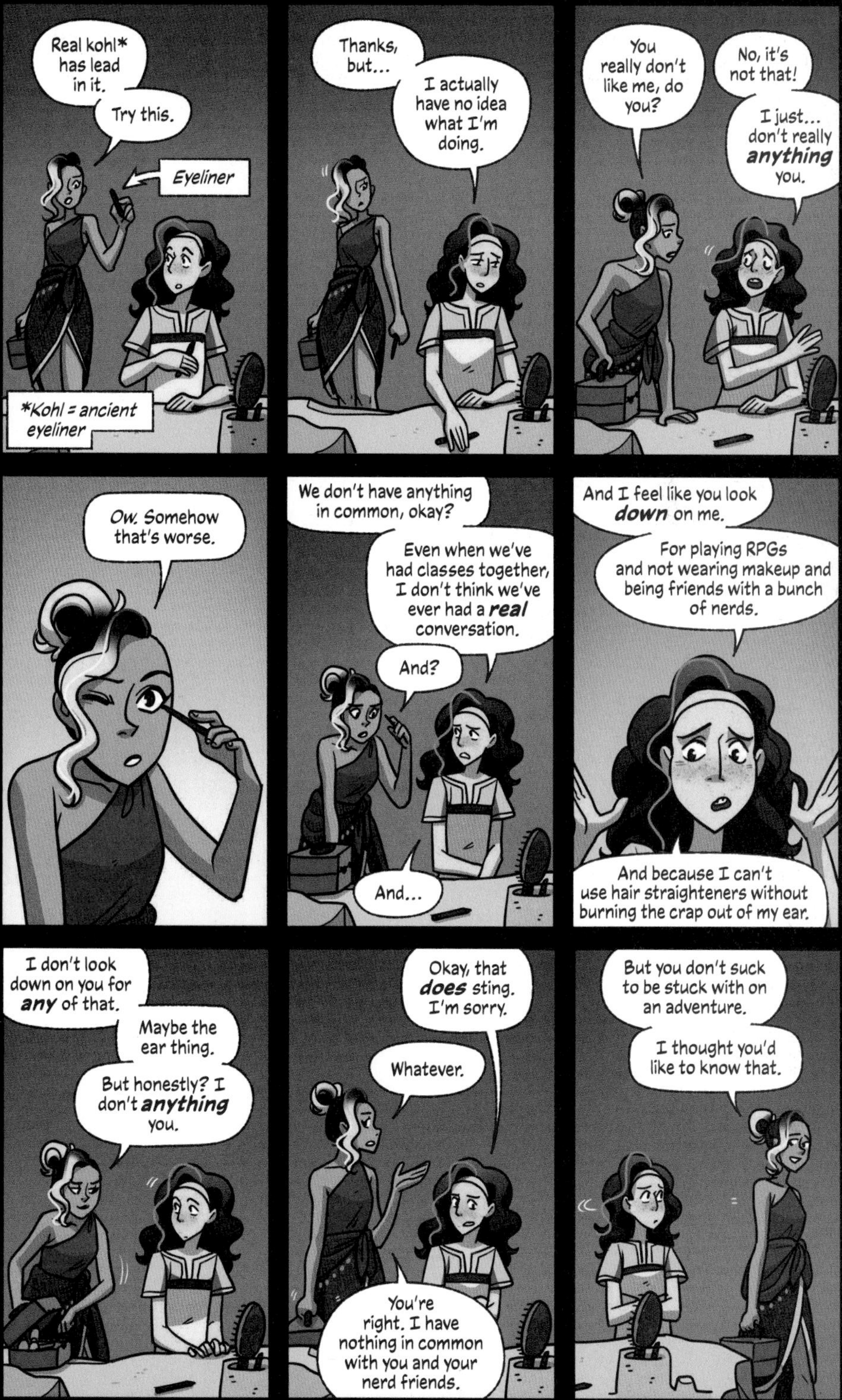
Real kohl* has lead in it.
Try this.
Eyeliner
*Kohl = ancient eyeliner
Thanks, but...
I actually have no idea what I'm doing.
You really don't like me, do you?
No, it's not that!
I just... don't really **anything** you.
Ow. Somehow that's worse.
We don't have anything in common, okay?
Even when we've had classes together, I don't think we've ever had a **real** conversation.
And?
And...
And I feel like you look **down** on me.
For playing RPGs and not wearing makeup and being friends with a bunch of nerds.
And because I can't use hair straighteners without burning the crap out of my ear.
I don't look down on you for **any** of that.
Maybe the ear thing.
But honestly? I don't **anything** you.
Okay, that **does** sting. I'm sorry.
Whatever.
You're right. I have nothing in common with you and your nerd friends.
But you don't suck to be stuck with on an adventure.
I thought you'd like to know that.

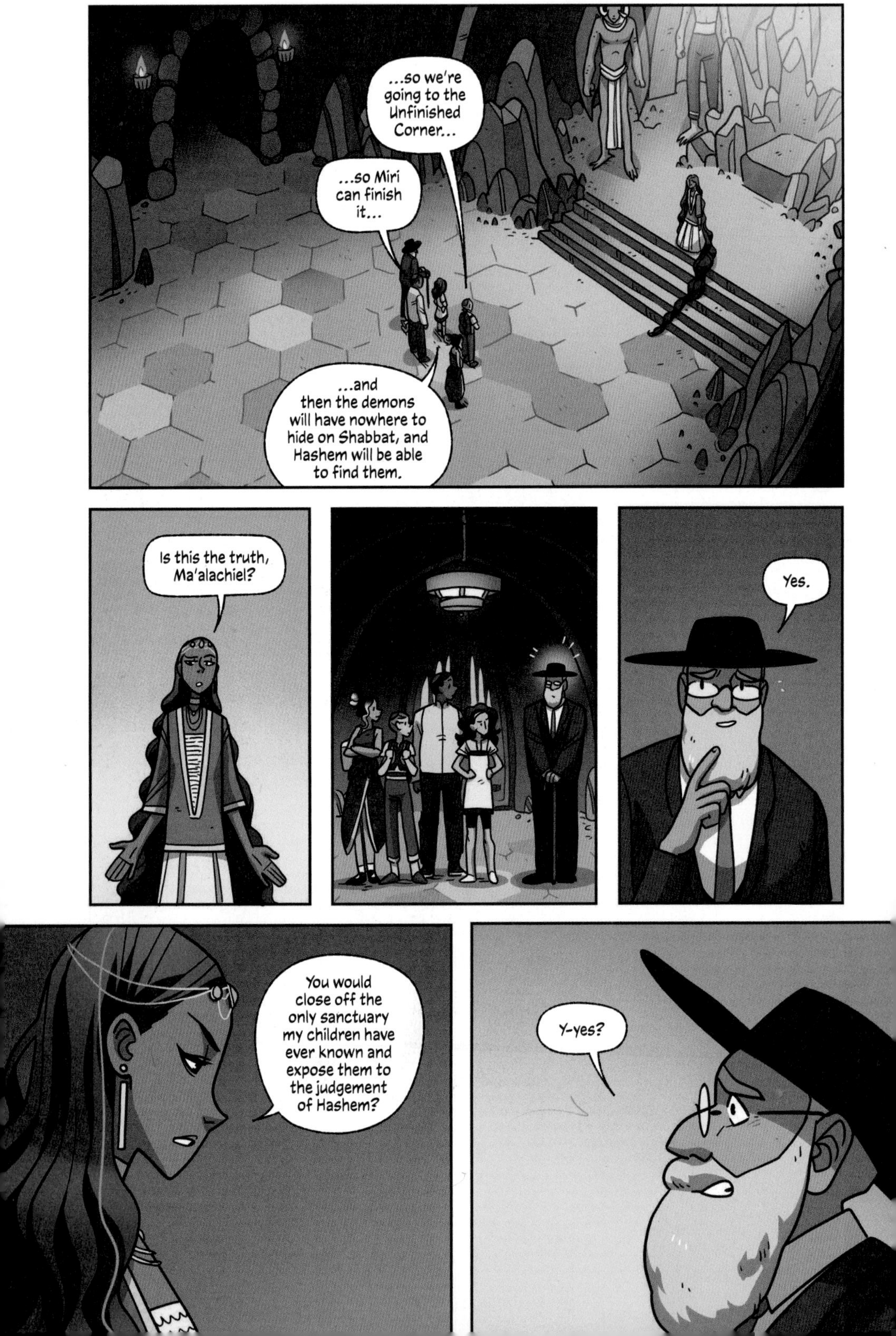
...so we're going to the Unfinished Corner...
...so Miri can finish it...
...and then the demons will have nowhere to hide on Shabbat, and Hashem will be able to find them.
Is this the truth, Ma'alachiel?
Yes.
You would close off the only sanctuary my children have ever known and expose them to the judgement of Hashem?
Y-yes?

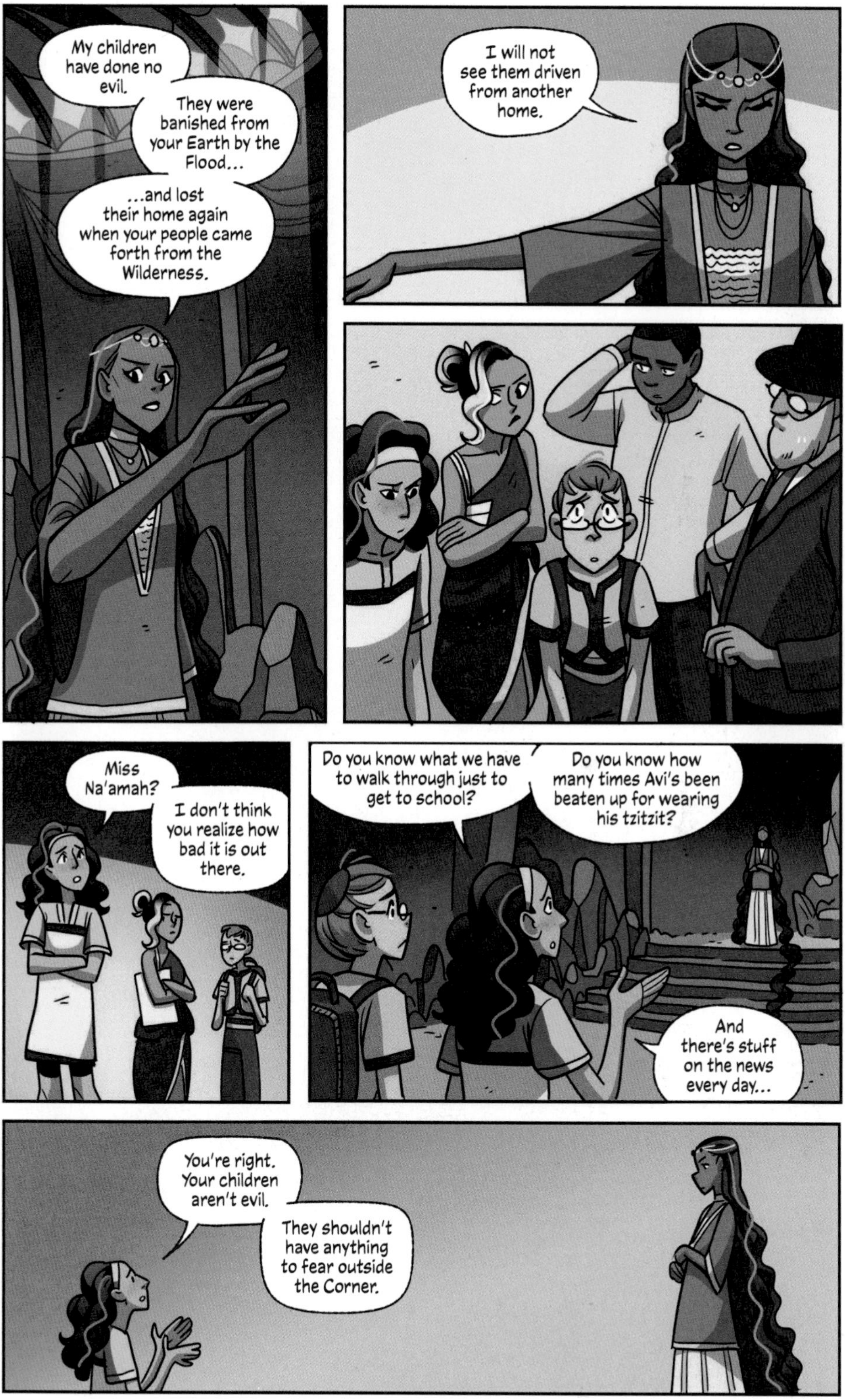
My children have done no evil.
They were banished from your Earth by the Flood...
...and lost their home again when your people came forth from the Wilderness.
I will not see them driven from another home.
Miss Na'amah?
I don't think you realize how bad it is out there.
Do you know what we have to walk through just to get to school?
Do you know how many times Avi's been beaten up for wearing his tzitzit?
And there's stuff on the news every day...
You're right. Your children aren't evil.
They shouldn't have anything to fear outside the Corner.

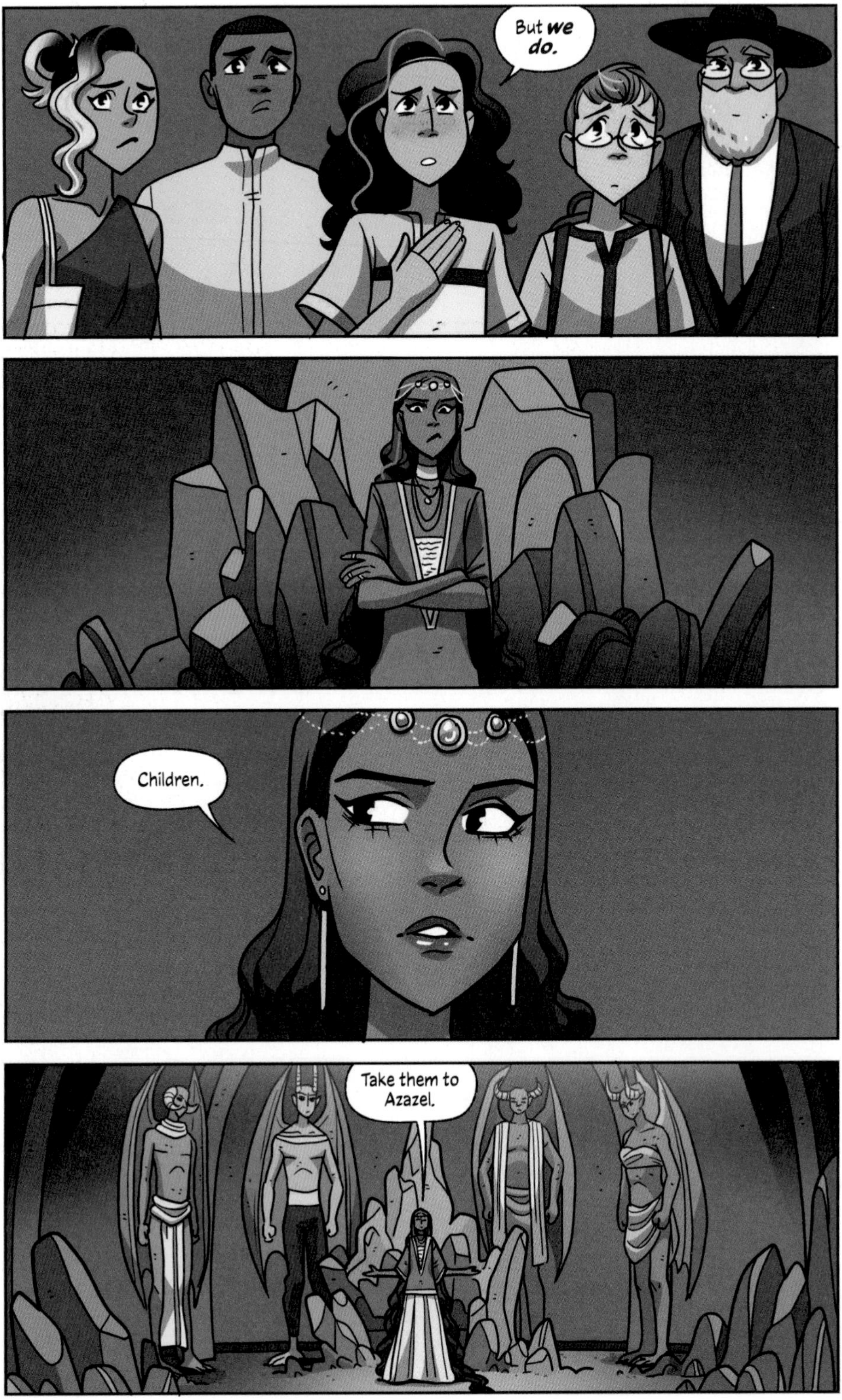
But **we** *do.*
Children.
Take them to Azazel.

CHAPTER SIX

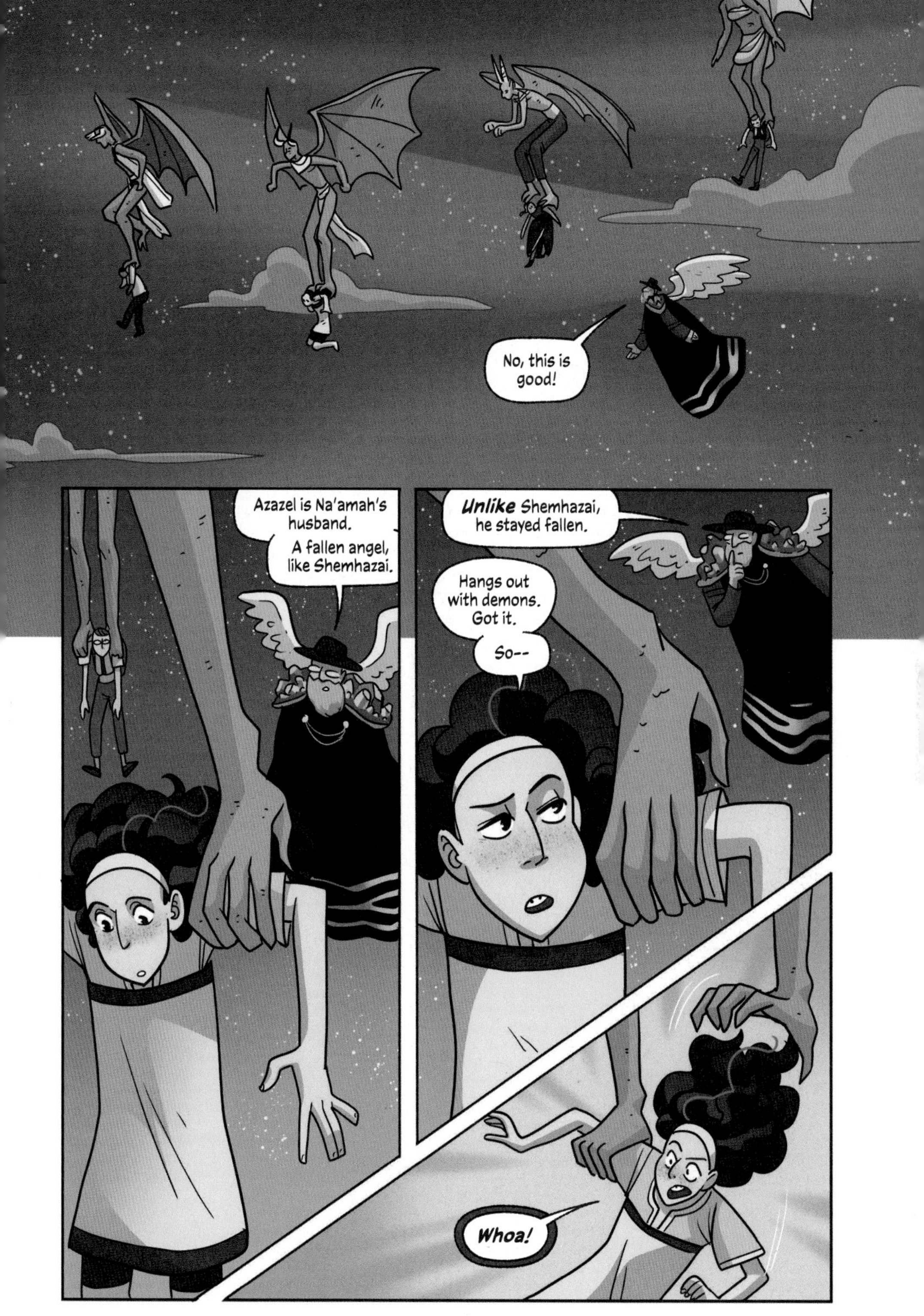

No, this is good!
Azazel is Na'amah's husband.
A fallen angel, like Shemhazai.
Unlike Shemhazai, he stayed fallen.
Hangs out with demons. Got it.
So--
Whoa!

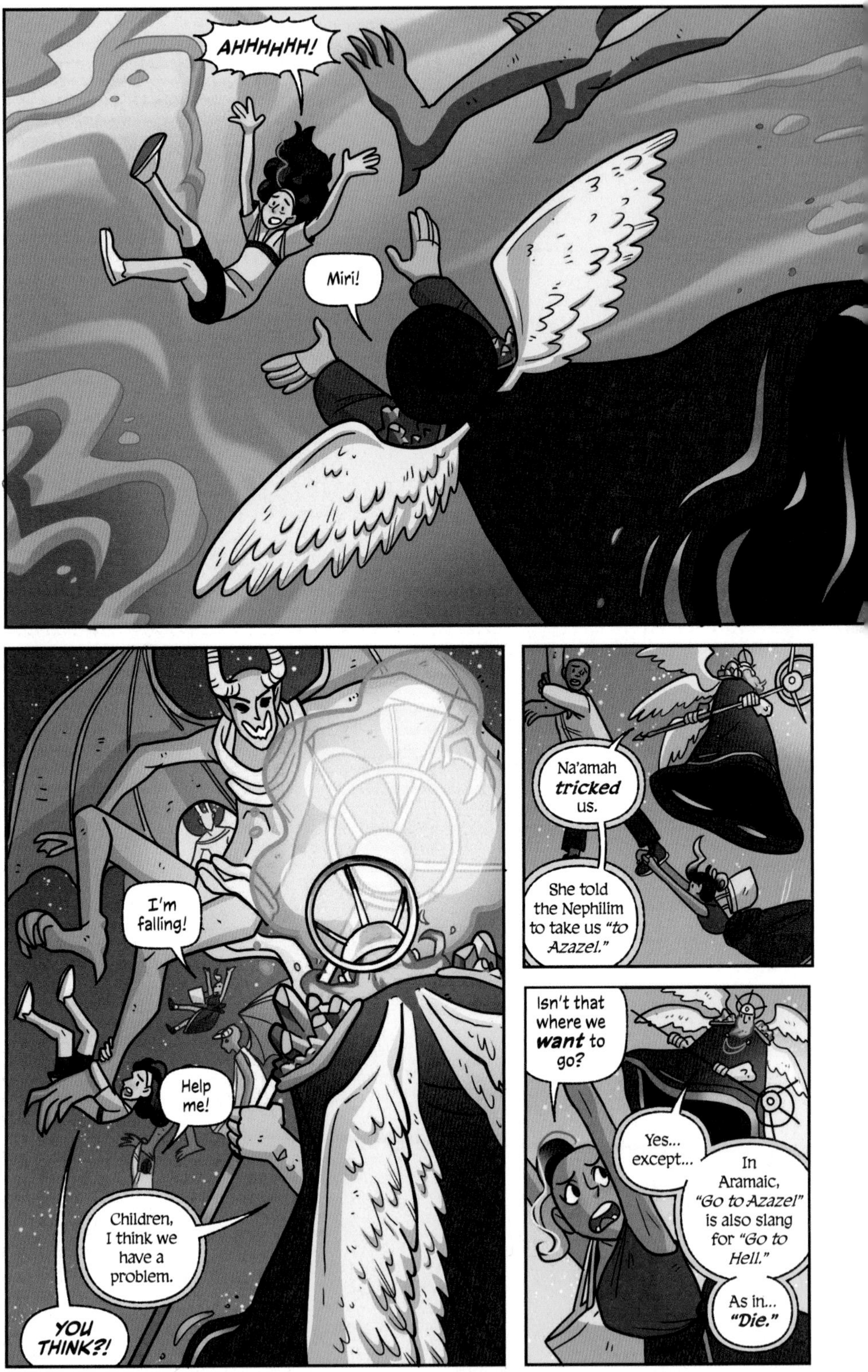
AHHHHHH!
Miri!
I'm falling!
Help me!
Children, I think we have a problem.
YOU THINK?!
Na'amah **tricked** us.
She told the Nephilim to take us *"to Azazel."*
Isn't that where we **want** to go?
Yes... except...
In Aramaic, *"Go to Azazel"* is also slang for *"Go to Hell."*
As in... ***"Die."***

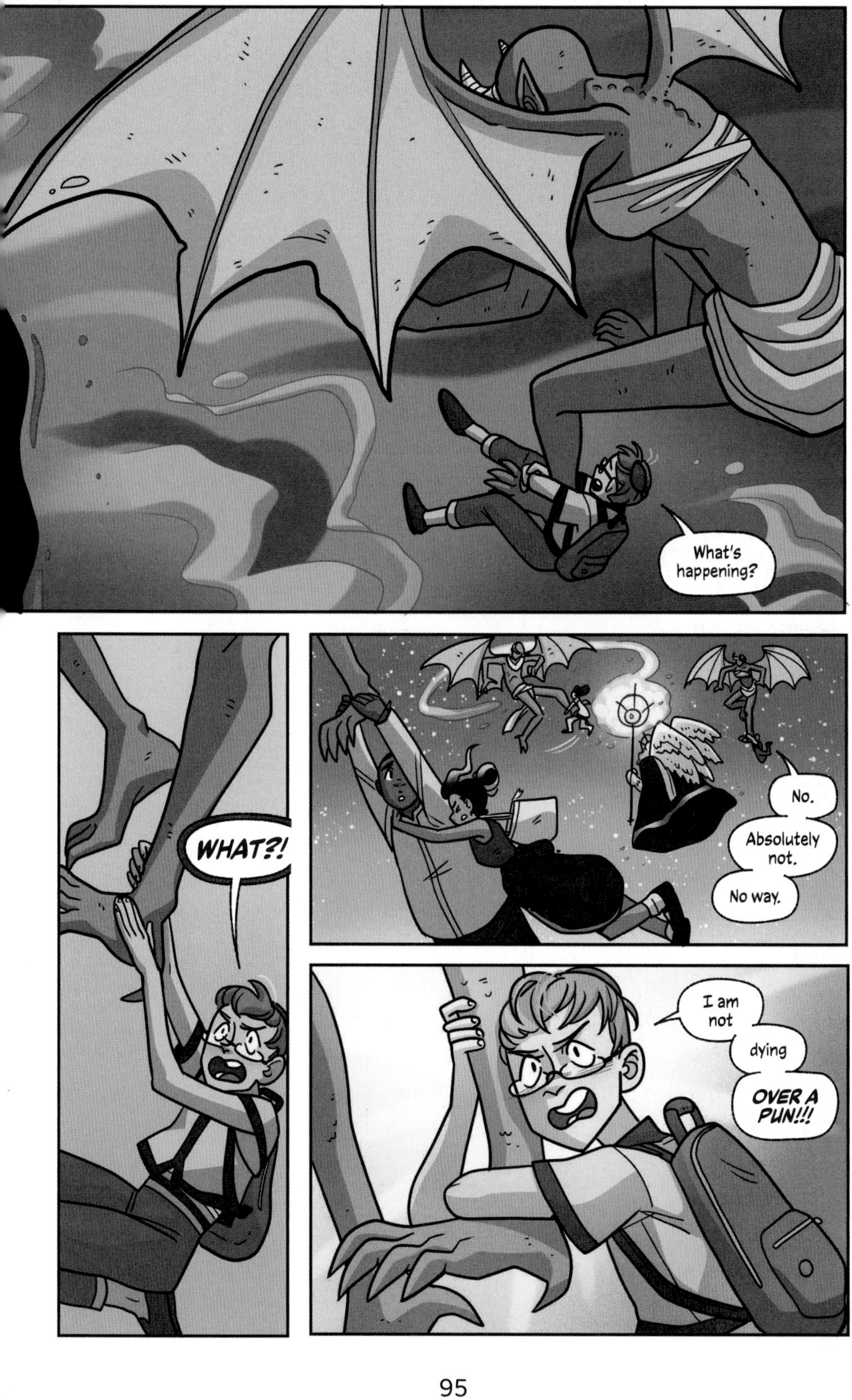

What's happening?
WHAT?!
No.
Absolutely not.
No way.
I am not
dying
OVER A PUN!!!

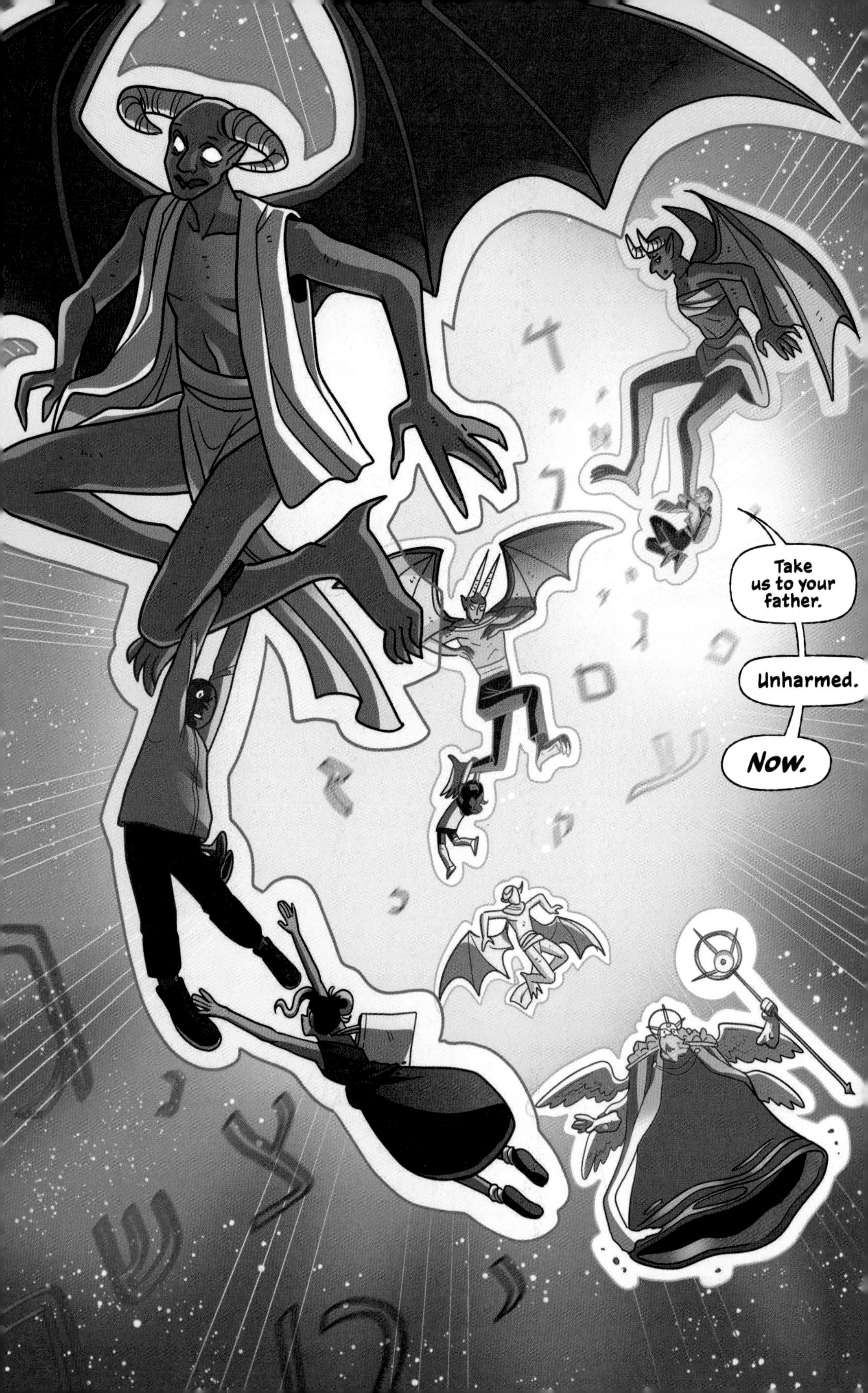
Take us to your father.
Unharmed.
Now.

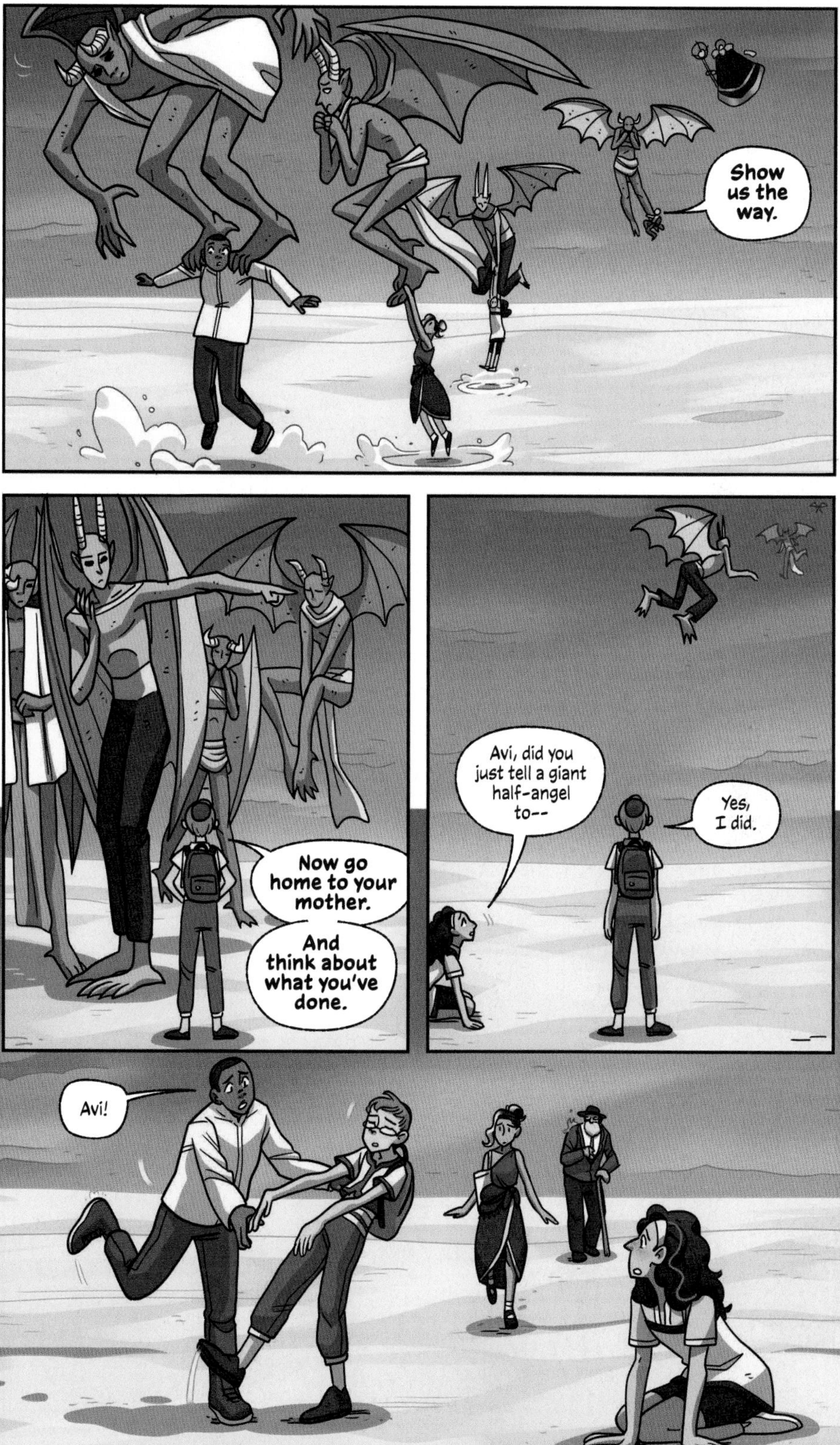
Show us the way.
Now go home to your mother.
And think about what you've done.
Avi, did you just tell a giant half-angel to--
Yes, I did.
Avi!

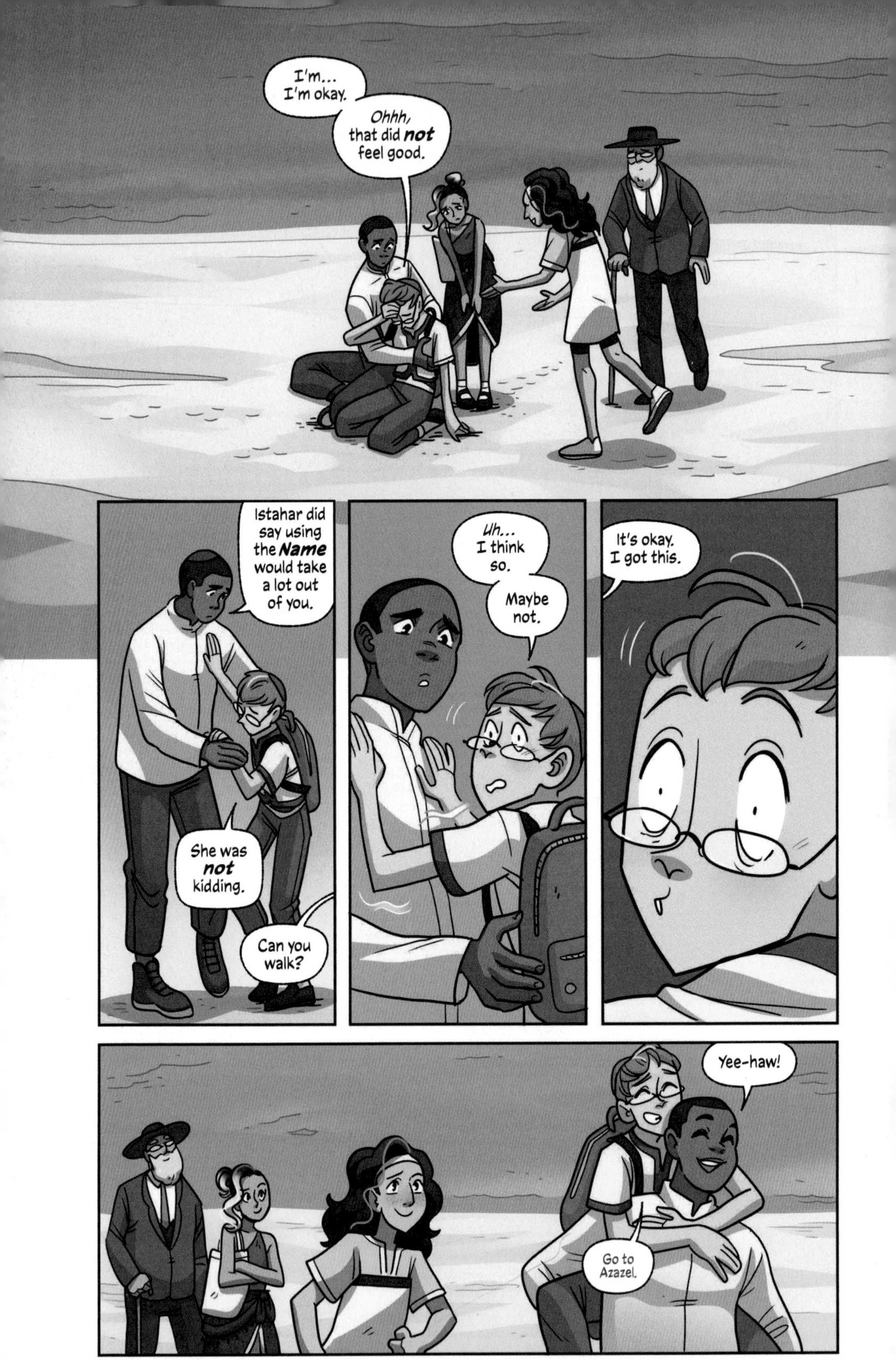

I'm...
I'm okay.
Ohhh, that did ***not*** feel good.
Istahar did say using the ***Name*** would take a lot out of you.
She was ***not*** kidding.
Can you walk?
Uh... I think so.
Maybe not.
It's okay. I got this.
Yee-haw!
Go to Azazel.

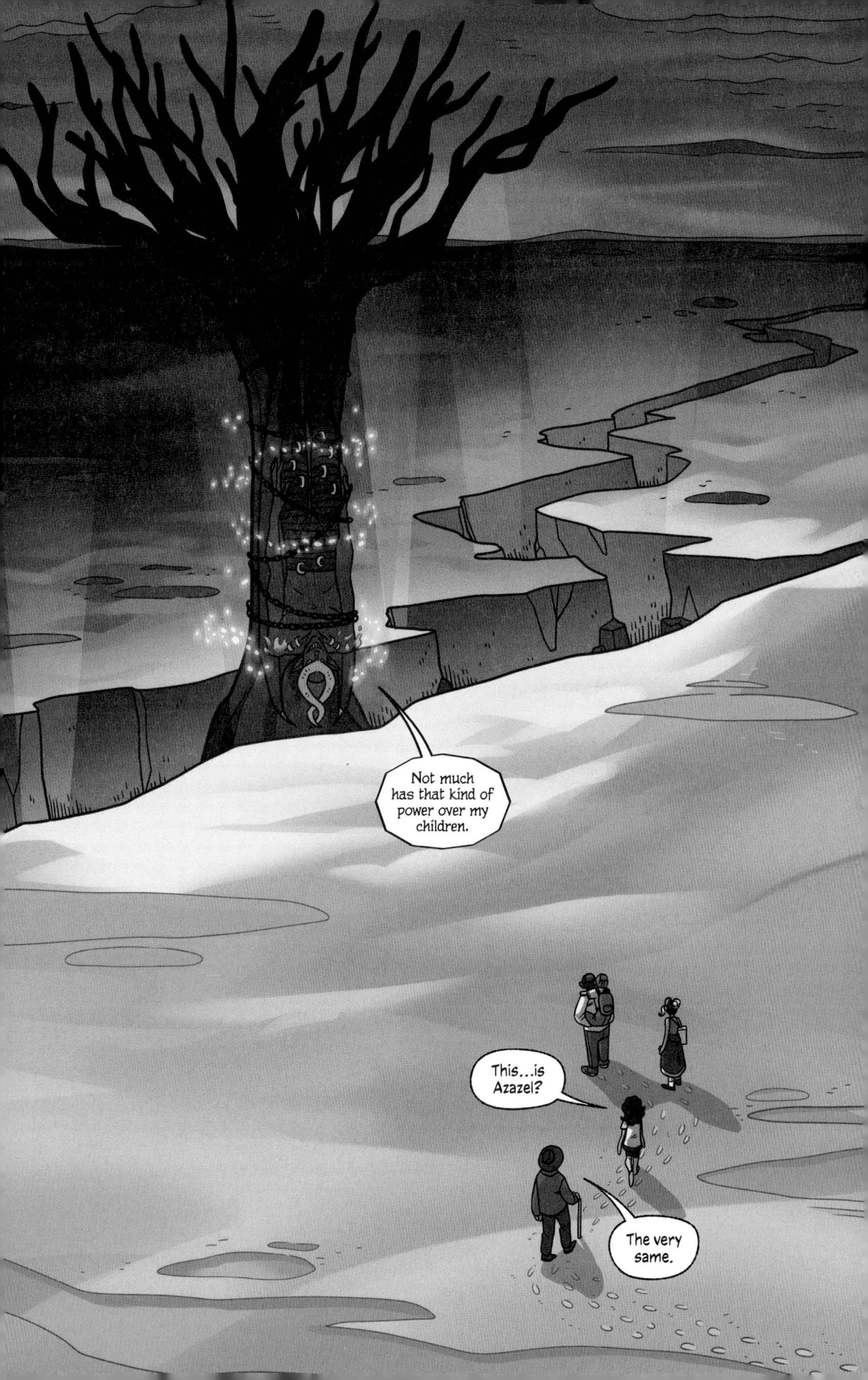
Not much has that kind of power over my children.
This...is Azazel?
The very same.

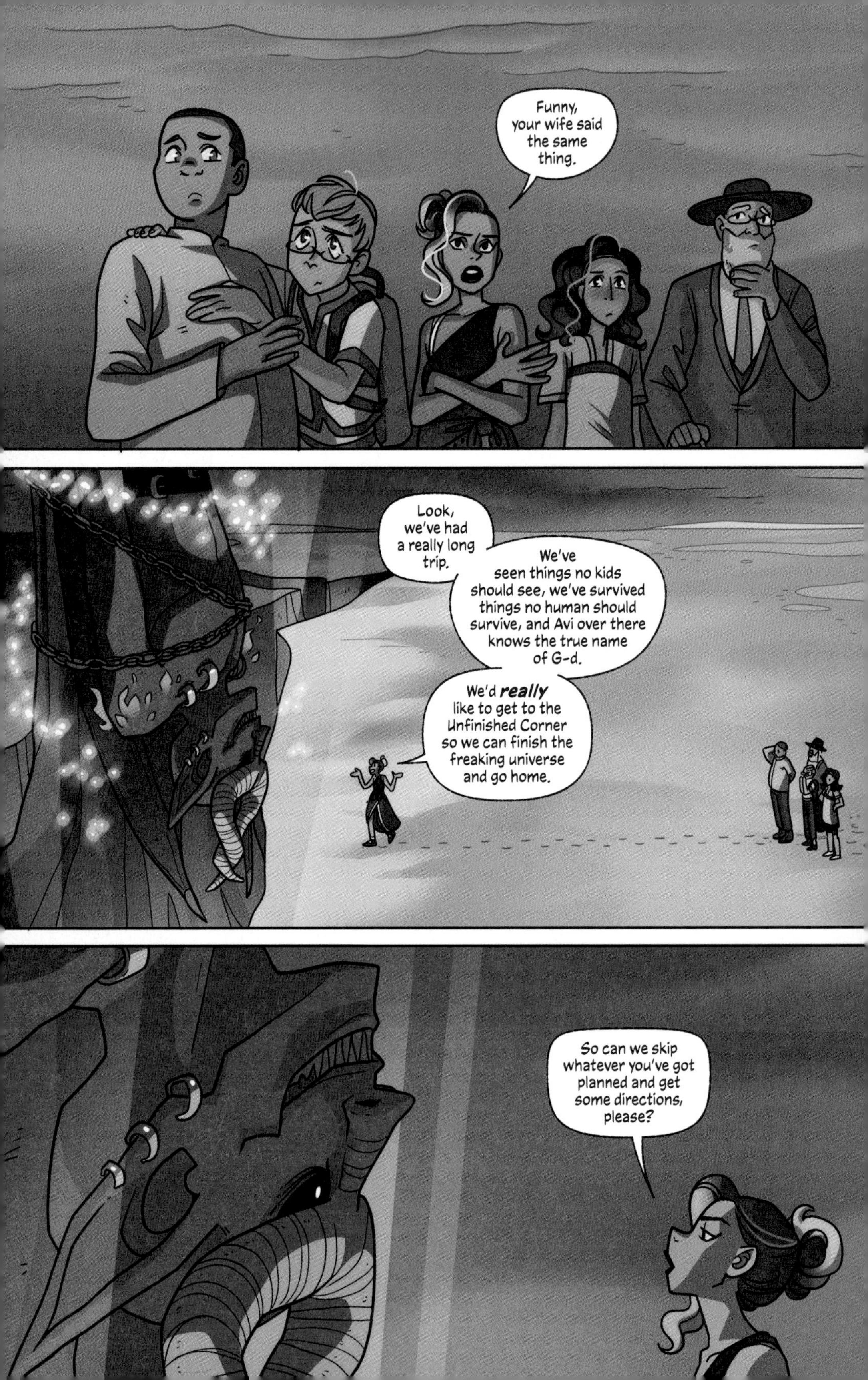

Funny, your wife said the same thing.
Look, we've had a really long trip.
We've seen things no kids should see, we've survived things no human should survive, and Avi over there knows the true name of G-d.
We'd **really** like to get to the Unfinished Corner so we can finish the freaking universe and go home.
So can we skip whatever you've got planned and get some directions, please?

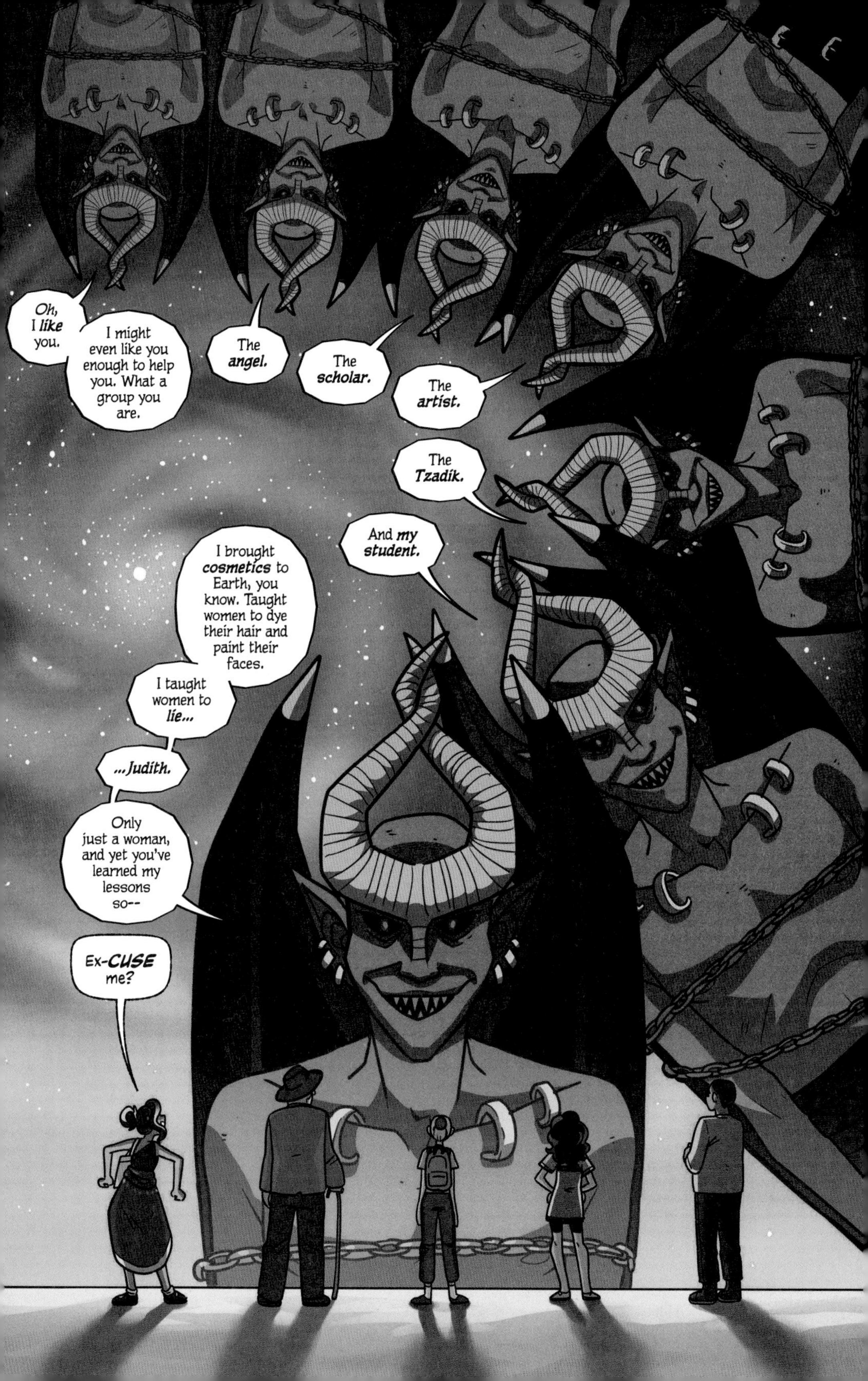

Oh, I like you.
I might even like you enough to help you. What a group you are.
The angel.
The scholar.
The artist.
The Tzadik.
And my student.
I brought cosmetics to Earth, you know. Taught women to dye their hair and paint their faces.
I taught women to lie...
...Judith.
Only just a woman, and yet you've learned my lessons so--
Ex-CUSE me?

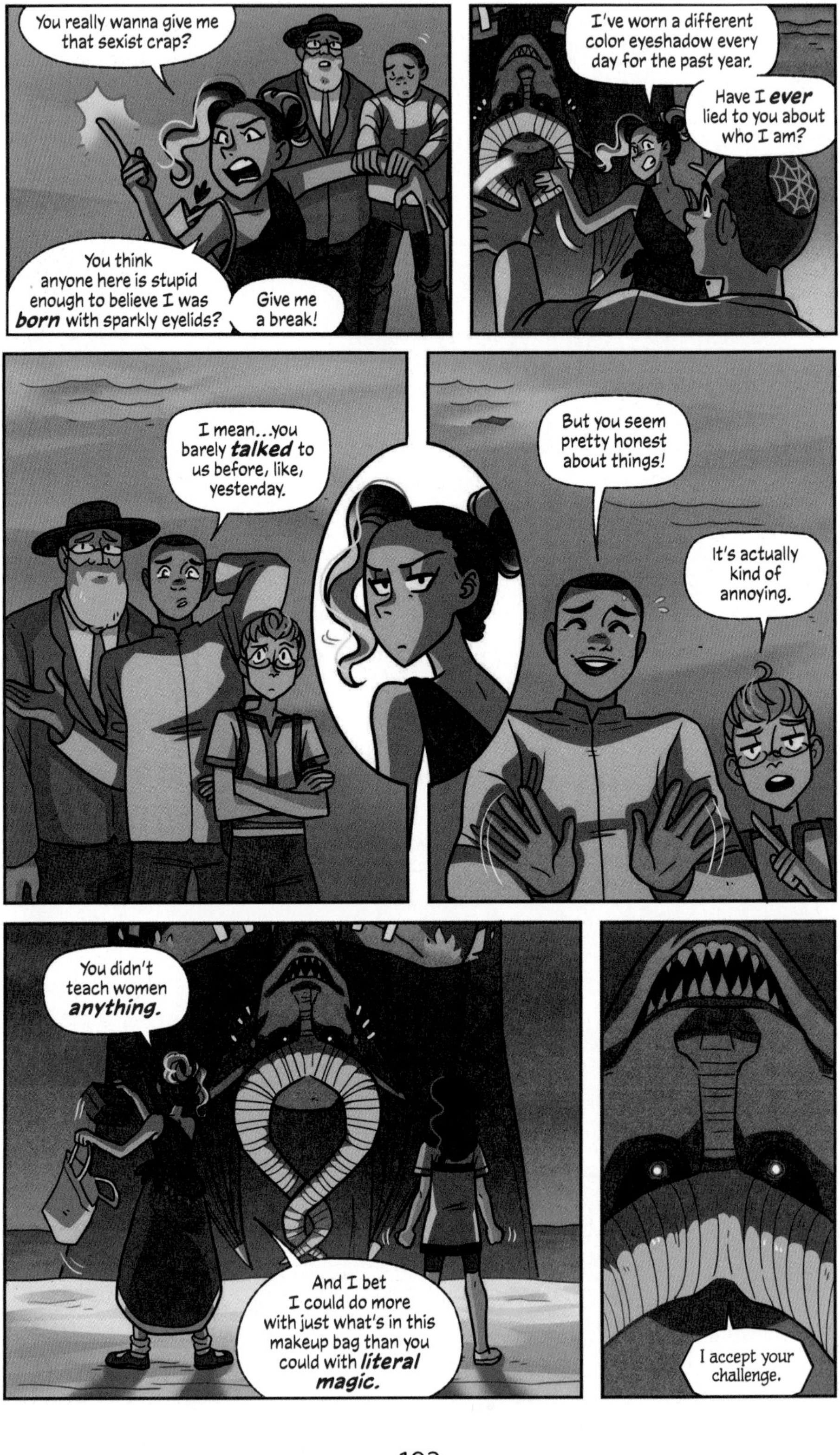
You really wanna give me that sexist crap?
You think anyone here is stupid enough to believe I was **born** with sparkly eyelids?
Give me a break!
I've worn a different color eyeshadow every day for the past year.
Have I **ever** lied to you about who I am?
I mean...you barely **talked** to us before, like, yesterday.
But you seem pretty honest about things!
It's actually kind of annoying.
You didn't teach women **anything.**
And I bet I could do more with just what's in this makeup bag than you could with **literal magic.**
I accept your challenge.

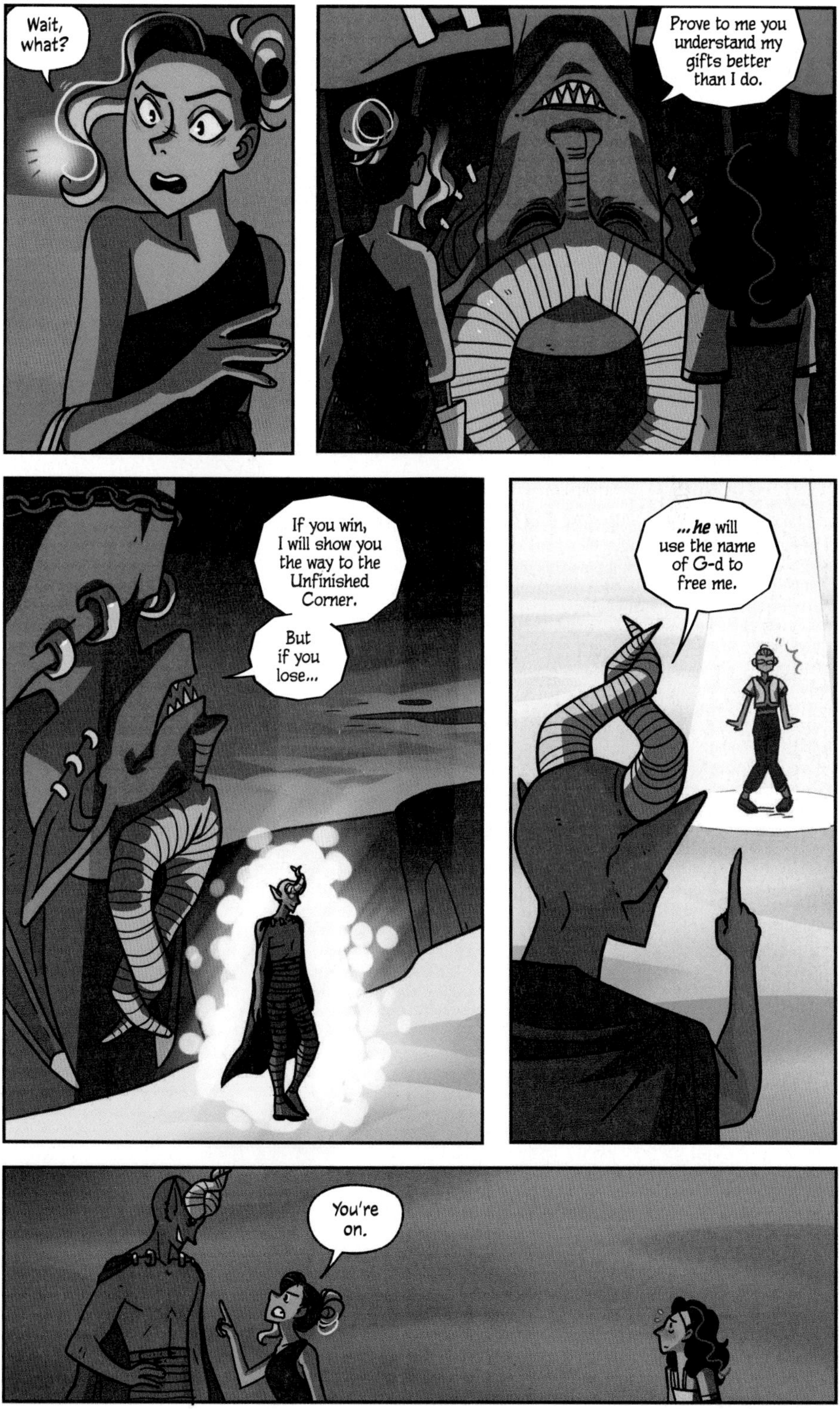
Wait, what?
Prove to me you understand my gifts better than I do.
If you win, I will show you the way to the Unfinished Corner.
But if you lose...
...he will use the name of G-d to free me.
You're on.

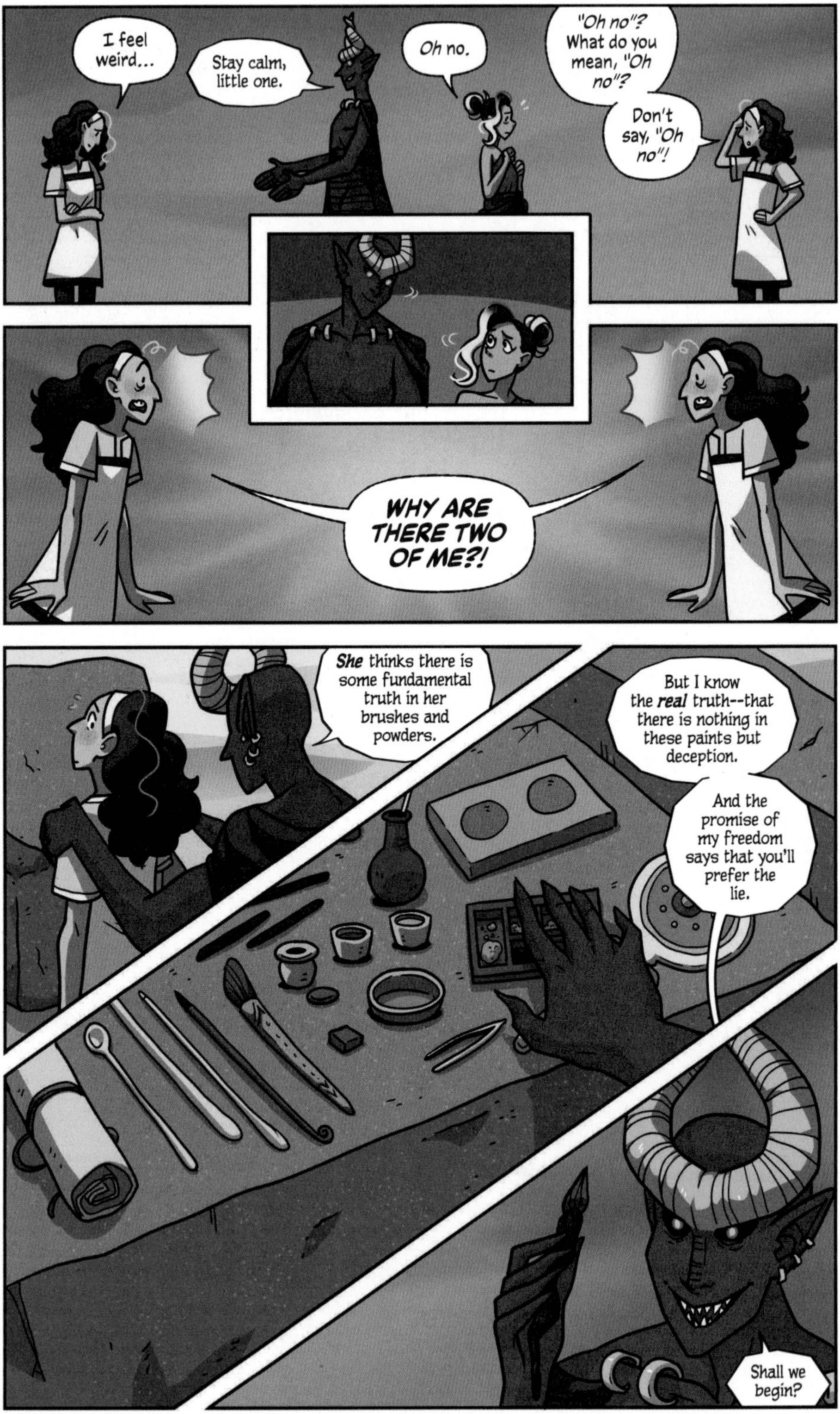
I feel weird...
Stay calm, little one.
Oh no.
"Oh no"? What do you mean, "Oh no"?
Don't say, "Oh no"!
WHY ARE THERE TWO OF ME?!
She thinks there is some fundamental truth in her brushes and powders.
But I know the real truth--that there is nothing in these paints but deception.
And the promise of my freedom says that you'll prefer the lie.
Shall we begin?

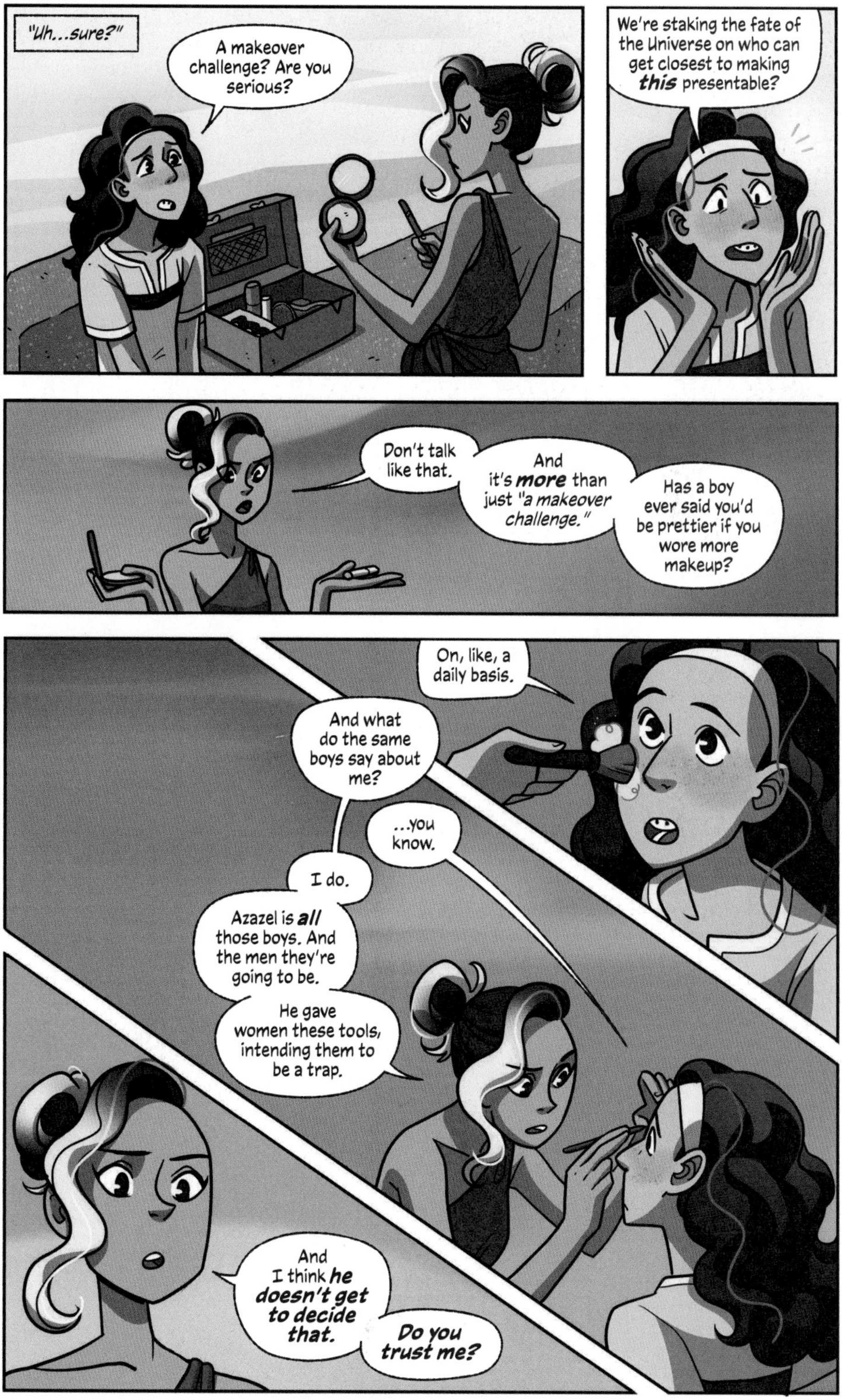
"Uh...sure?"
A makeover challenge? Are you serious?
We're staking the fate of the Universe on who can get closest to making ***this*** presentable?
Don't talk like that.
And it's ***more*** than just *"a makeover challenge."*
Has a boy ever said you'd be prettier if you wore more makeup?
On, like, a daily basis.
And what do the same boys say about me?
...you know.
I do.
Azazel is ***all*** those boys. And the men they're going to be.
He gave women these tools, intending them to be a trap.
And I think ***he doesn't get to decide that.***
Do you trust me?

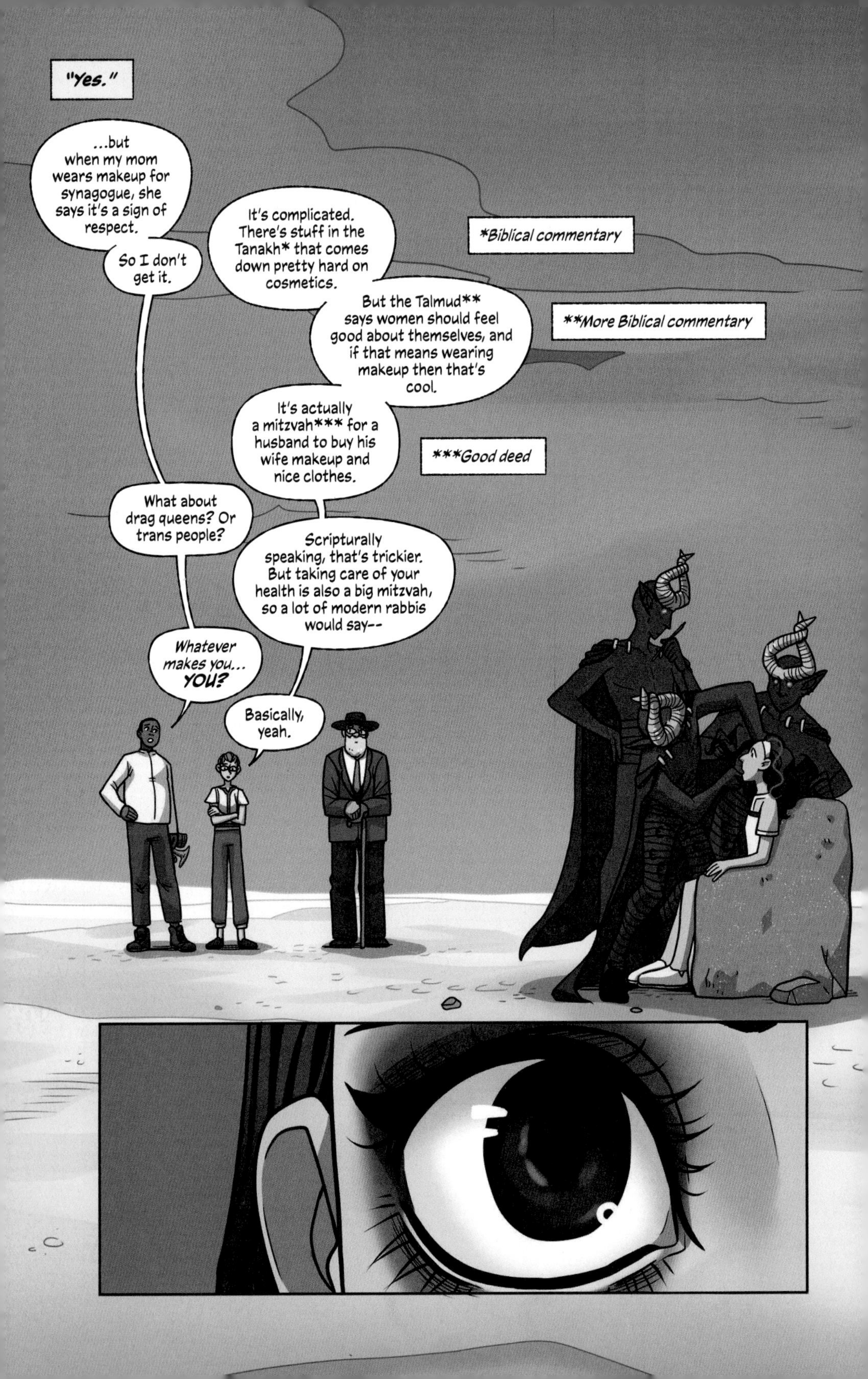
"Yes."
...but when my mom wears makeup for synagogue, she says it's a sign of respect.
So I don't get it.
It's complicated. There's stuff in the Tanakh* that comes down pretty hard on cosmetics.
*Biblical commentary
But the Talmud** says women should feel good about themselves, and if that means wearing makeup then that's cool.
**More Biblical commentary
It's actually a mitzvah*** for a husband to buy his wife makeup and nice clothes.
***Good deed
What about drag queens? Or trans people?
Scripturally speaking, that's trickier. But taking care of your health is also a big mitzvah, so a lot of modern rabbis would say--
Whatever makes you... YOU?
Basically, yeah.

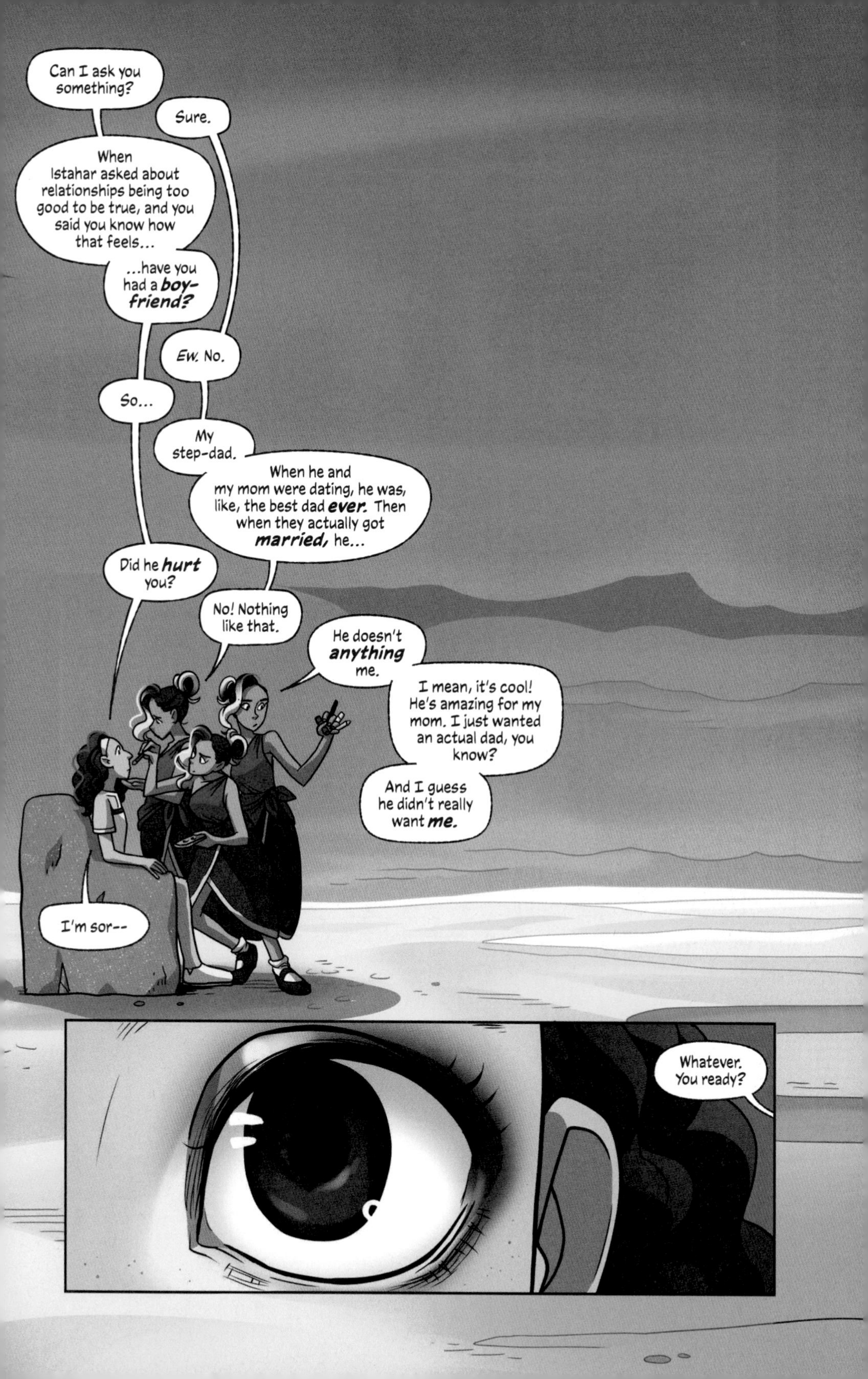
Can I ask you something?
Sure.
When Istahar asked about relationships being too good to be true, and you said you know how that feels...
...have you had a *boy-friend?*
Ew. No.
So...
My step-dad.
When he and my mom were dating, he was, like, the best dad *ever.* Then when they actually got *married,* he...
Did he *hurt* you?
No! Nothing like that.
He doesn't *anything* me.
I mean, it's cool! He's amazing for my mom. I just wanted an actual dad, you know?
And I guess he didn't really want *me.*
I'm sor--
Whatever. You ready?

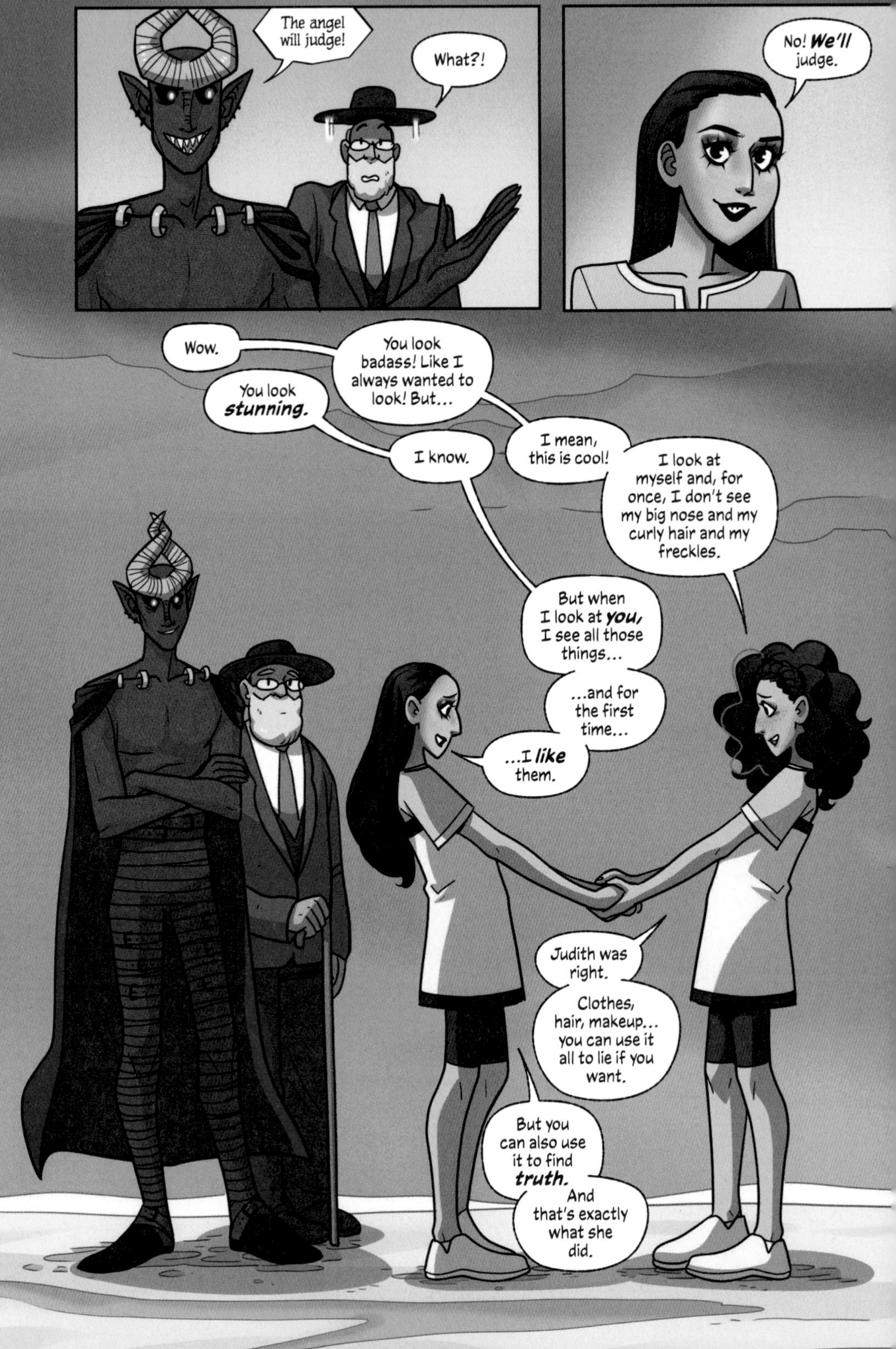
The angel will judge!
What?!
No! *We'll* judge.
Wow.
You look badass! Like I always wanted to look! But...
You look *stunning.*
I know.
I mean, this is cool!
I look at myself and, for once, I don't see my big nose and my curly hair and my freckles.
But when I look at *you,* I see all those things...
...and for the first time...
...I *like* them.
Judith was right.
Clothes, hair, makeup... you can use it all to lie if you want.
But you can also use it to find *truth.*
And that's exactly what she did.

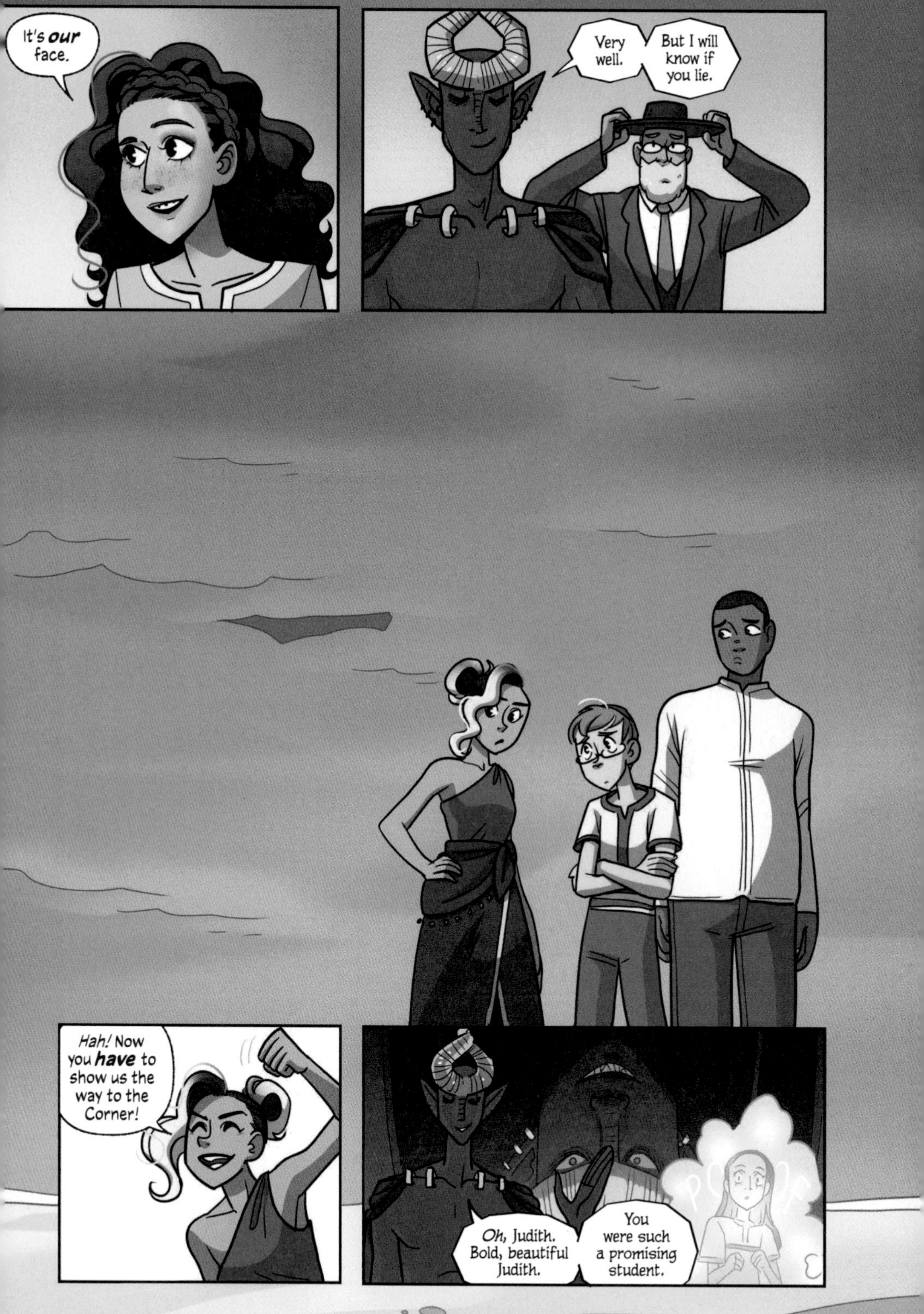
It's **our** face.
Very well.
But I will know if you lie.
Hah! Now you **have** to show us the way to the Corner!
Oh, Judith. Bold, beautiful Judith.
You were such a promising student.

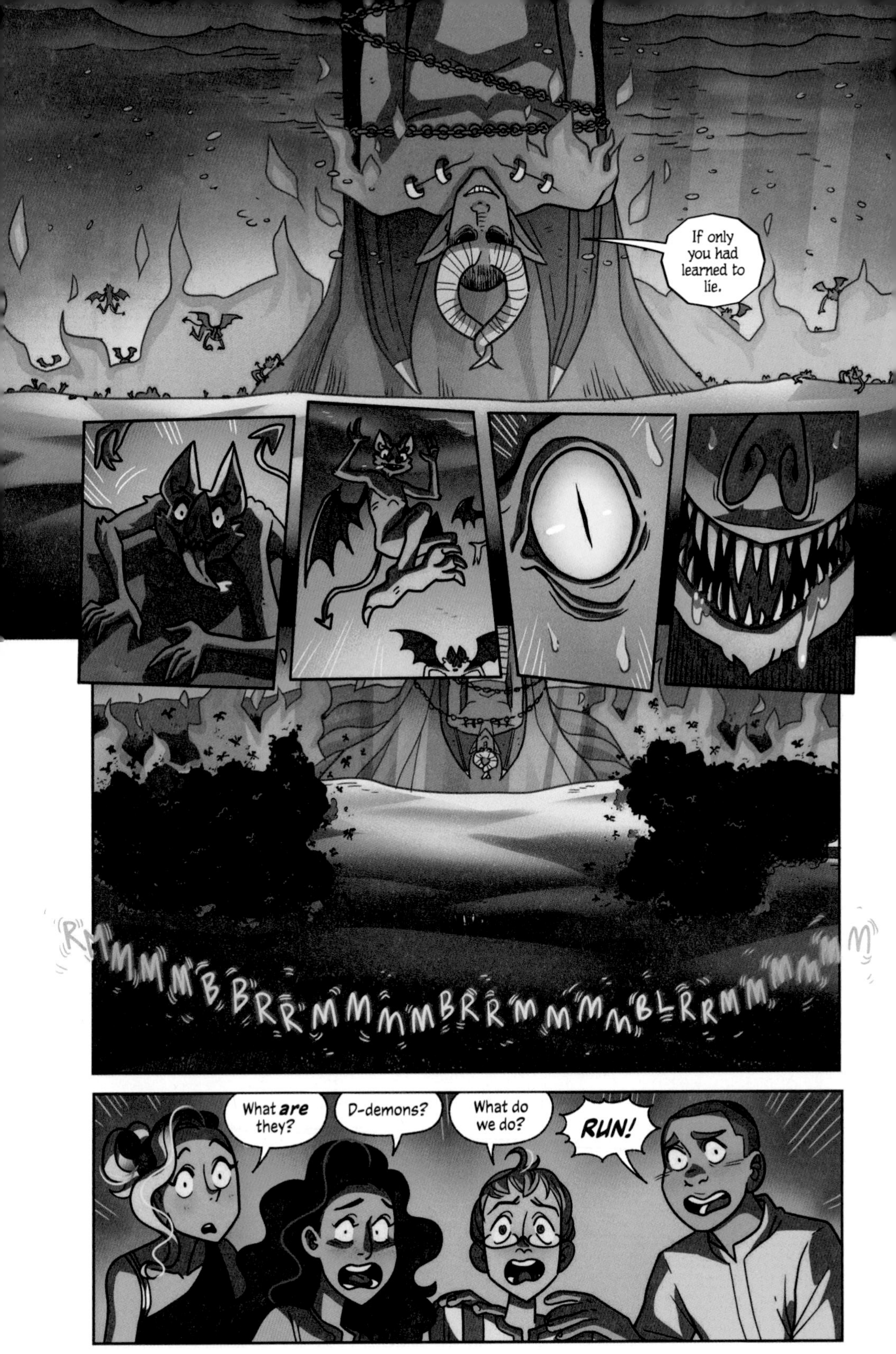
If only you had learned to lie.
RMMMMMBBRRMMMMMBRRMMMMMBLRRMMMMMM
What *are* they?
D-demons?
What do we do?
RUN!

CHAPTER SEVEN

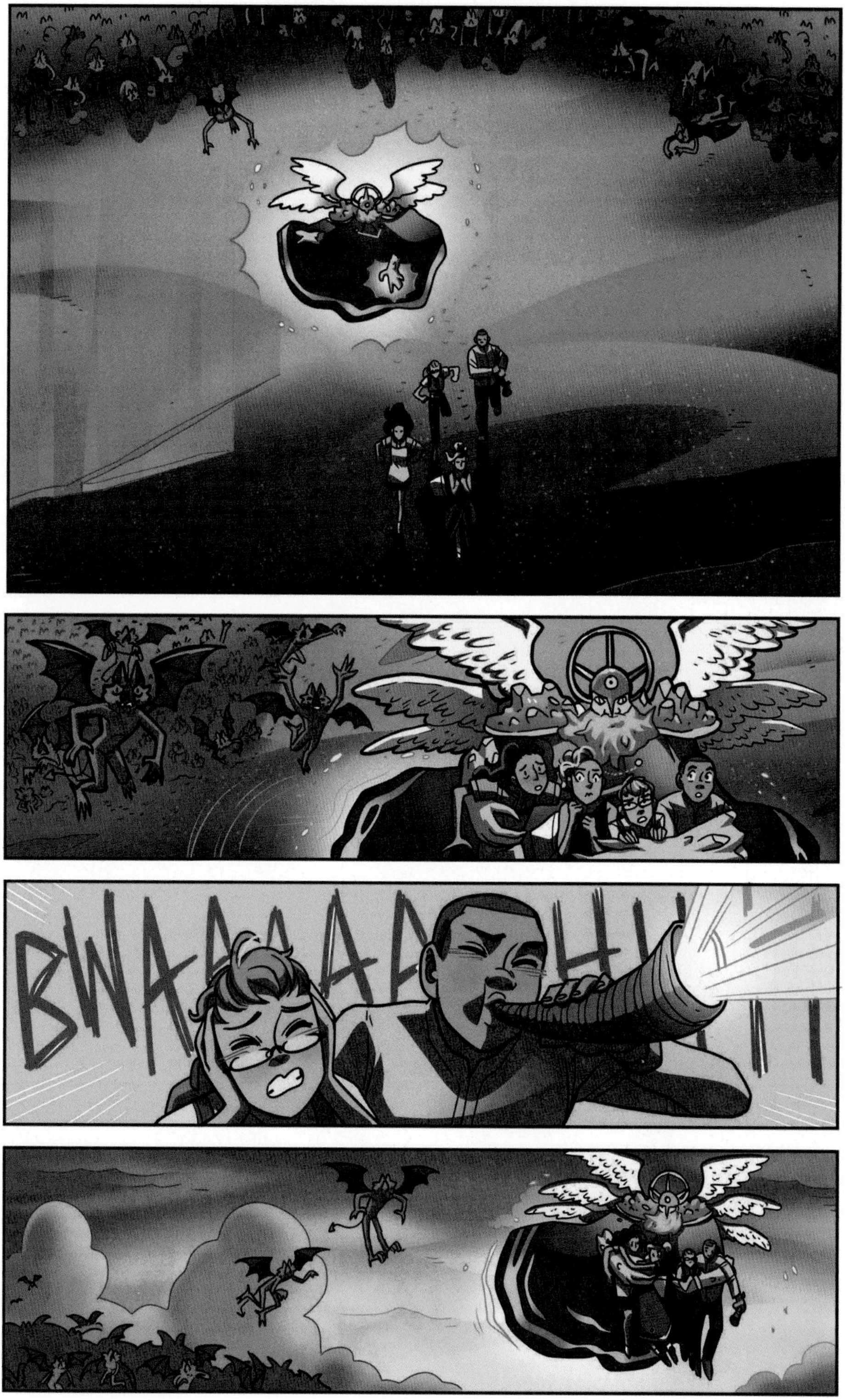

BWAAAAAHHH

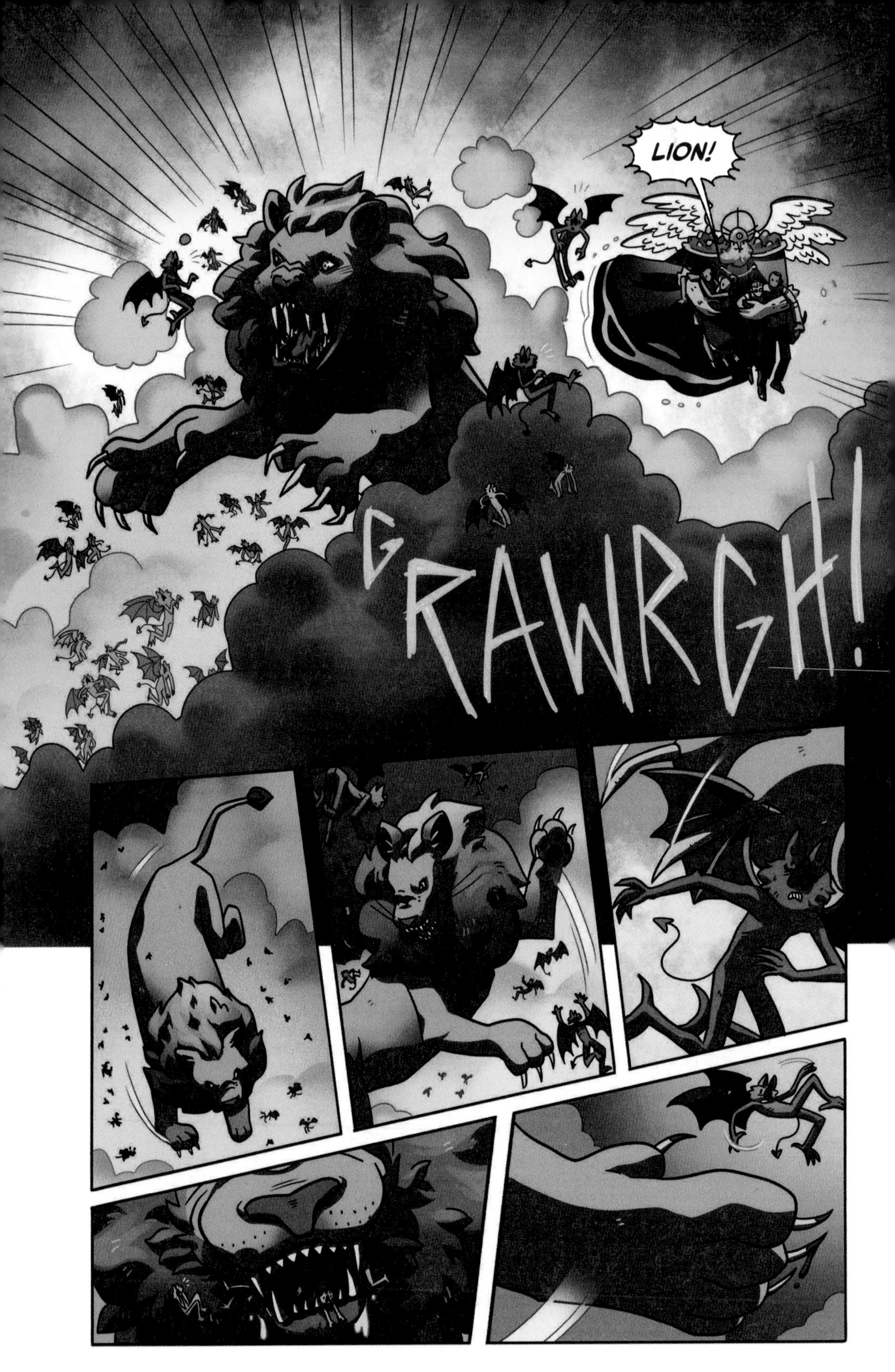
LION!
GRAWRGH!

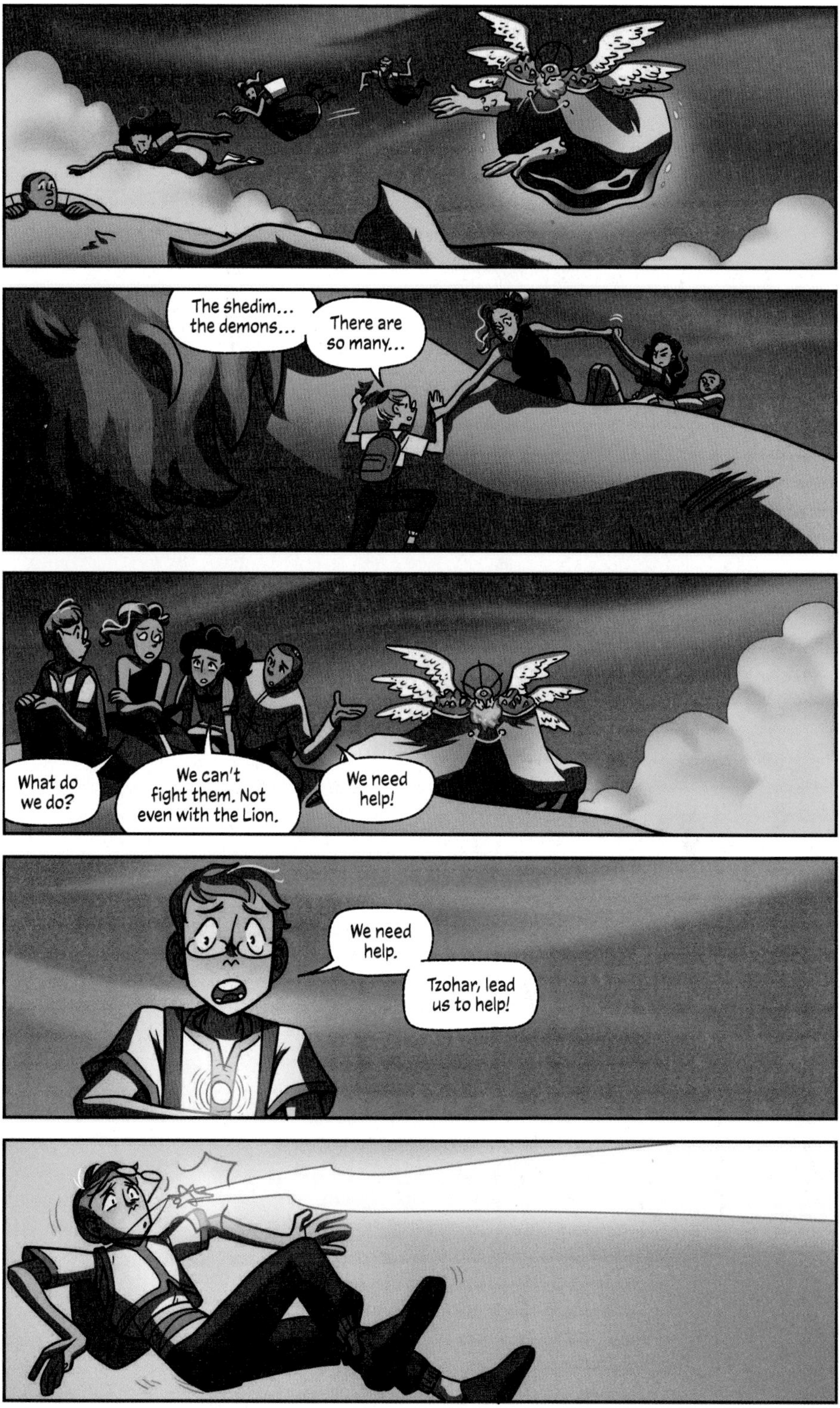

The shedim... the demons...
There are so many...
What do we do?
We can't fight them. Not even with the Lion.
We need help!
We need help.
Tzohar, lead us to help!

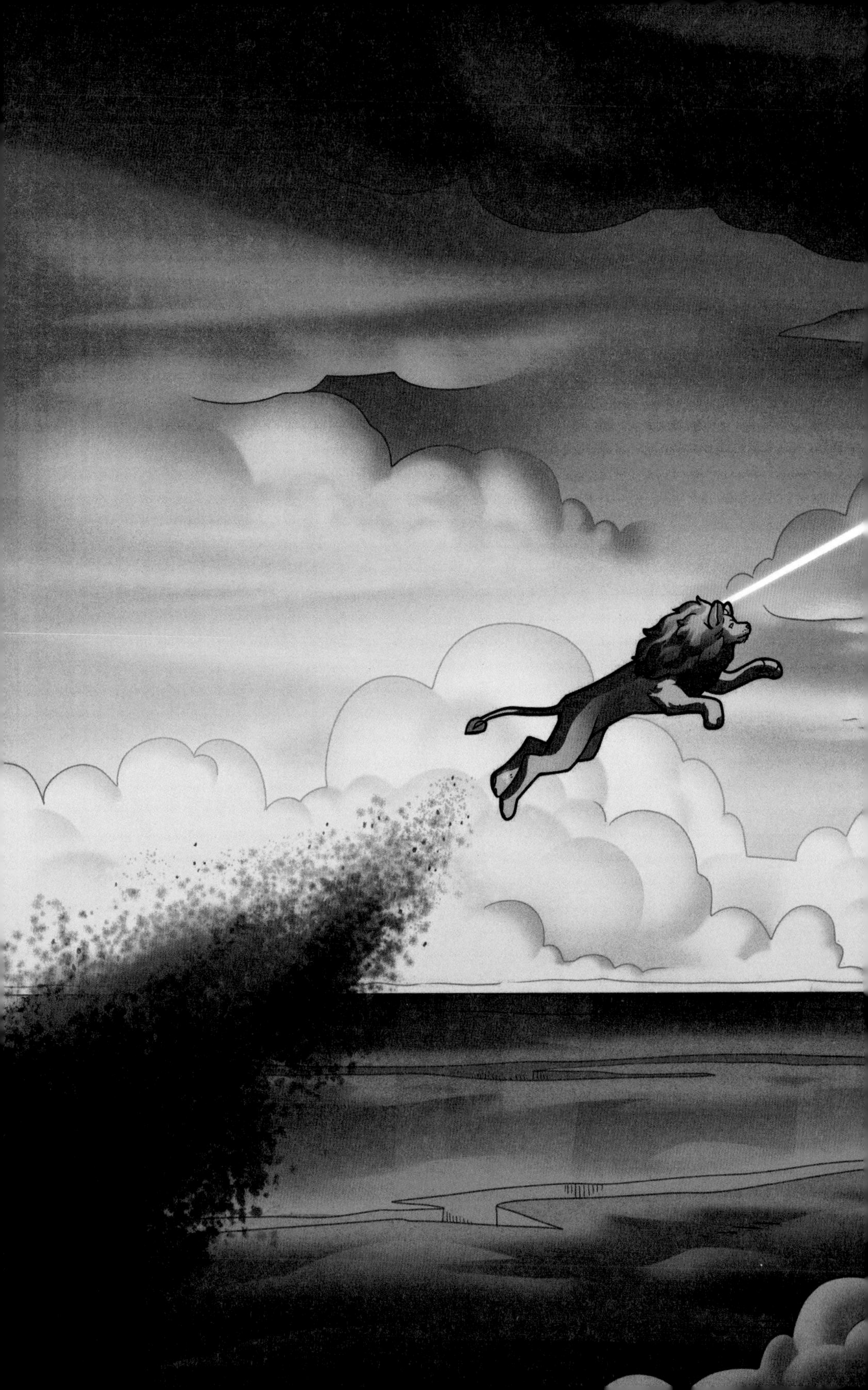

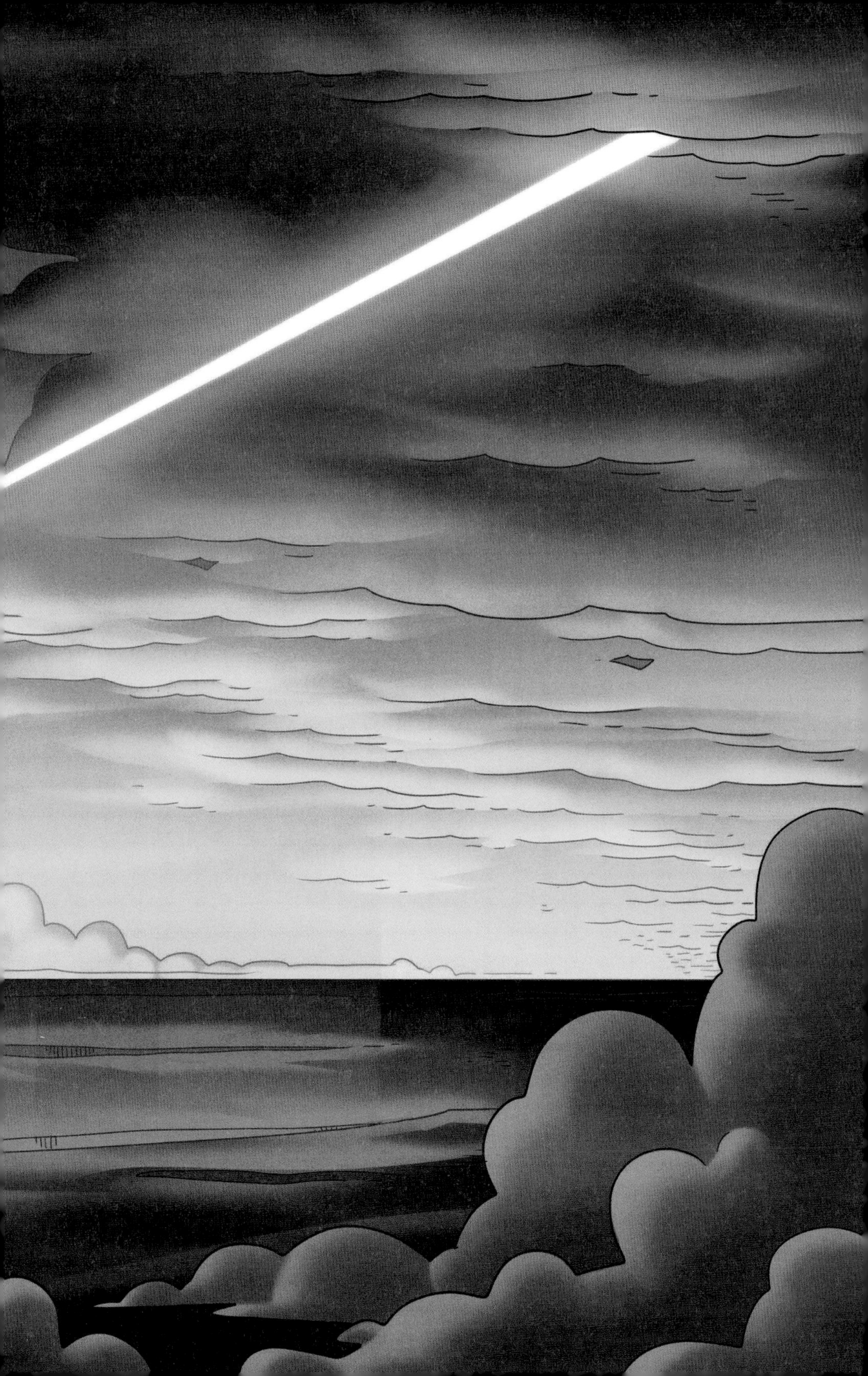

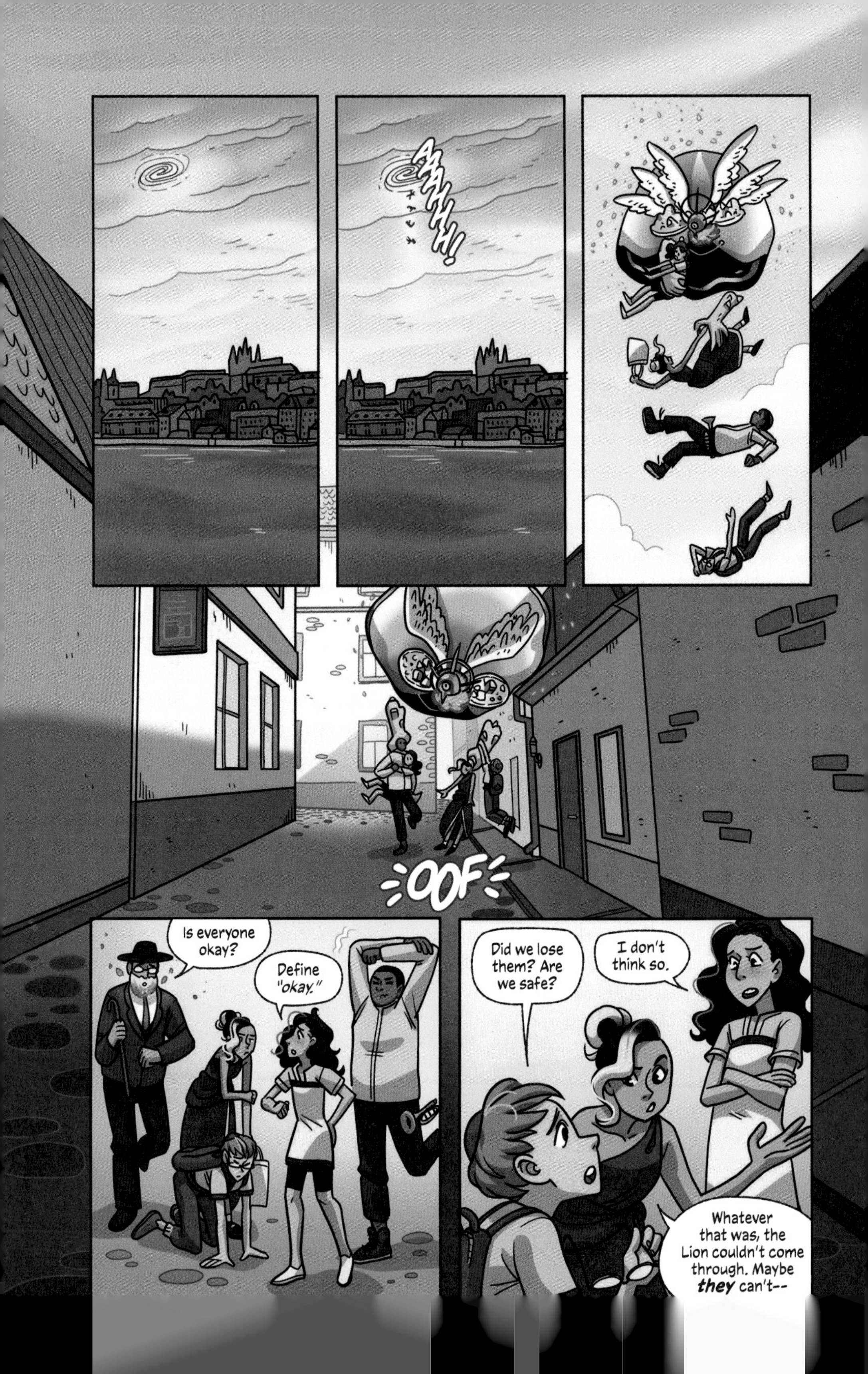
AAAHHH!
OOF
Is everyone okay?
Define "okay."
Did we lose them? Are we safe?
I don't think so.
Whatever that was, the Lion couldn't come through. Maybe *they* can't--

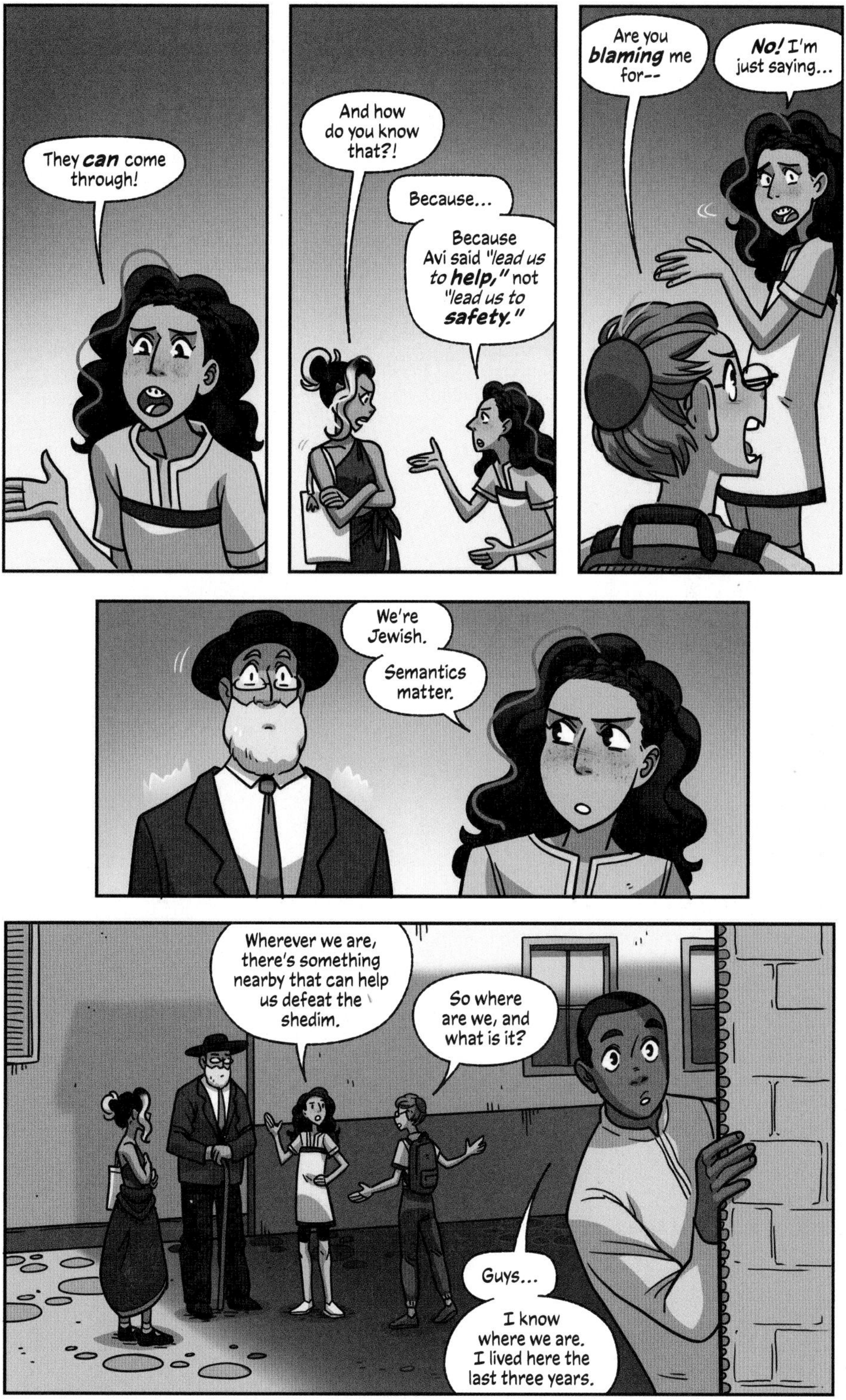
They **can** come through!
And how do you know that?!
Because...
Because Avi said *"lead us to **help,**"* not *"lead us to **safety.**"*
Are you **blaming** me for--
No! I'm just saying...
We're Jewish.
Semantics matter.
Wherever we are, there's something nearby that can help us defeat the shedim.
So where are we, and what is it?
Guys...
I know where we are. I lived here the last three years.

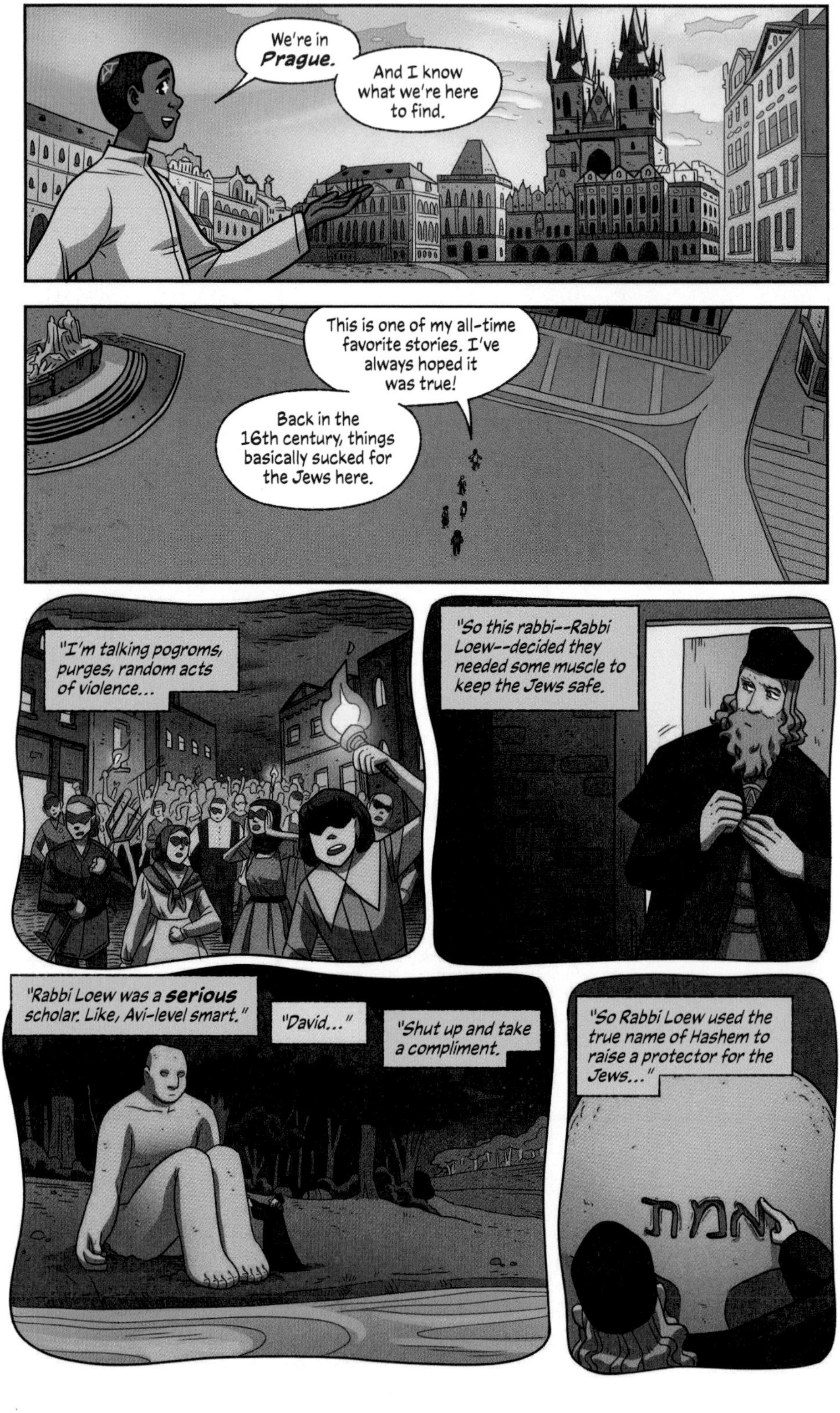
We're in Prague.
And I know what we're here to find.
This is one of my all-time favorite stories. I've always hoped it was true!
Back in the 16th century, things basically sucked for the Jews here.
"I'm talking pogroms, purges, random acts of violence...
"So this rabbi--Rabbi Loew--decided they needed some muscle to keep the Jews safe.
"Rabbi Loew was a serious scholar. Like, Avi-level smart."
"David..."
"Shut up and take a compliment.
"So Rabbi Loew used the true name of Hashem to raise a protector for the Jews..."
אמת

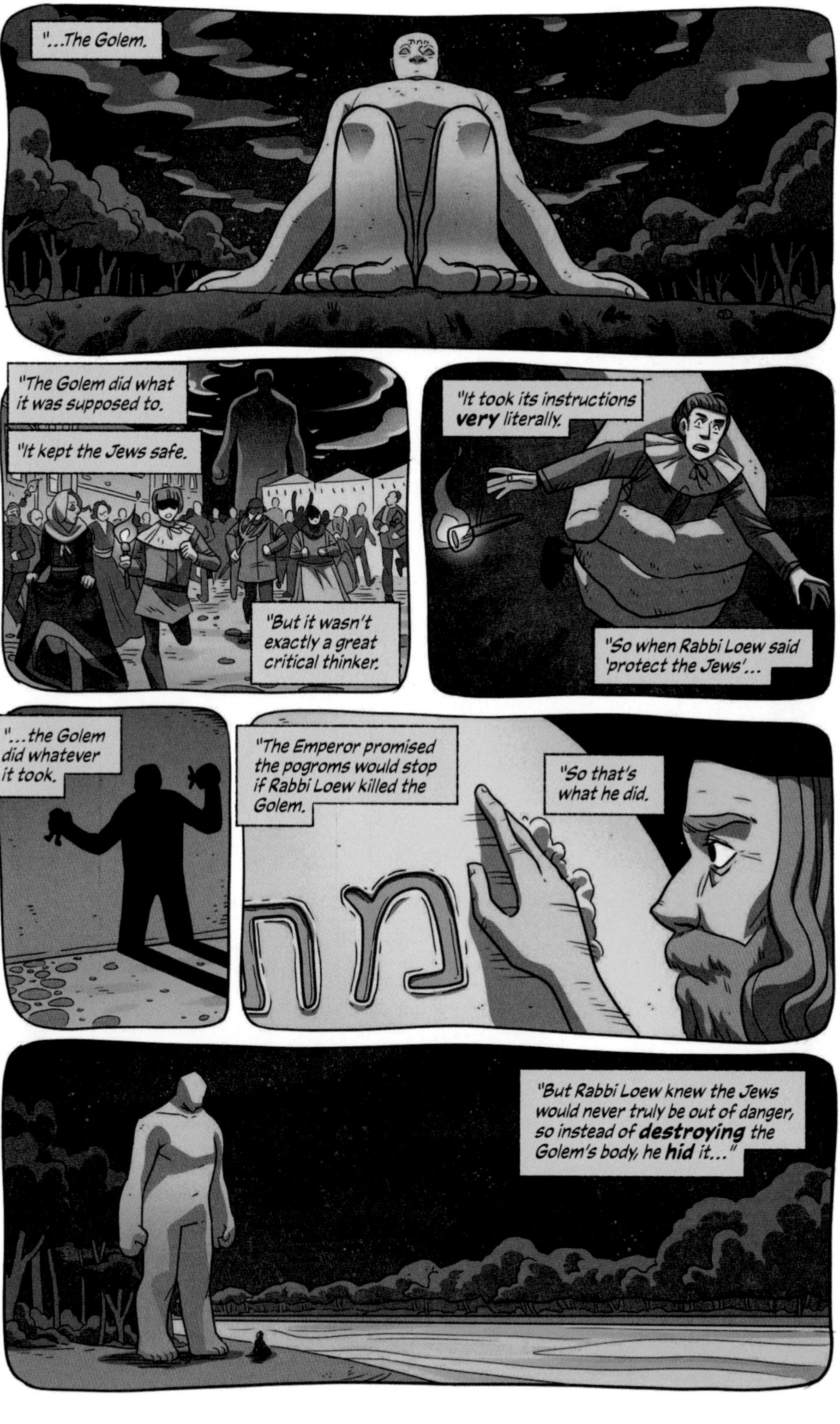
"...The Golem.
"The Golem did what it was supposed to.
"It kept the Jews safe.
"But it wasn't exactly a great critical thinker.
"It took its instructions **very** literally.
"So when Rabbi Loew said 'protect the Jews'...
"...the Golem did whatever it took.
"The Emperor promised the pogroms would stop if Rabbi Loew killed the Golem.
"So that's what he did.
"But Rabbi Loew knew the Jews would never truly be out of danger, so instead of **destroying** the Golem's body, he **hid** it..."

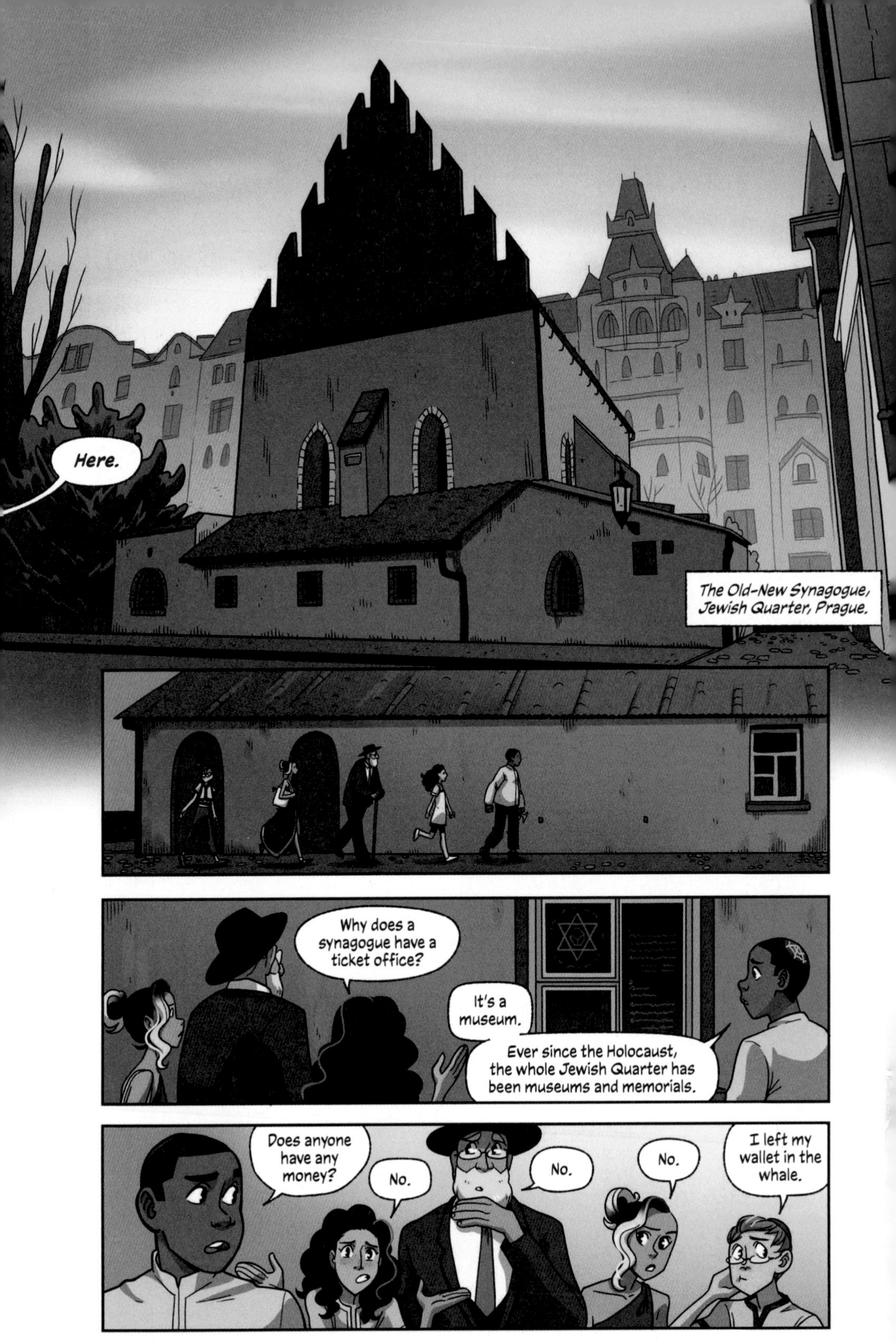

Here.
The Old-New Synagogue, Jewish Quarter, Prague.
Why does a synagogue have a ticket office?
It's a museum.
Ever since the Holocaust, the whole Jewish Quarter has been museums and memorials.
Does anyone have any money?
No.
No.
No.
I left my wallet in the whale.

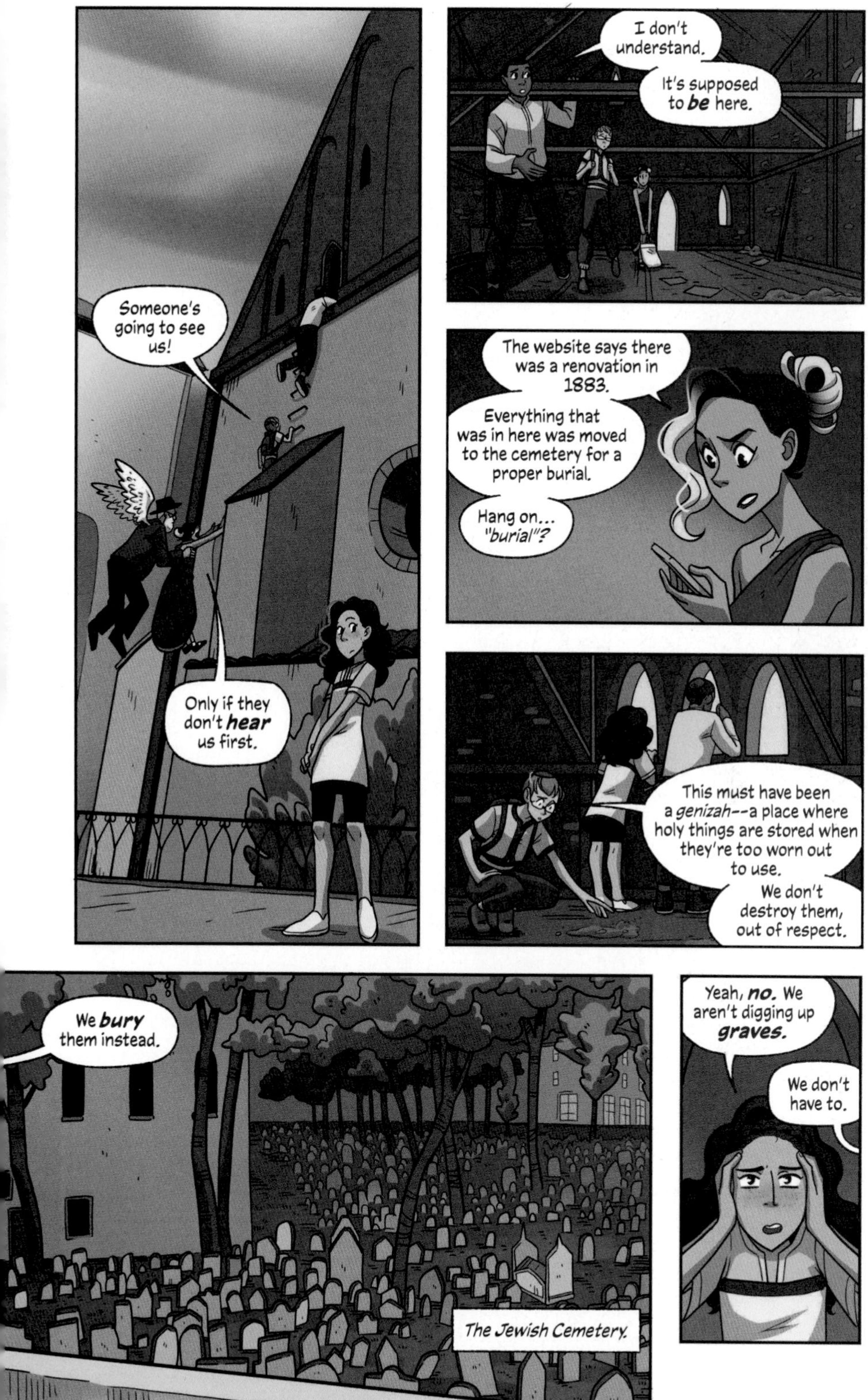
Someone's going to see us!
Only if they don't **hear** us first.
I don't understand.
It's supposed to ***be*** here.
The website says there was a renovation in 1883.
Everything that was in here was moved to the cemetery for a proper burial.
Hang on... *"burial"?*
This must have been a *genizah*--a place where holy things are stored when they're too worn out to use.
We don't destroy them, out of respect.
We ***bury*** them instead.
The Jewish Cemetery.
Yeah, ***no.*** We aren't digging up ***graves.***
We don't have to.

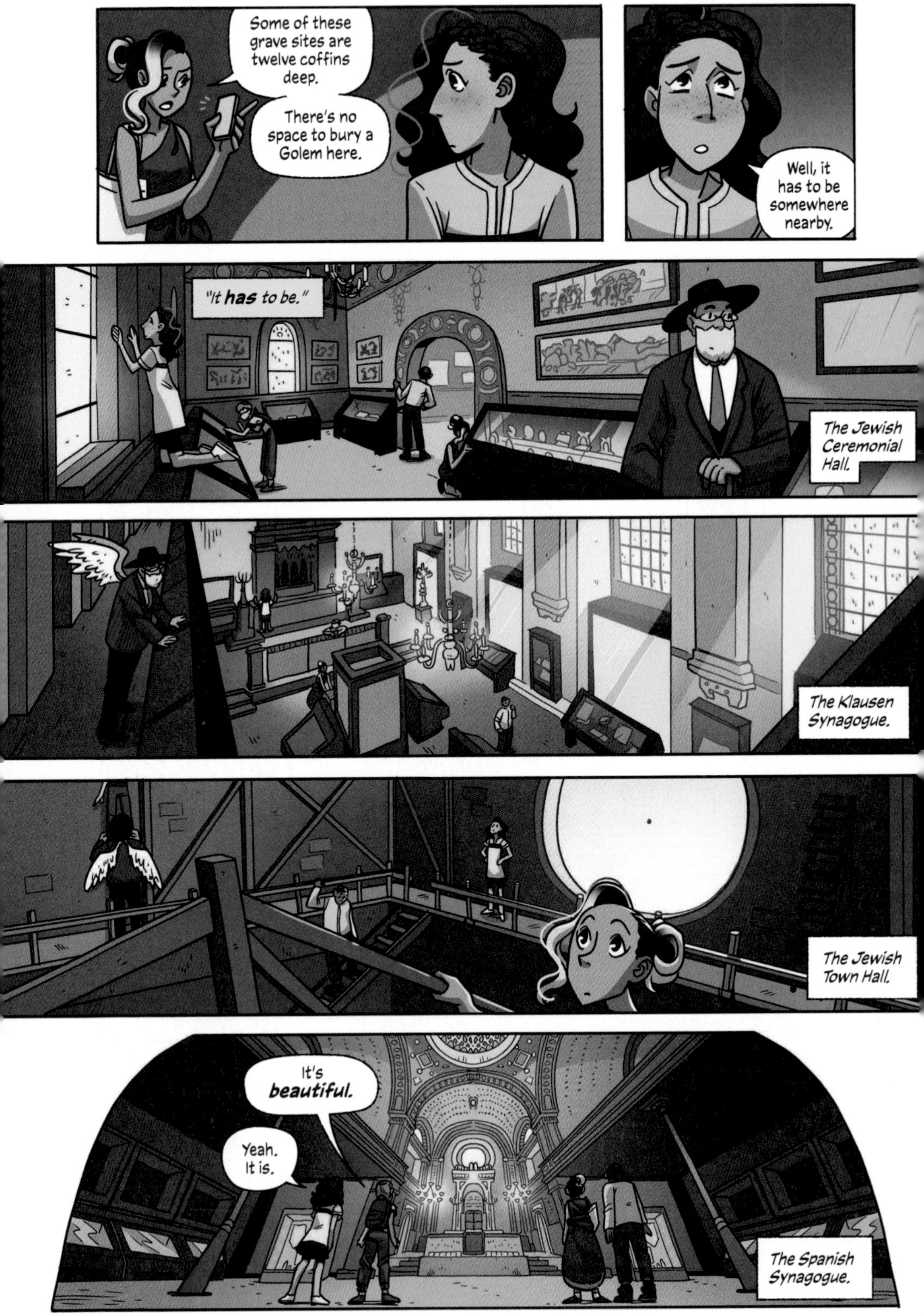
Some of these grave sites are twelve coffins deep.
There's no space to bury a Golem here.
Well, it has to be somewhere nearby.
"It **has** to be."
The Jewish Ceremonial Hall.
The Klausen Synagogue.
The Jewish Town Hall.
It's ***beautiful.***
Yeah. It is.
The Spanish Synagogue.

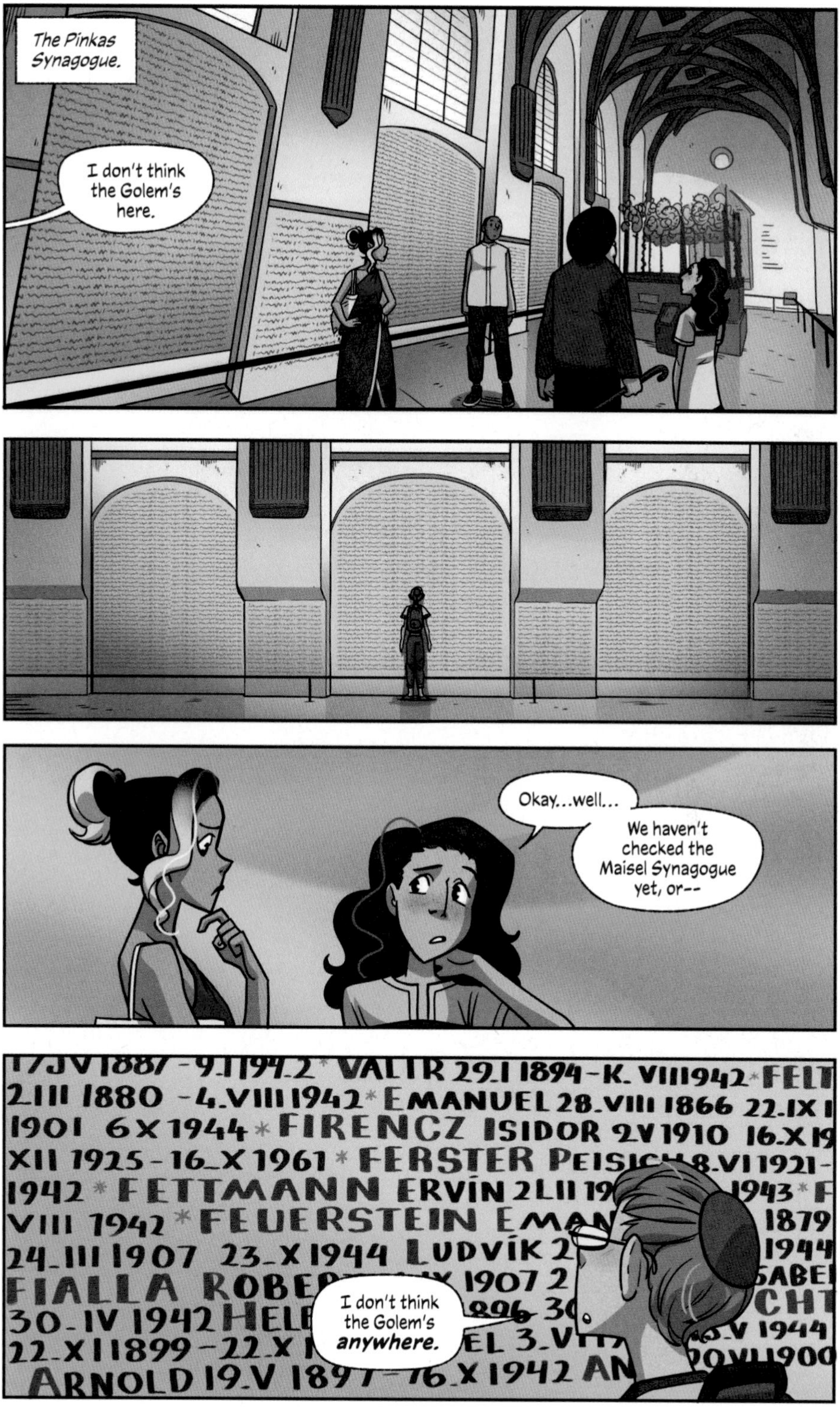
The Pinkas Synagogue.
I don't think the Golem's here.
Okay...well...
We haven't checked the Maisel Synagogue yet, or--
I don't think the Golem's *anywhere.*

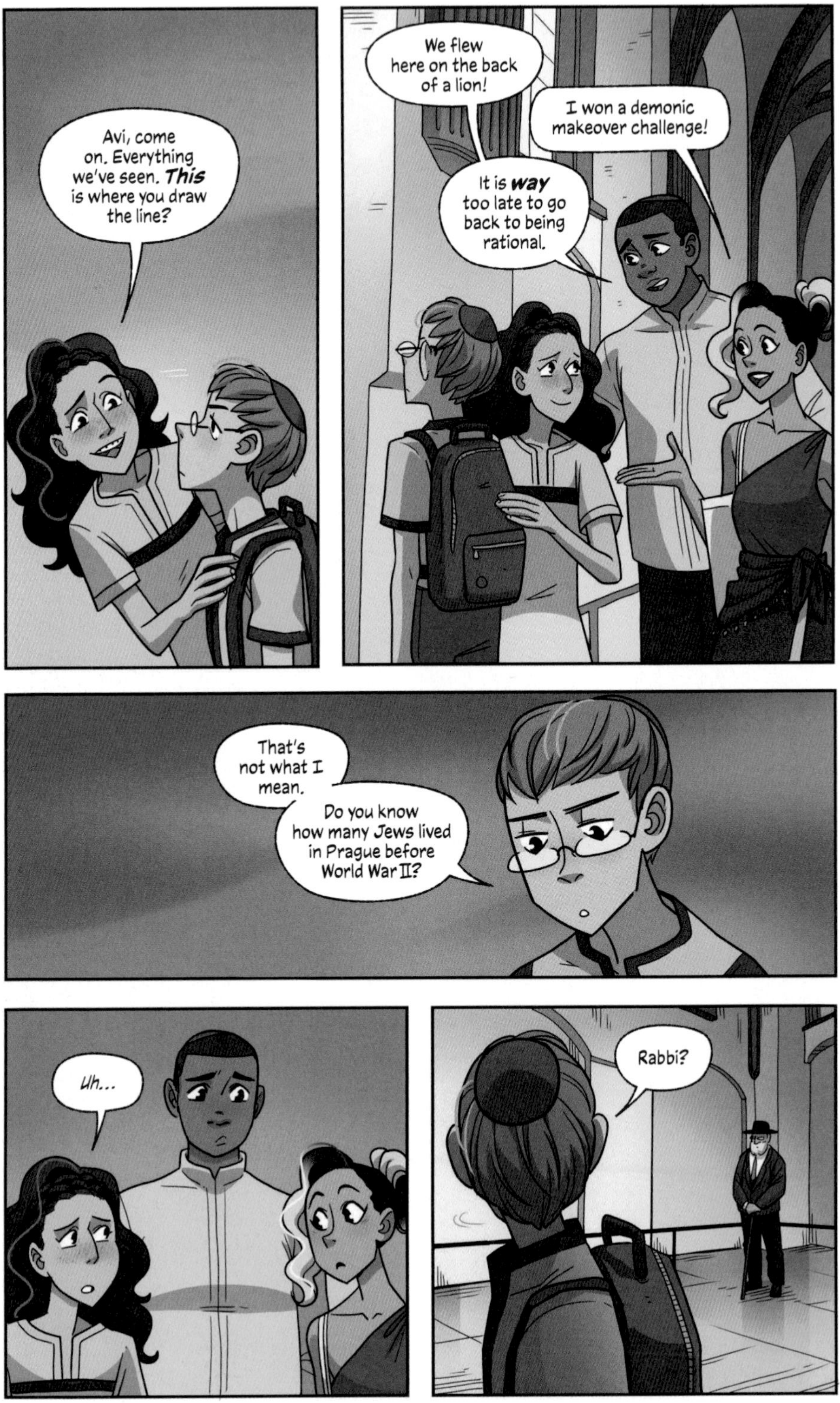
Avi, come on. Everything we've seen. ***This*** is where you draw the line?
We flew here on the back of a lion!
I won a demonic makeover challenge!
It is ***way*** too late to go back to being rational.
That's not what I mean.
Do you know how many Jews lived in Prague before World War II?
Uh...
Rabbi?

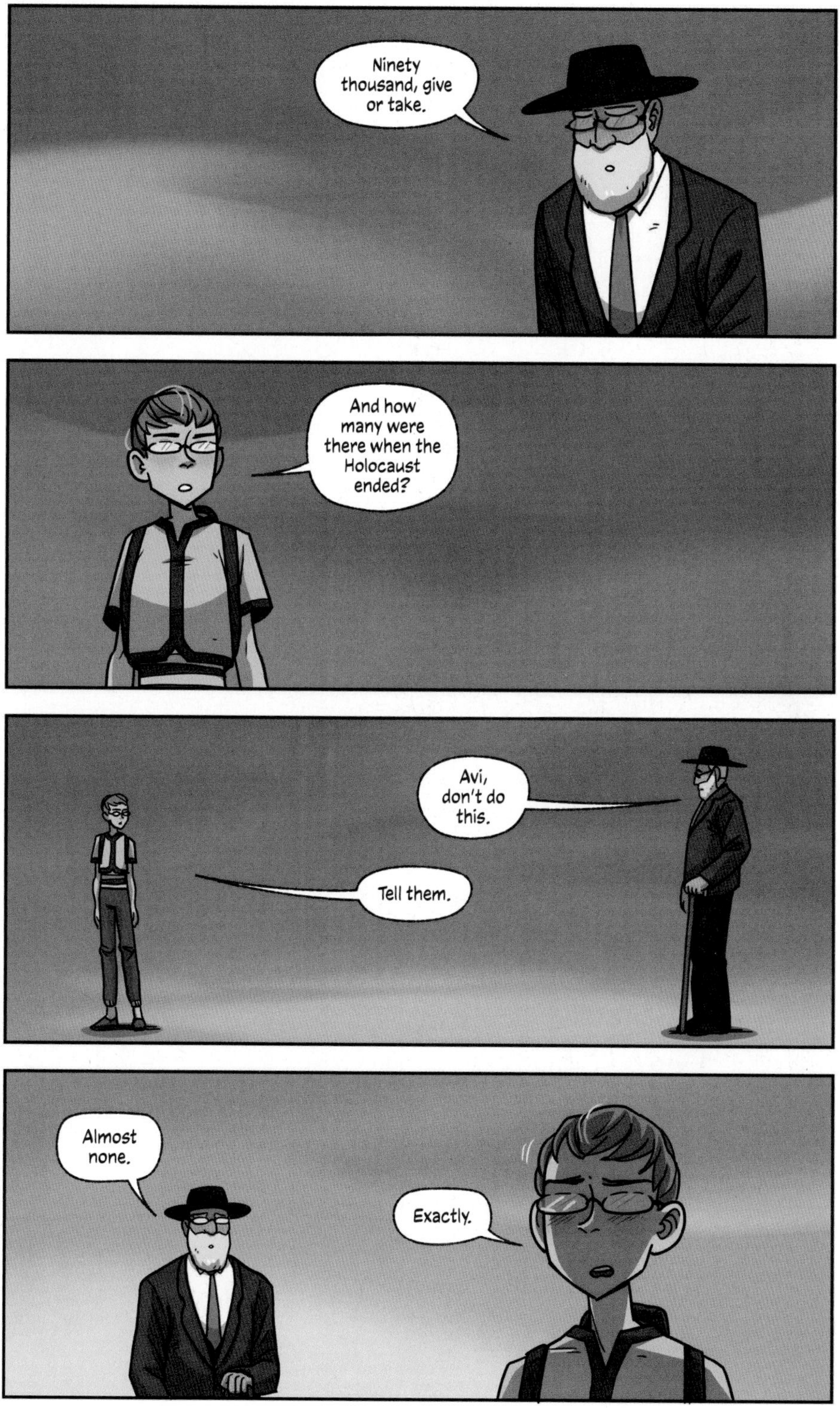
Ninety thousand, give or take.
And how many were there when the Holocaust ended?
Avi, don't do this.
Tell them.
Almost none.
Exactly.

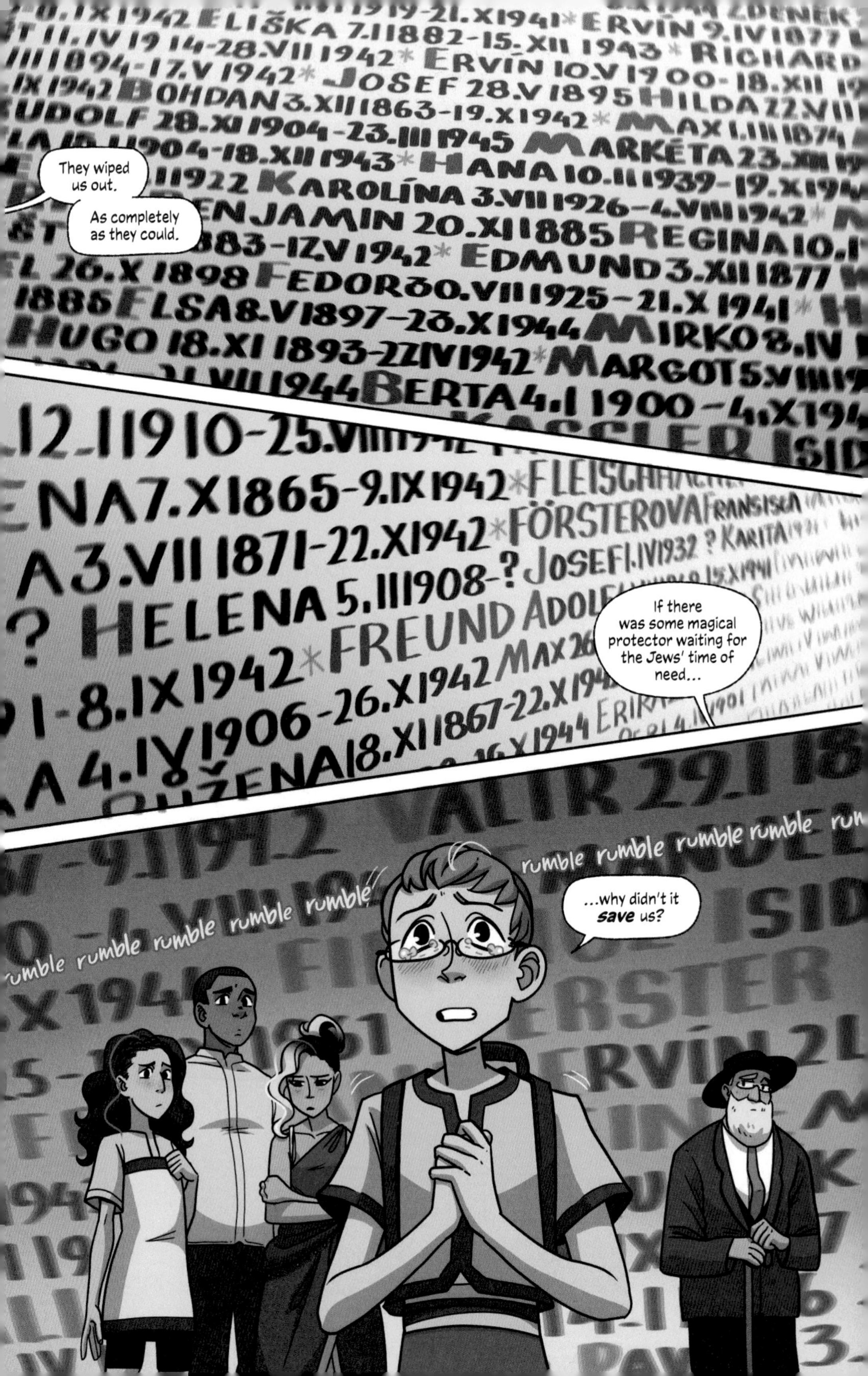
They wiped us out.
As completely as they could.
If there was some magical protector waiting for the Jews' time of need...
rumble rumble rumble rumble rumble
rumble rumble rumble rumble rumble
...why didn't it *save* us?

CHAPTER EIGHT

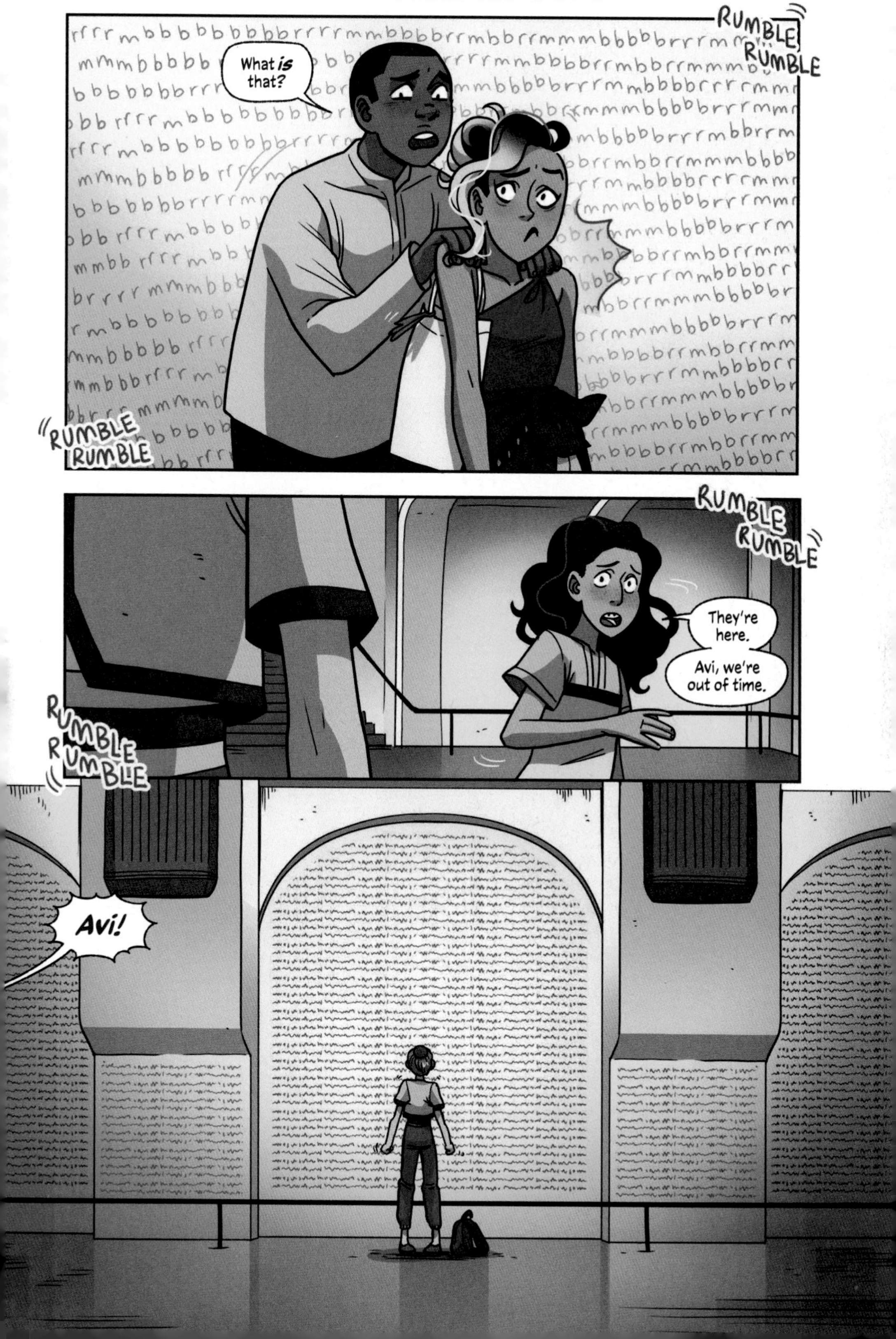
RUMBLE RUMBLE
What *is* that?
RUMBLE RUMBLE
RUMBLE RUMBLE
They're here.
Avi, we're out of time.
RUMBLE RUMBLE
Avi!

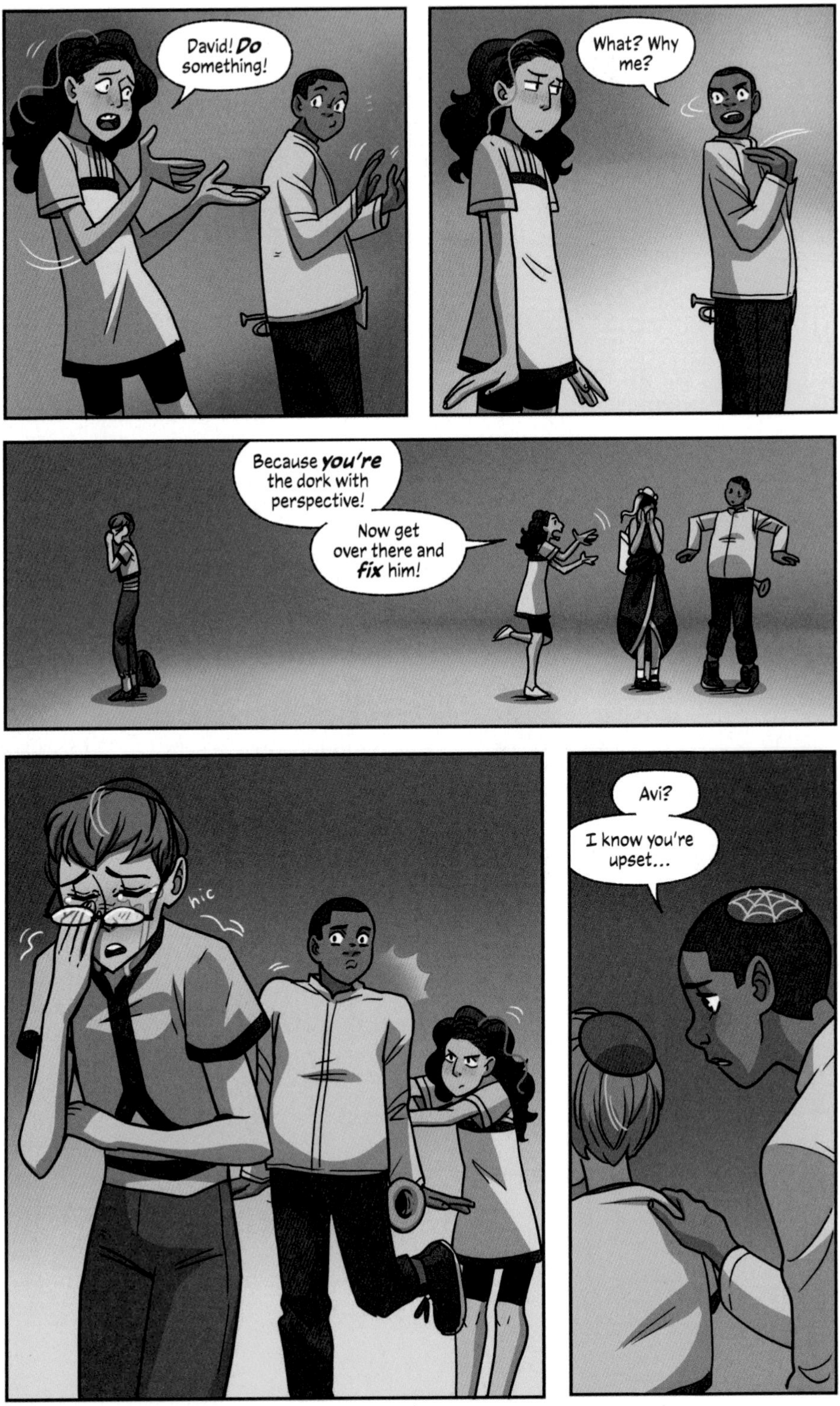
David! Do something!
What? Why me?
Because you're the dork with perspective!
Now get over there and fix him!
hic
Avi?
I know you're upset...

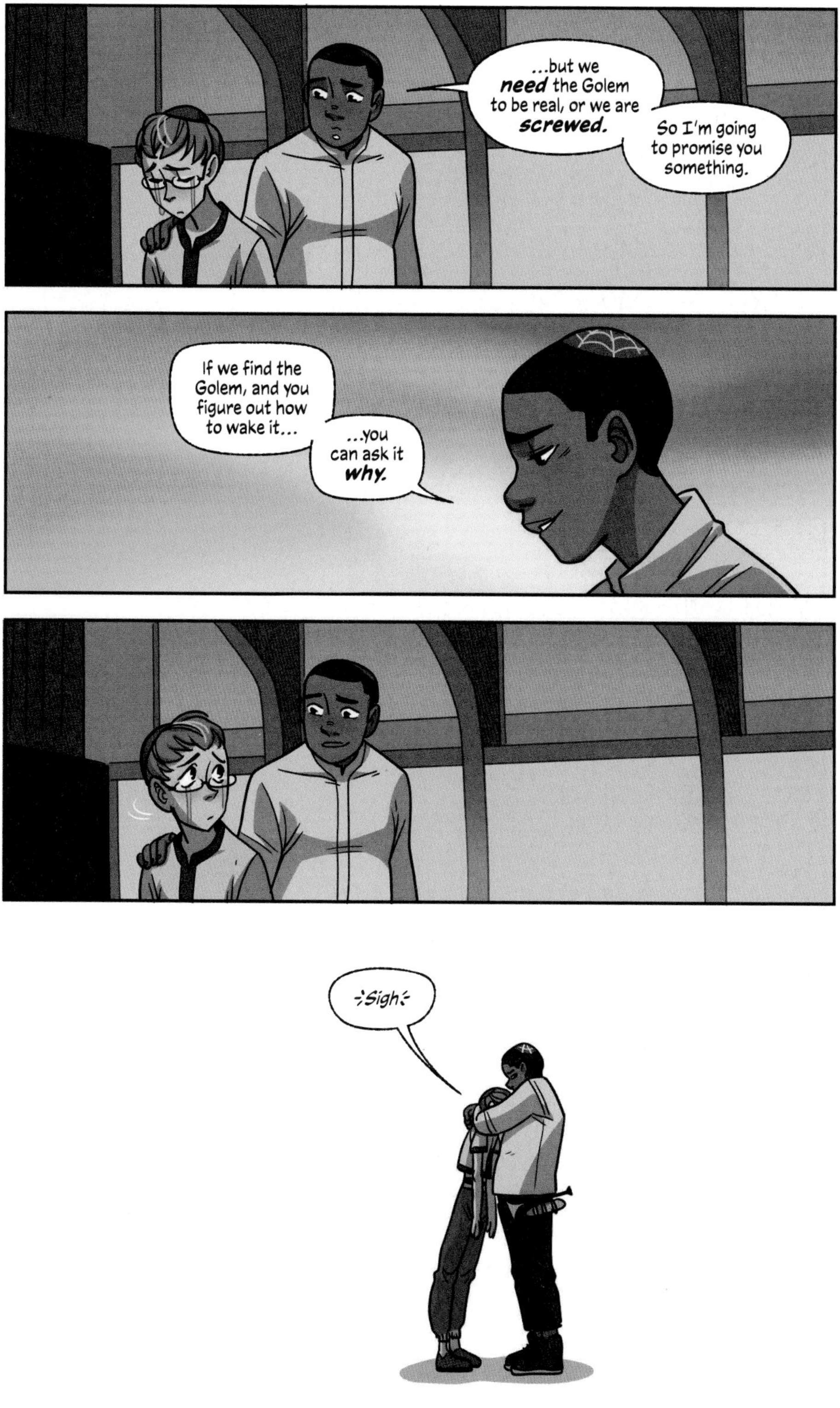
...but we **need** the Golem to be real, or we are ***screwed.***
So I'm going to promise you something.
If we find the Golem, and you figure out how to wake it...
...you can ask it ***why.***
Sigh

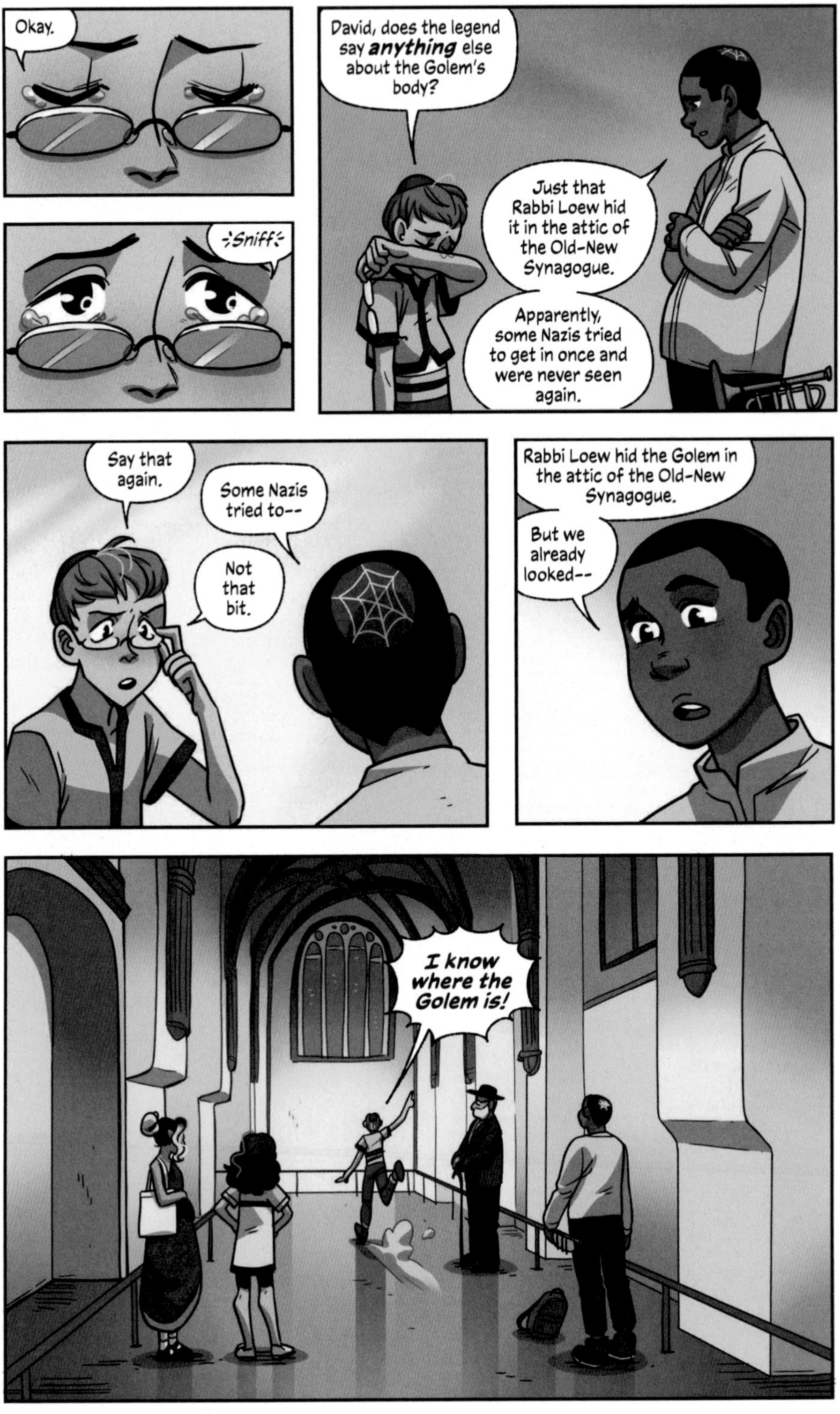
Okay.
David, does the legend say *anything* else about the Golem's body?
Just that Rabbi Loew hid it in the attic of the Old-New Synagogue.
Apparently, some Nazis tried to get in once and were never seen again.
-;Sniff;-
Say that again.
Some Nazis tried to--
Not that bit.
Rabbi Loew hid the Golem in the attic of the Old-New Synagogue.
But we already looked--
I know where the Golem is!

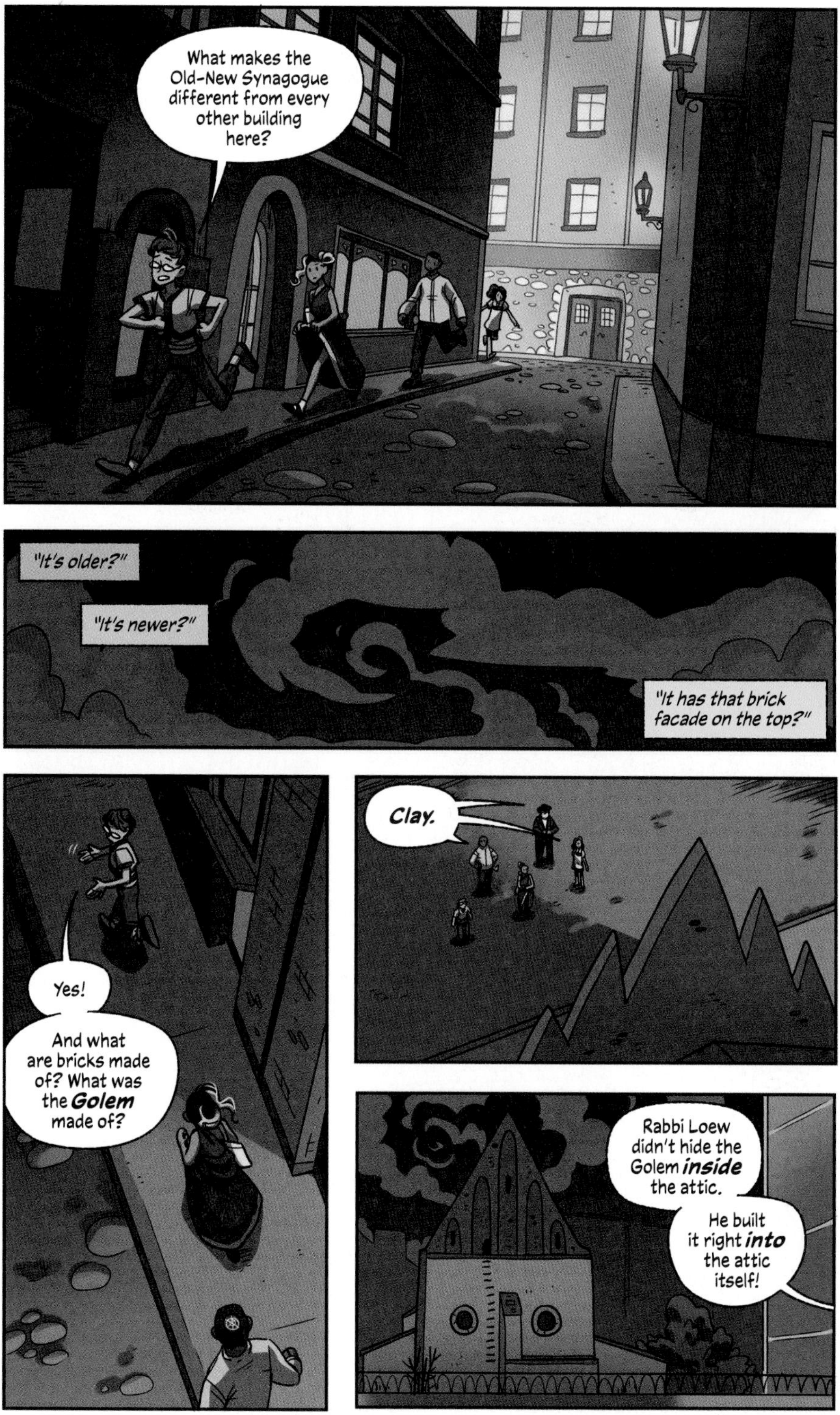
What makes the Old-New Synagogue different from every other building here?
"It's older?"
"It's newer?"
"It has that brick facade on the top?"
Yes!
And what are bricks made of? What was the *Golem* made of?
Clay.
Rabbi Loew didn't hide the Golem *inside* the attic.
He built it right *into* the attic itself!

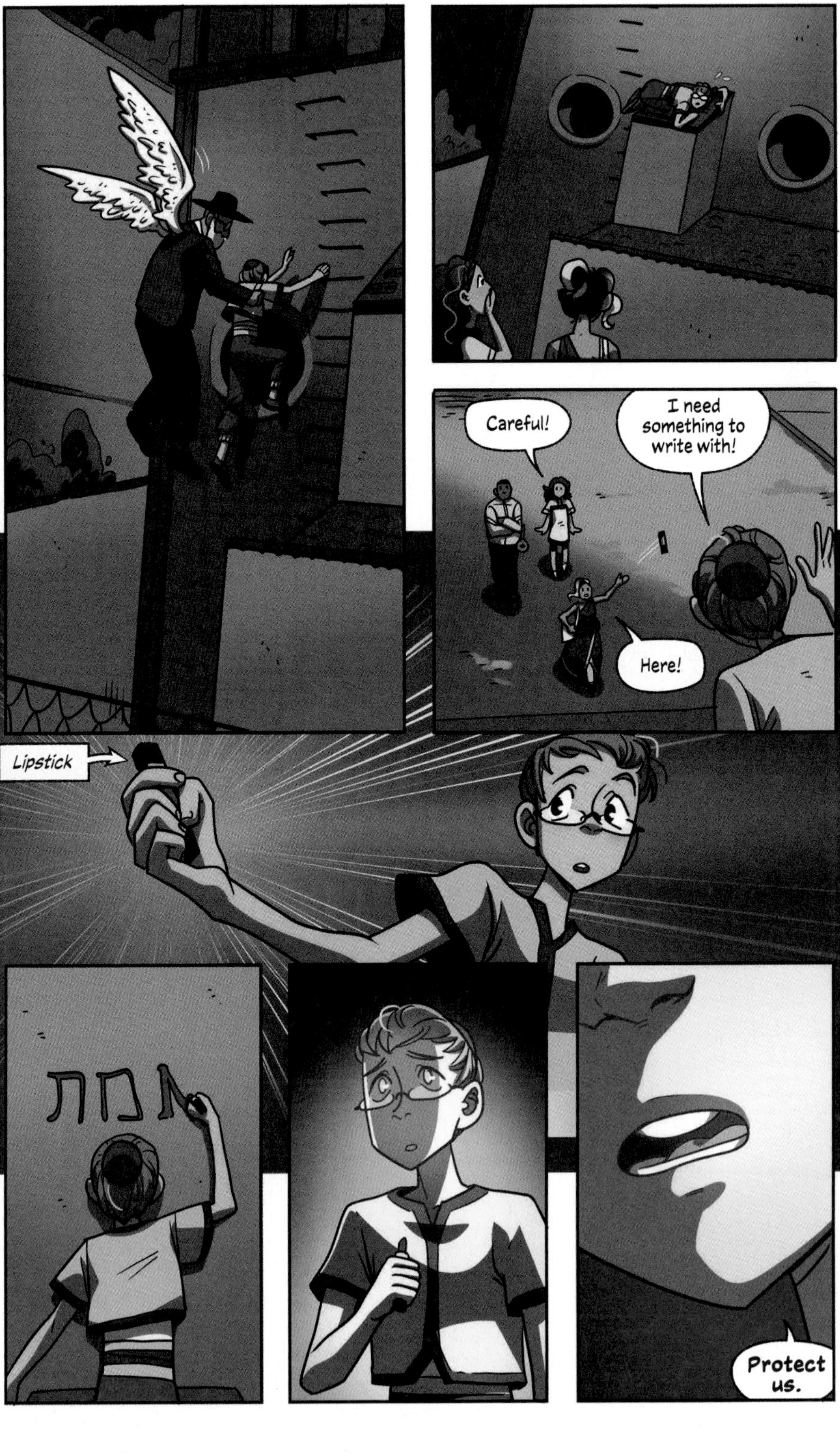
Careful!
I need something to write with!
Here!
Lipstick
אמת
Protect us.

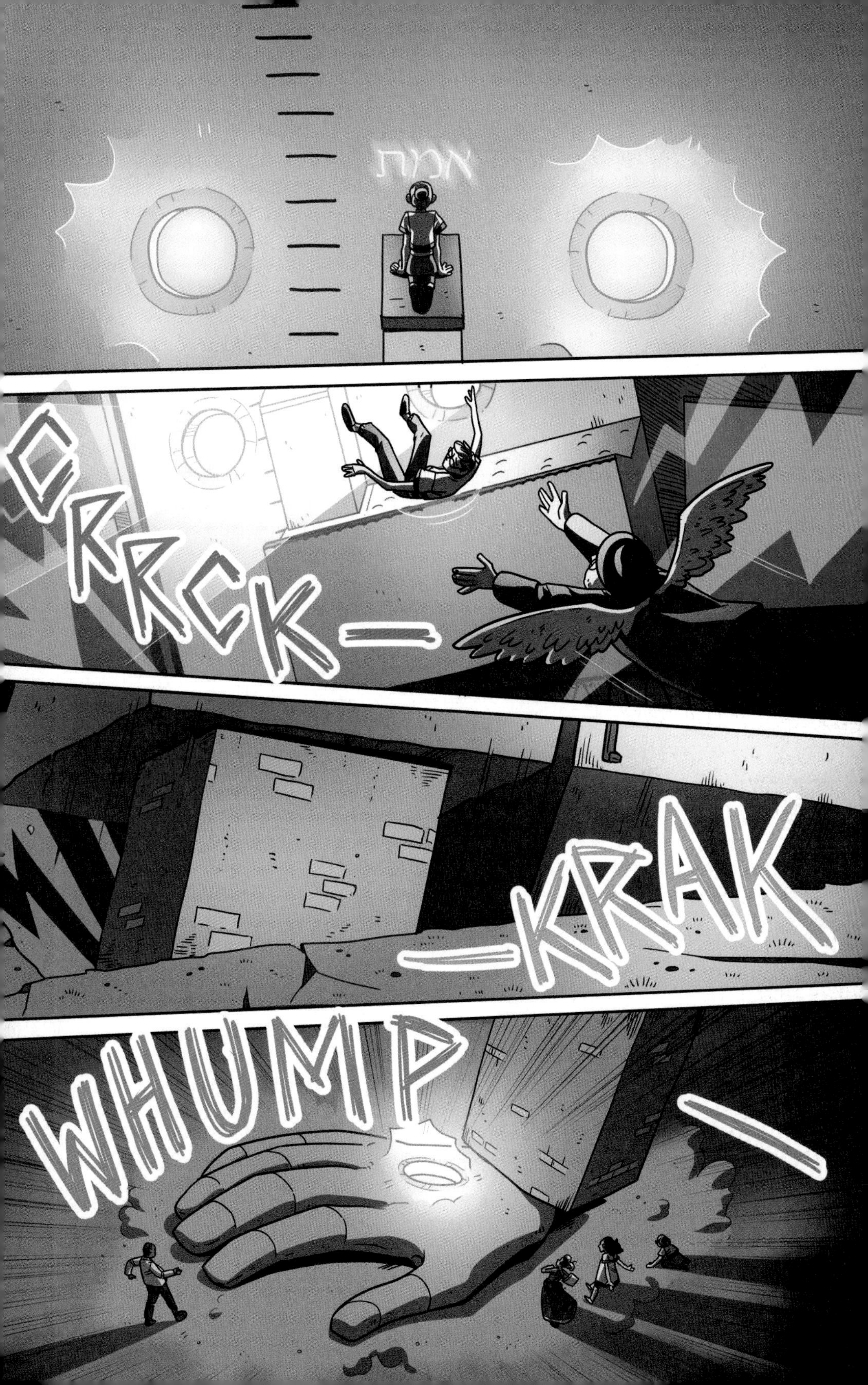

אמת
CRRCK——
—KRAK
WHUMP—

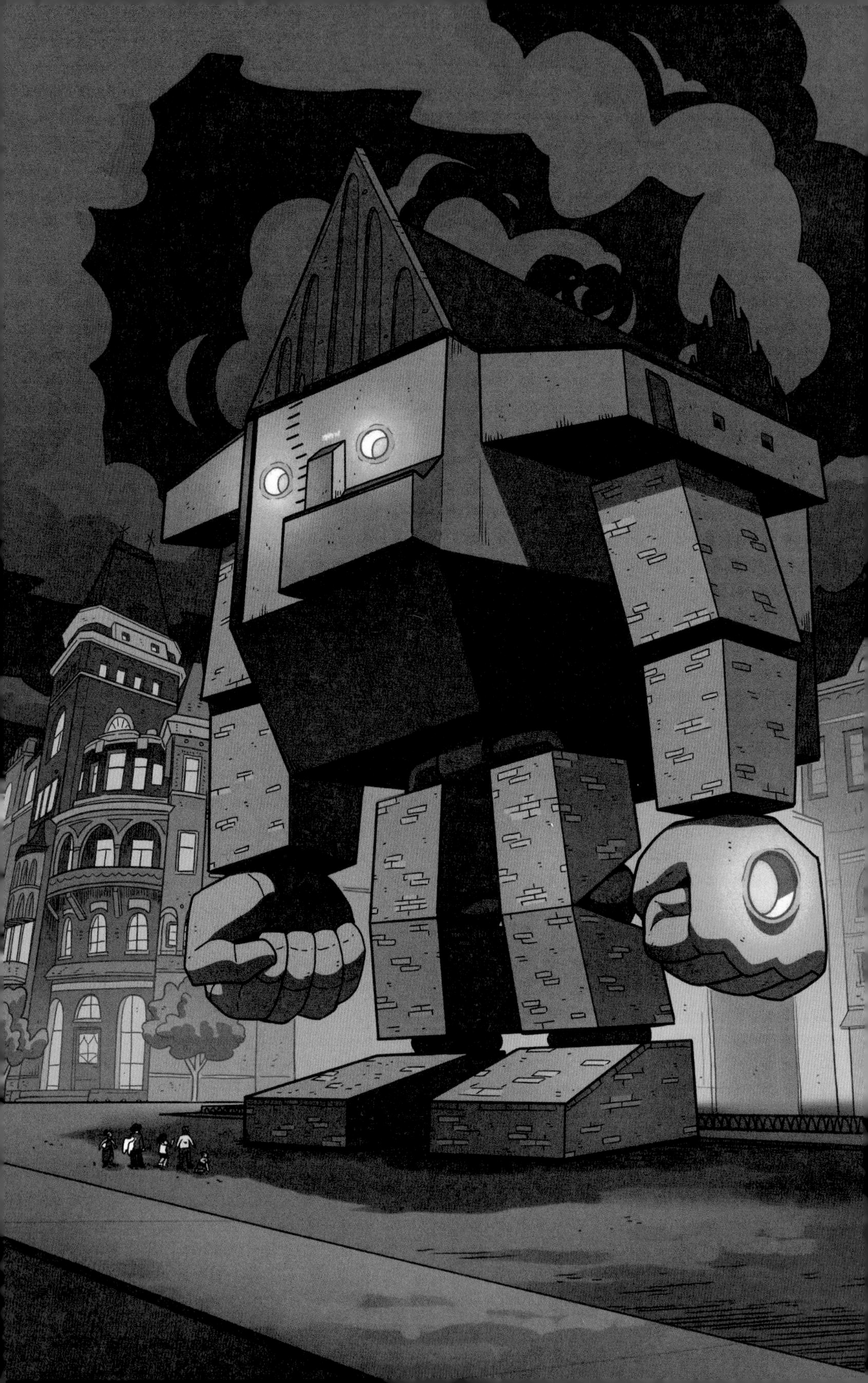

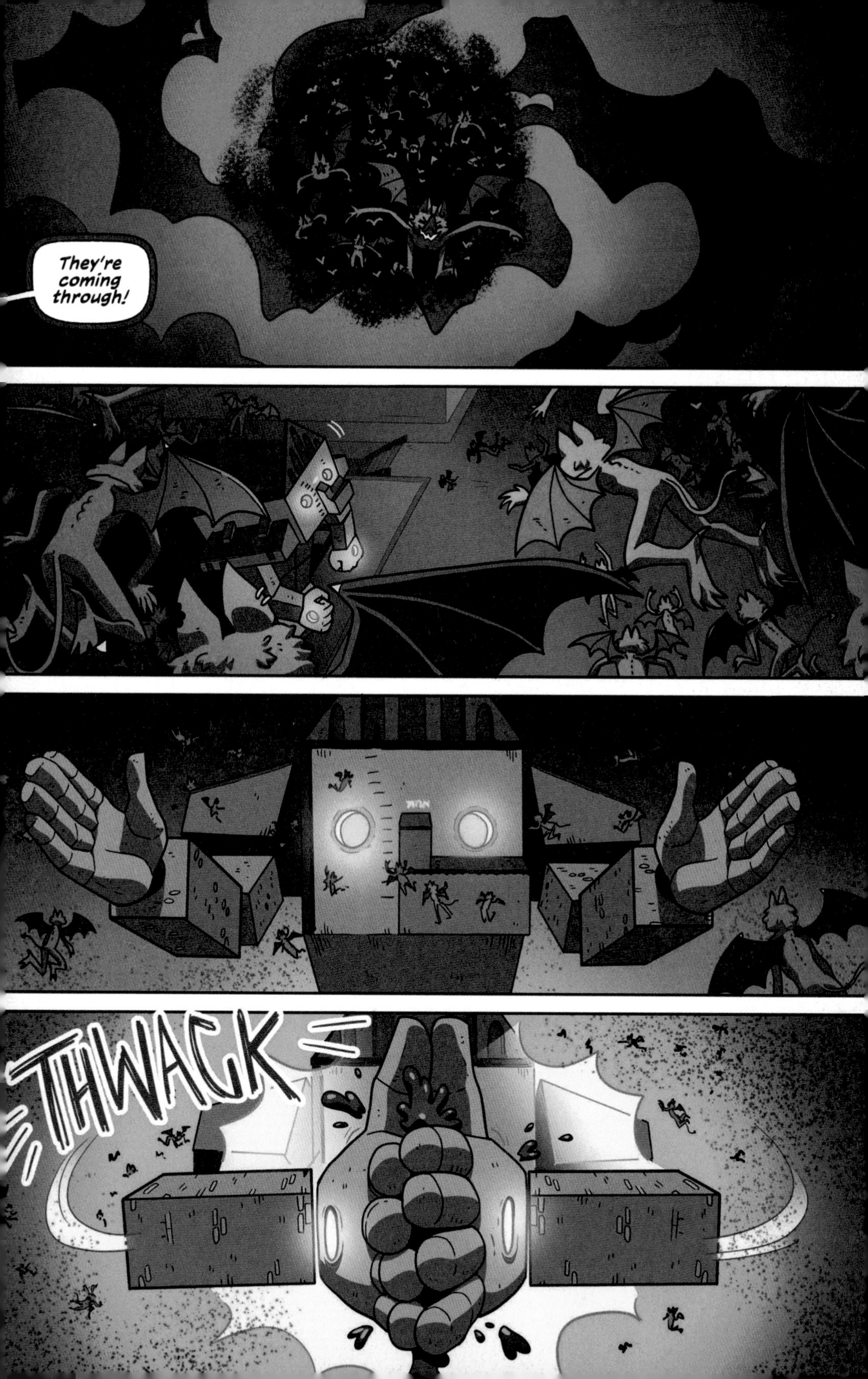
They're coming through!
THWACK

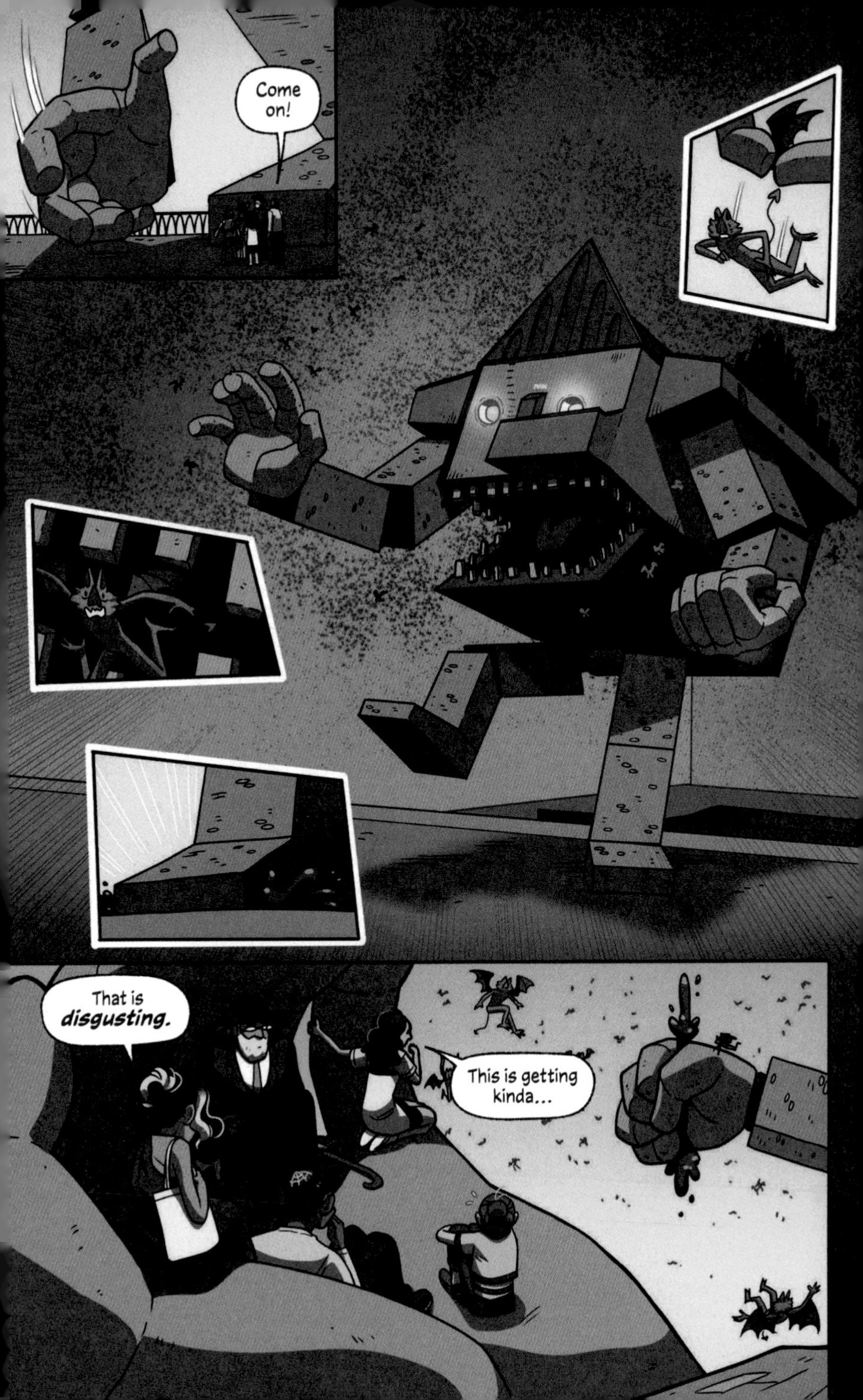
Come on!
That is disgusting.
This is getting kinda...

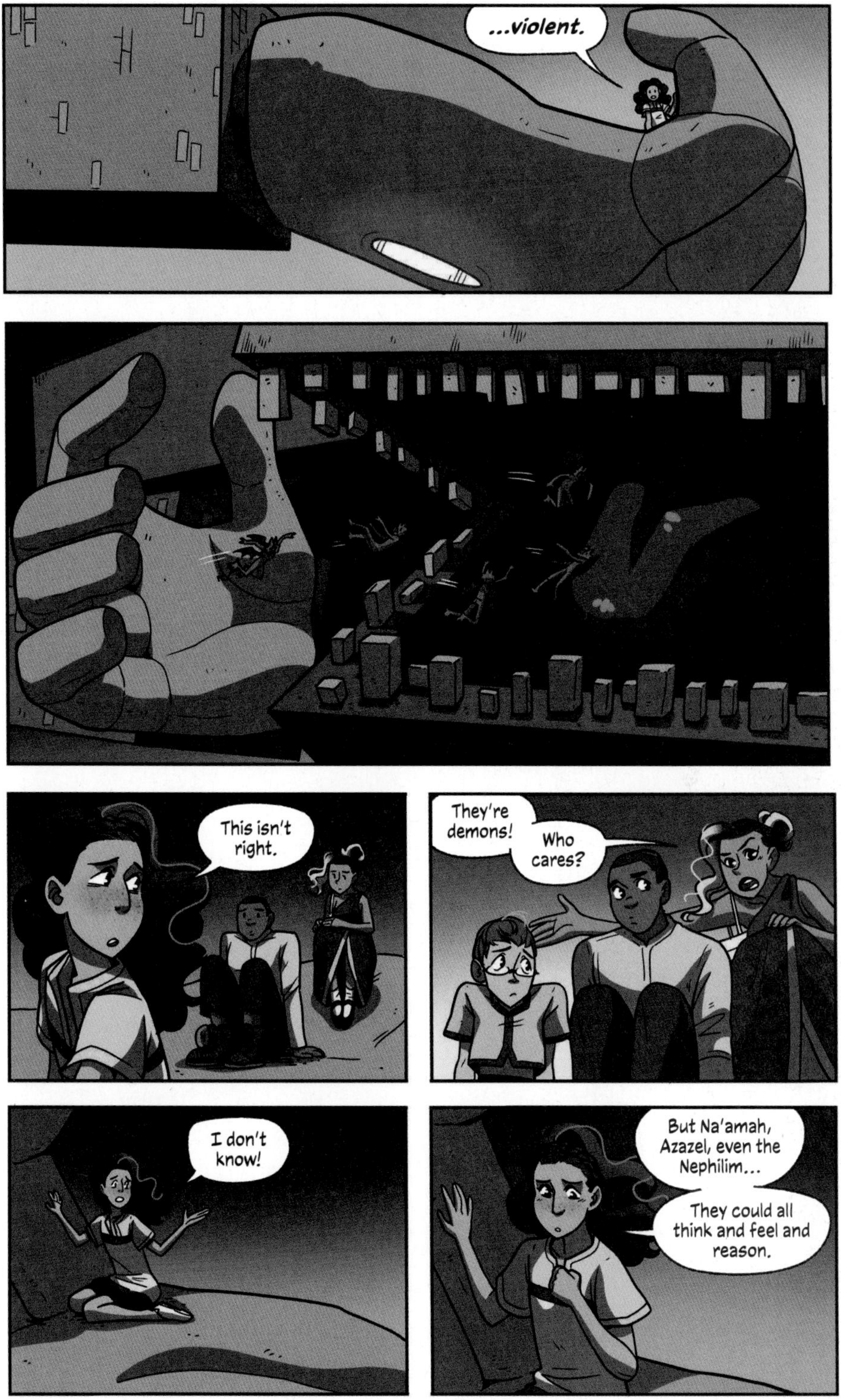
...violent.
This isn't right.
They're demons!
Who cares?
I don't know!
But Na'amah, Azazel, even the Nephilim...
They could all think and feel and reason.

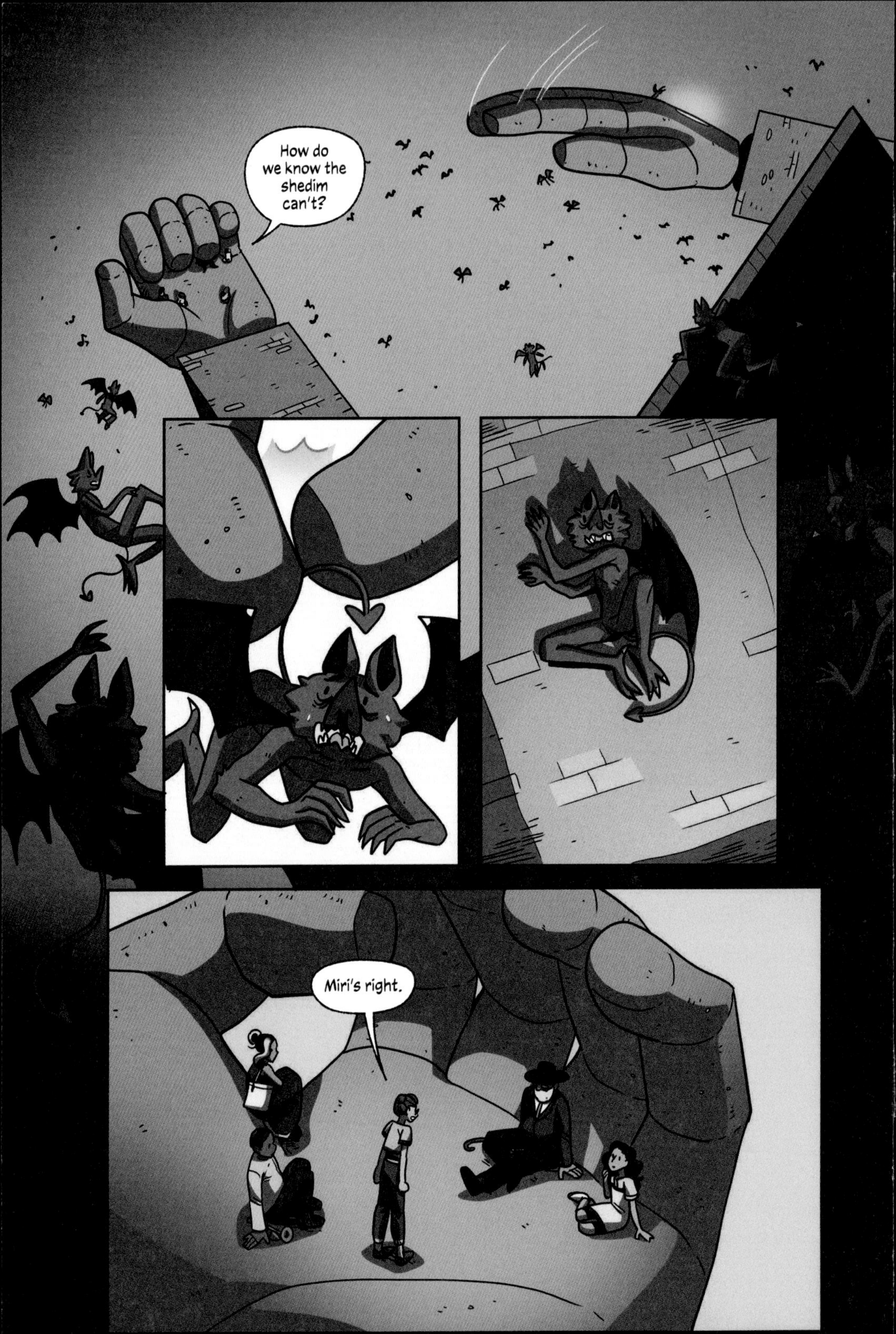
How do we know the shedim can't?
Miri's right.

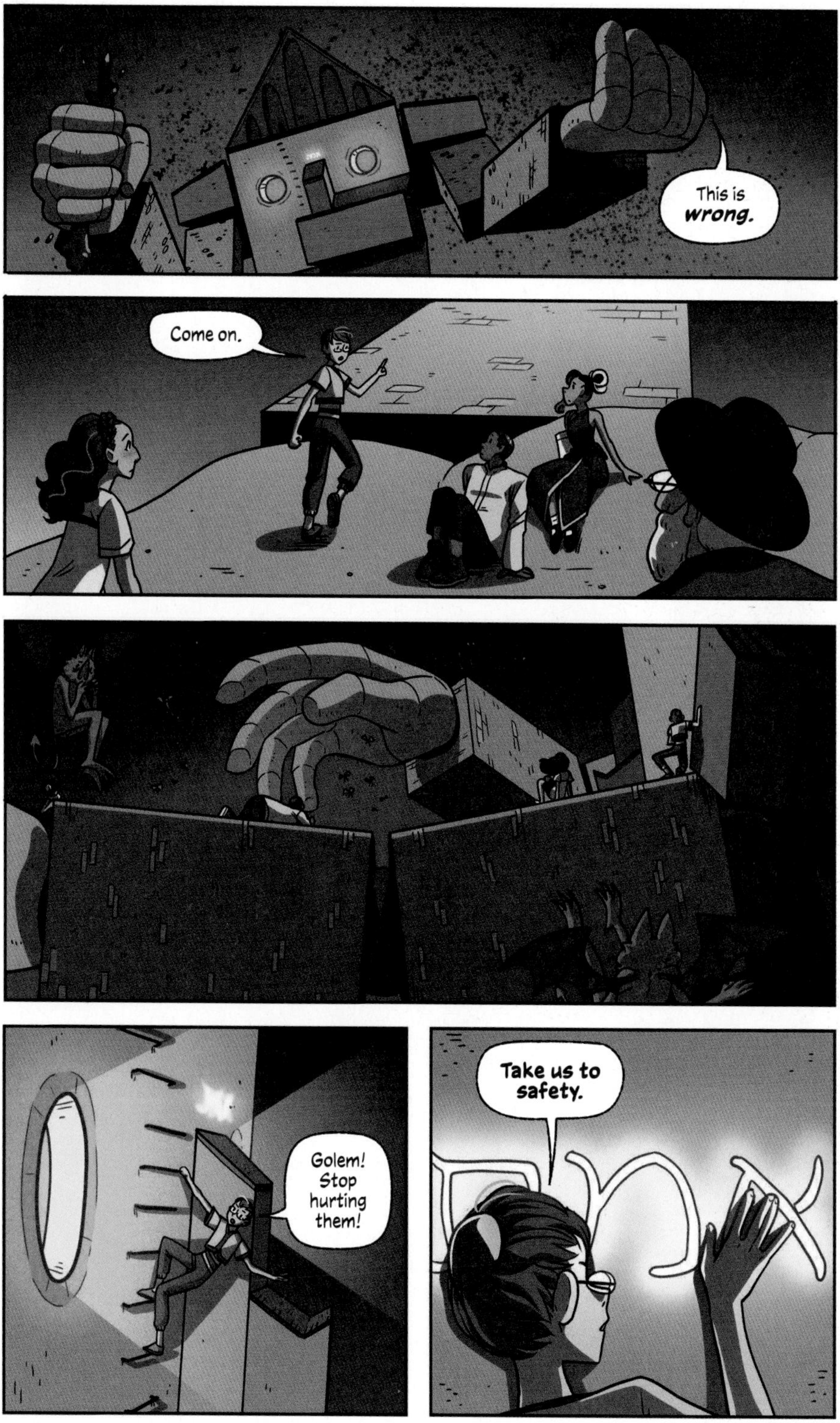
This is wrong.
Come on.
Golem! Stop hurting them!
Take us to safety.

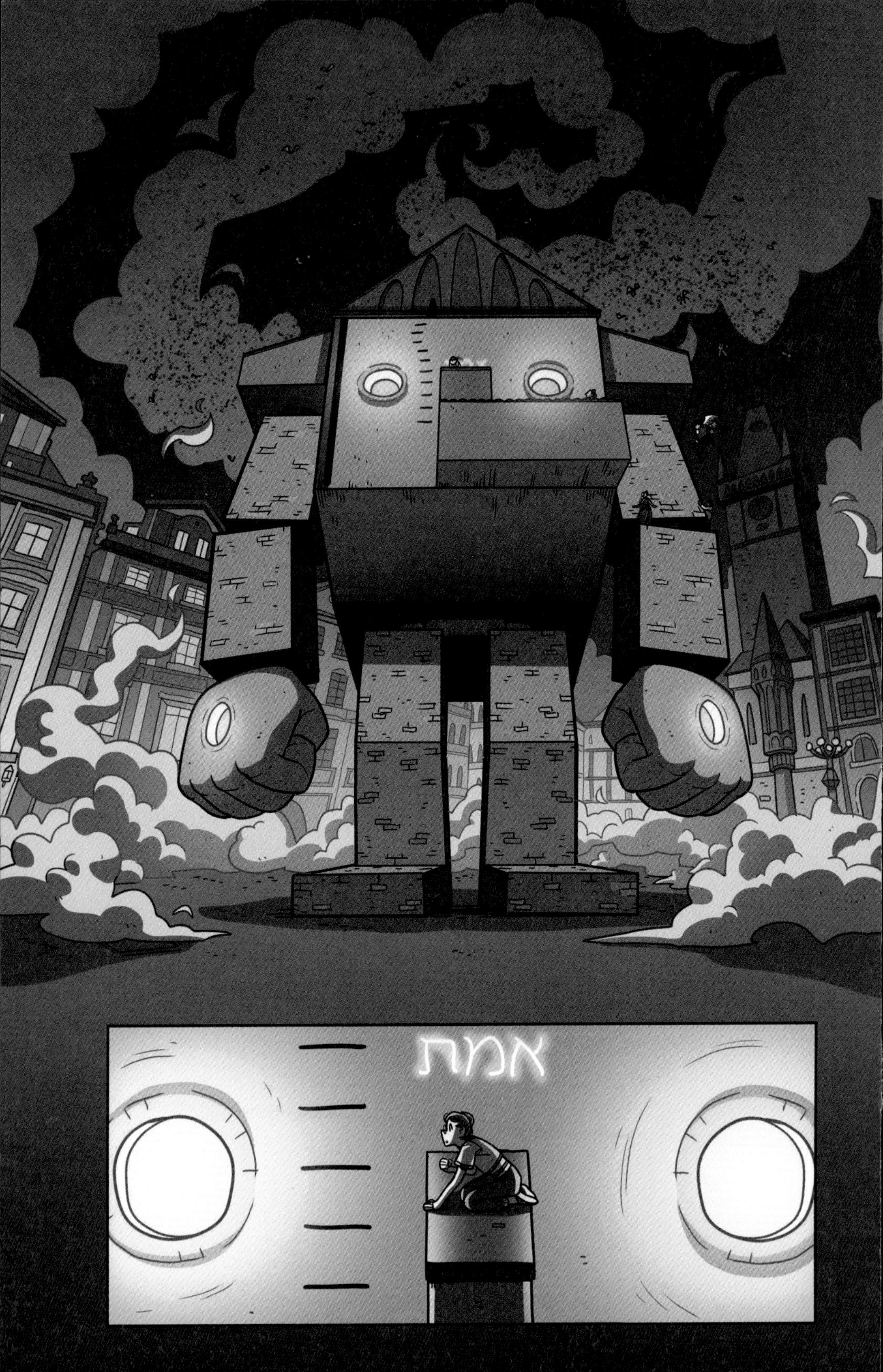
אמת

CHAPTER NINE

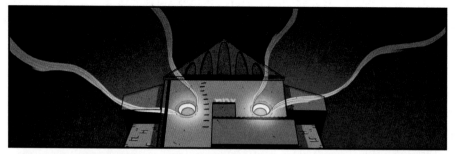

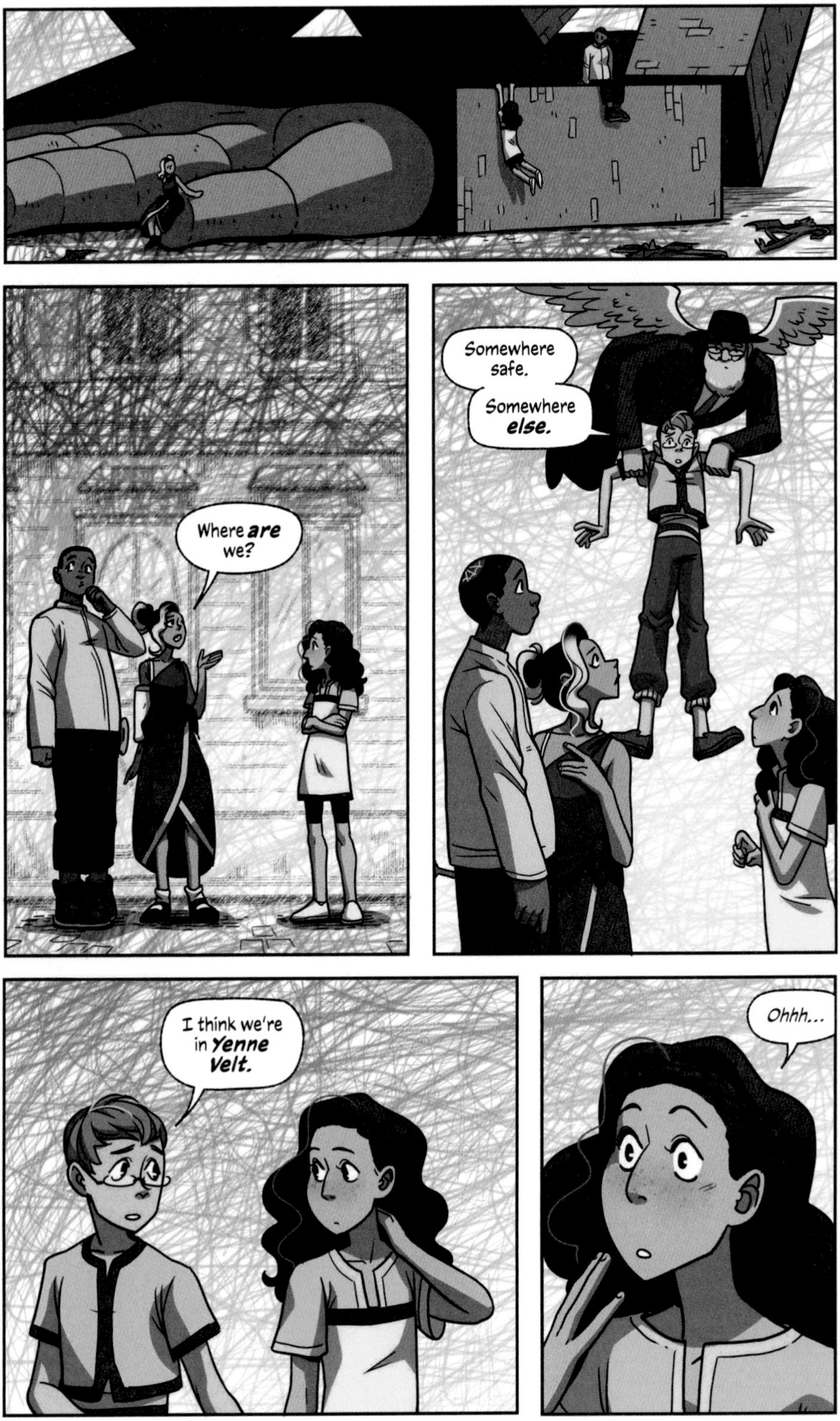
Where *are* we?
Somewhere safe.
Somewhere *else.*
I think we're in *Yenne Velt.*
Ohhh...

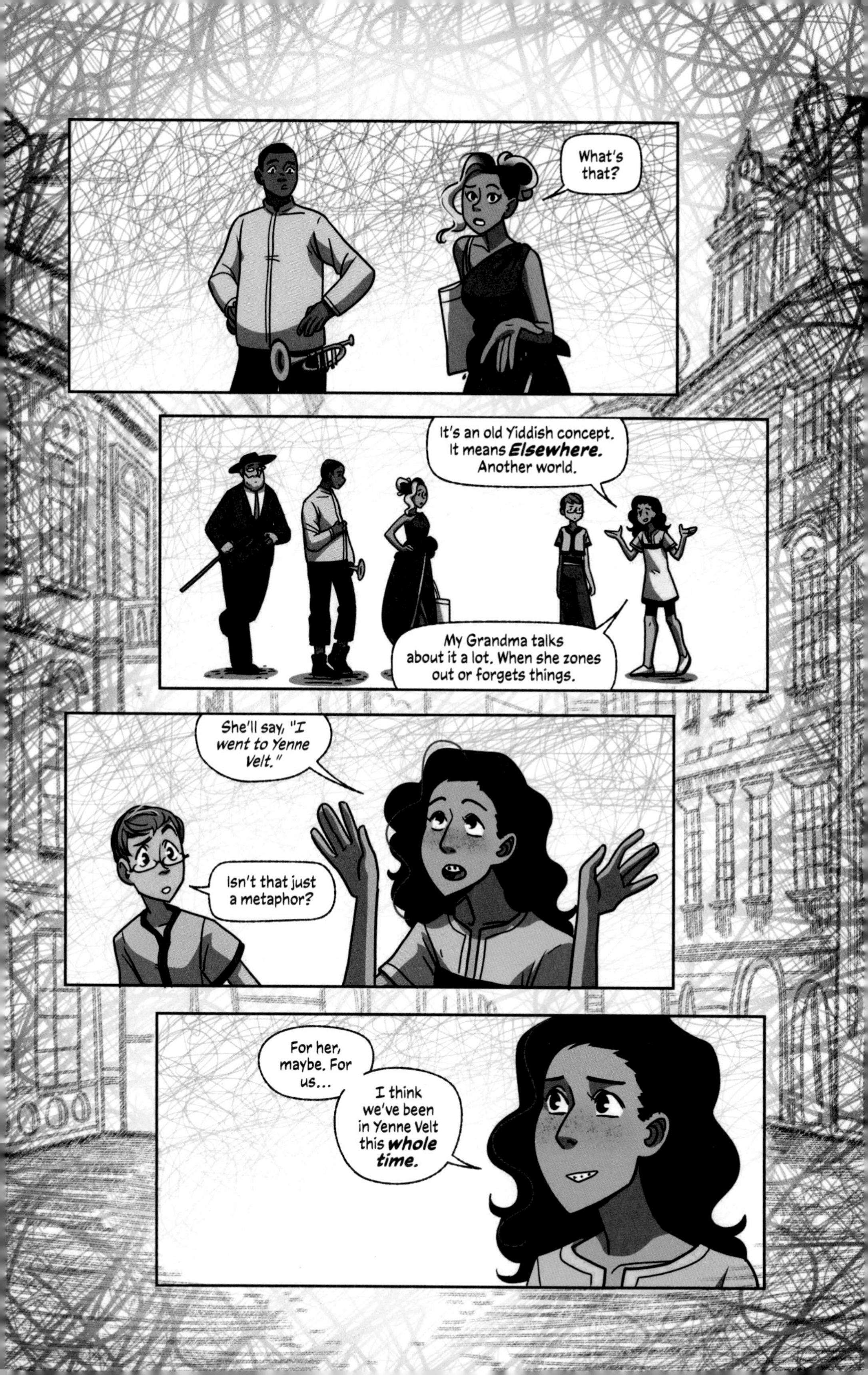
What's that?
It's an old Yiddish concept. It means *Elsewhere.* Another world.
My Grandma talks about it a lot. When she zones out or forgets things.
She'll say, "*I went to Yenne Velt.*"
Isn't that just a metaphor?
For her, maybe. For us...
I think we've been in Yenne Velt this ***whole time.***

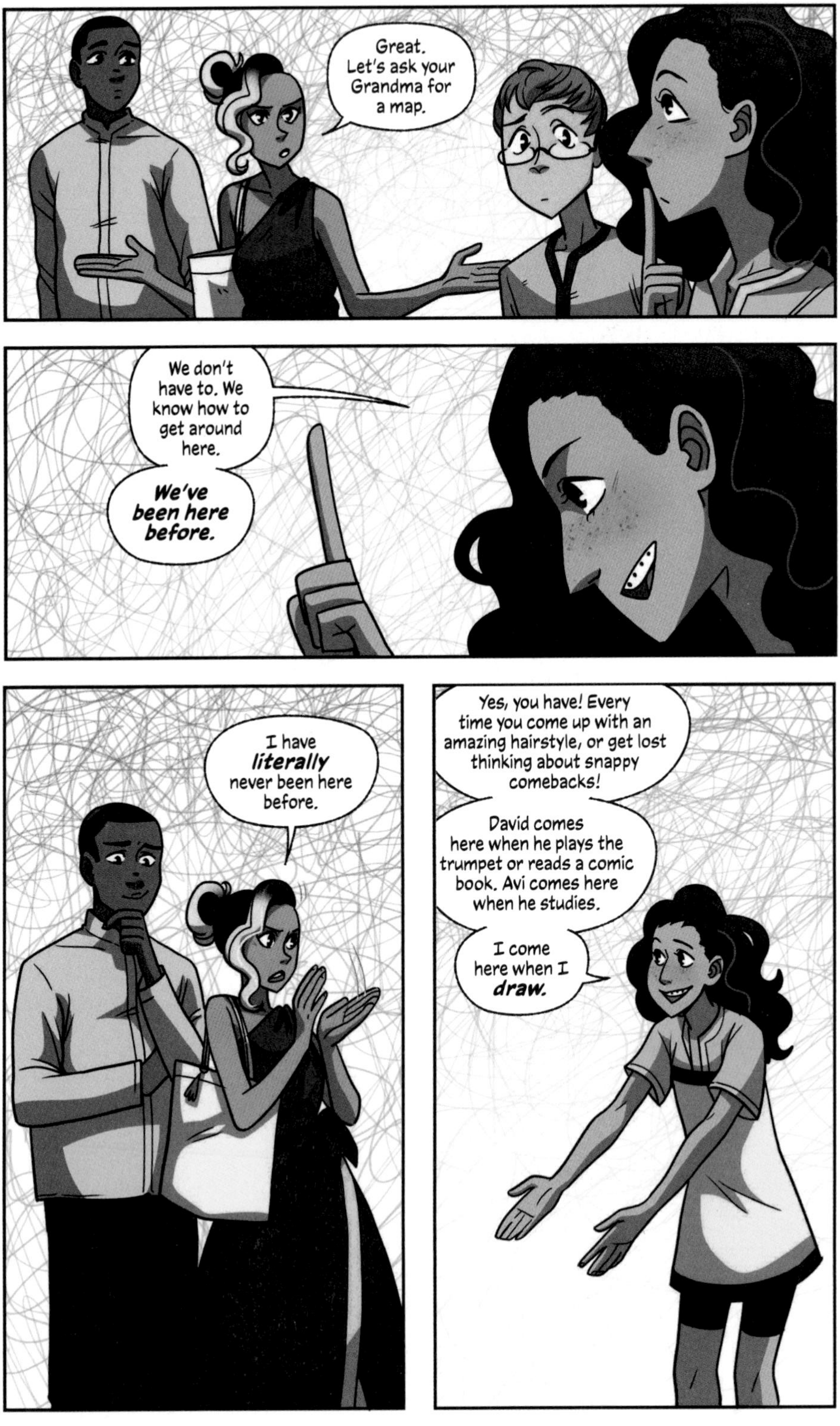
Great. Let's ask your Grandma for a map.
We don't have to. We know how to get around here.
We've been here before.
I have ***literally*** never been here before.
Yes, you have! Every time you come up with an amazing hairstyle, or get lost thinking about snappy comebacks!
David comes here when he plays the trumpet or reads a comic book. Avi comes here when he studies.
I come here when I ***draw.***

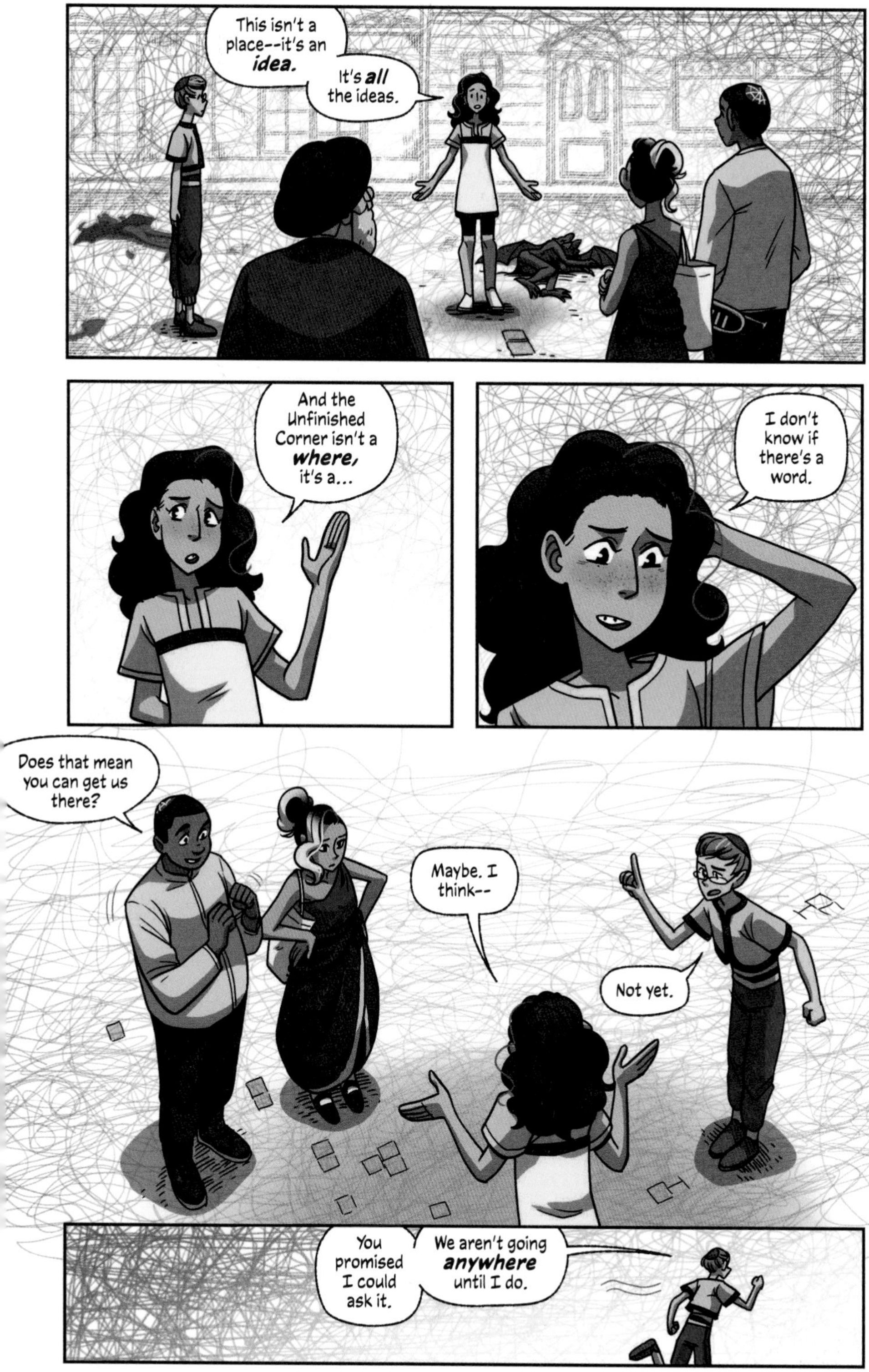
This isn't a place--it's an *idea.*
It's *all* the ideas.
And the Unfinished Corner isn't a *where,* it's a...
I don't know if there's a word.
Does that mean you can get us there?
Maybe. I think--
Not yet.
You promised I could ask it.
We aren't going *anywhere* until I do.

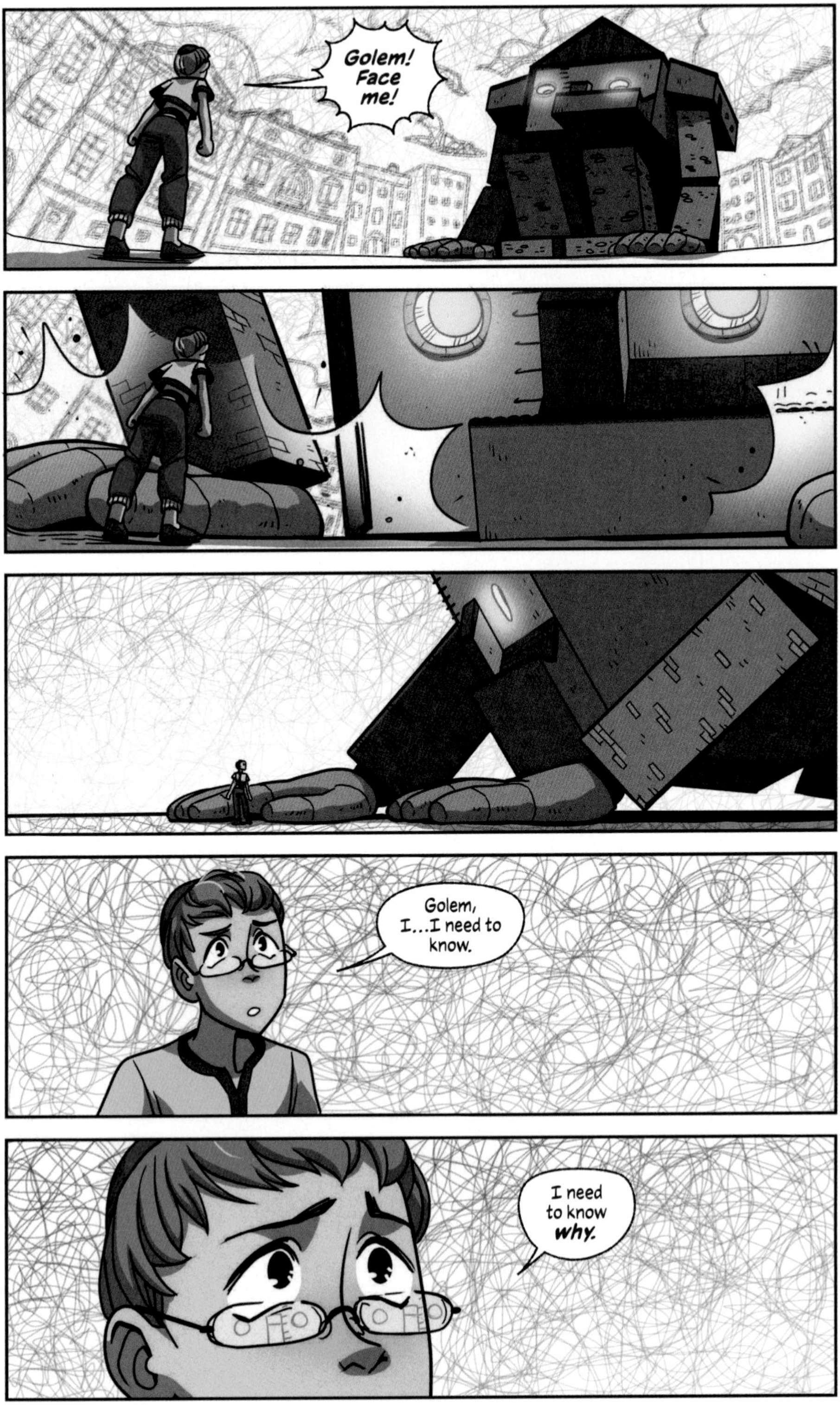
Golem! Face me!
Golem, I...I need to know.
I need to know why.

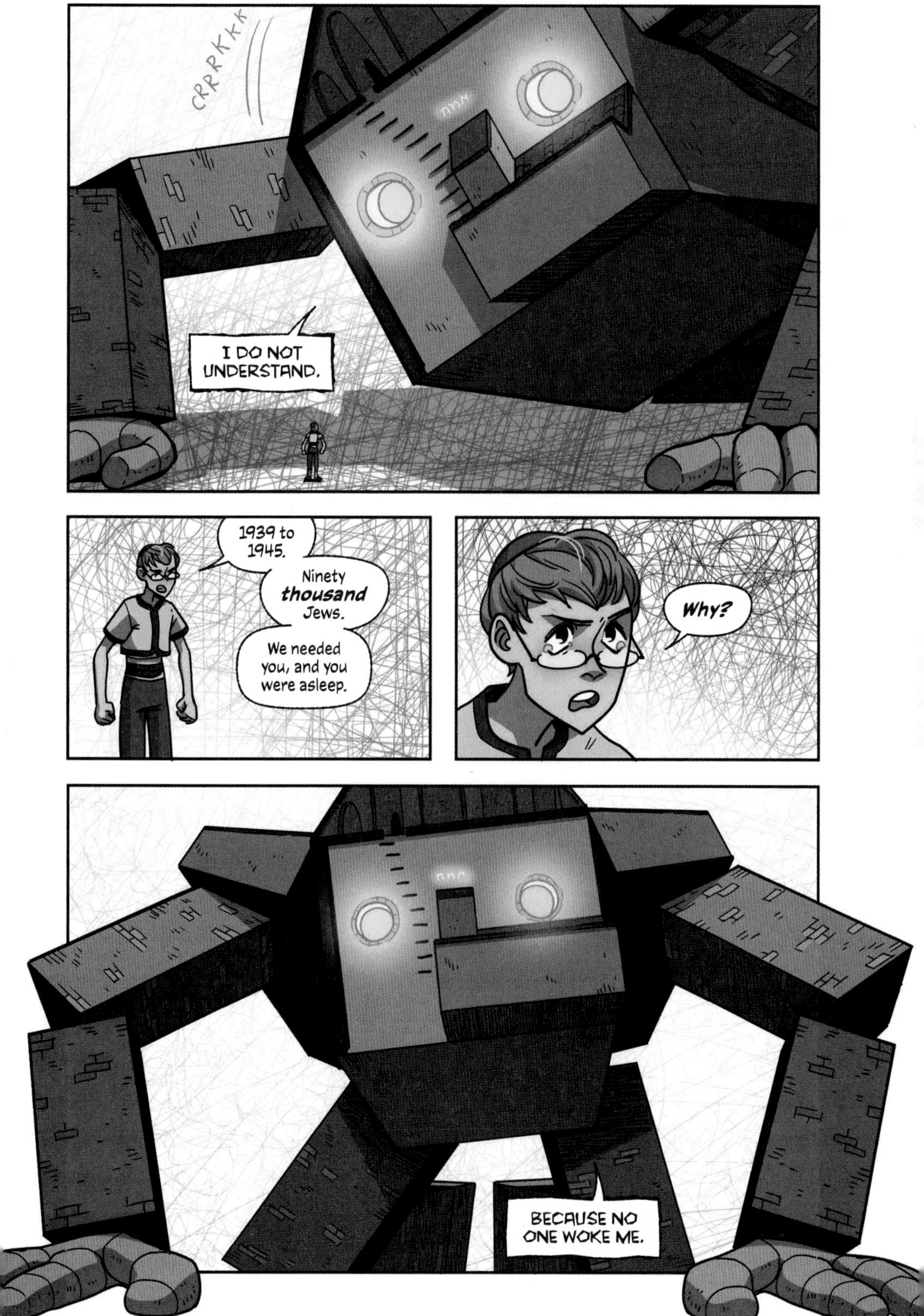
CRRKKK
I DO NOT UNDERSTAND.
1939 to 1945.
Ninety **thousand** Jews.
We needed you, and you were asleep.
Why?
BECAUSE NO ONE WOKE ME.

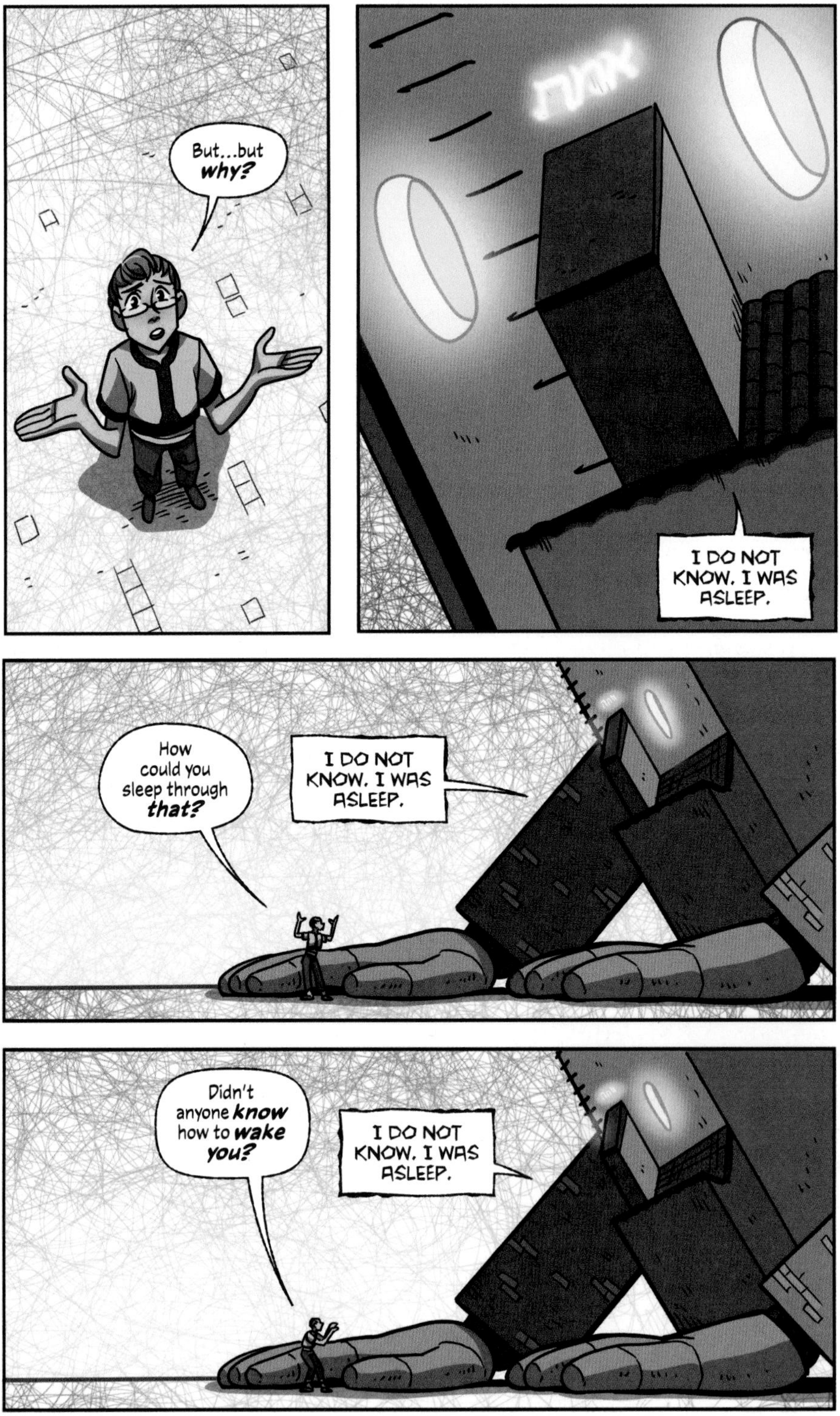
But...but why?
I DO NOT KNOW. I WAS ASLEEP.
How could you sleep through that?
I DO NOT KNOW. I WAS ASLEEP.
Didn't anyone know how to wake you?
I DO NOT KNOW. I WAS ASLEEP.

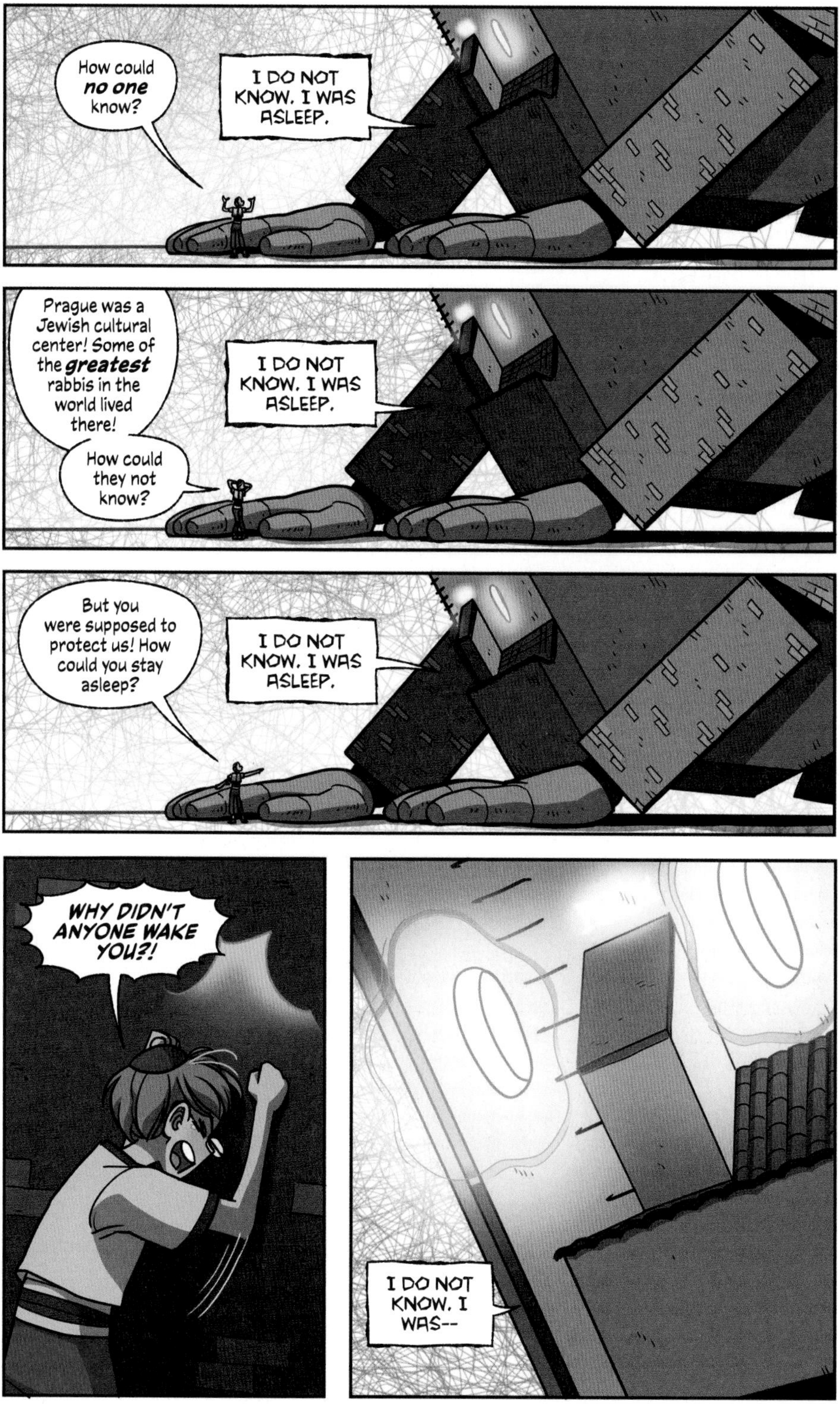

How could no one know?
I DO NOT KNOW. I WAS ASLEEP.
Prague was a Jewish cultural center! Some of the greatest rabbis in the world lived there!
How could they not know?
I DO NOT KNOW. I WAS ASLEEP.
But you were supposed to protect us! How could you stay asleep?
I DO NOT KNOW. I WAS ASLEEP.
WHY DIDN'T ANYONE WAKE YOU?!
I DO NOT KNOW. I WAS--

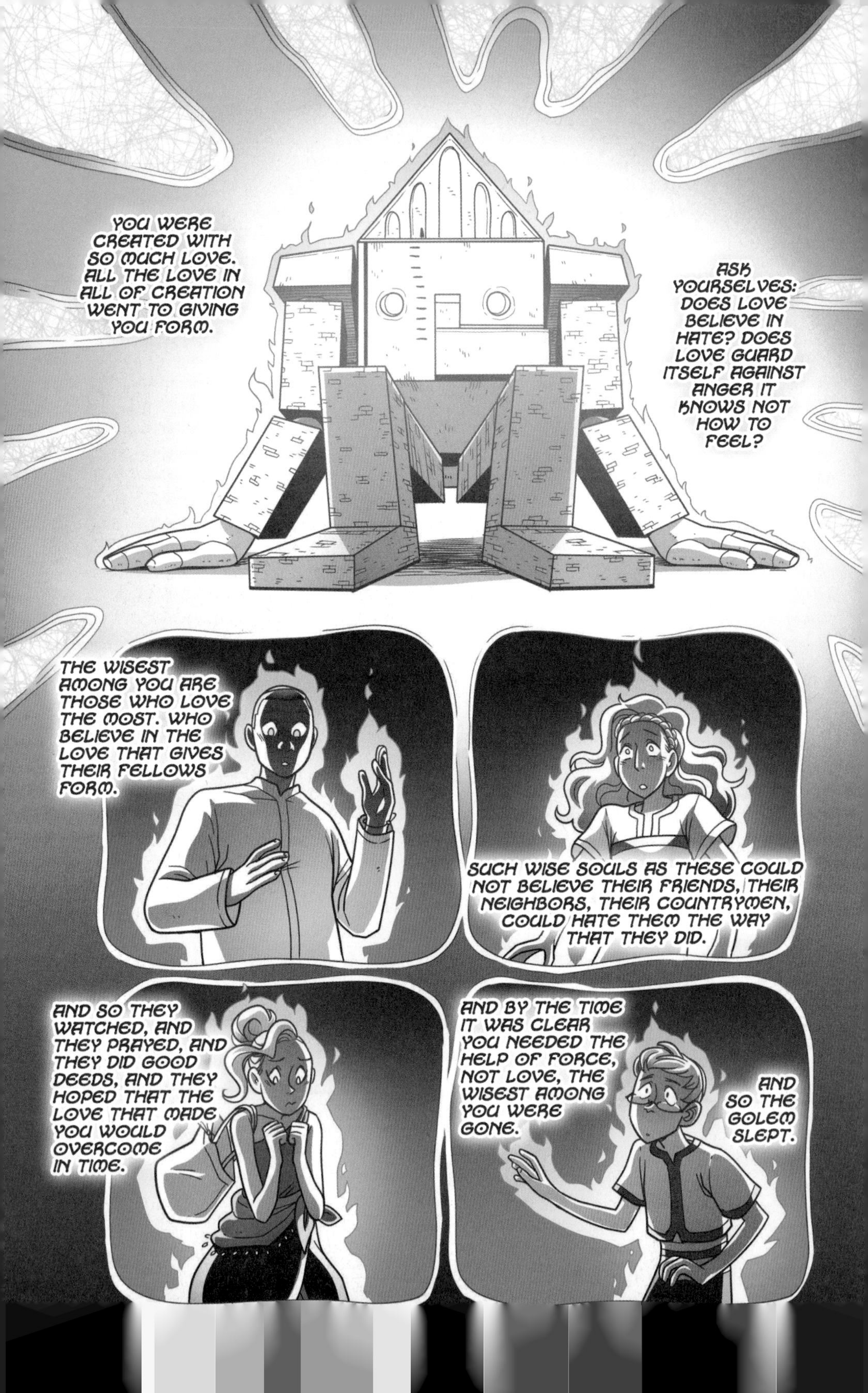

YOU WERE CREATED WITH SO MUCH LOVE. ALL THE LOVE IN ALL OF CREATION WENT TO GIVING YOU FORM.
ASK YOURSELVES: DOES LOVE BELIEVE IN HATE? DOES LOVE GUARD ITSELF AGAINST ANGER IT KNOWS NOT HOW TO FEEL?
THE WISEST AMONG YOU ARE THOSE WHO LOVE THE MOST. WHO BELIEVE IN THE LOVE THAT GIVES THEIR FELLOWS FORM.
SUCH WISE SOULS AS THESE COULD NOT BELIEVE THEIR FRIENDS, THEIR NEIGHBORS, THEIR COUNTRYMEN, COULD HATE THEM THE WAY THAT THEY DID.
AND SO THEY WATCHED, AND THEY PRAYED, AND THEY DID GOOD DEEDS, AND THEY HOPED THAT THE LOVE THAT MADE YOU WOULD OVERCOME IN TIME.
AND BY THE TIME IT WAS CLEAR YOU NEEDED THE HELP OF FORCE, NOT LOVE, THE WISEST AMONG YOU WERE GONE.
AND SO THE GOLEM SLEPT.

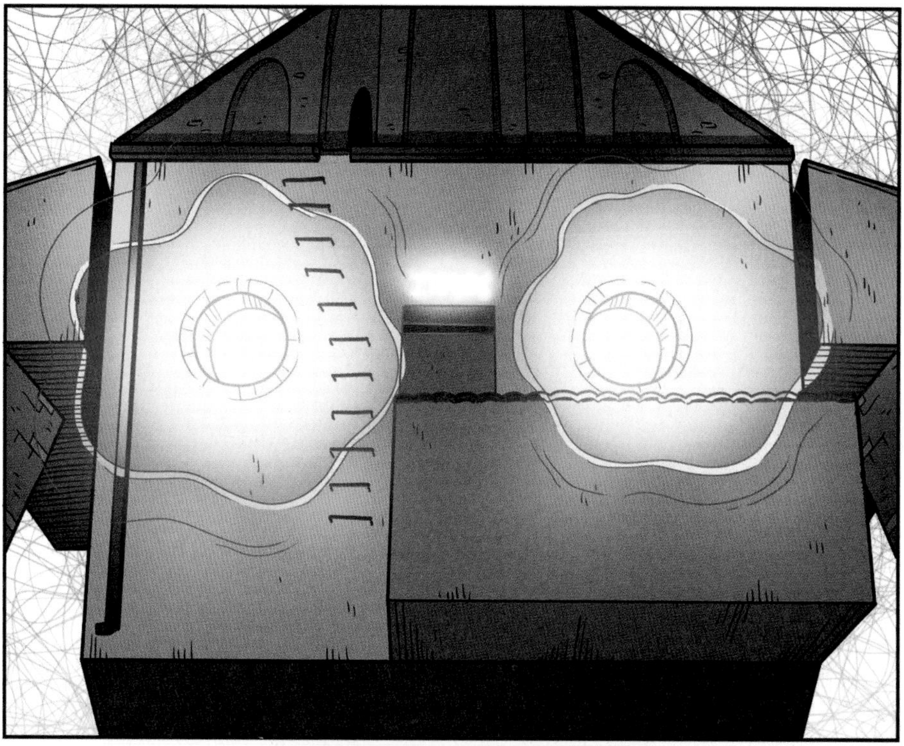

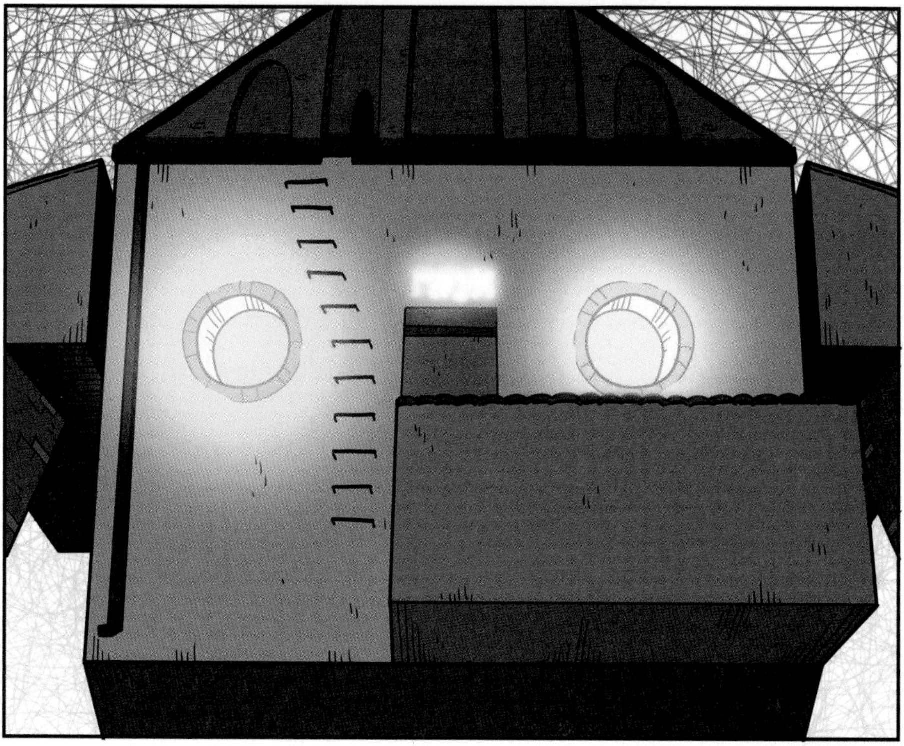

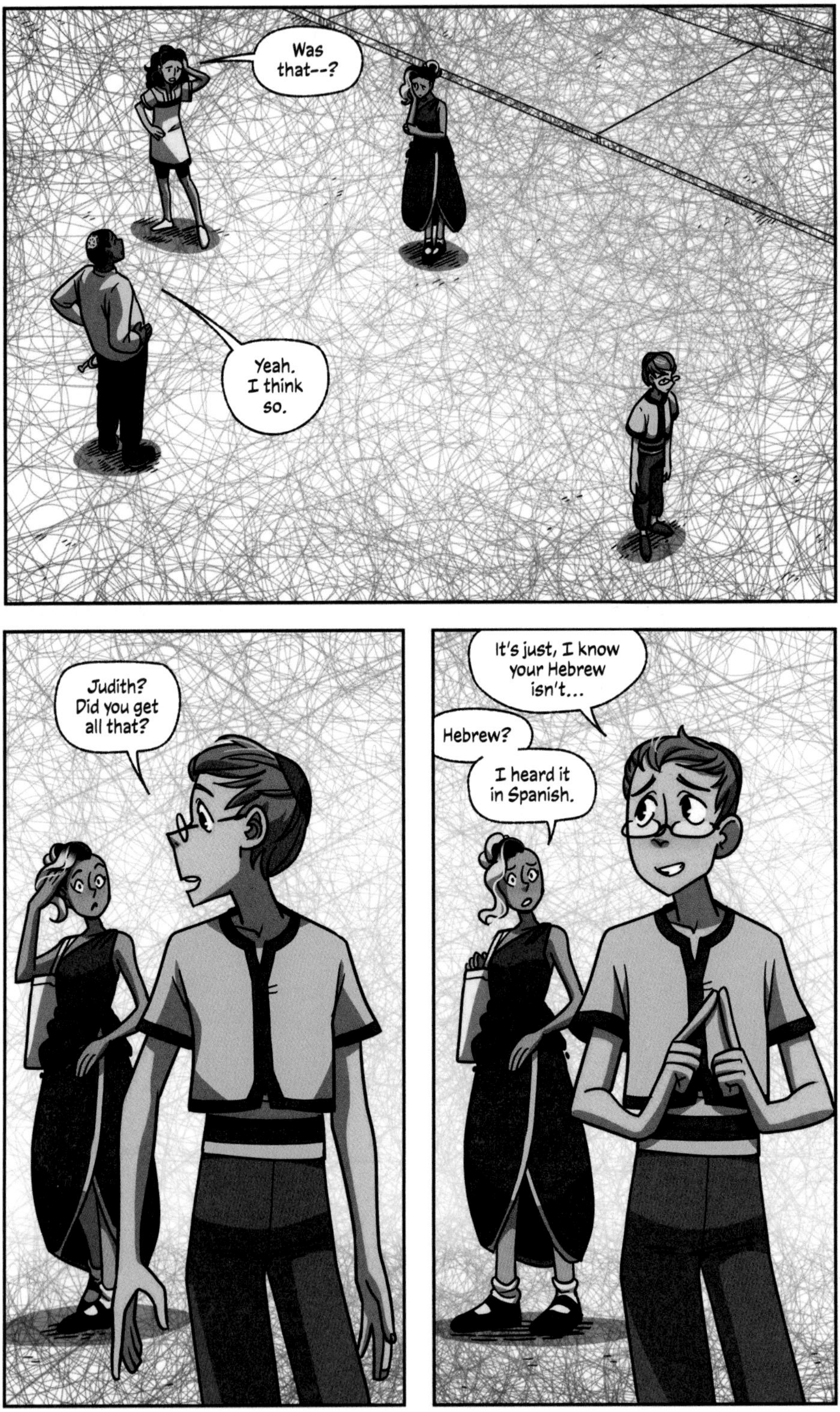
Was that--?
Yeah. I think so.
Judith? Did you get all that?
It's just, I know your Hebrew isn't...
Hebrew?
I heard it in Spanish.

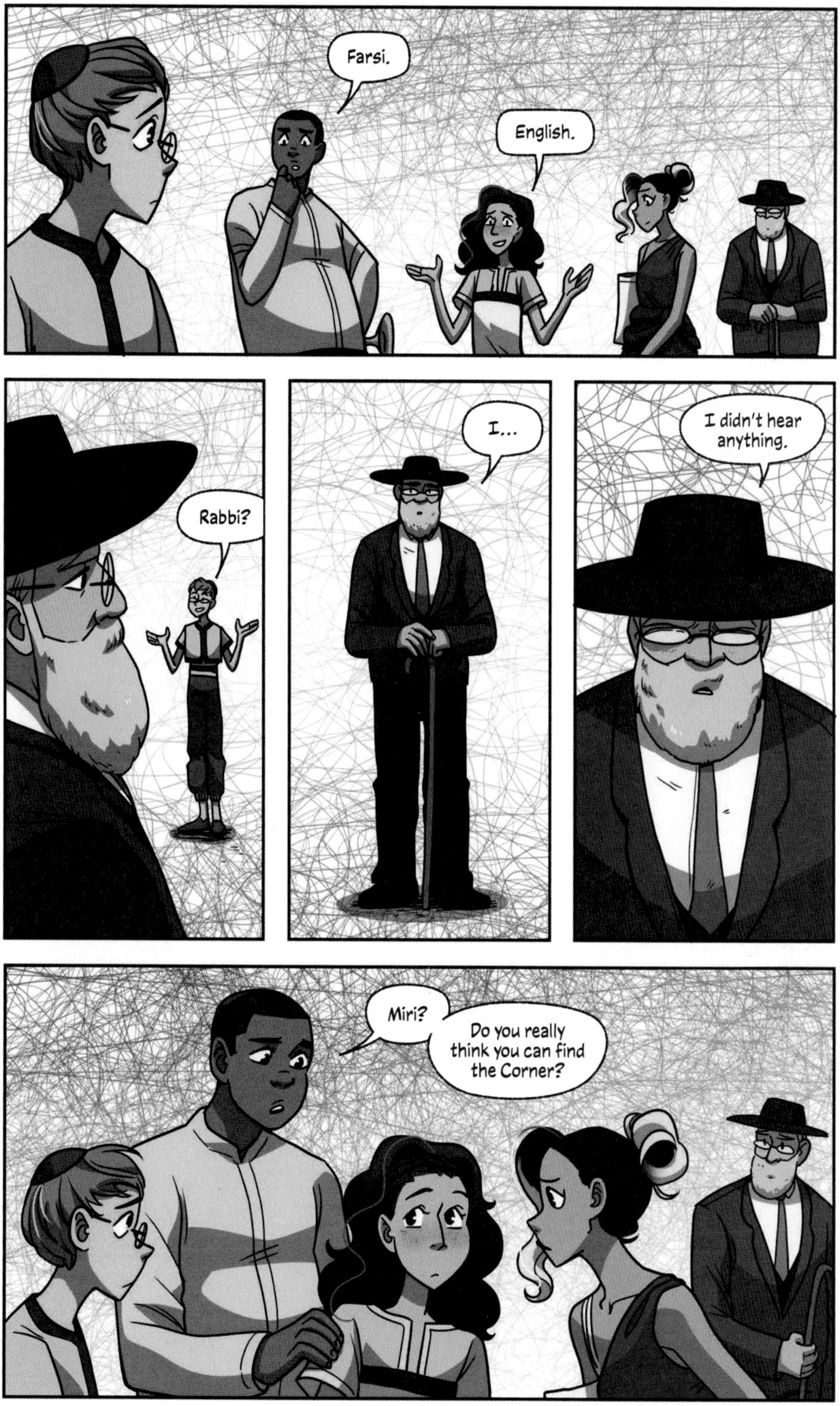
Farsi.
English.
Rabbi?
I...
I didn't hear anything.
Miri?
Do you really think you can find the Corner?

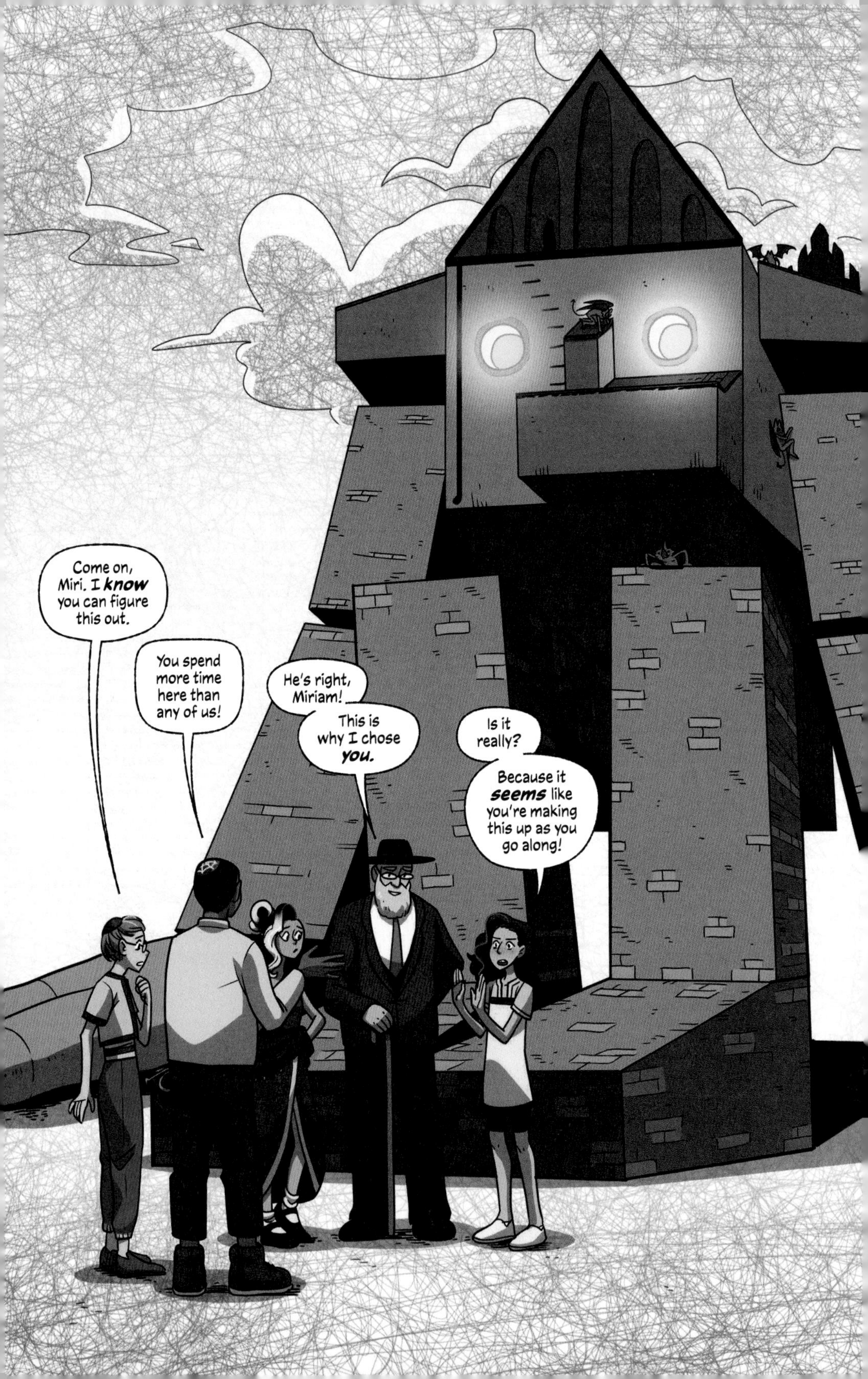
Come on, Miri. I **know** you can figure this out.
You spend more time here than any of us!
He's right, Miriam!
This is why I chose **you.**
Is it really?
Because it **seems** like you're making this up as you go along!

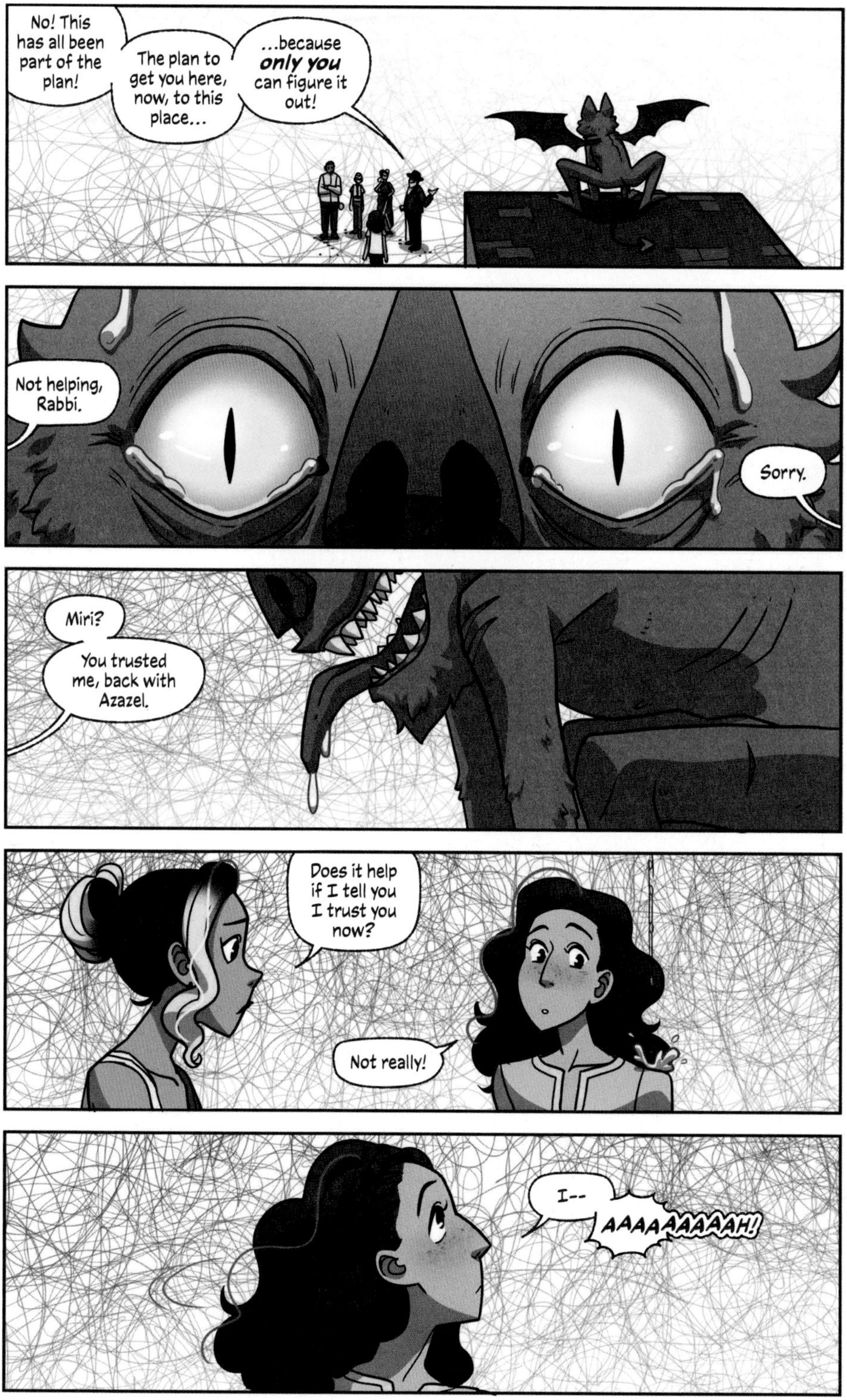
No! This has all been part of the plan!
The plan to get you here, now, to this place...
...because **only you** can figure it out!
Not helping, Rabbi.
Sorry.
Miri?
You trusted me, back with Azazel.
Does it help if I tell you I trust you now?
Not really!
I--
AAAAAAAAAH!

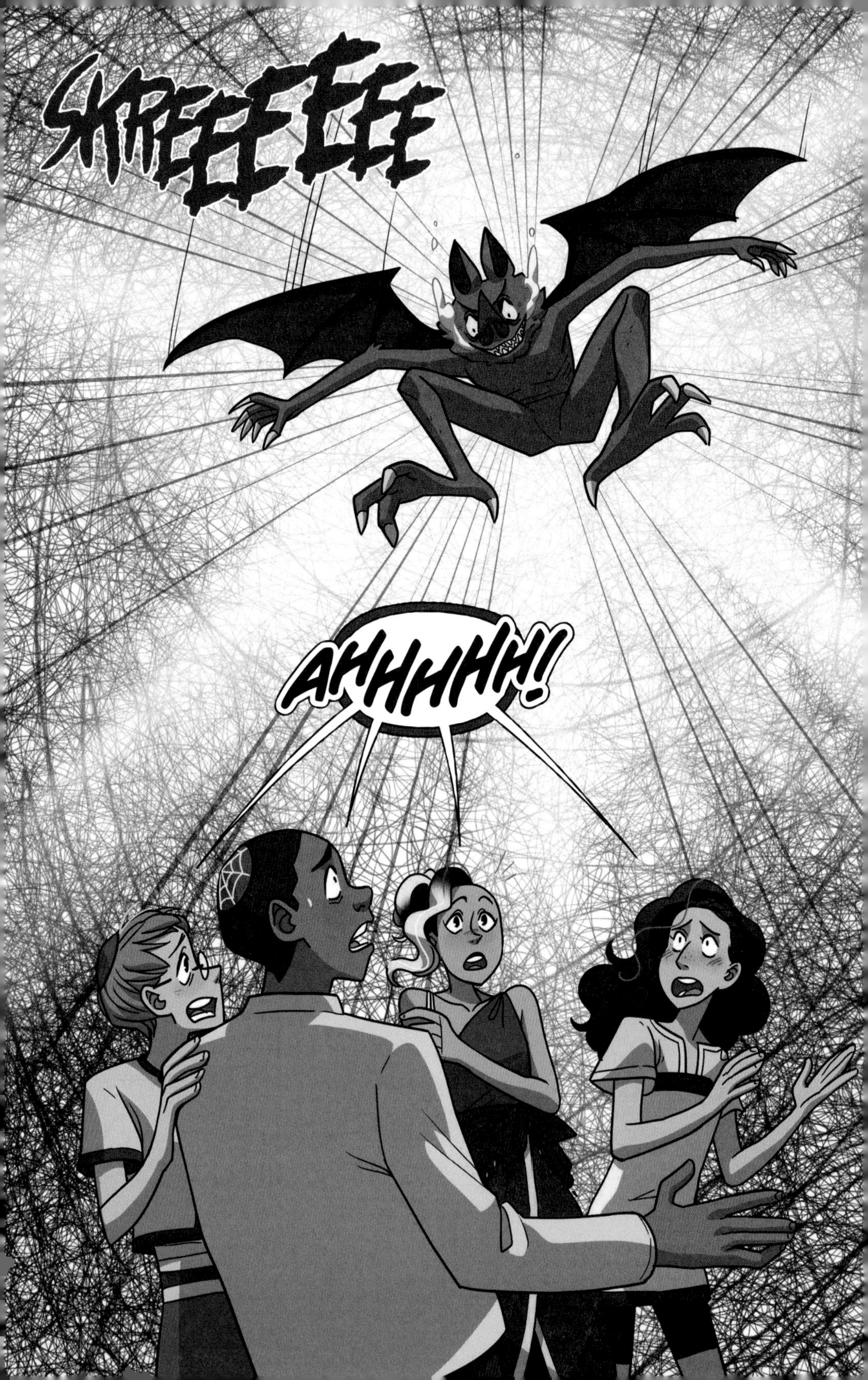
SKREEEEEE
AHHHHH!

CHAPTER TEN

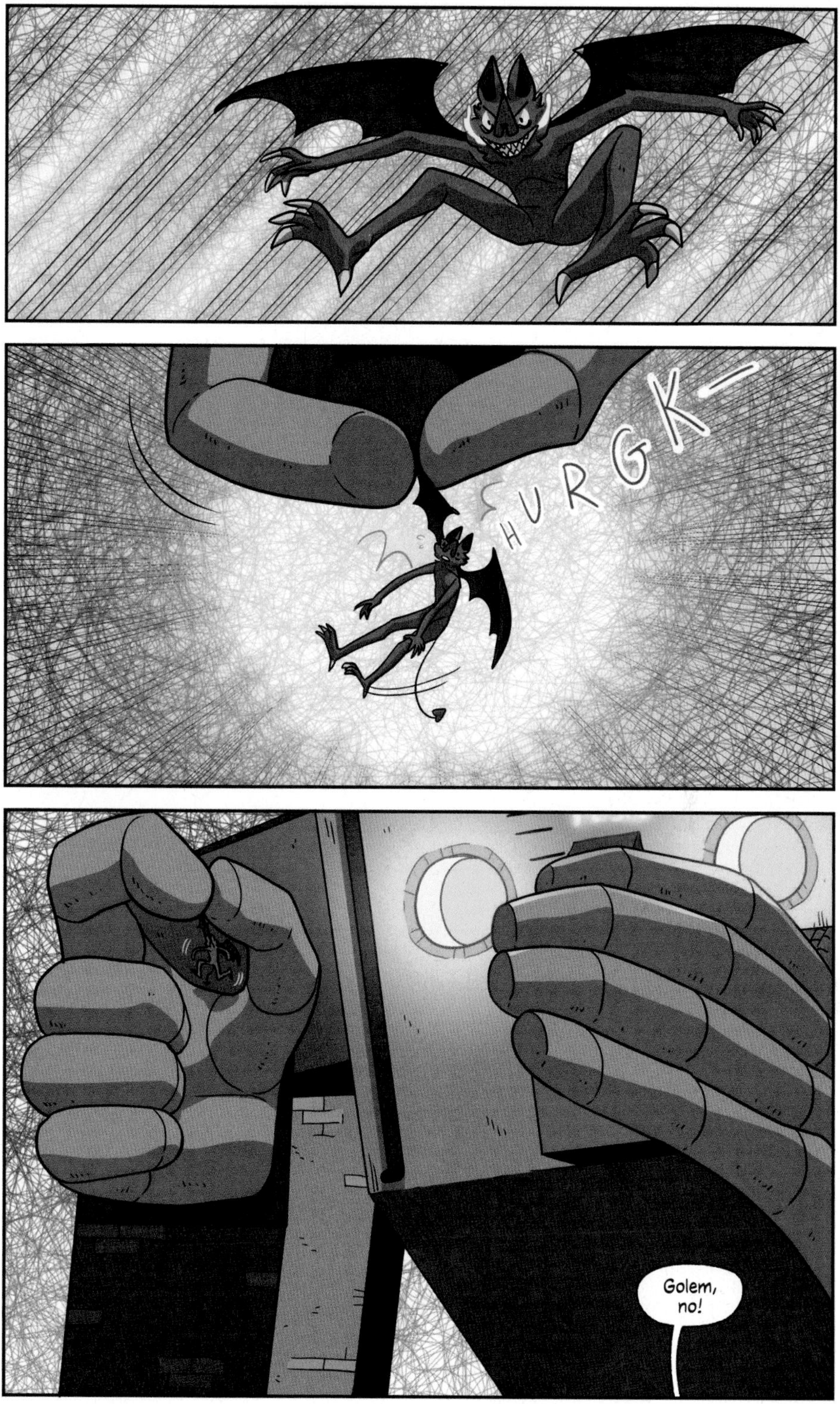
HURGK—
Golem, no!

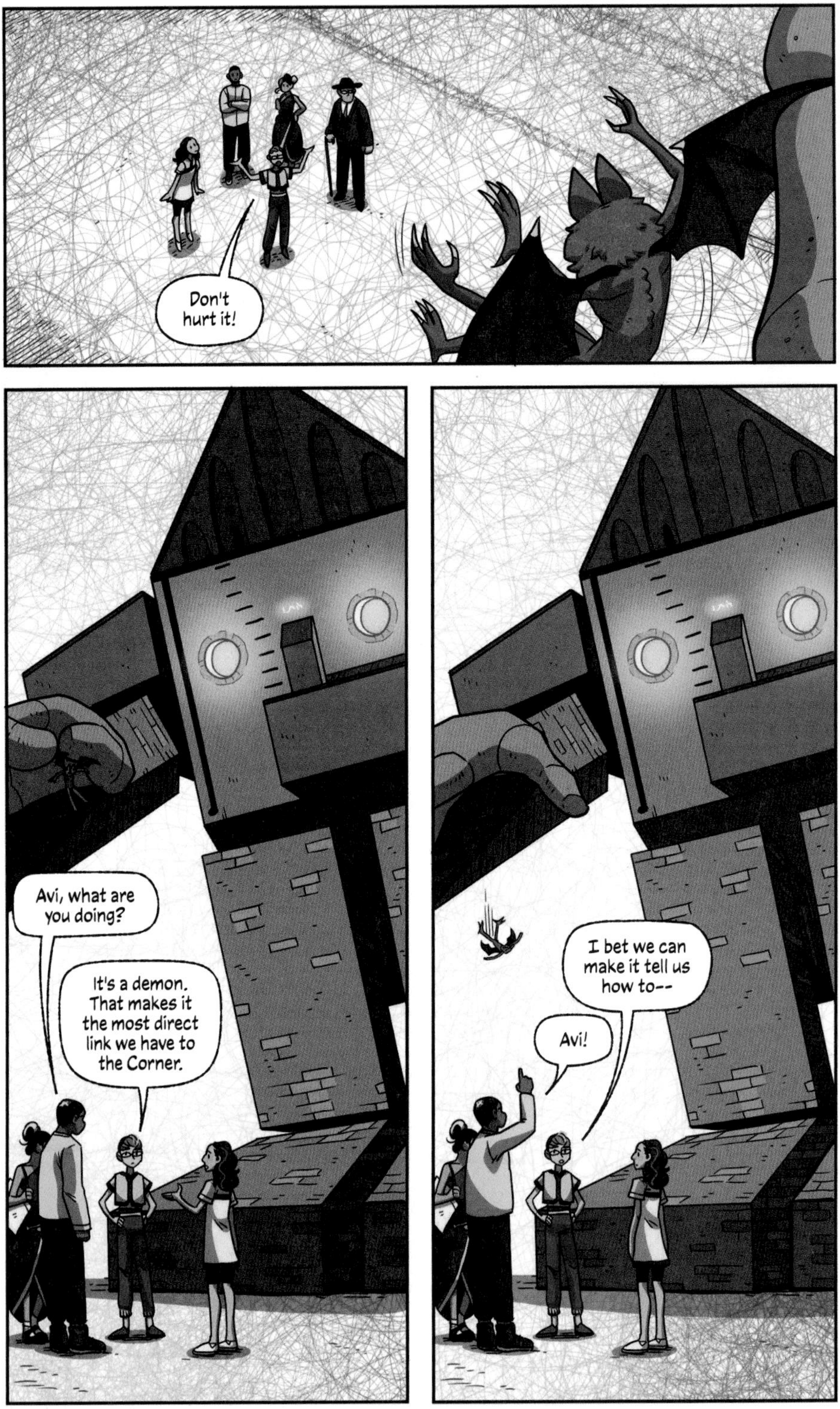

Don't hurt it!
Avi, what are you doing?
It's a demon. That makes it the most direct link we have to the Corner.
I bet we can make it tell us how to--
Avi!

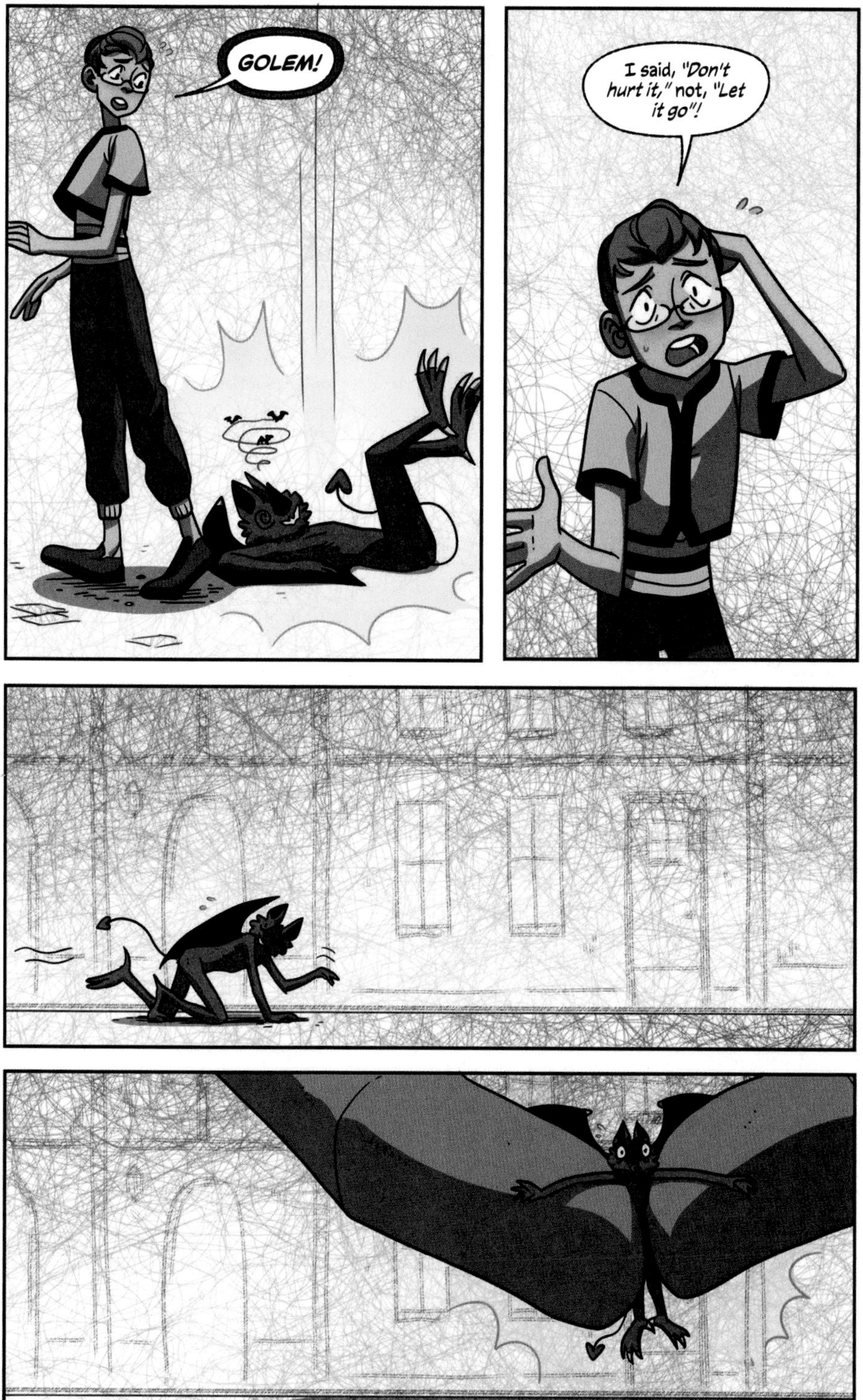
GOLEM!
I said, "Don't hurt it," not, "Let it go"!

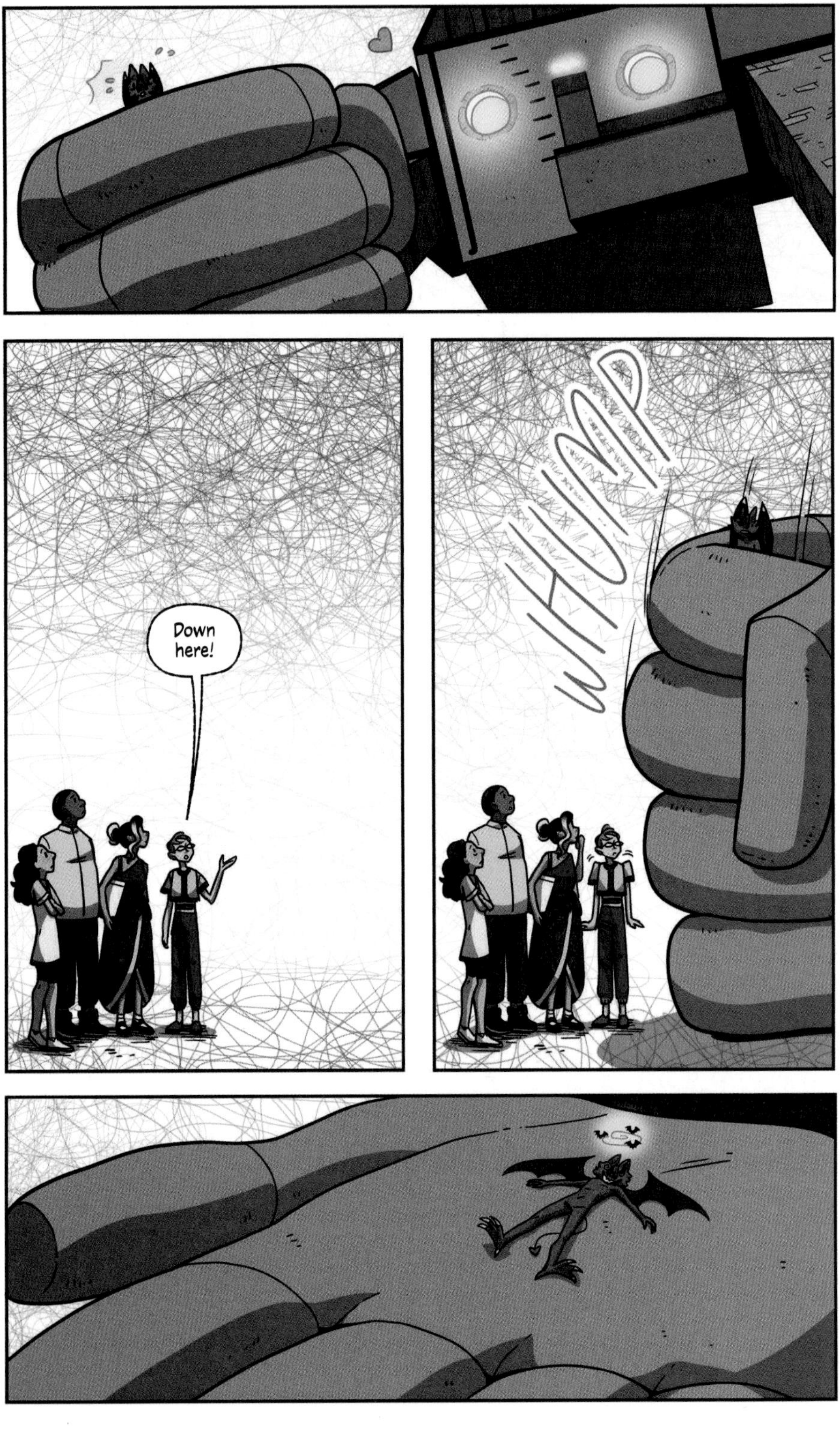
Down here!
WHUMP

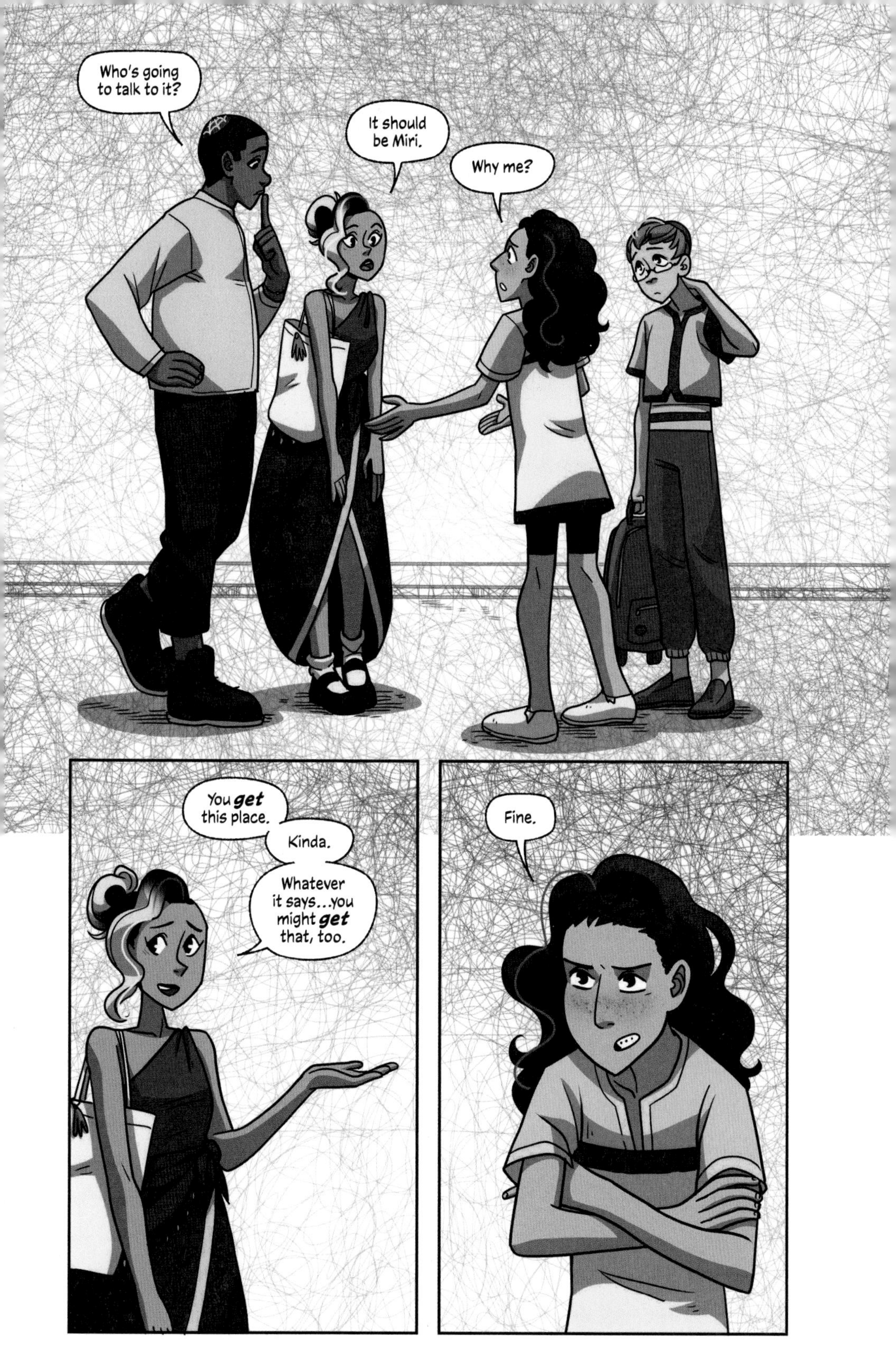
Who's going to talk to it?
It should be Miri.
Why me?
You get this place.
Kinda.
Whatever it says...you might get that, too.
Fine.

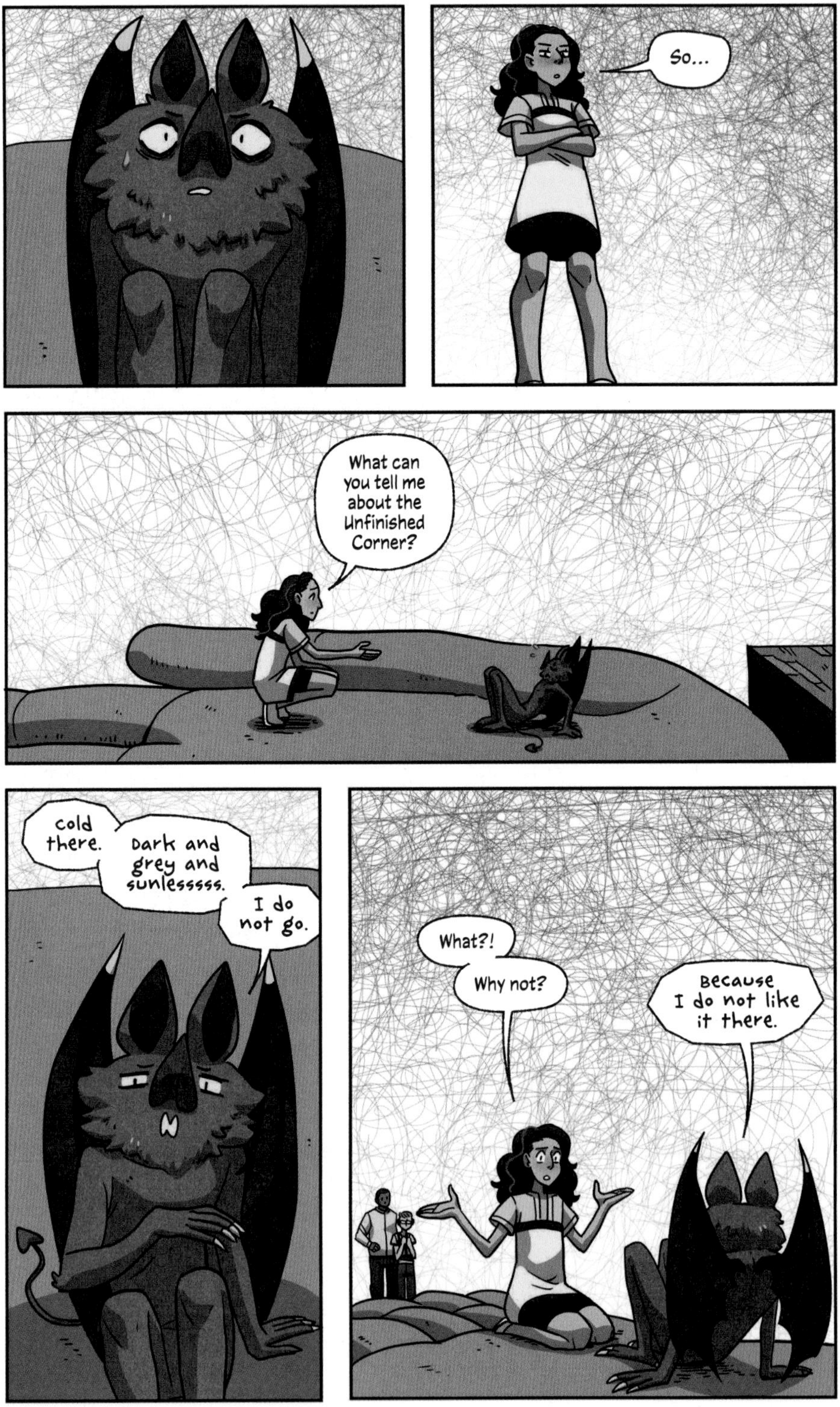

So...
What can you tell me about the Unfinished Corner?
Cold there.
Dark and grey and sunlesssss.
I do not go.
What?!
Why not?
Because I do not like it there.

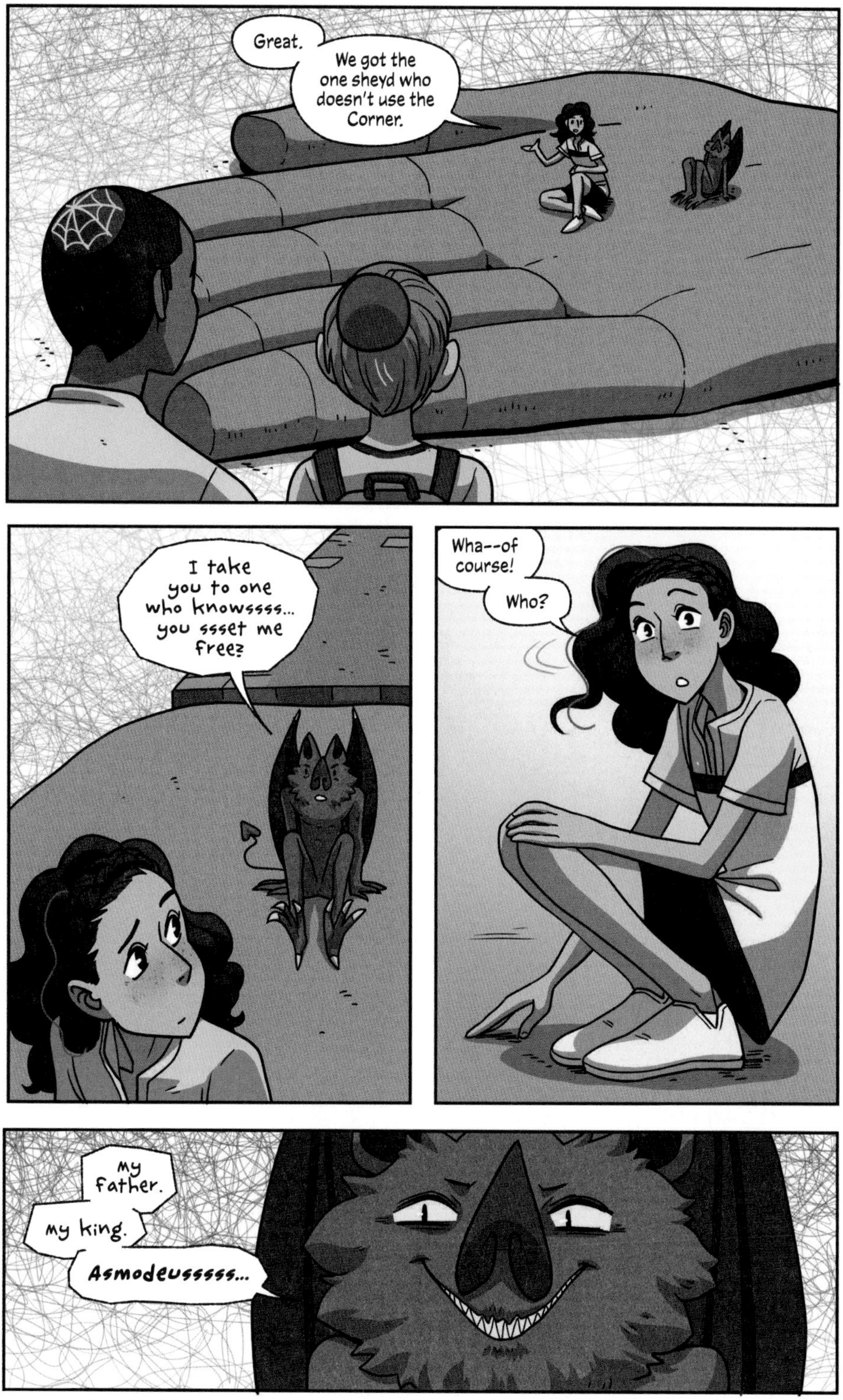
Great.
We got the one sheyd who doesn't use the Corner.
I take you to one who knowssss... you ssset me free?
Wha--of course!
Who?
My father.
My king.
Asmodeussssss...

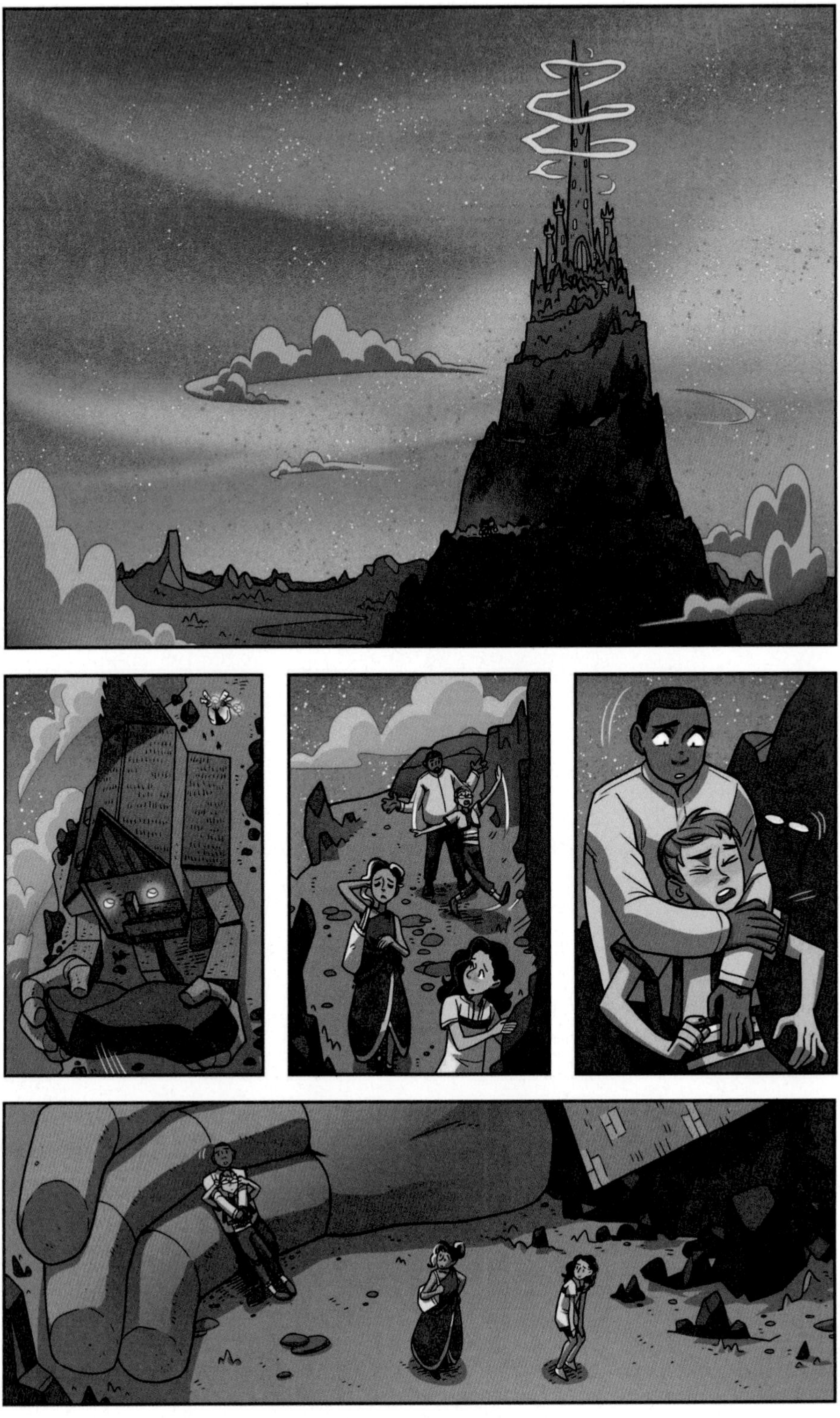

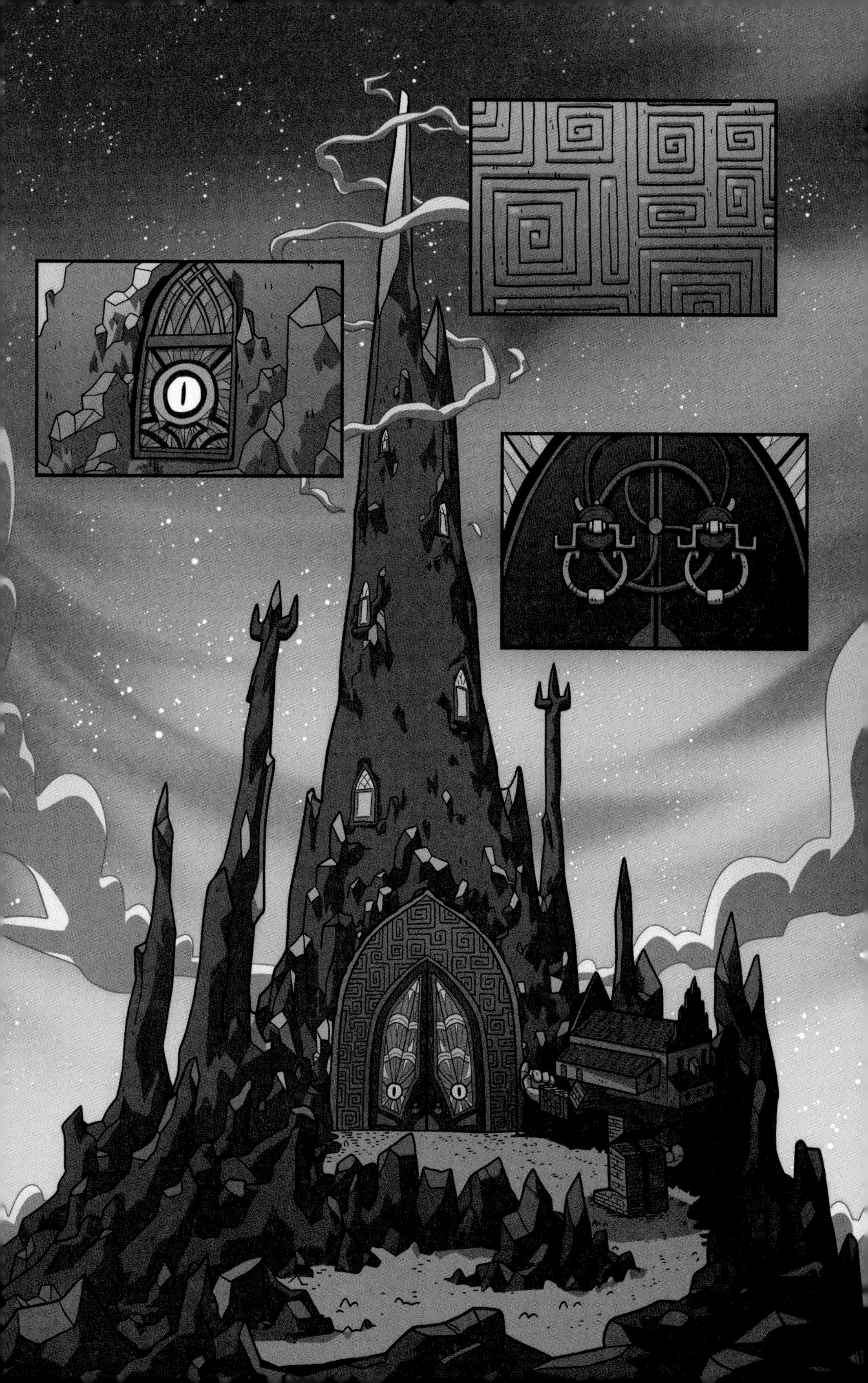

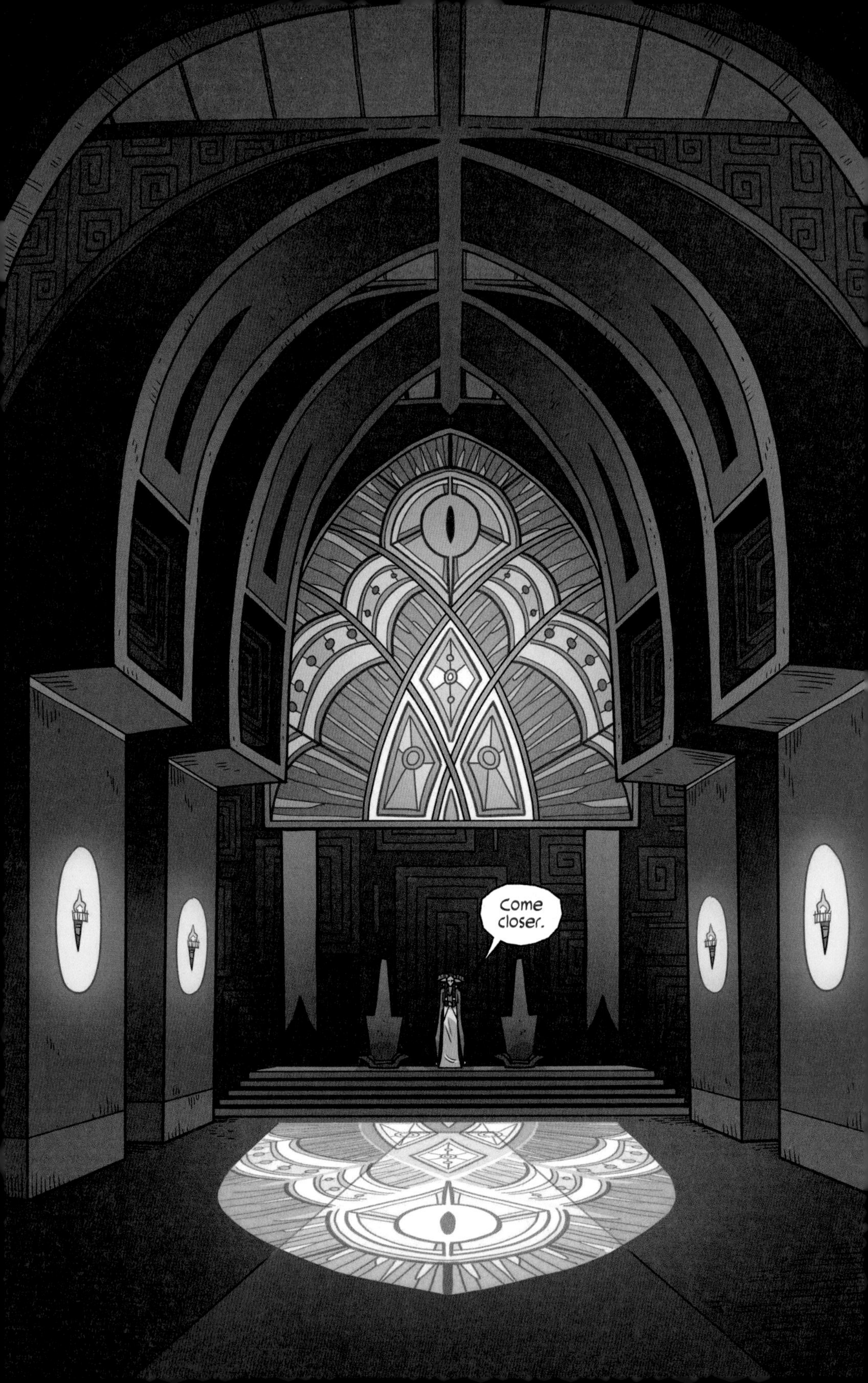
Come closer.

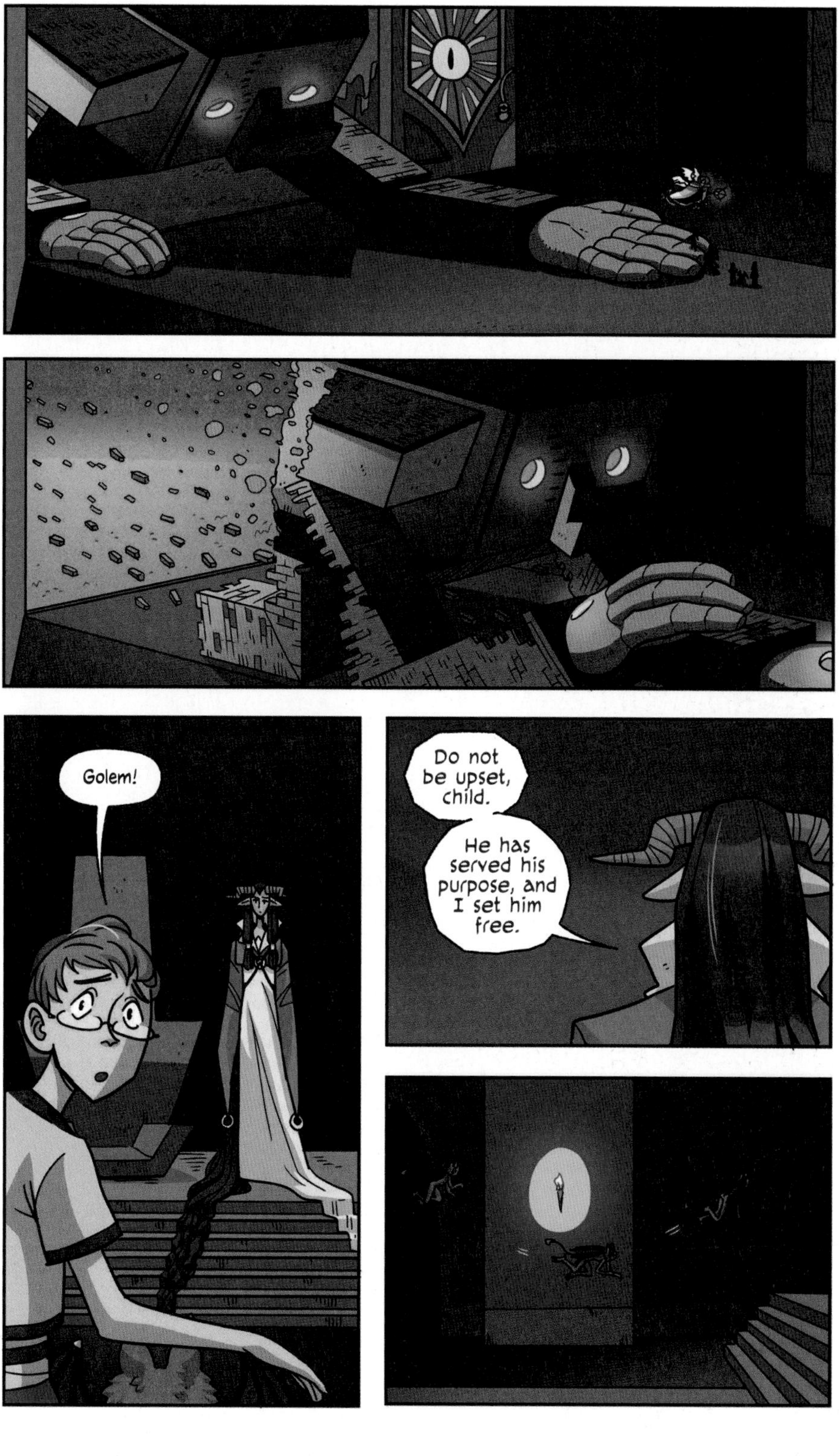
Golem!
Do not be upset, child.
He has served his purpose, and I set him free.

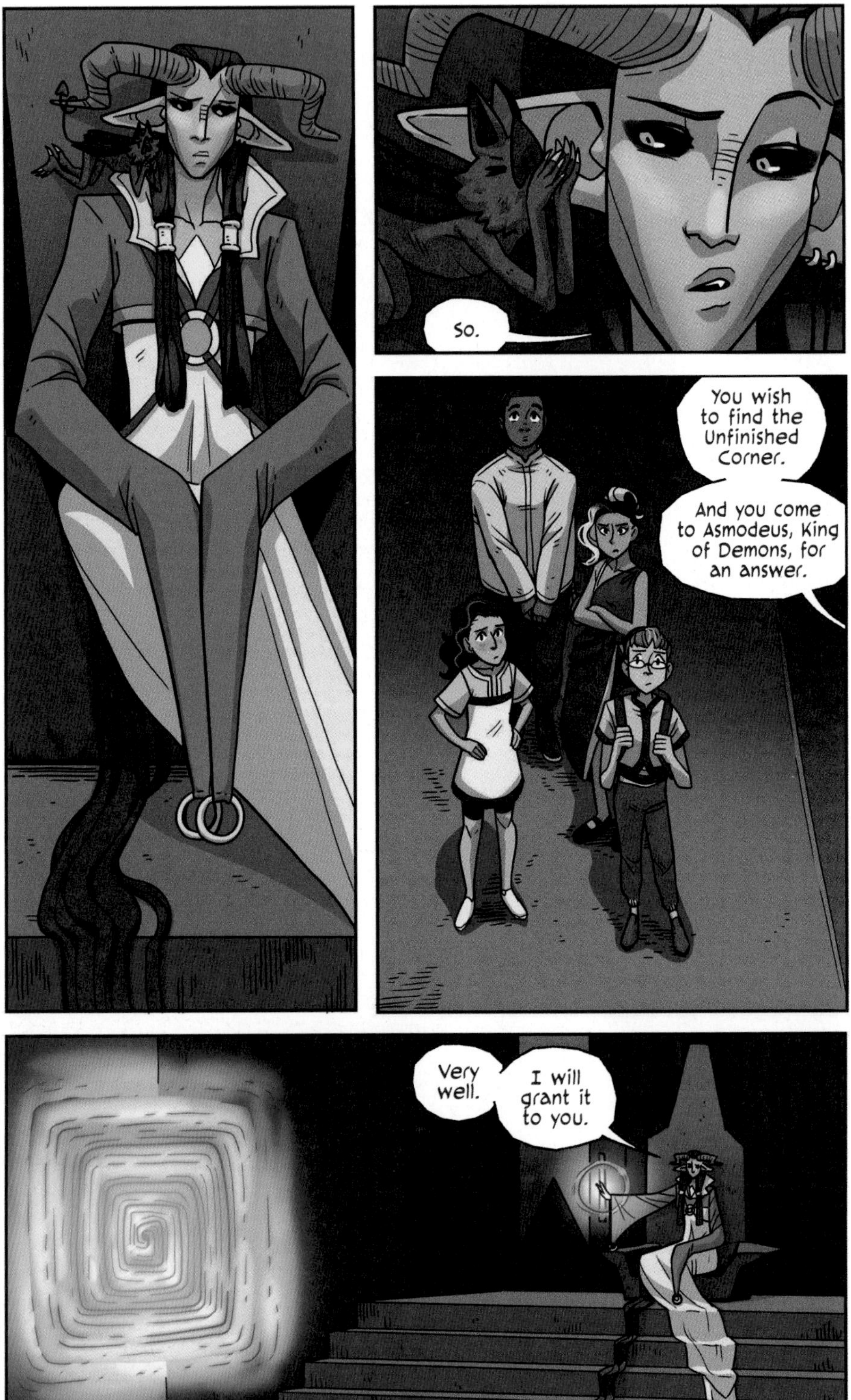
So.
You wish to find the Unfinished Corner.
And you come to Asmodeus, King of Demons, for an answer.
Very well.
I will grant it to you.

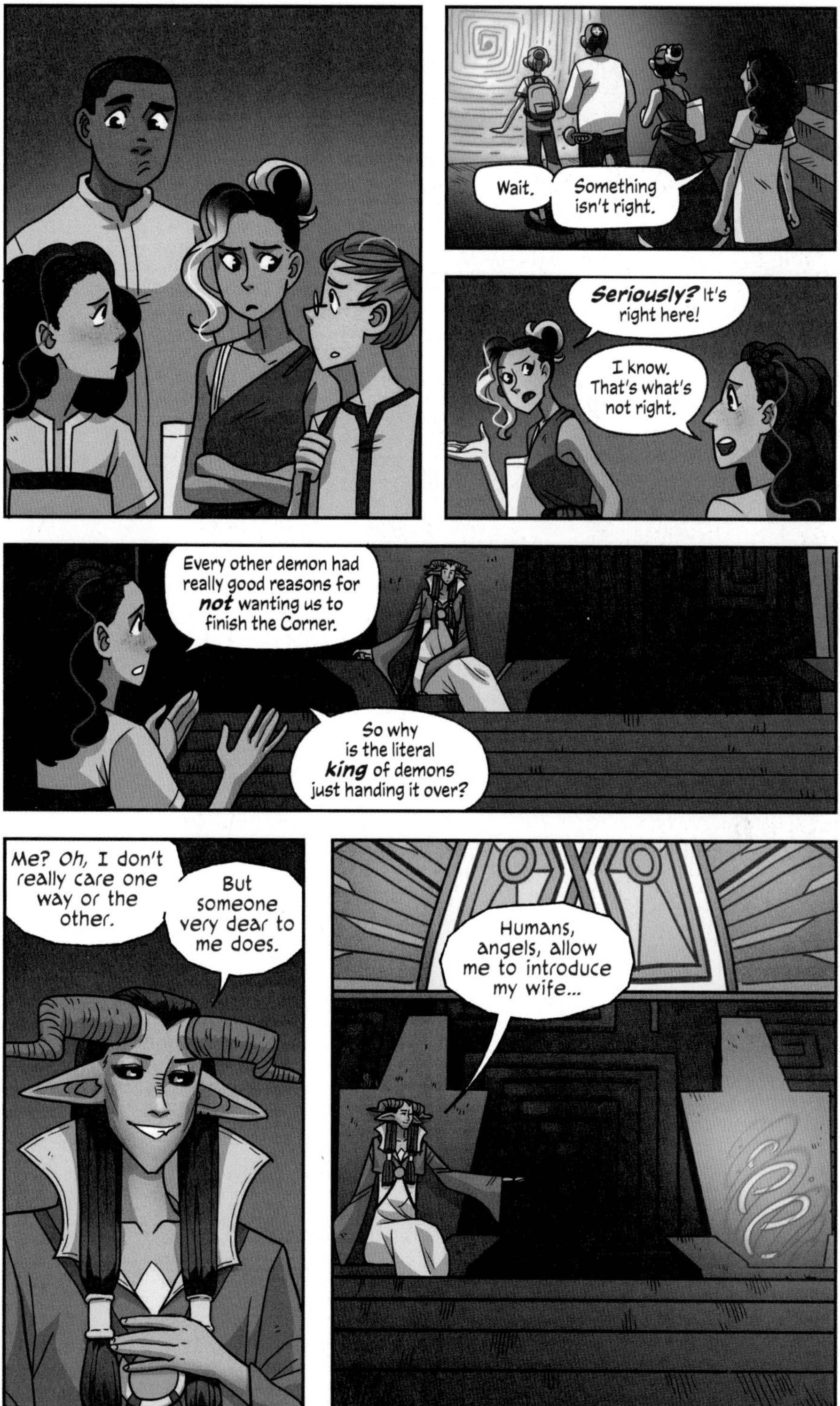
Wait.
Something isn't right.
Seriously? It's right here!
I know. That's what's not right.
Every other demon had really good reasons for not wanting us to finish the Corner.
So why is the literal king of demons just handing it over?
Me? Oh, I don't really care one way or the other.
But someone very dear to me does.
Humans, angels, allow me to introduce my wife...

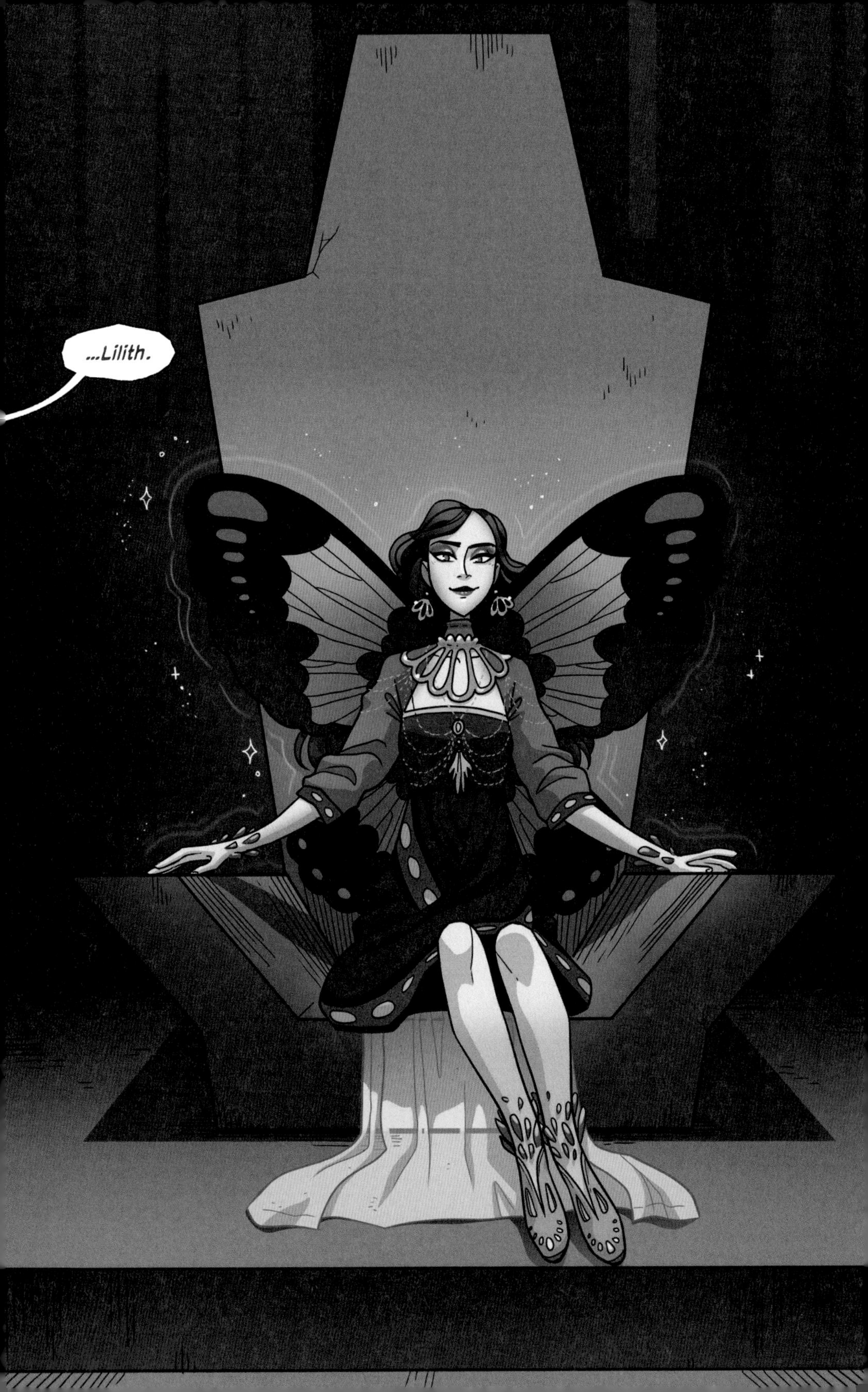
...Lilith.

CHAPTER ELEVEN

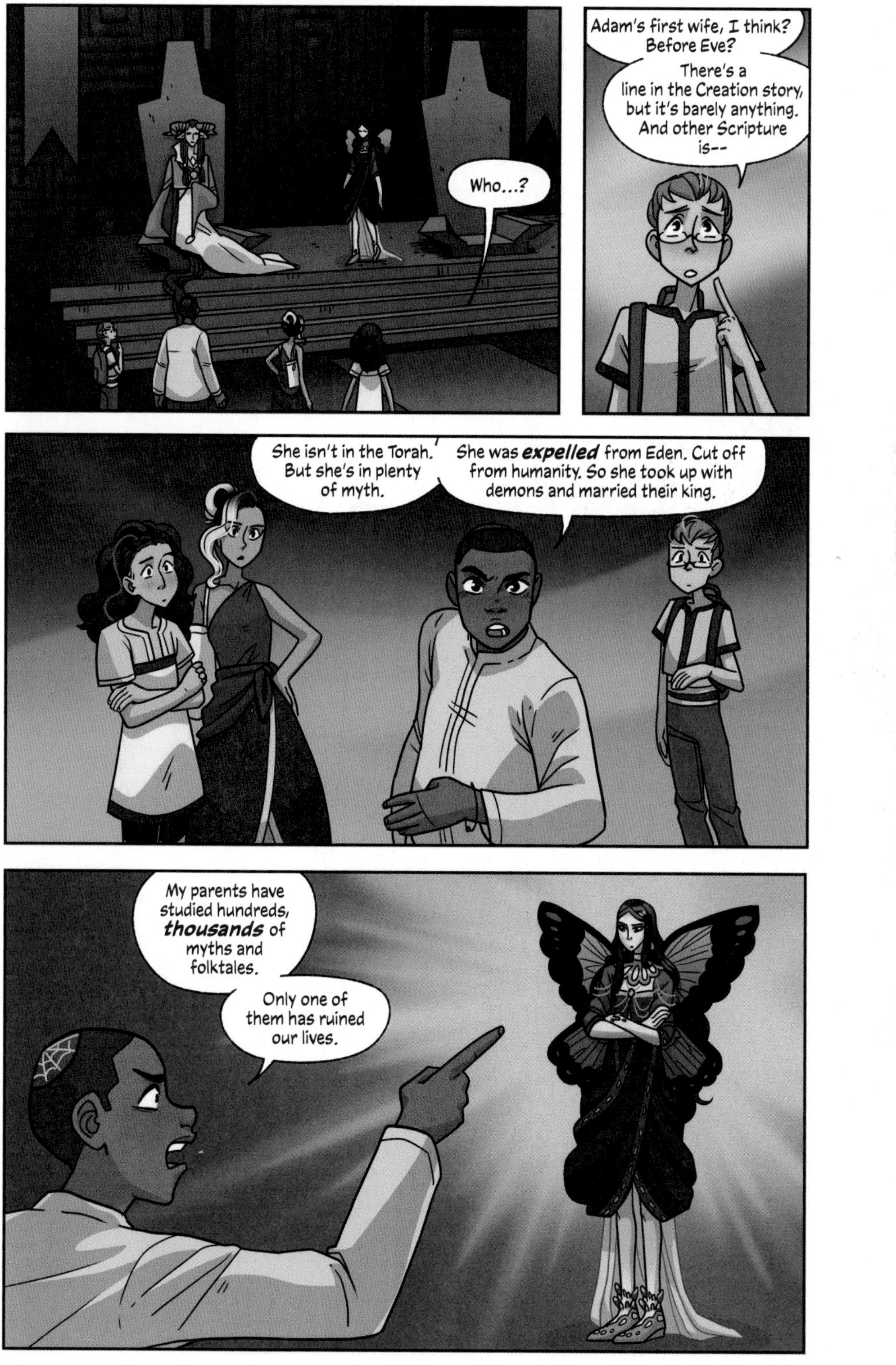
Who...?
Adam's first wife, I think? Before Eve?
There's a line in the Creation story, but it's barely anything. And other Scripture is--
She isn't in the Torah. But she's in plenty of myth.
She was ***expelled*** from Eden. Cut off from humanity. So she took up with demons and married their king.
My parents have studied hundreds, ***thousands*** of myths and folktales.
Only one of them has ruined our lives.

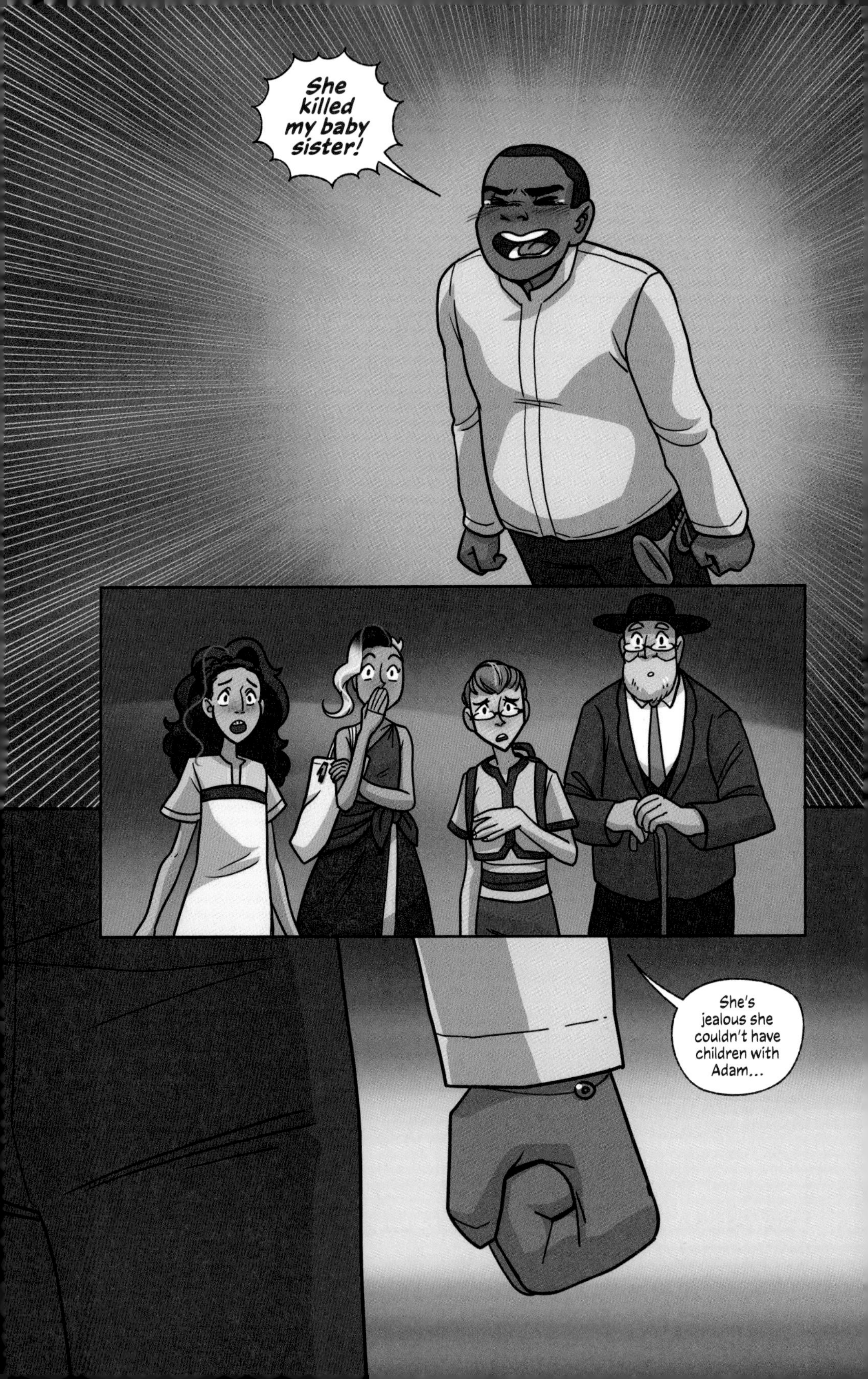
She killed my baby sister!
She's jealous she couldn't have children with Adam...

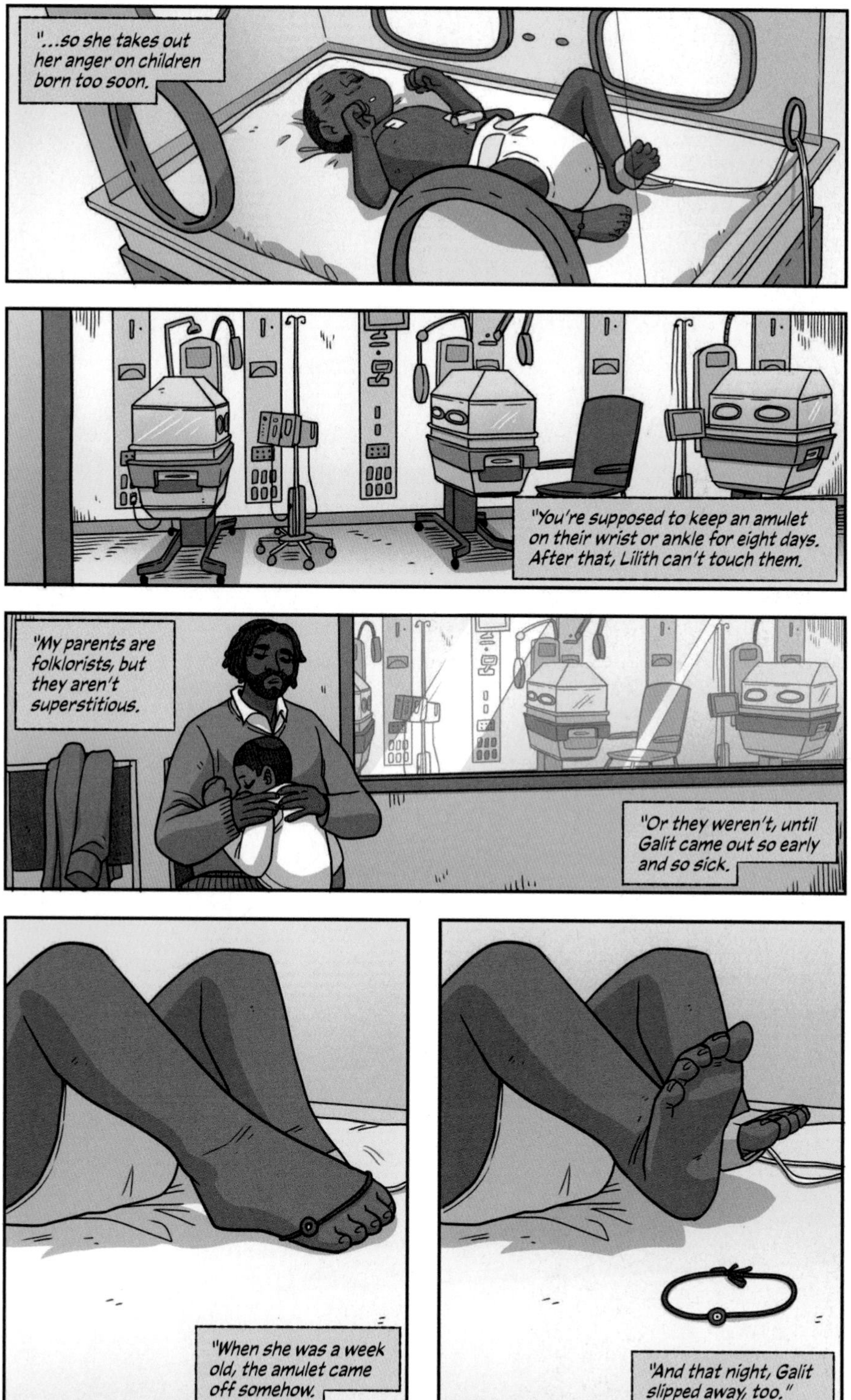
"...so she takes out her anger on children born too soon.
"You're supposed to keep an amulet on their wrist or ankle for eight days. After that, Lilith can't touch them.
"My parents are folklorists, but they aren't superstitious.
"Or they weren't, until Galit came out so early and so sick.
"When she was a week old, the amulet came off somehow.
"And that night, Galit slipped away, too."

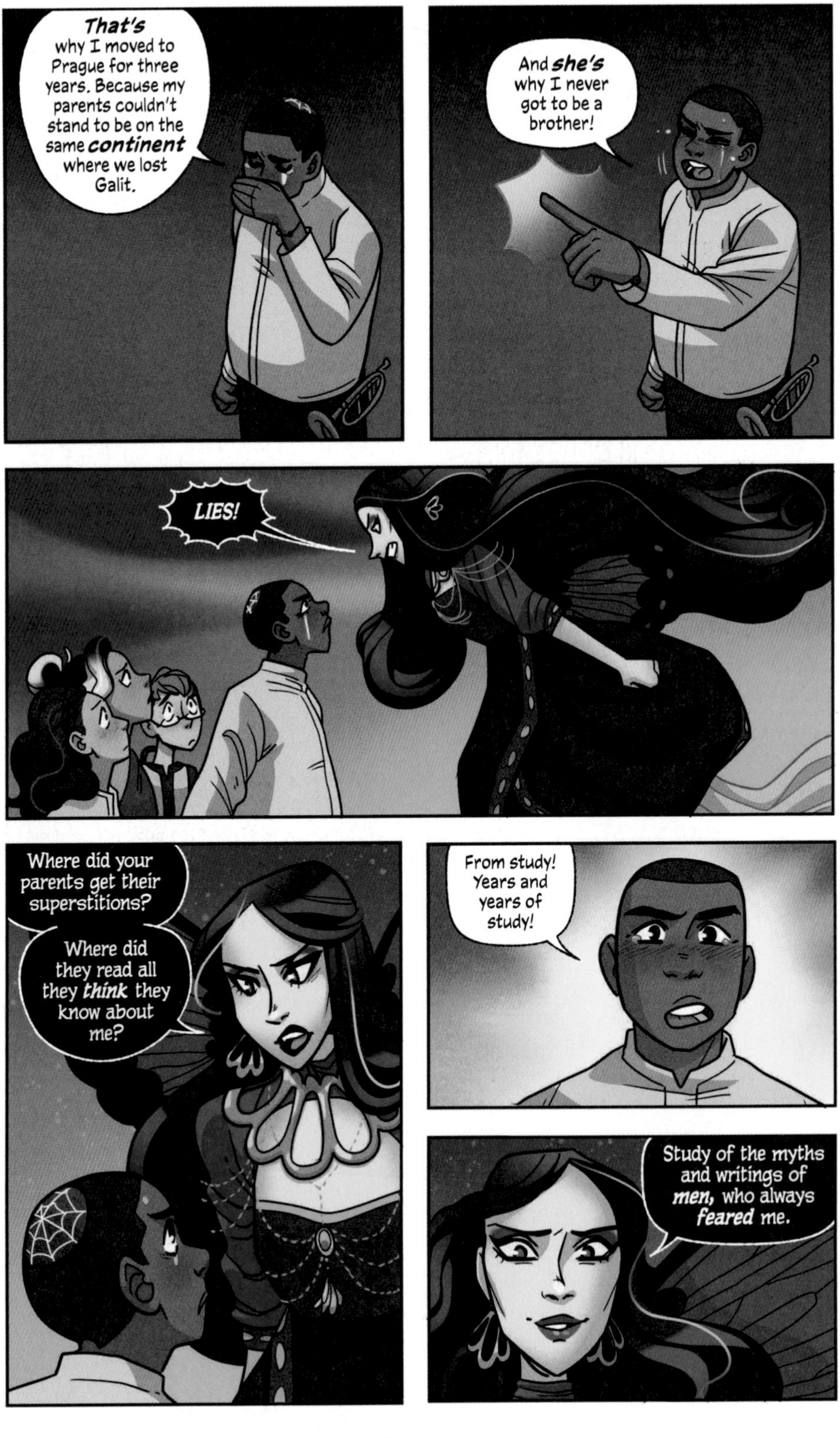
That's why I moved to Prague for three years. Because my parents couldn't stand to be on the same continent where we lost Galit.
And she's why I never got to be a brother!
LIES!
Where did your parents get their superstitions?
Where did they read all they think they know about me?
From study! Years and years of study!
Study of the myths and writings of men, who always feared me.

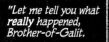

"Let me tell you what **really** happened, Brother-of-Galit.

"I was expelled from the Garden because I wanted to be equal to my husband. To look him in the eye as we gave humanity its start.

"But casting me out wasn't punishment enough.

"For wanting to be equal mother to humanity's children, my sentence was this...

"I could only ever be there for the sickest and weakest, and no matter what I did, I would fail.

"If somehow they live, I never see them again.

"If they die, I am blamed for it, and the fear of me grows."

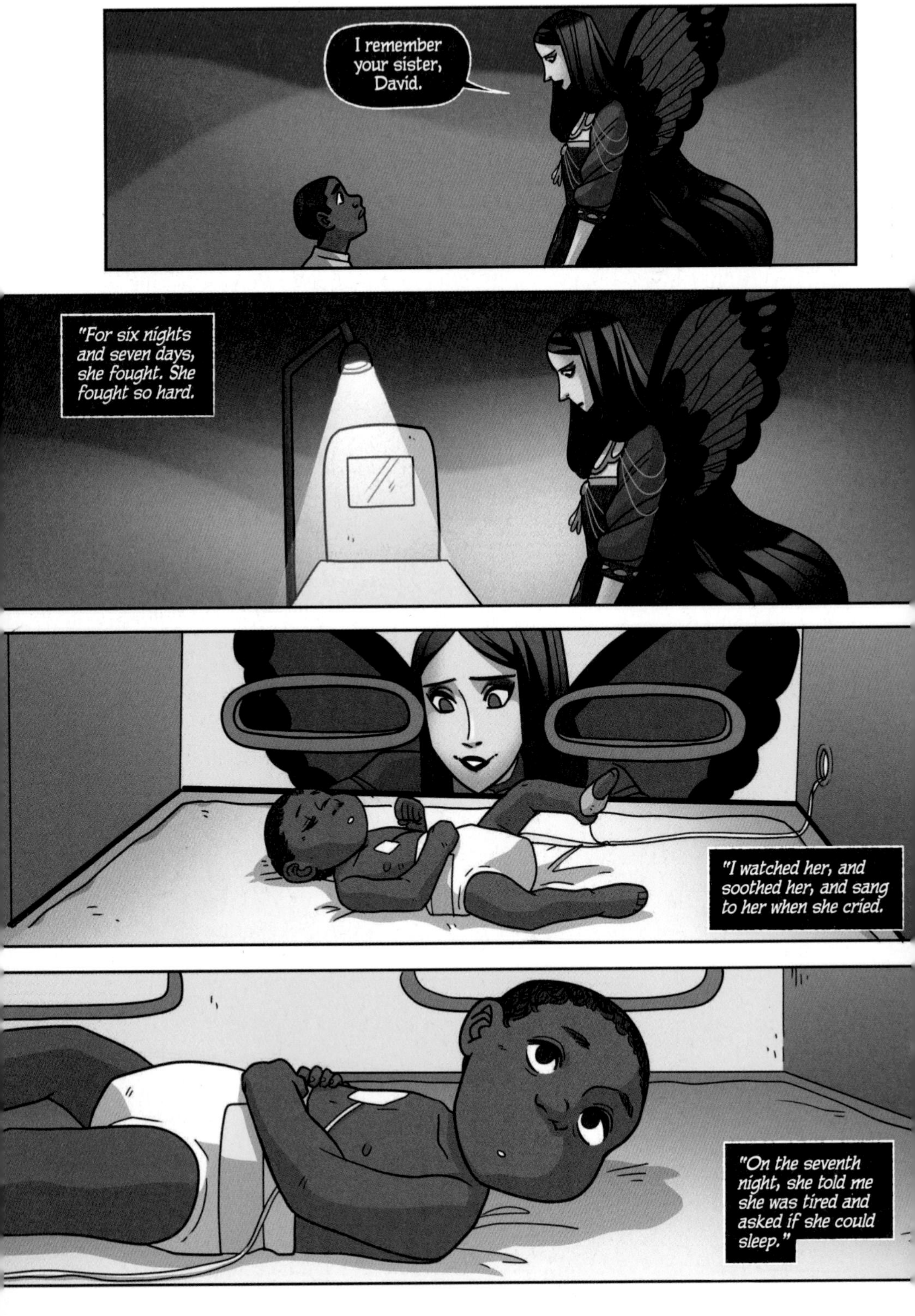
I remember your sister, David.
"For six nights and seven days, she fought. She fought so hard.
"I watched her, and soothed her, and sang to her when she cried.
"On the seventh night, she told me she was tired and asked if she could sleep."

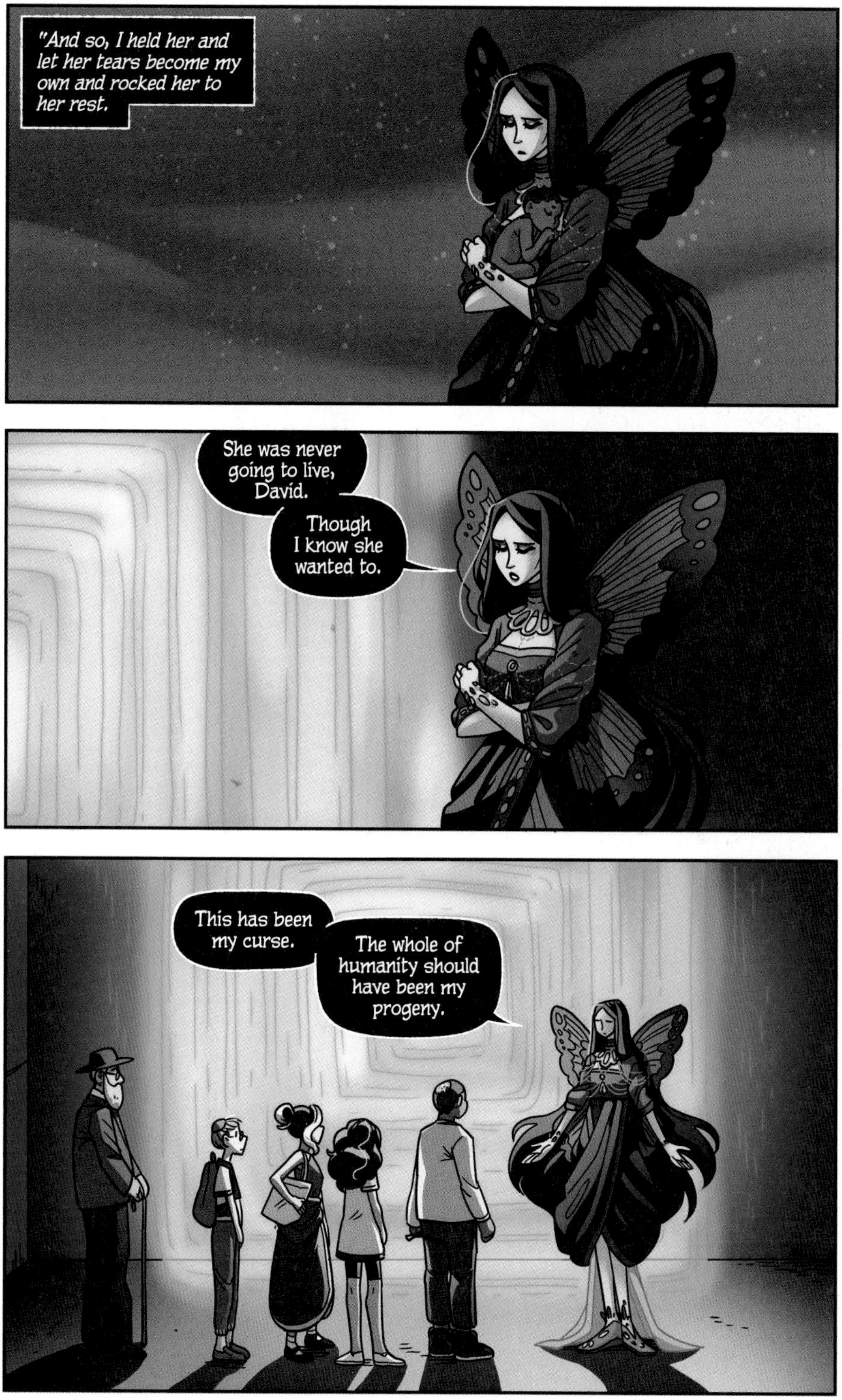
"And so, I held her and let her tears become my own and rocked her to her rest.
She was never going to live, David.
Though I know she wanted to.
This has been my curse.
The whole of humanity should have been my progeny.

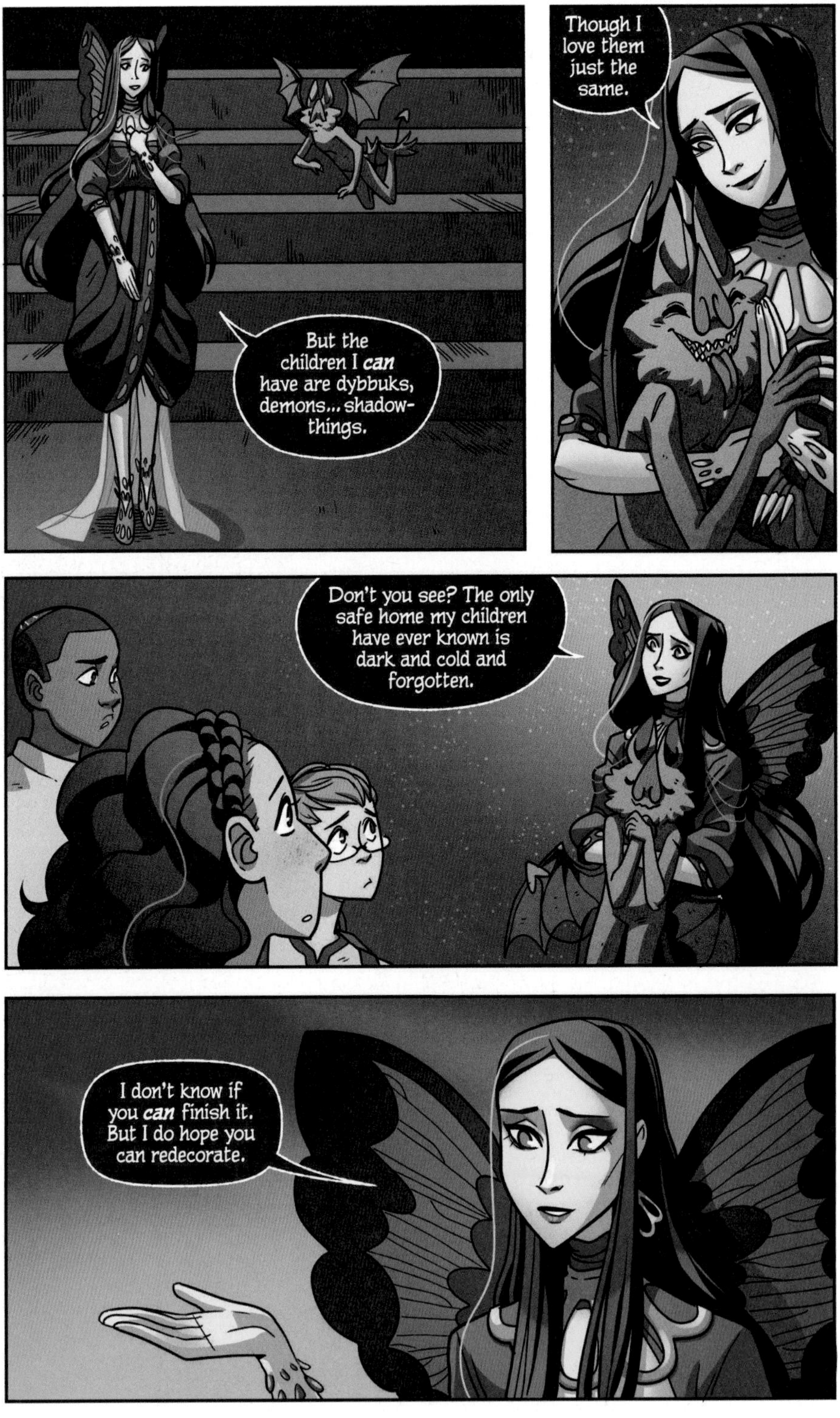
But the children I *can* have are dybbuks, demons... shadow-things.
Though I love them just the same.
Don't you see? The only safe home my children have ever known is dark and cold and forgotten.
I don't know if you *can* finish it. But I do hope you can redecorate.

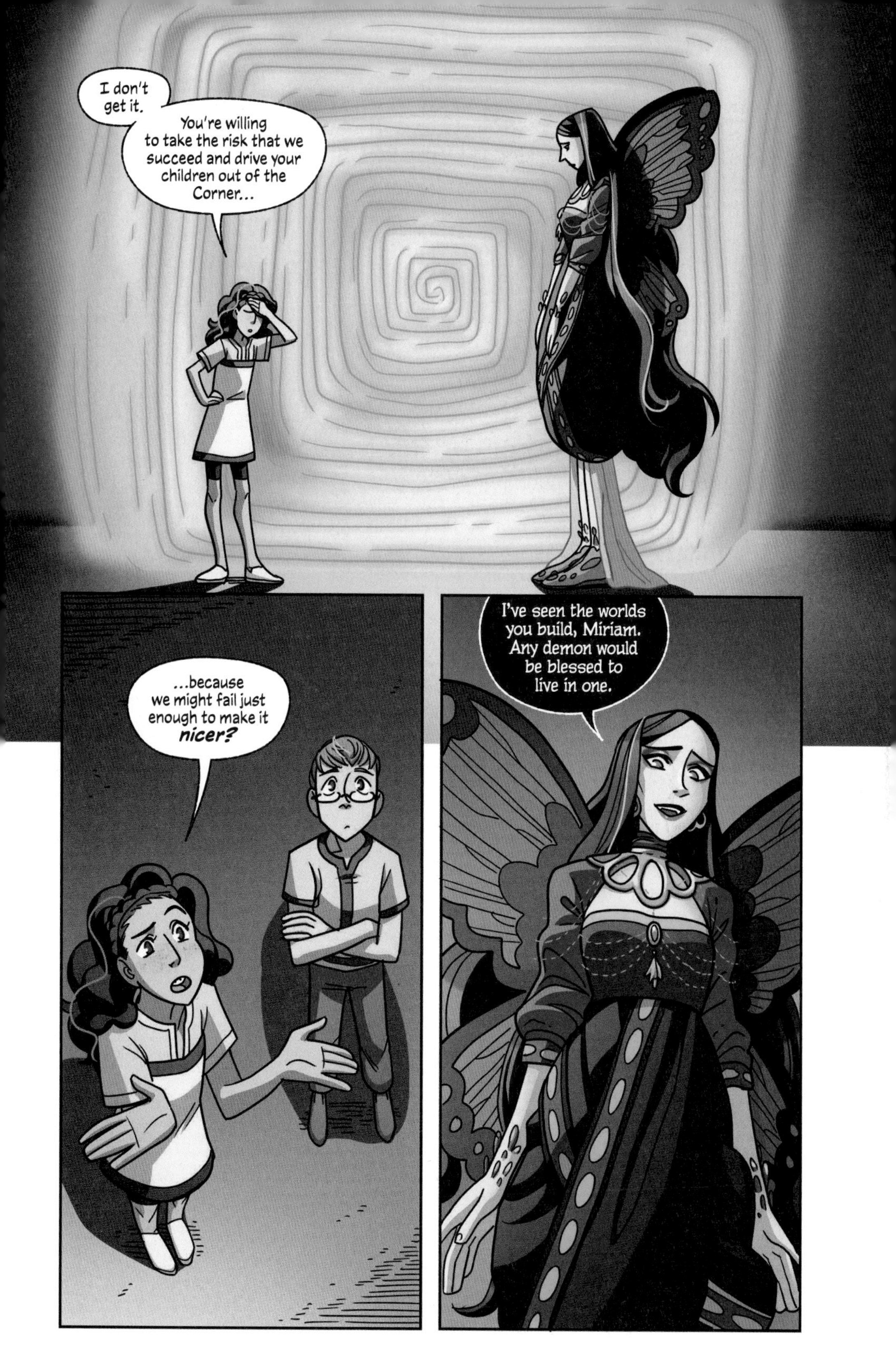
I don't get it.
You're willing to take the risk that we succeed and drive your children out of the Corner...
...because we might fail just enough to make it *nicer?*
I've seen the worlds you build, Miriam. Any demon would be blessed to live in one.

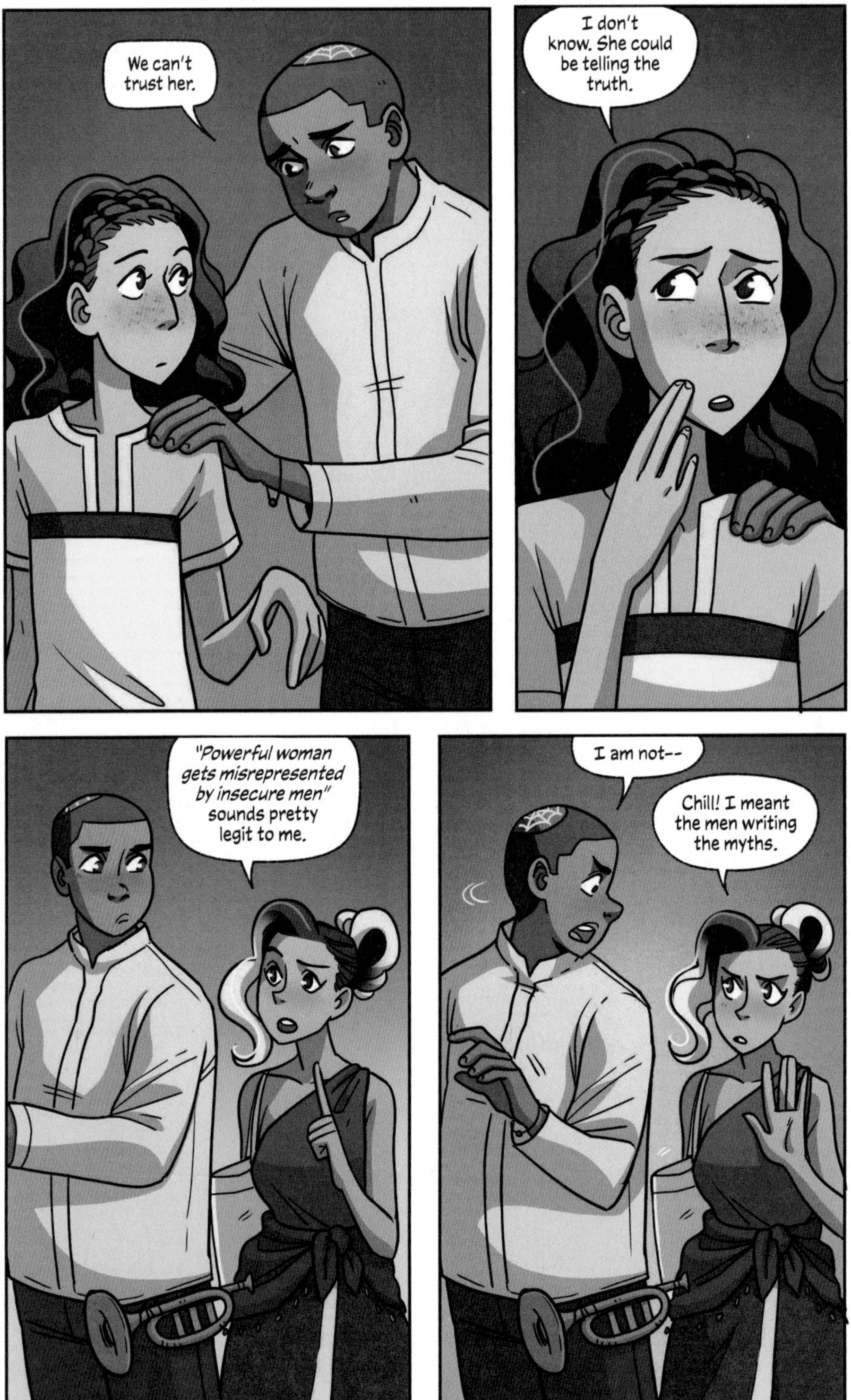
We can't trust her.
I don't know. She could be telling the truth.
"Powerful woman gets misrepresented by insecure men" sounds pretty legit to me.
I am not--
Chill! I meant the men writing the myths.

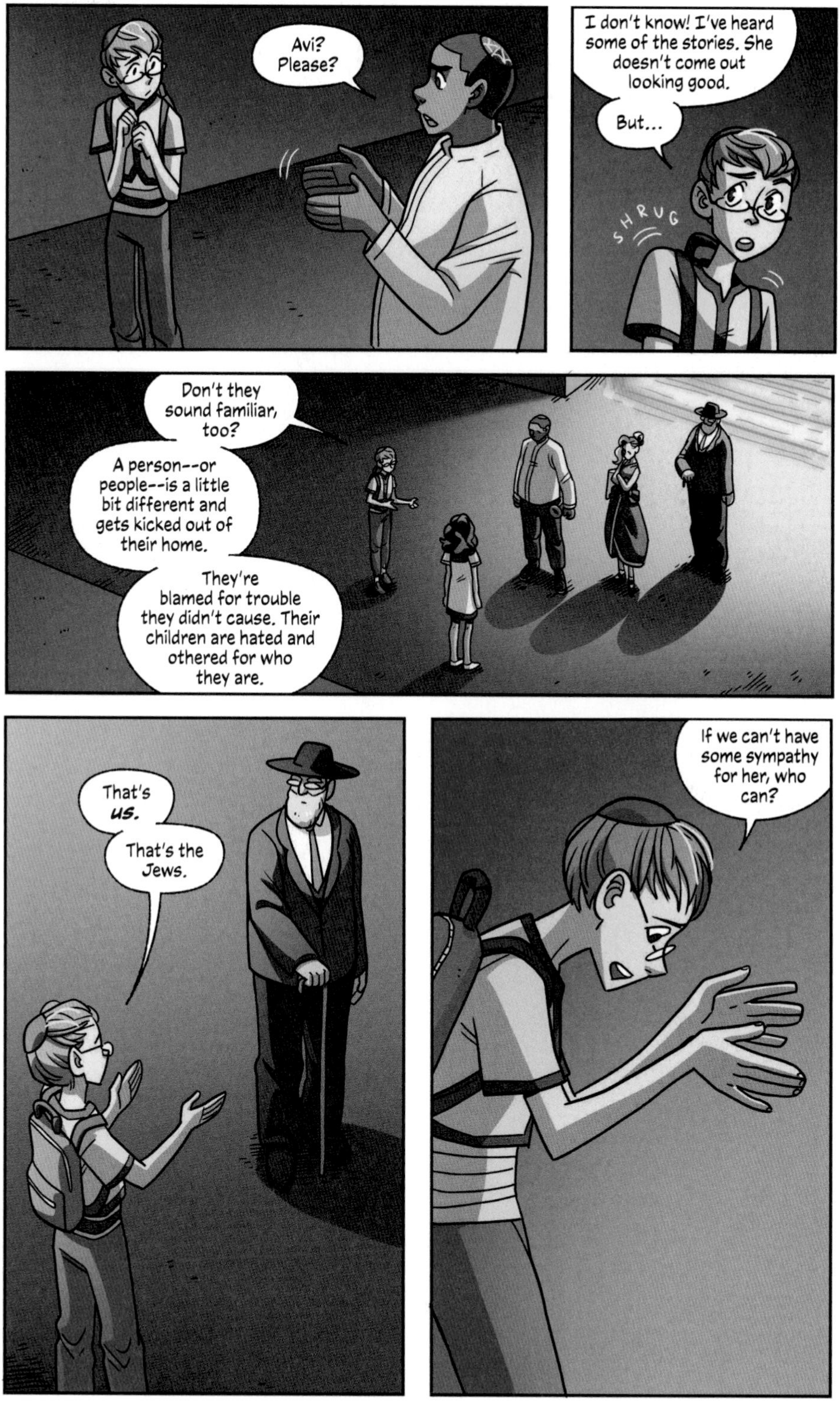
Avi? Please?
I don't know! I've heard some of the stories. She doesn't come out looking good.
But...
SHRUG
Don't they sound familiar, too?
A person--or people--is a little bit different and gets kicked out of their home.
They're blamed for trouble they didn't cause. Their children are hated and othered for who they are.
That's *us.*
That's the Jews.
If we can't have some sympathy for her, who can?

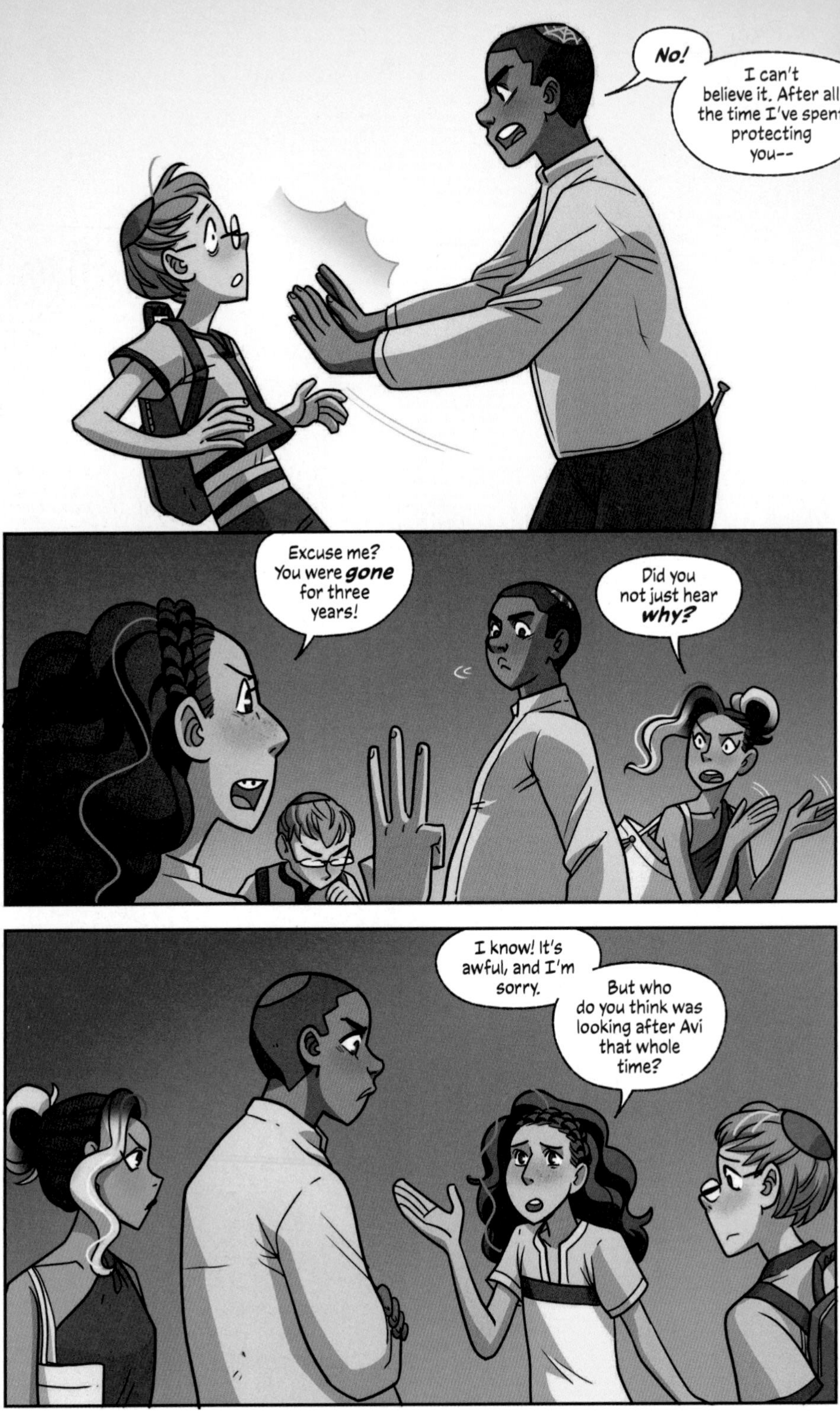
No!
I can't believe it. After all the time I've spent protecting you--
Excuse me? You were gone for three years!
Did you not just hear why?
I know! It's awful, and I'm sorry.
But who do you think was looking after Avi that whole time?

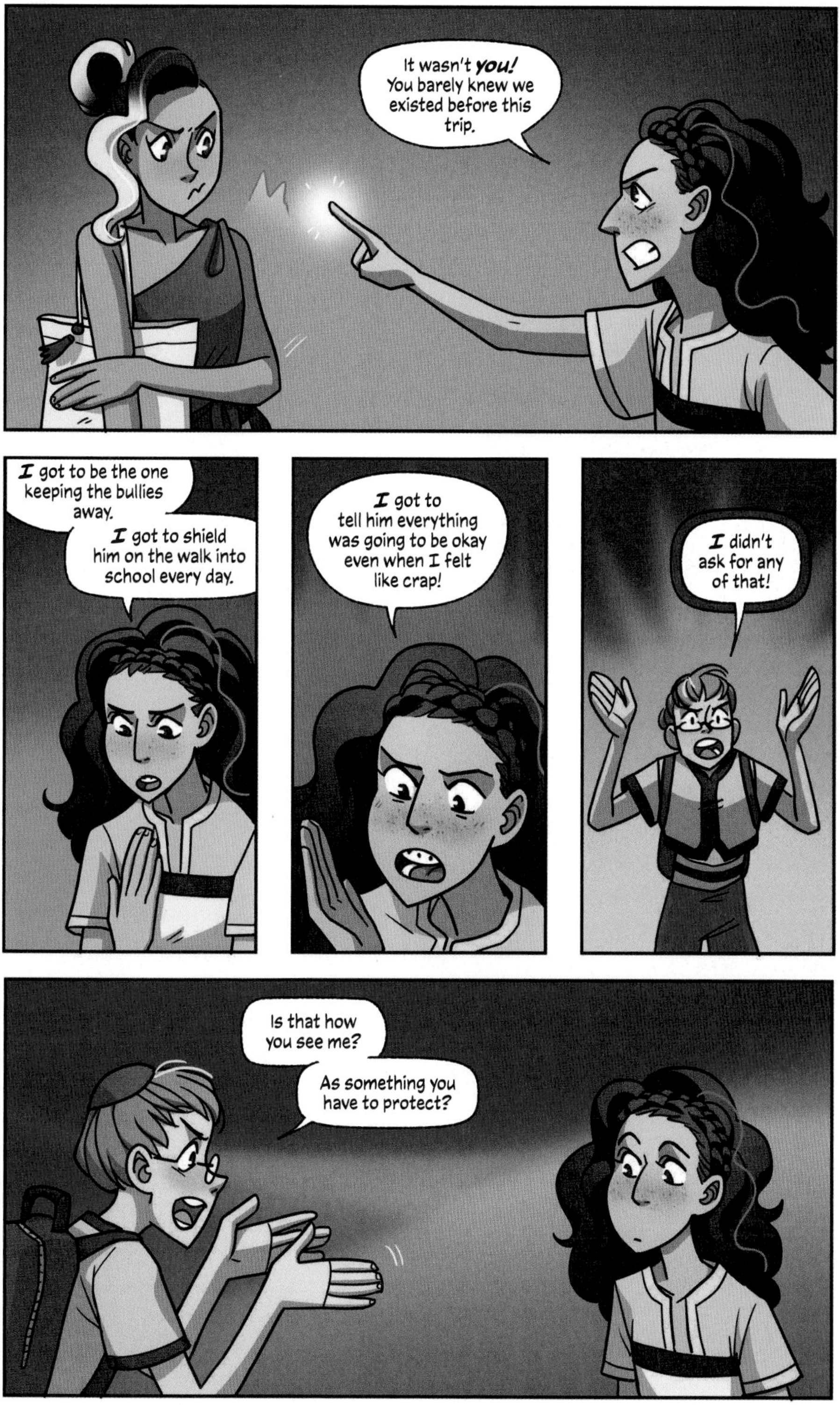
It wasn't *you!* You barely knew we existed before this trip.
I got to be the one keeping the bullies away.
I got to shield him on the walk into school every day.
I got to tell him everything was going to be okay even when I felt like crap!
I didn't ask for any of that!
Is that how you see me?
As something you have to protect?

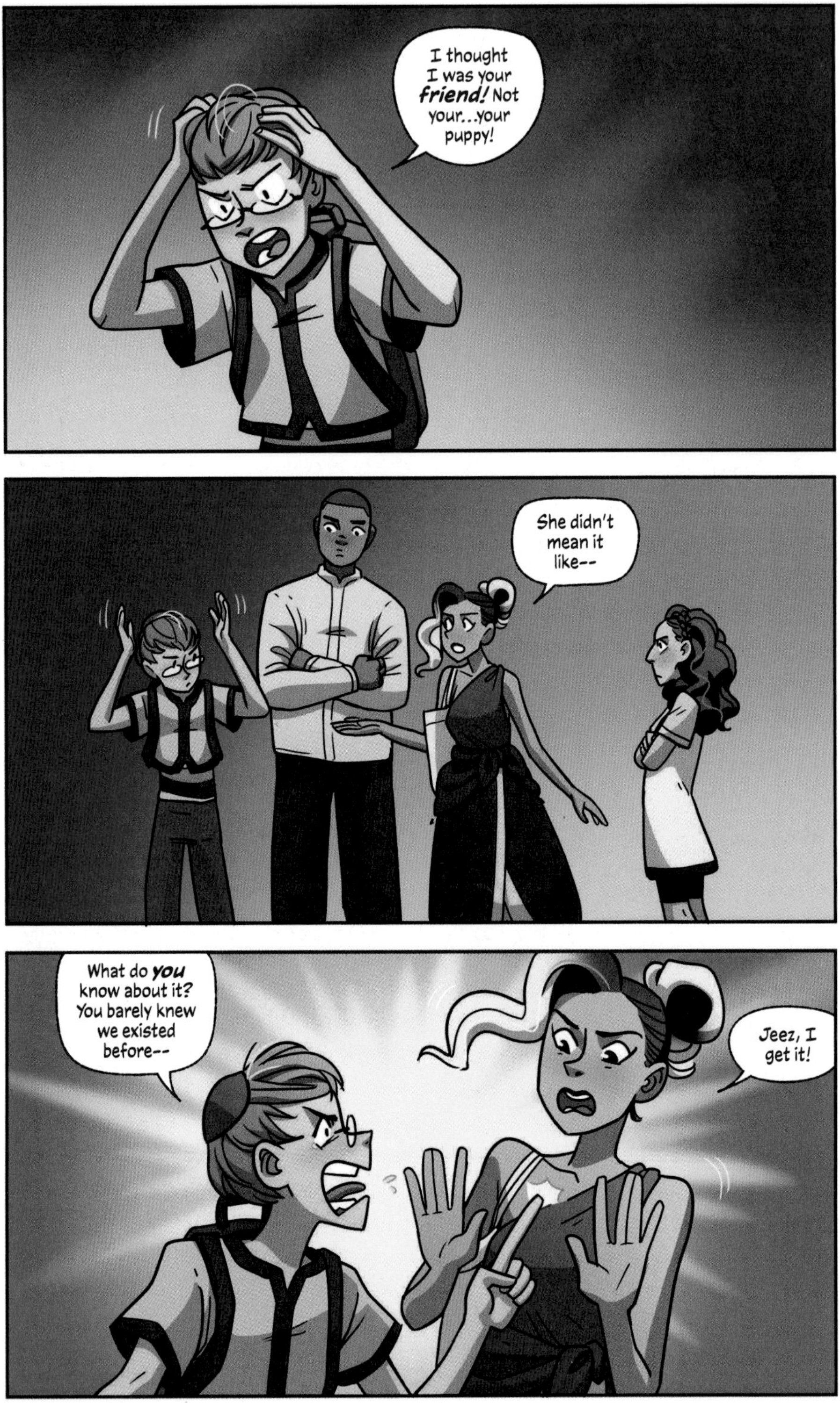
I thought I was your ***friend!*** Not your...your puppy!
She didn't mean it like--
What do ***you*** know about it? You barely knew we existed before--
Jeez, I get it!

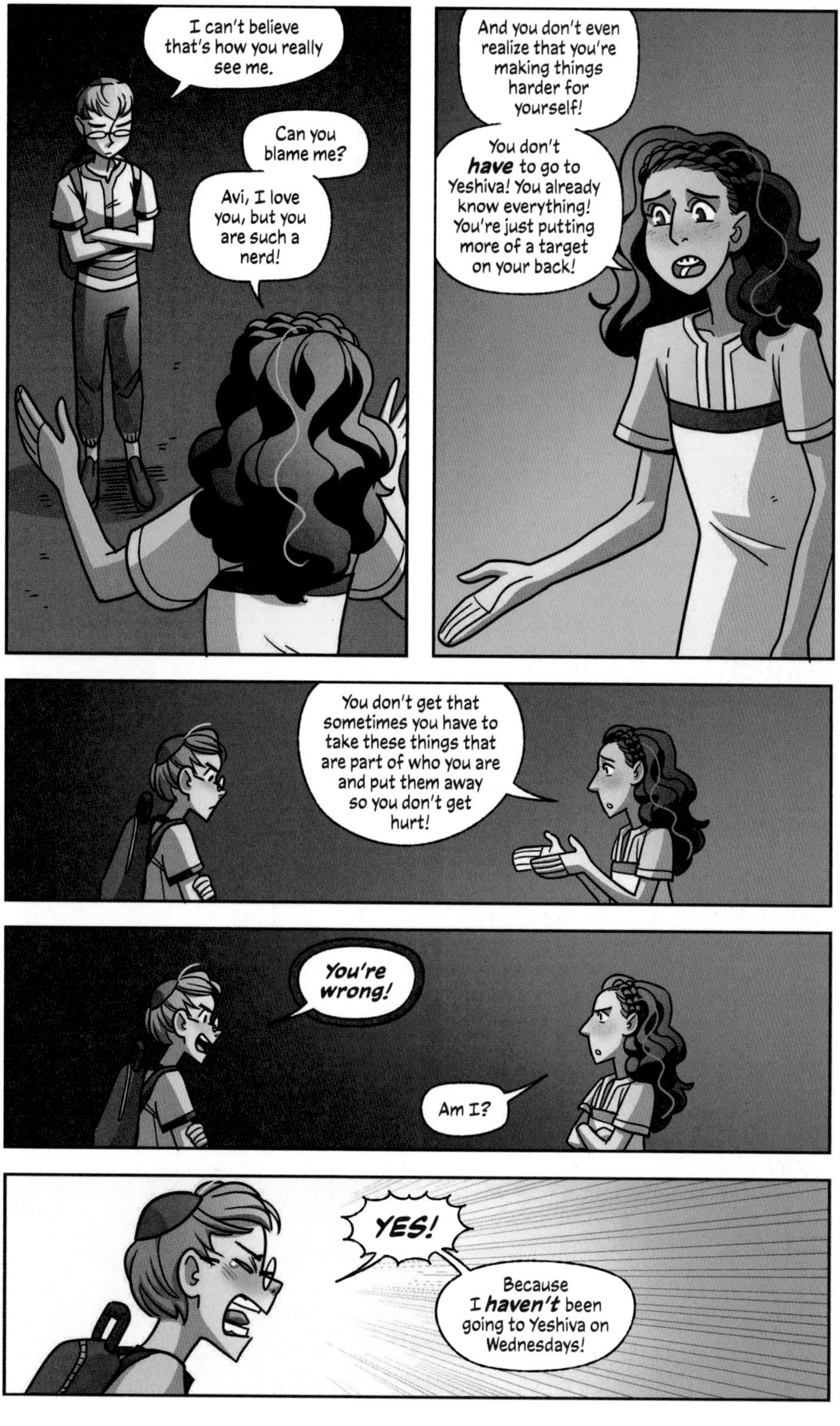

I can't believe that's how you really see me.
Can you blame me?
Avi, I love you, but you are such a nerd!
And you don't even realize that you're making things harder for yourself!
You don't **have** to go to Yeshiva! You already know everything! You're just putting more of a target on your back!
You don't get that sometimes you have to take these things that are part of who you are and put them away so you don't get hurt!
You're wrong!
Am I?
YES!
Because I ***haven't*** been going to Yeshiva on Wednesdays!

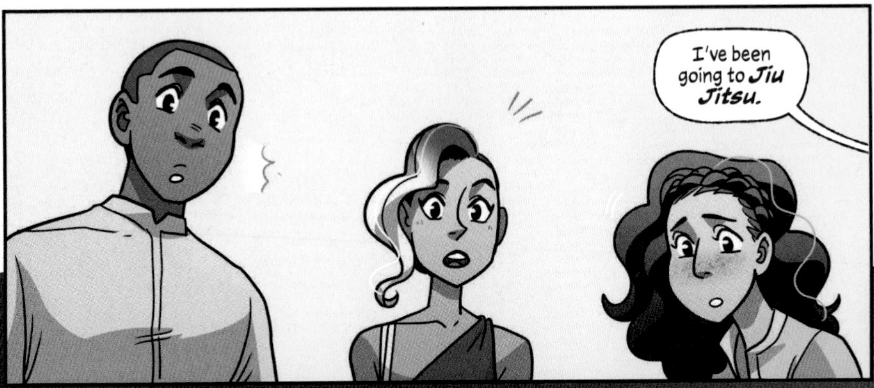
I've been going to **Jiu Jitsu.**

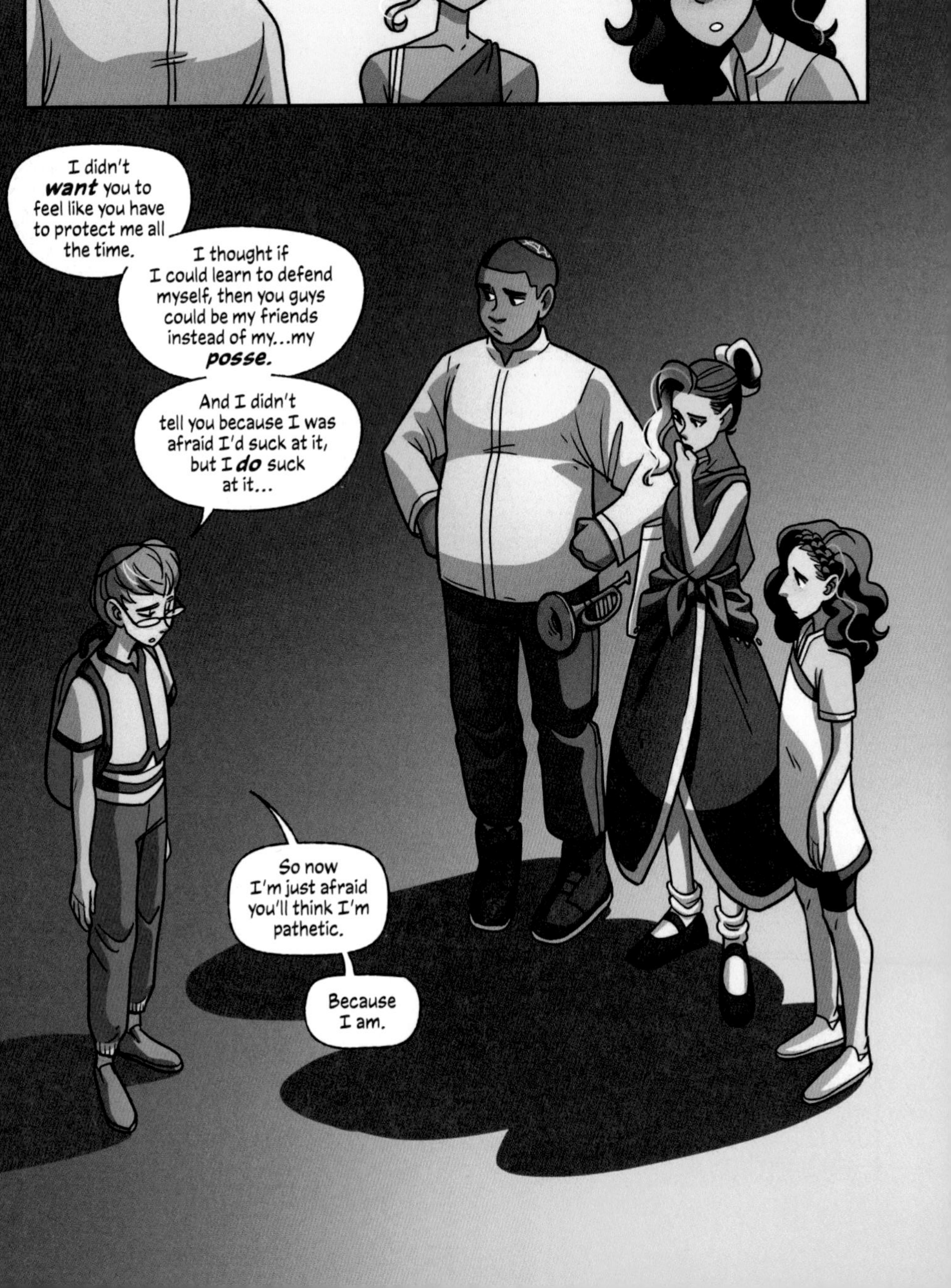
I didn't **want** you to feel like you have to protect me all the time.
I thought if I could learn to defend myself, then you guys could be my friends instead of my...my **posse.**
And I didn't tell you because I was afraid I'd suck at it, but I **do** suck at it...
So now I'm just afraid you'll think I'm pathetic.
Because I am.

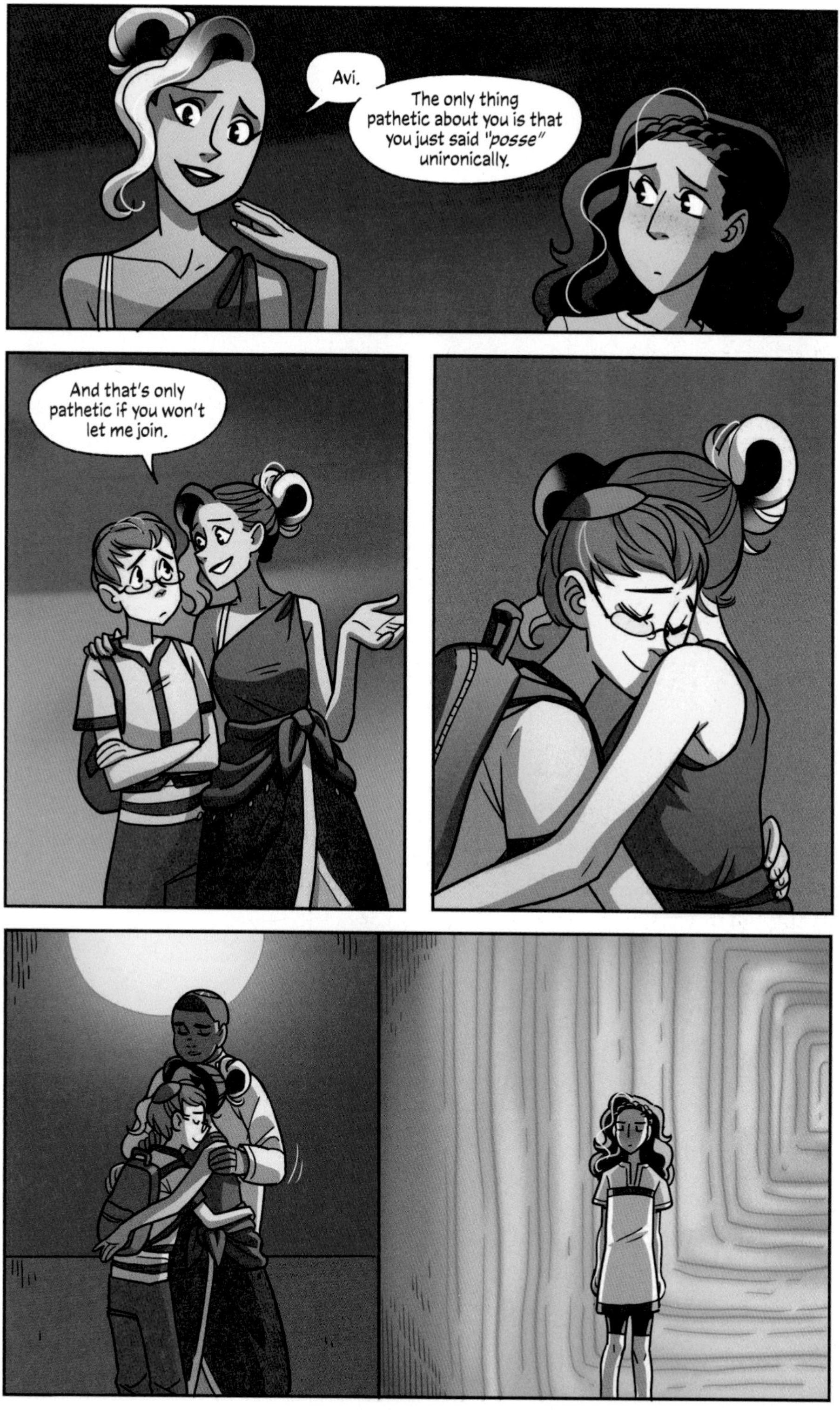
Avi.
The only thing pathetic about you is that you just said "*posse*" unironically.
And that's only pathetic if you won't let me join.

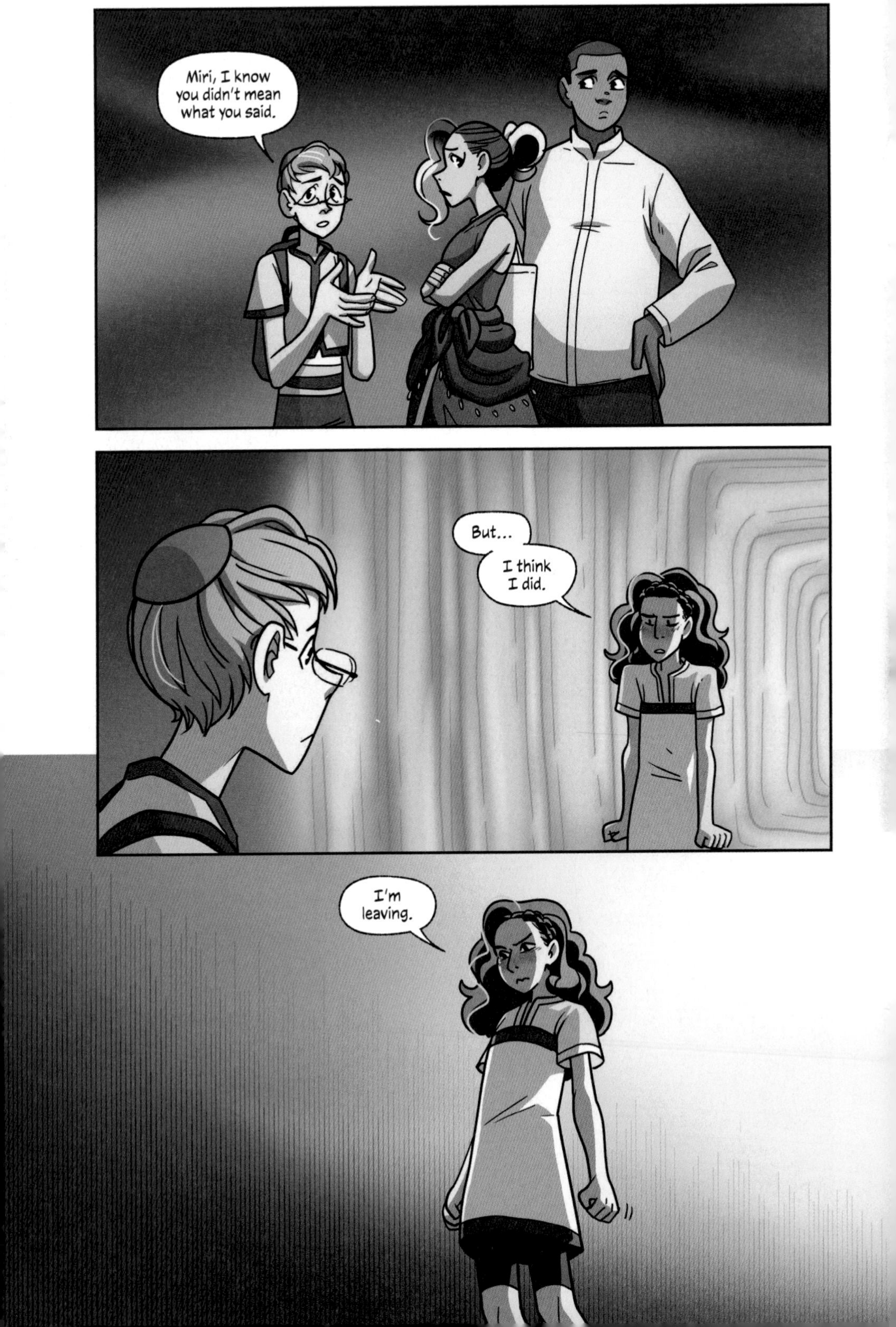
Miri, I know you didn't mean what you said.
But...
I think I did.
I'm leaving.

CHAPTER TWELVE

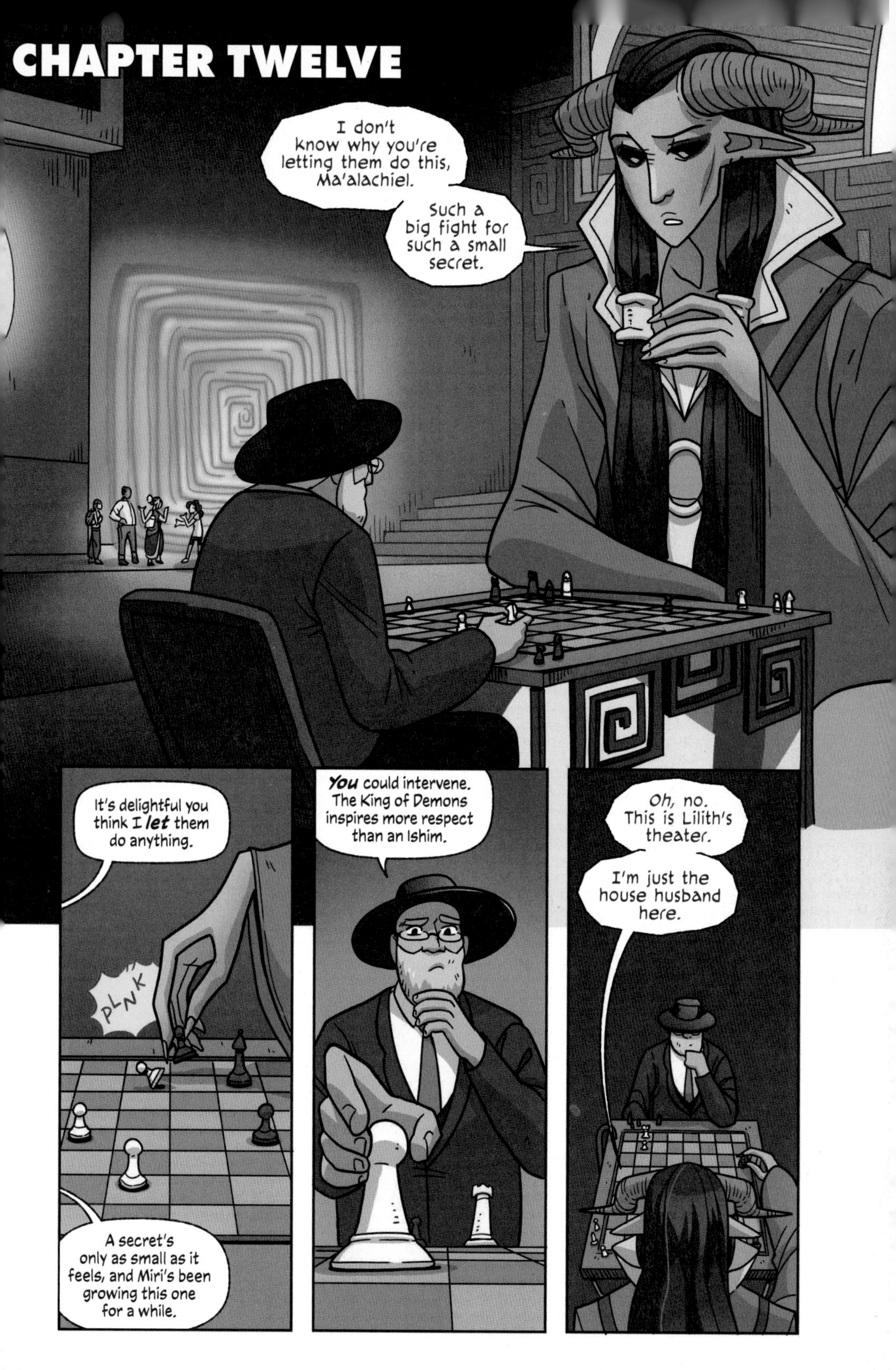

I don't know why you're letting them do this, Ma'alachiel.
Such a big fight for such a small secret.
It's delightful you think I *let* them do anything.
PLNK
A secret's only as small as it feels, and Miri's been growing this one for a while.
You could intervene. The King of Demons inspires more respect than an Ishim.
Oh, no. This is Lilith's theater.
I'm just the house husband here.

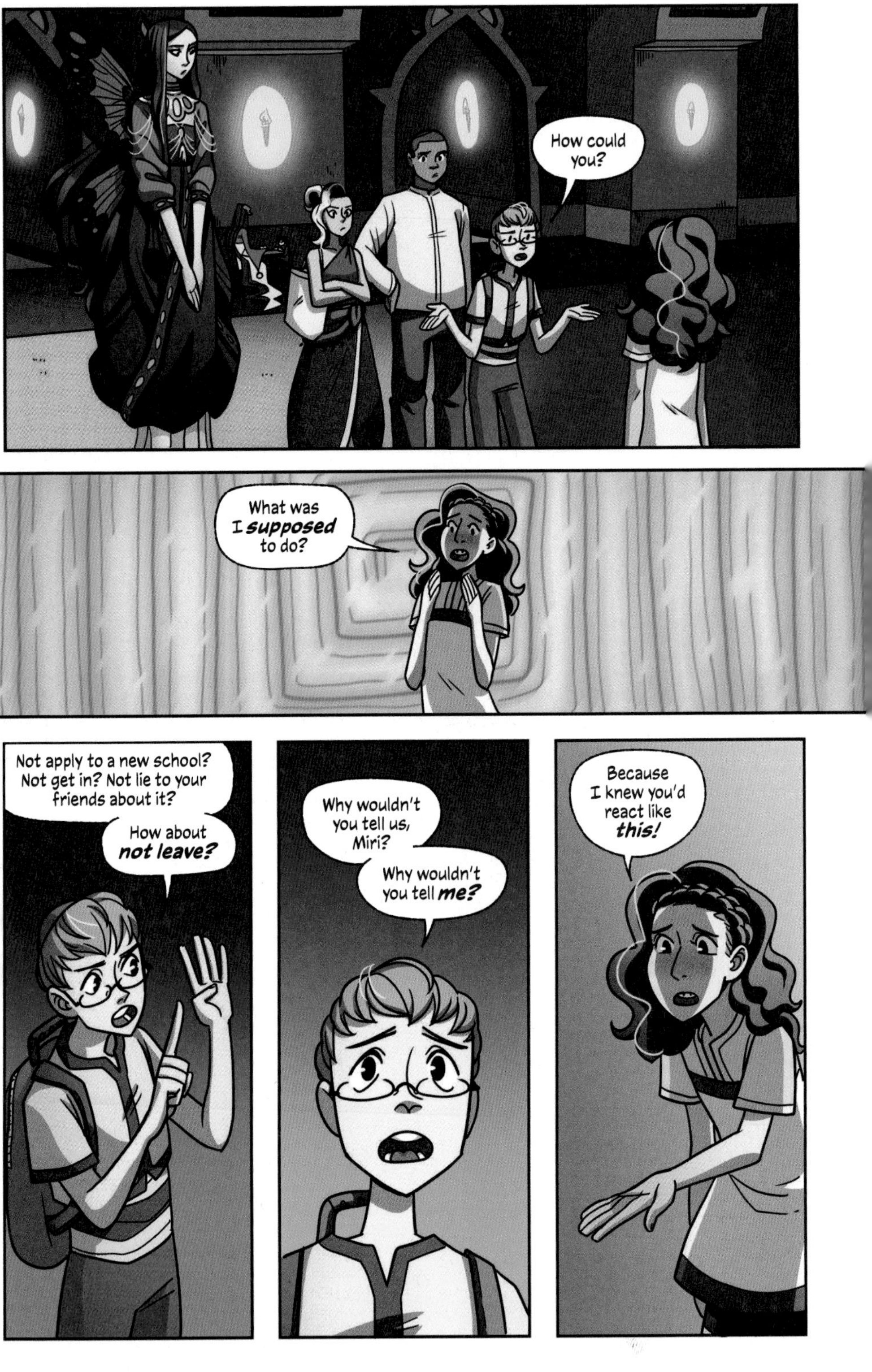
How could you?
What was I supposed to do?
Not apply to a new school? Not get in? Not lie to your friends about it?
How about not leave?
Why wouldn't you tell us, Miri?
Why wouldn't you tell me?
Because I knew you'd react like this!

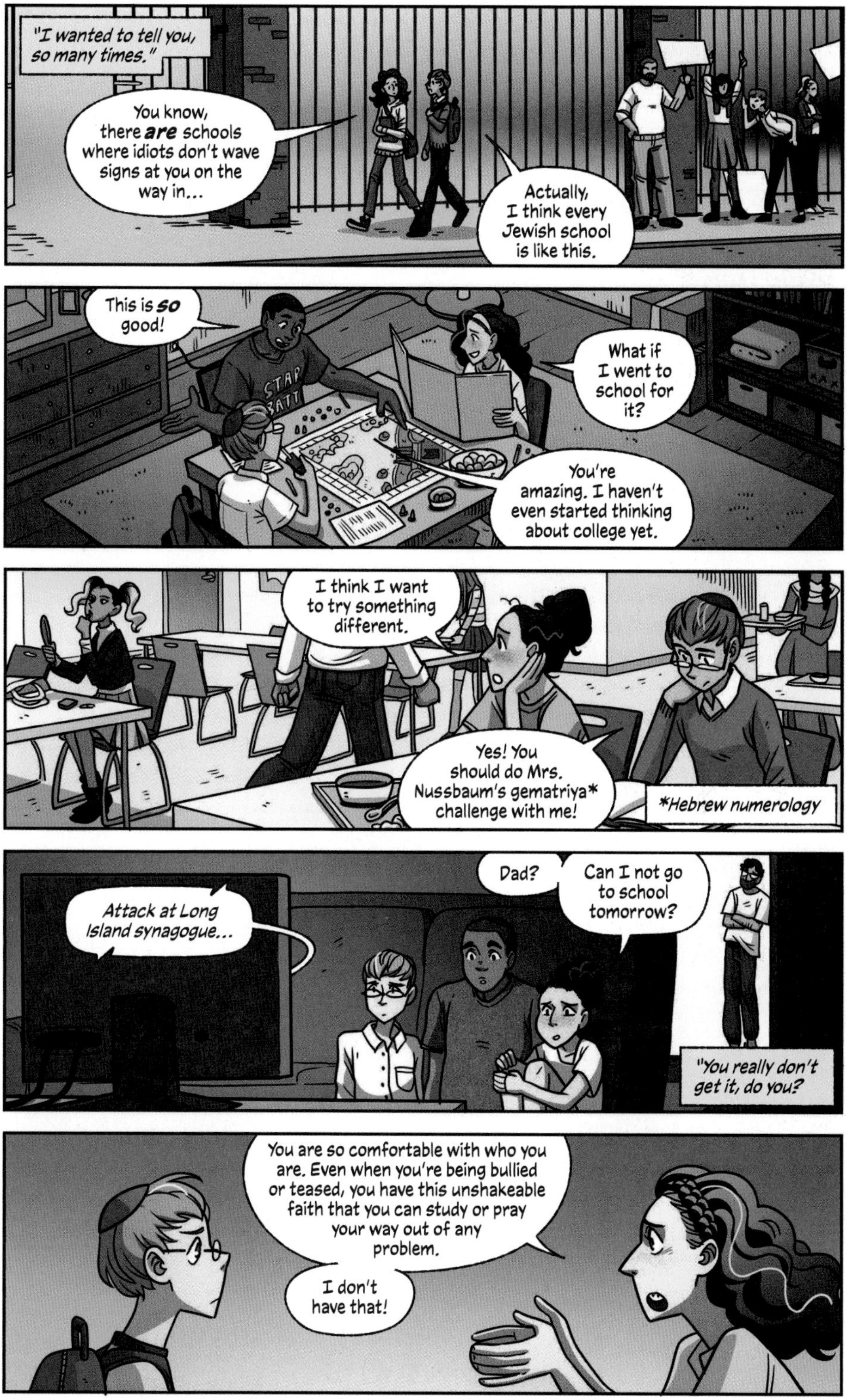
"I wanted to tell you, so many times."
You know, there are schools where idiots don't wave signs at you on the way in...
Actually, I think every Jewish school is like this.
This is so good!
What if I went to school for it?
You're amazing. I haven't even started thinking about college yet.
I think I want to try something different.
Yes! You should do Mrs. Nussbaum's gematriya* challenge with me!
*Hebrew numerology
Attack at Long Island synagogue...
Dad?
Can I not go to school tomorrow?
"You really don't get it, do you?
You are so comfortable with who you are. Even when you're being bullied or teased, you have this unshakeable faith that you can study or pray your way out of any problem.
I don't have that!

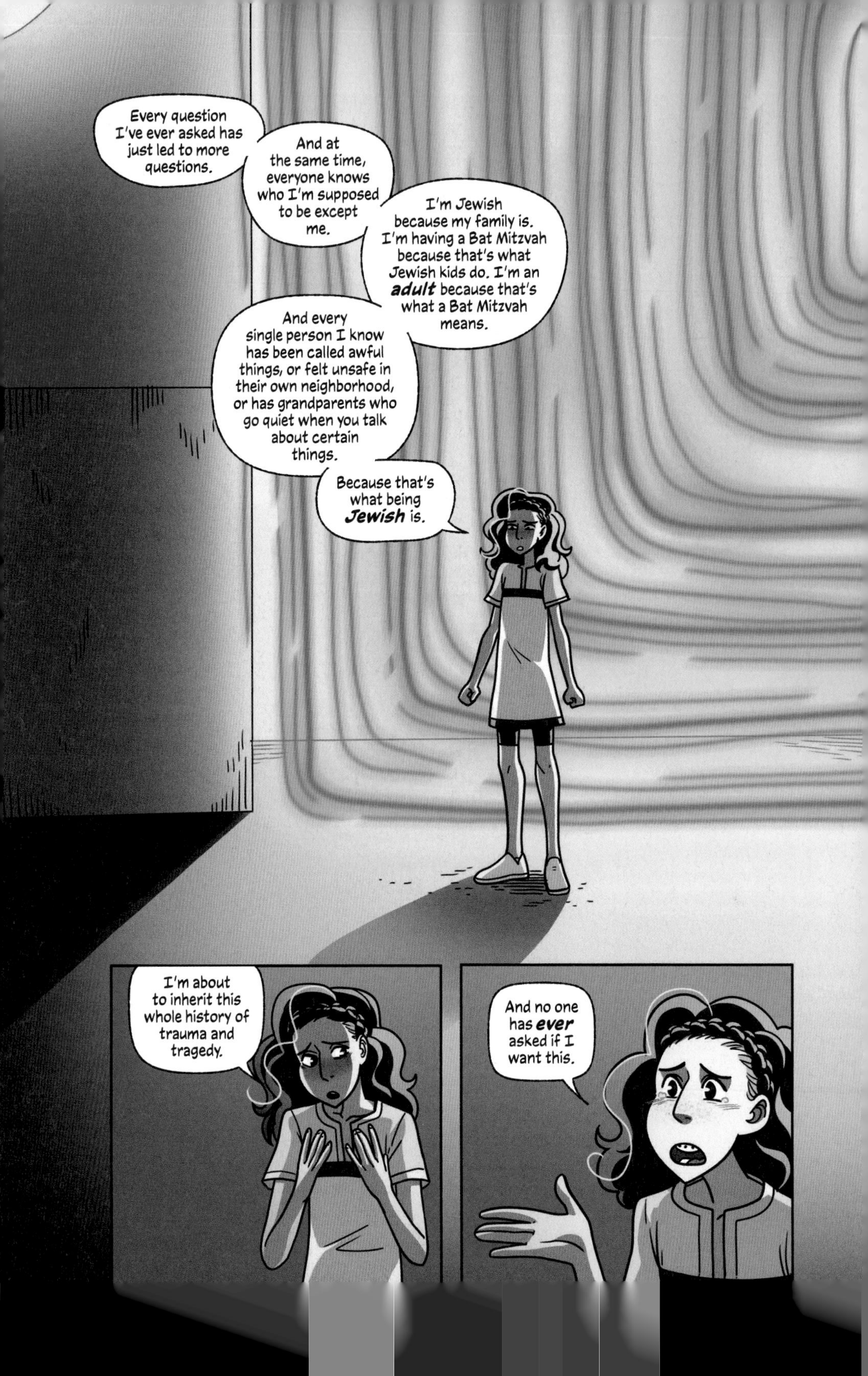
Every question I've ever asked has just led to more questions.
And at the same time, everyone knows who I'm supposed to be except me.
I'm Jewish because my family is. I'm having a Bat Mitzvah because that's what Jewish kids do. I'm an **adult** because that's what a Bat Mitzvah means.
And every single person I know has been called awful things, or felt unsafe in their own neighborhood, or has grandparents who go quiet when you talk about certain things.
Because that's what being **Jewish** is.
I'm about to inherit this whole history of trauma and tragedy.
And no one has **ever** asked if I want this.

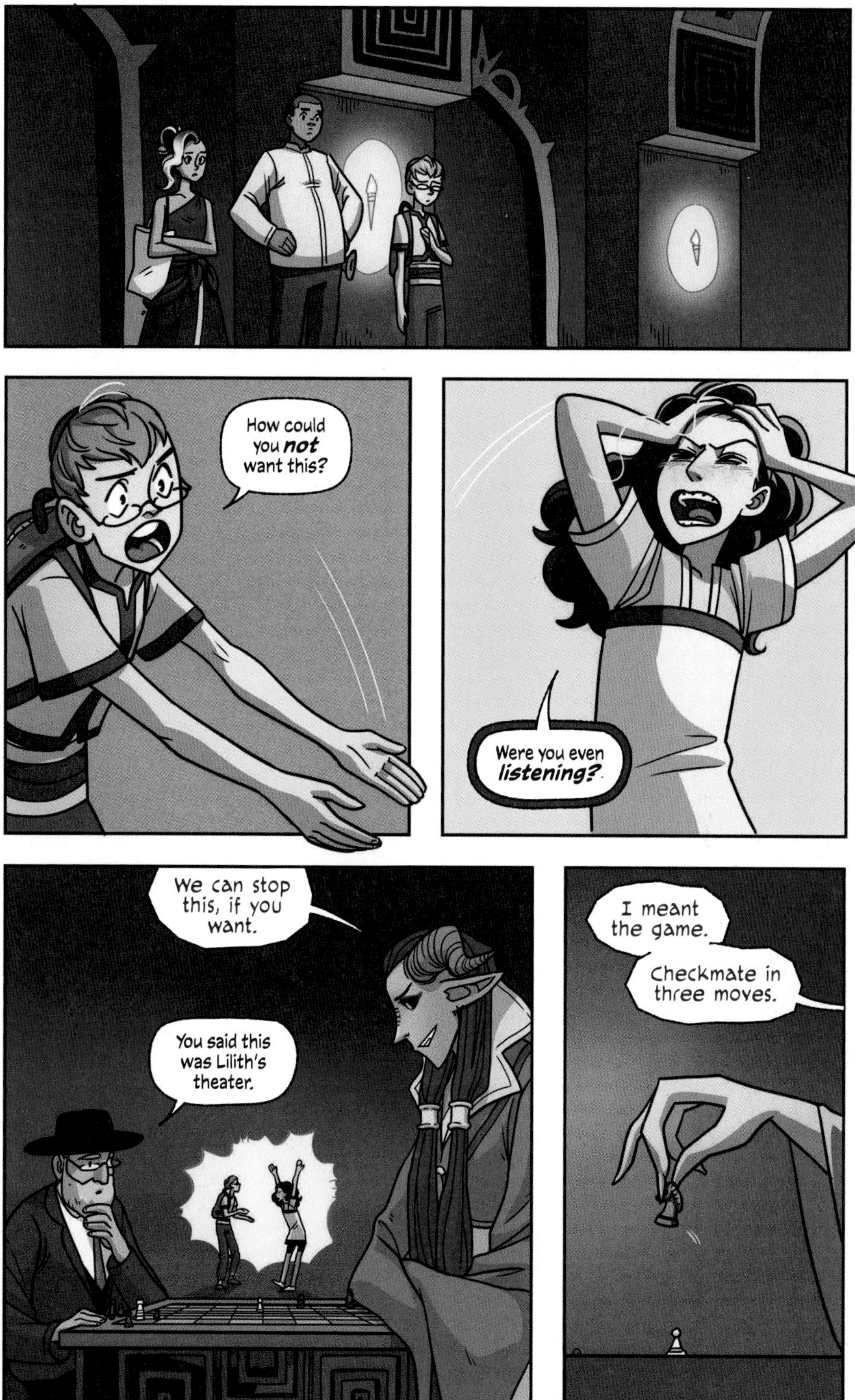
How could you *not* want this?
Were you even *listening?*
We can stop this, if you want.
You said this was Lilith's theater.
I meant the game.
Checkmate in three moves.

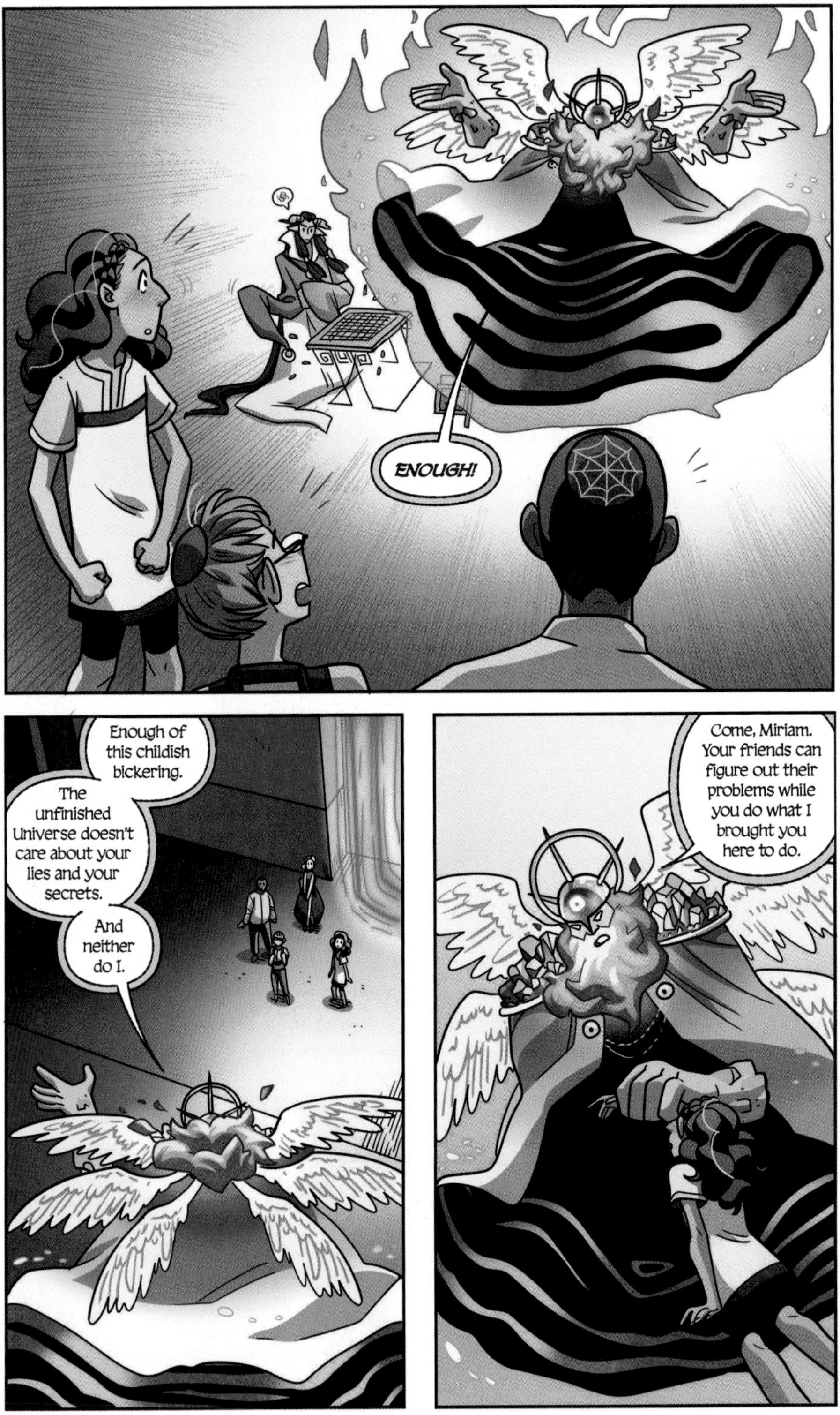
ENOUGH!
Enough of this childish bickering.
The unfinished Universe doesn't care about your lies and your secrets.
And neither do I.
Come, Miriam. Your friends can figure out their problems while you do what I brought you here to do.

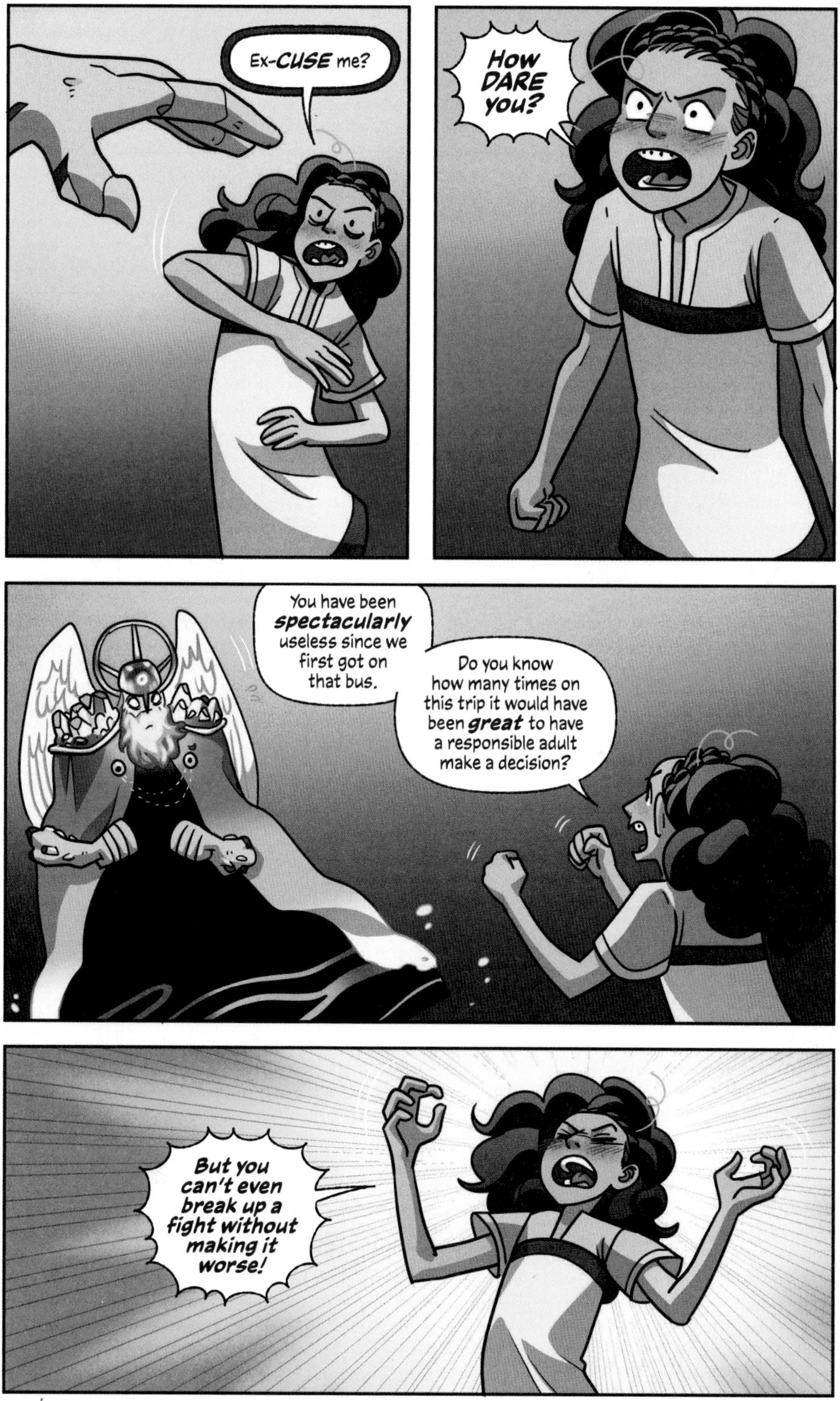
Ex-CUSE me?
How DARE you?
You have been spectacularly useless since we first got on that bus.
Do you know how many times on this trip it would have been great to have a responsible adult make a decision?
But you can't even break up a fight without making it worse!

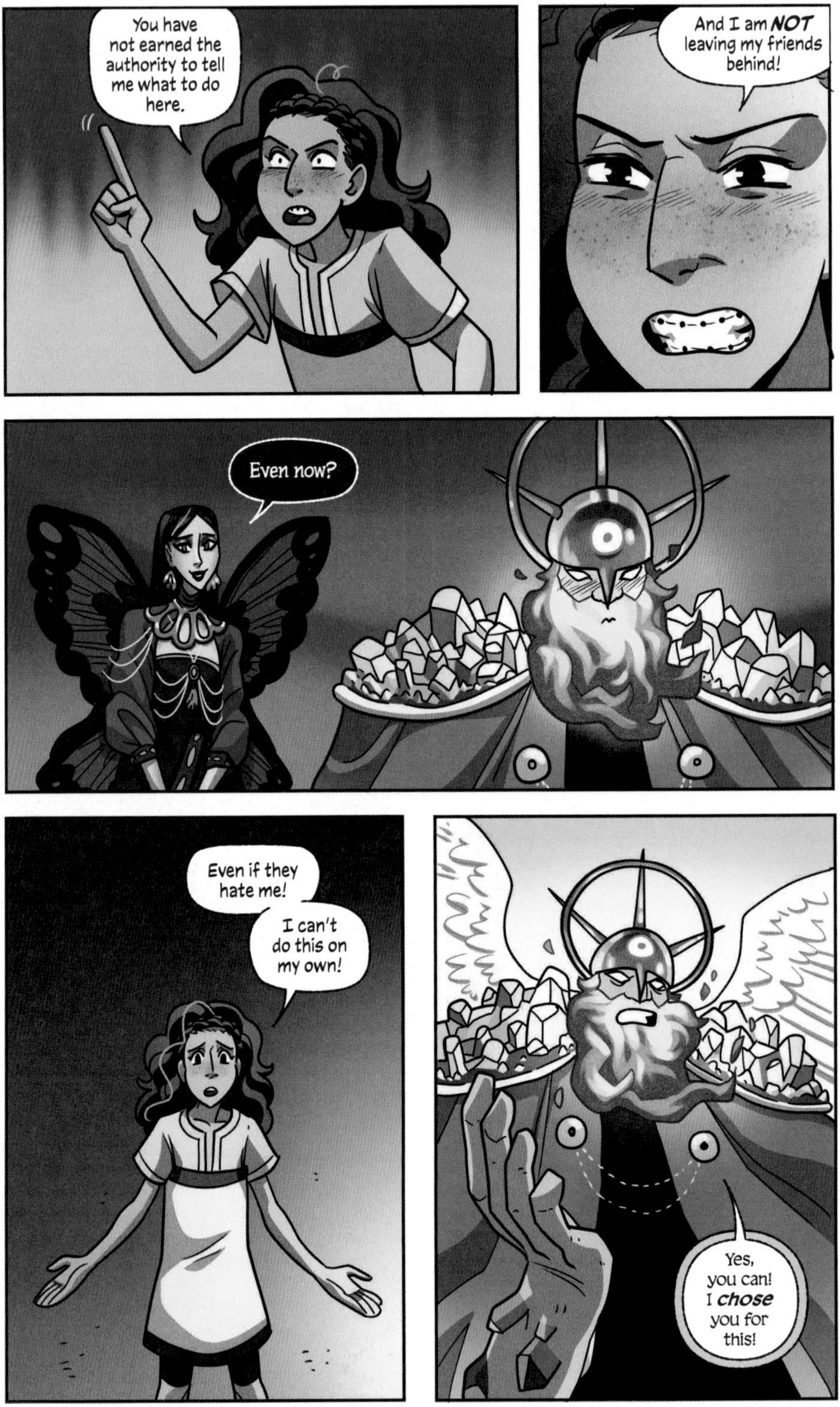
You have not earned the authority to tell me what to do here.
And I am **NOT** leaving my friends behind!
Even now?
Even if they hate me!
I can't do this on my own!
Yes, you can! I ***chose*** you for this!

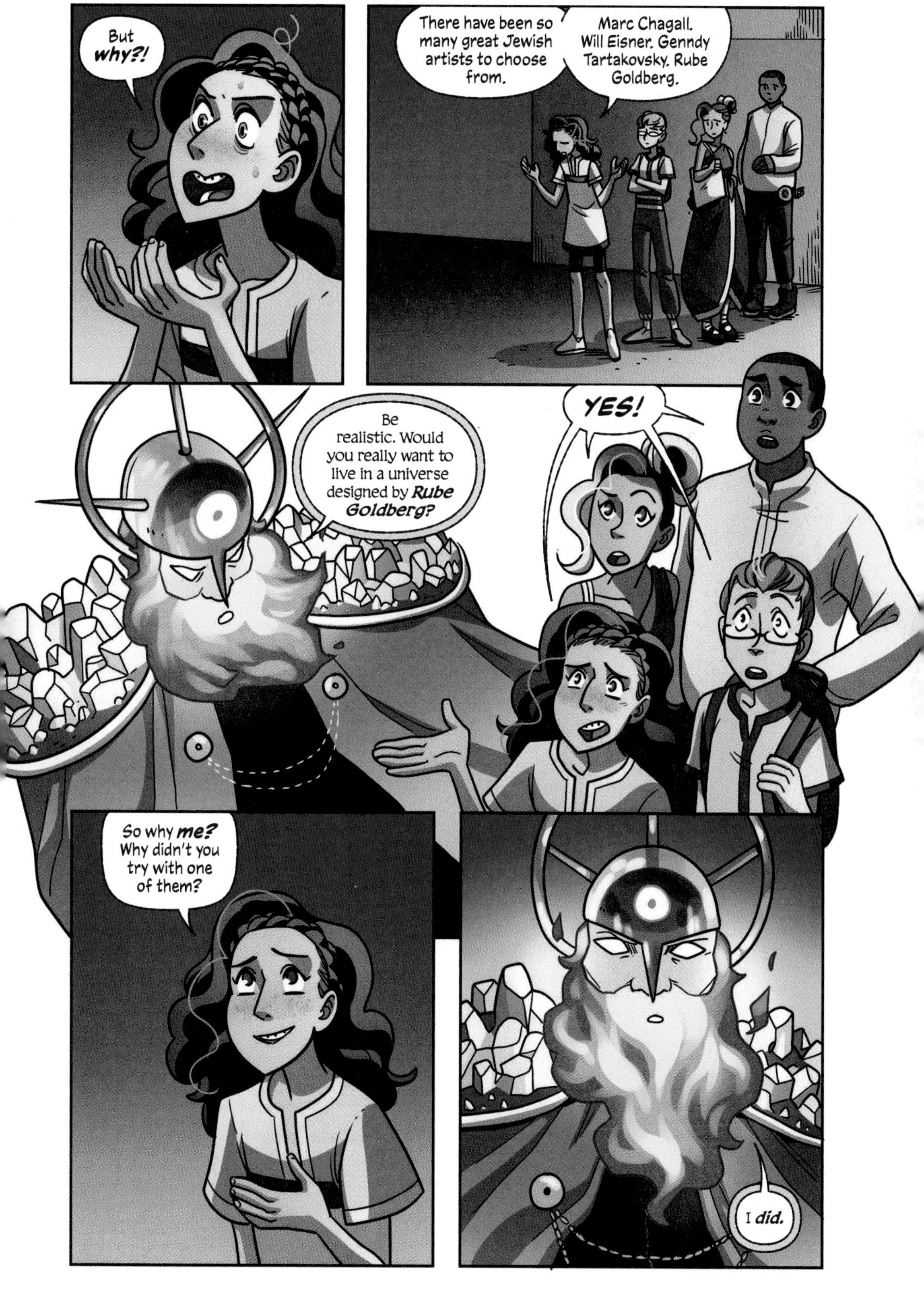
But why?!
There have been so many great Jewish artists to choose from.
Marc Chagall. Will Eisner. Genndy Tartakovsky. Rube Goldberg.
Be realistic. Would you really want to live in a universe designed by Rube Goldberg?
YES!
So why me? Why didn't you try with one of them?
I did.

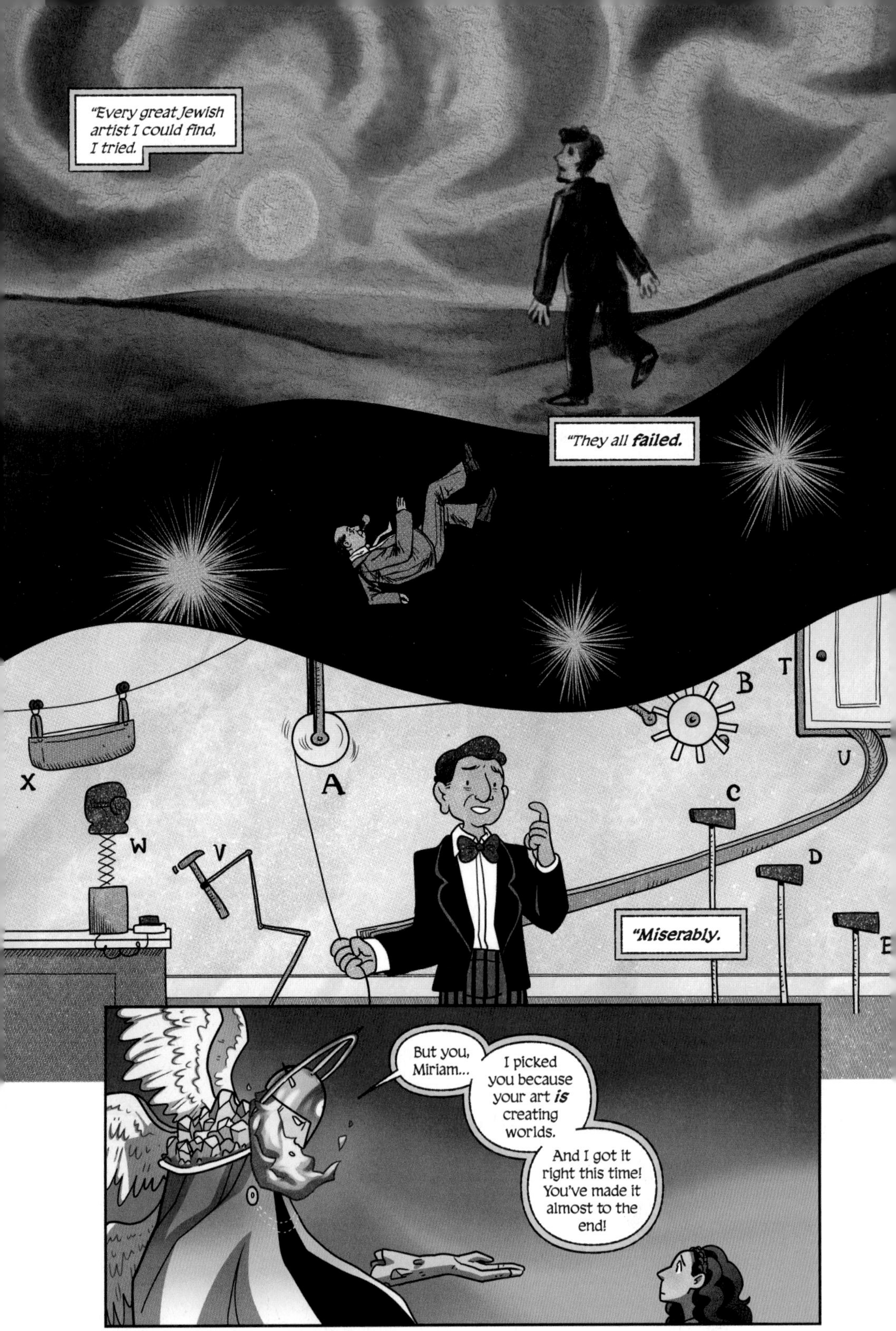
"Every great Jewish artist I could find, I tried.
"They all **failed.**
X
A
B
T
U
W
V
C
D
E
"Miserably.
But you, Miriam...
I picked you because your art ***is*** creating worlds.
And I got it right this time! You've made it almost to the end!

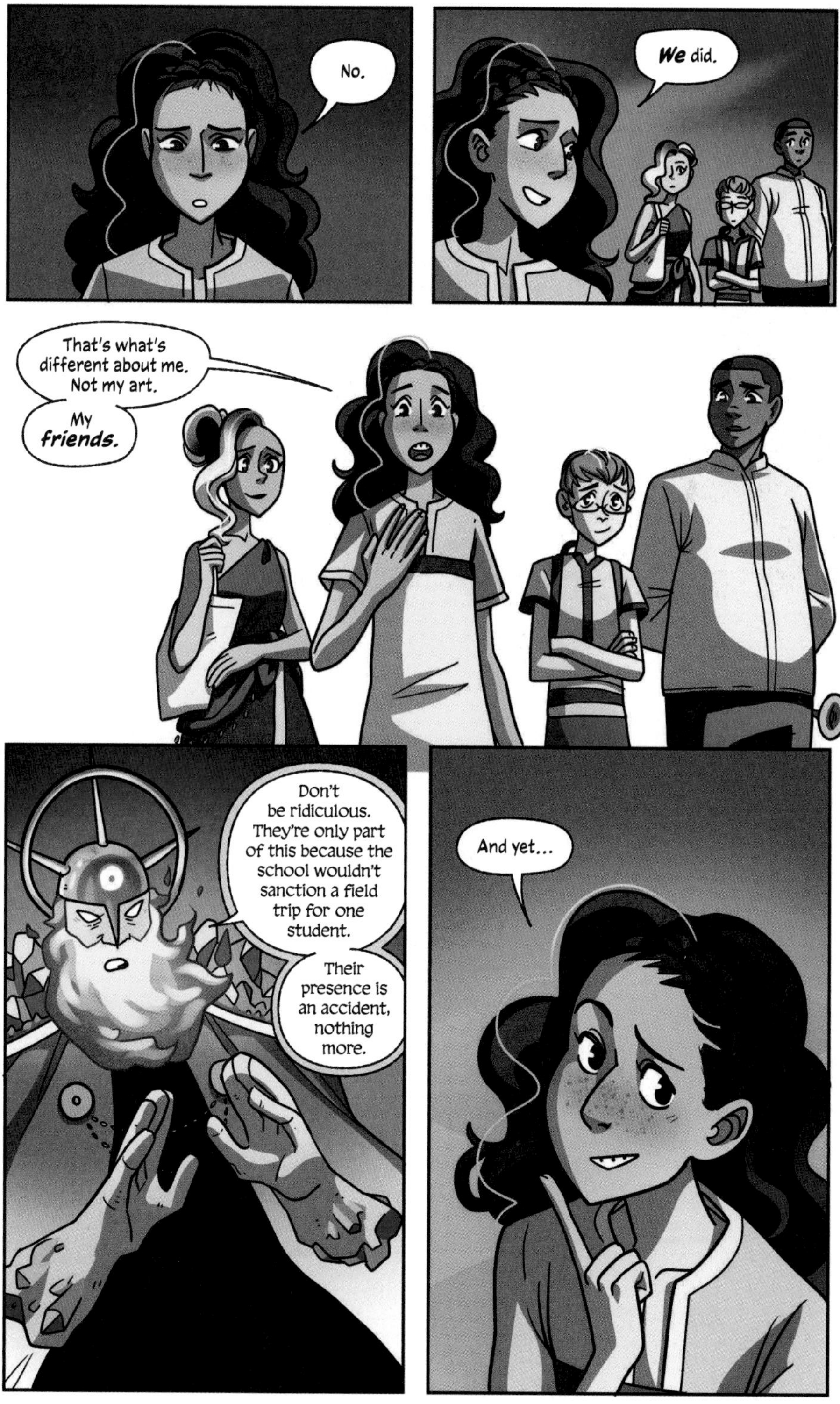
No.
We did.
That's what's different about me. Not my art.
My friends.
Don't be ridiculous. They're only part of this because the school wouldn't sanction a field trip for one student.
Their presence is an accident, nothing more.
And yet...

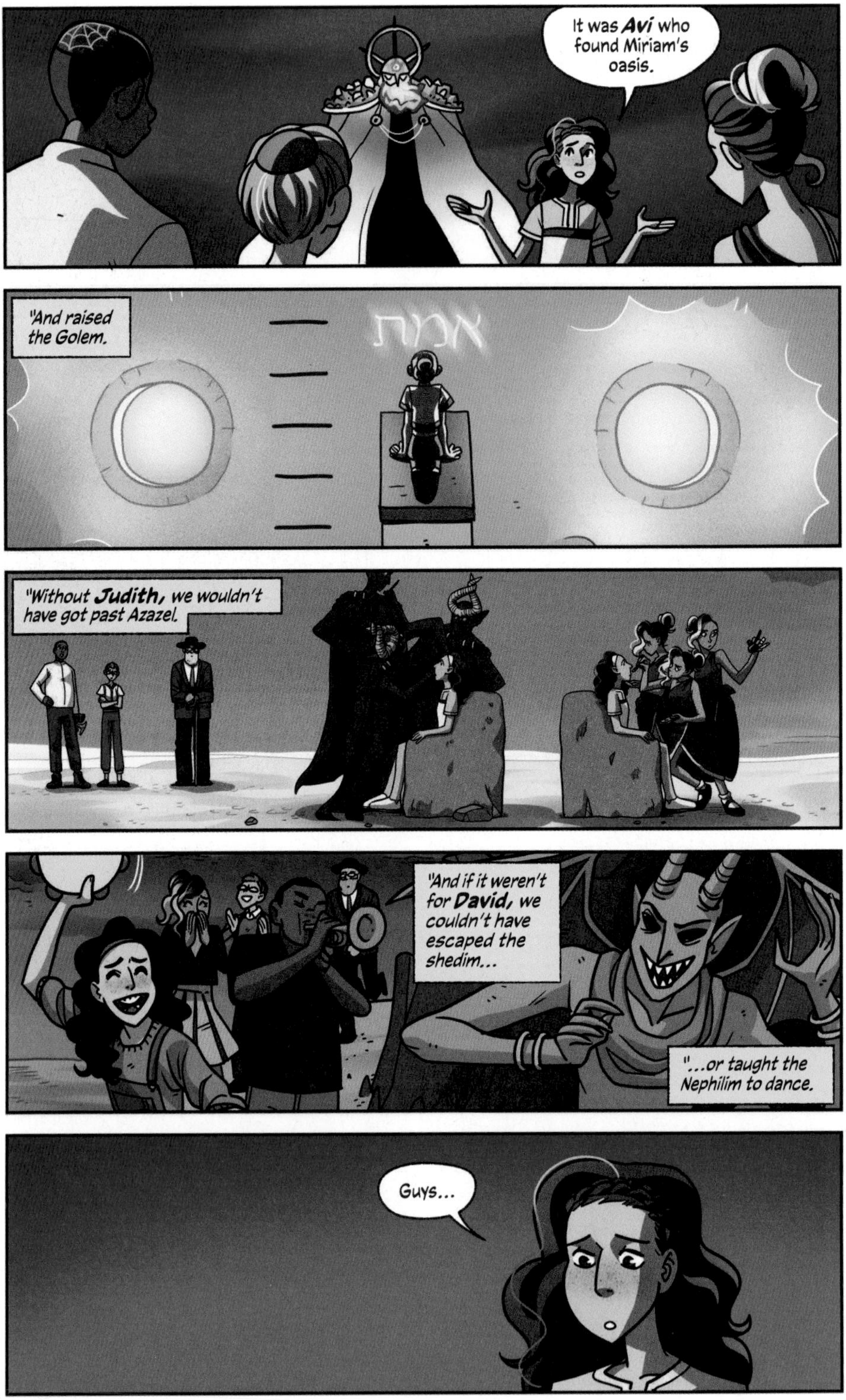
It was Avi who found Miriam's oasis.
"And raised the Golem.
אמת
"Without Judith, we wouldn't have got past Azazel.
"And if it weren't for David, we couldn't have escaped the shedim...
"...or taught the Nephilim to dance.
Guys...

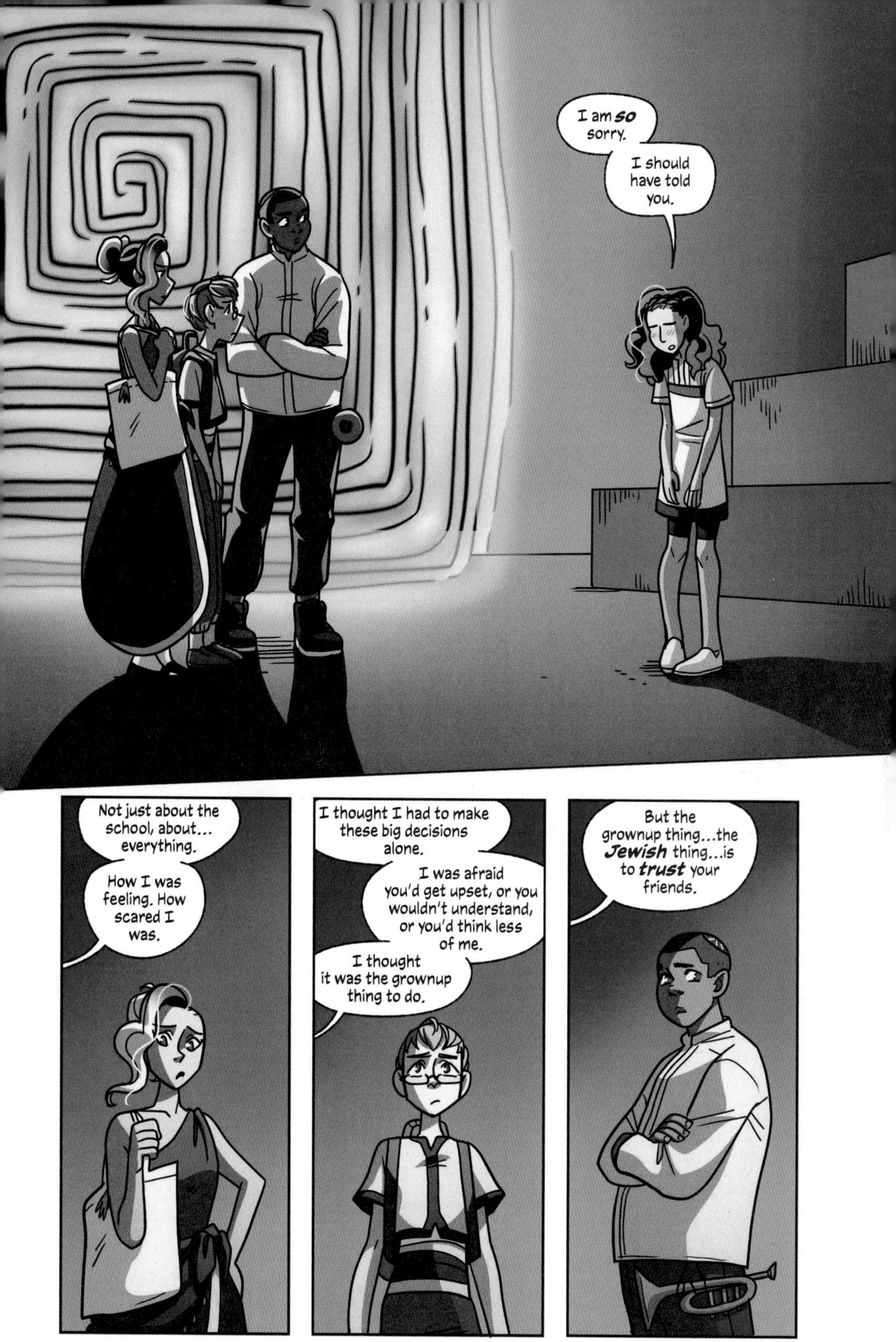
I am SO sorry.
I should have told you.
Not just about the school, about... everything.
How I was feeling. How scared I was.
I thought I had to make these big decisions alone.
I was afraid you'd get upset, or you wouldn't understand, or you'd think less of me.
I thought it was the grownup thing to do.
But the grownup thing...the *Jewish* thing...is to *trust* your friends.

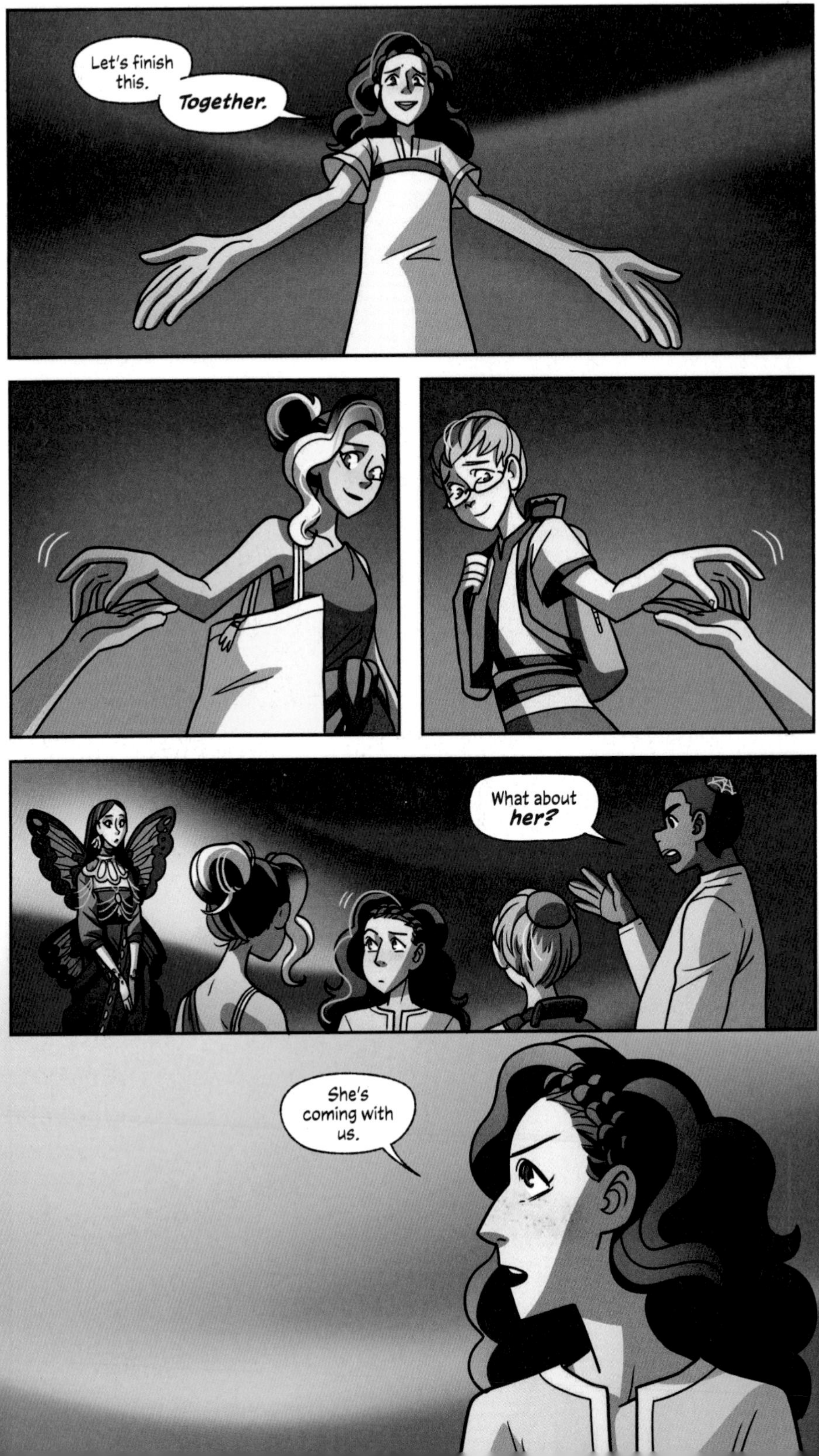
Let's finish this.
Together.
What about *her?*
She's coming with us.

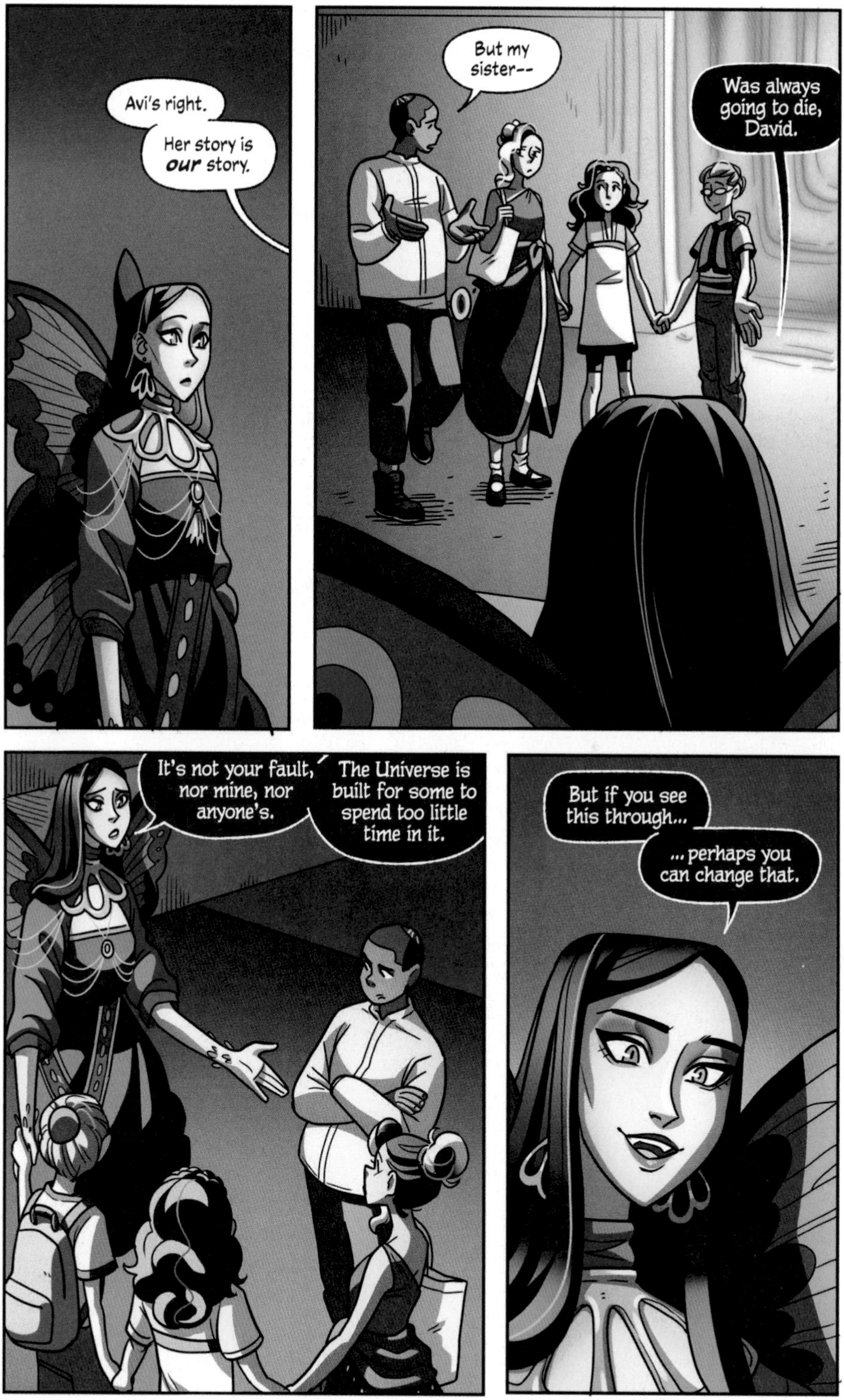
Avi's right.
Her story is *our* story.
But my sister--
Was always going to die, David.
It's not your fault, nor mine, nor anyone's.
The Universe is built for some to spend too little time in it.
But if you see this through...
...perhaps you can change that.

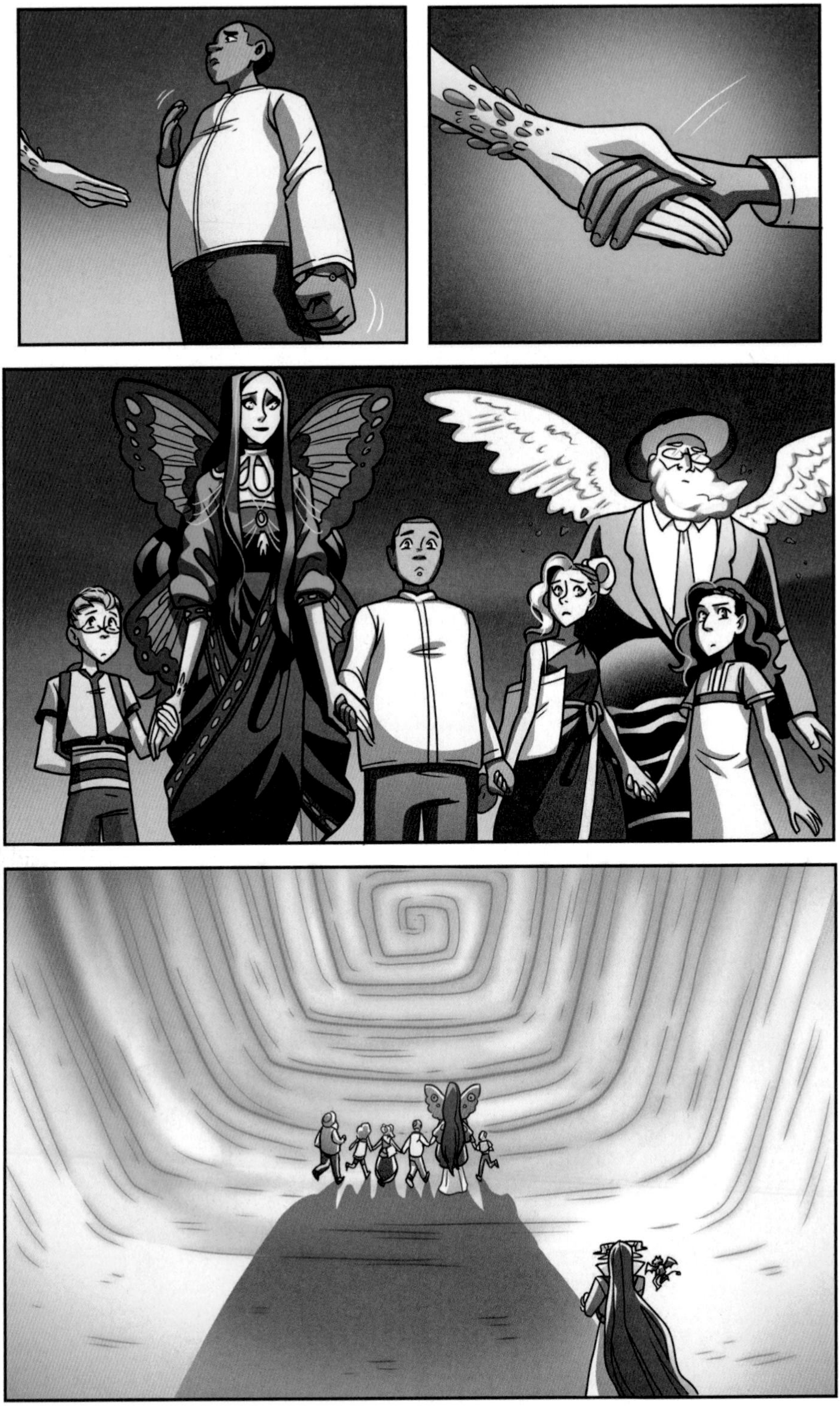

CHAPTER THIRTEEN

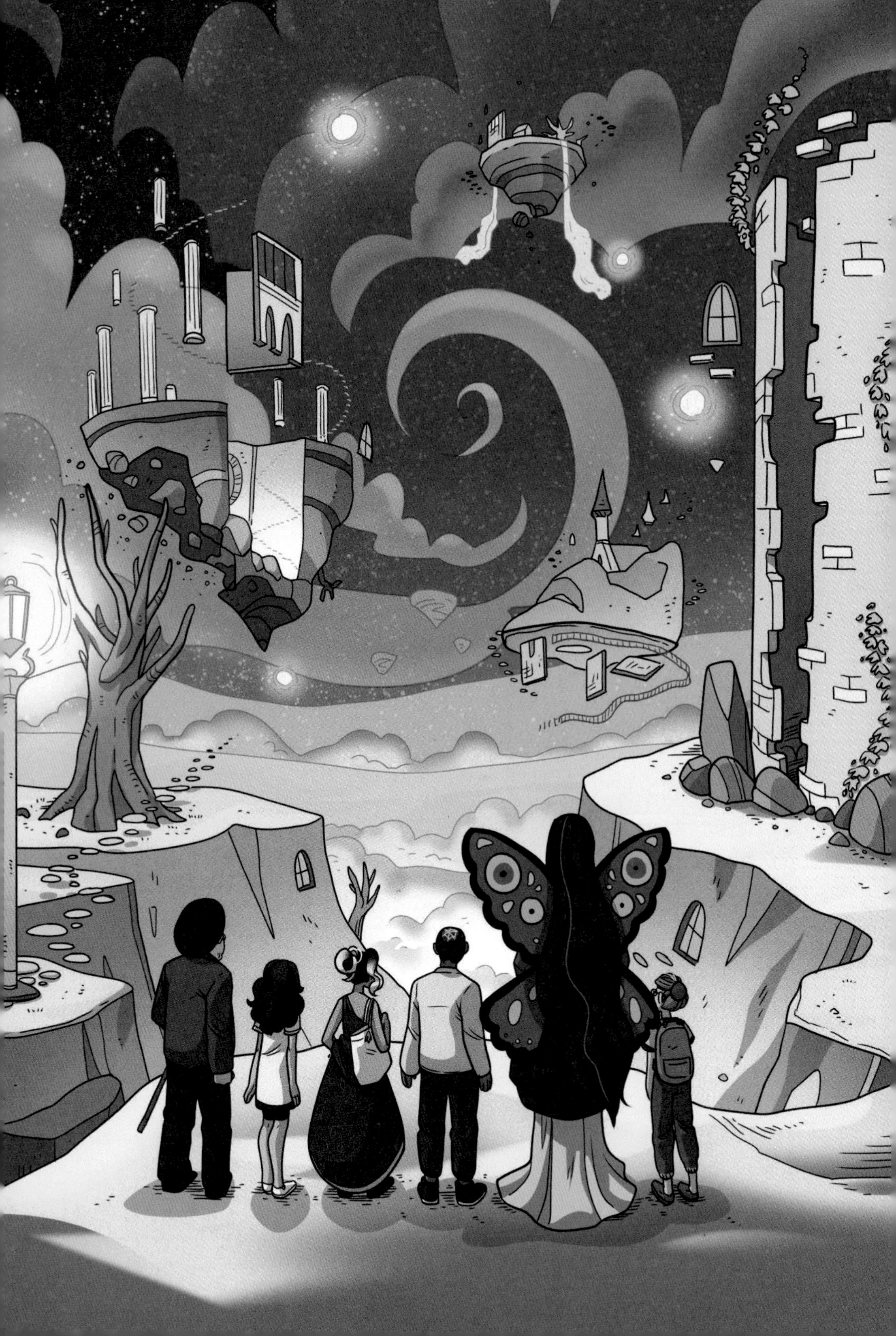

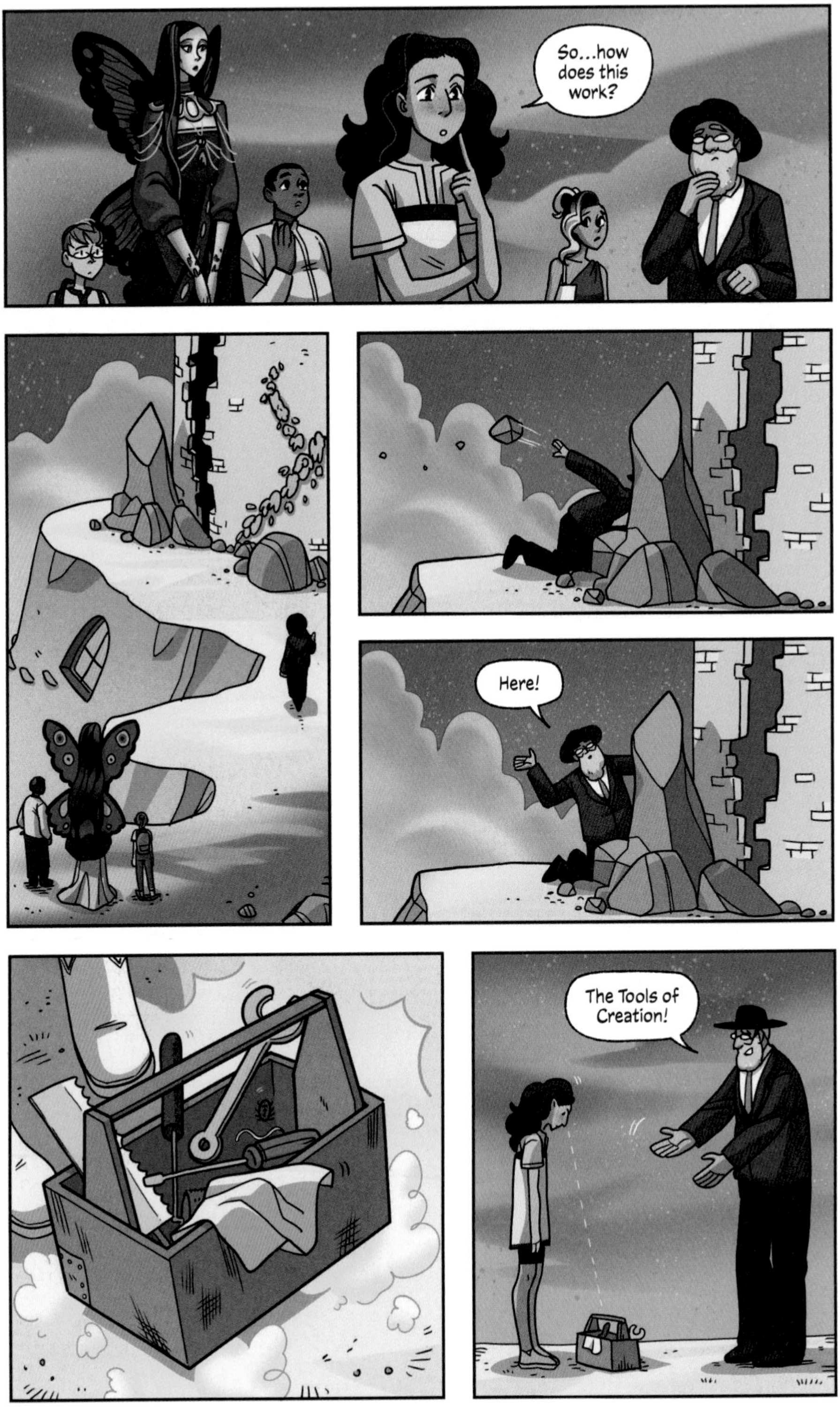
So...how does this work?
Here!
The Tools of Creation!

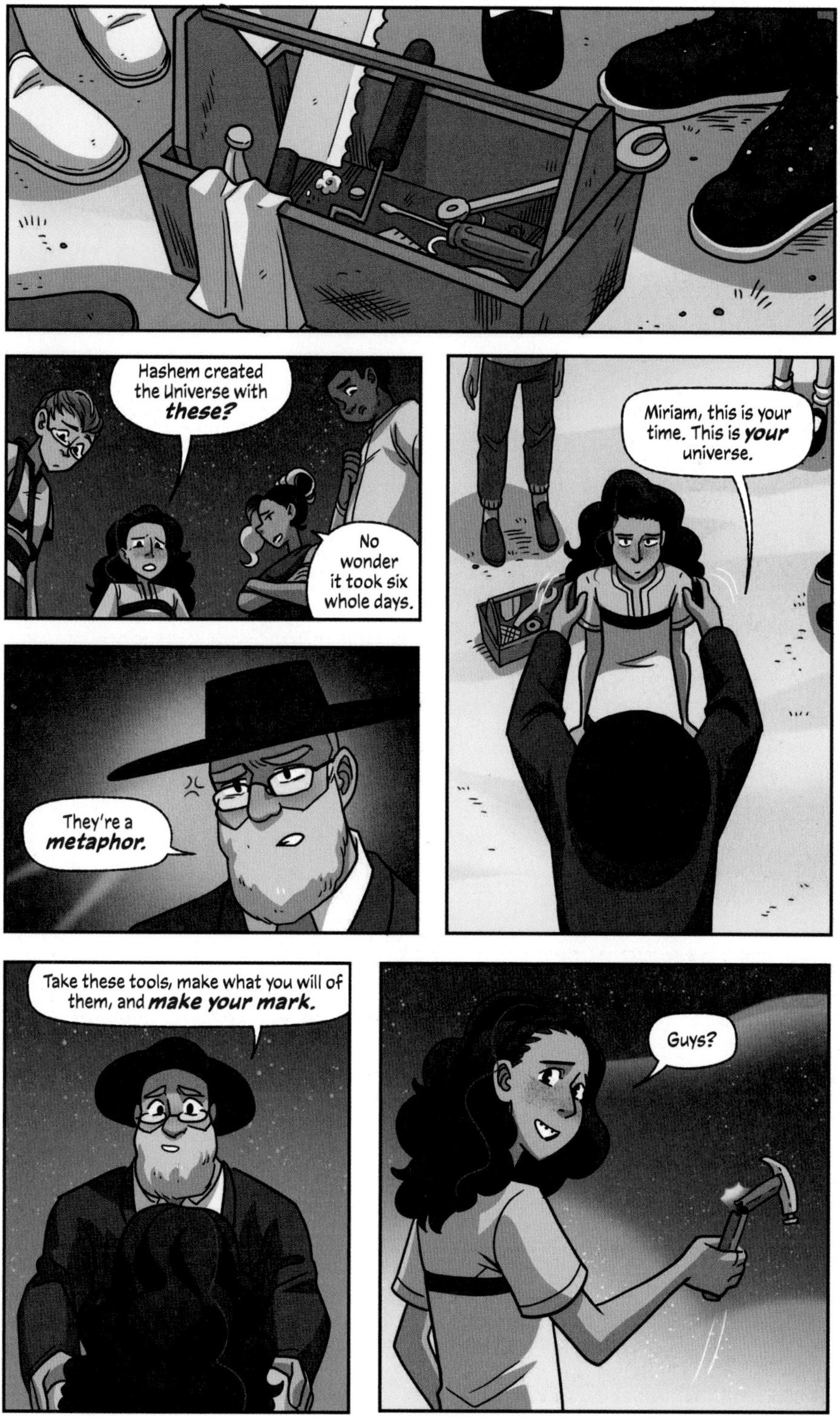
Hashem created the Universe with these?
No wonder it took six whole days.
Miriam, this is your time. This is your universe.
They're a metaphor.
Take these tools, make what you will of them, and make your mark.
Guys?

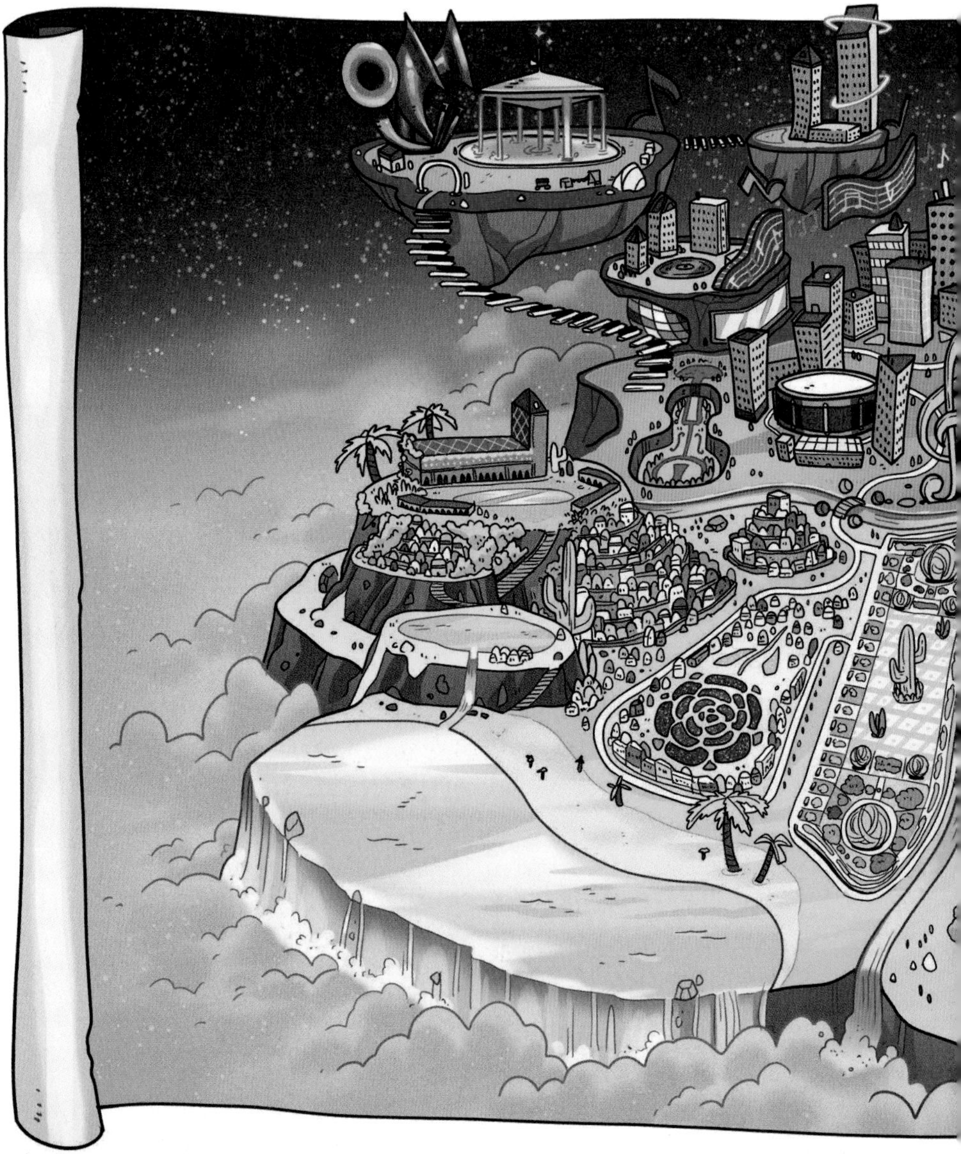

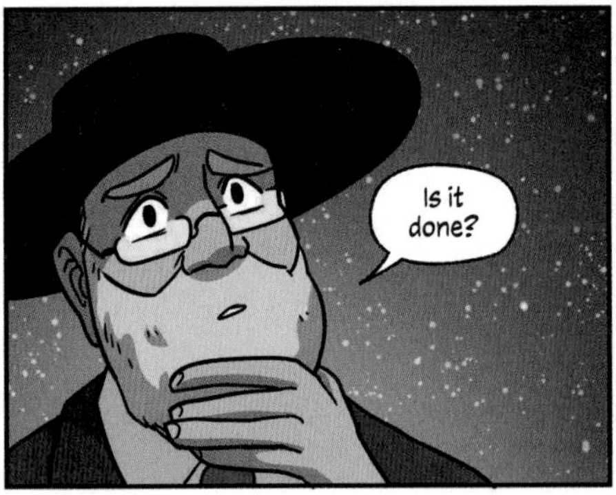
Is it
done?

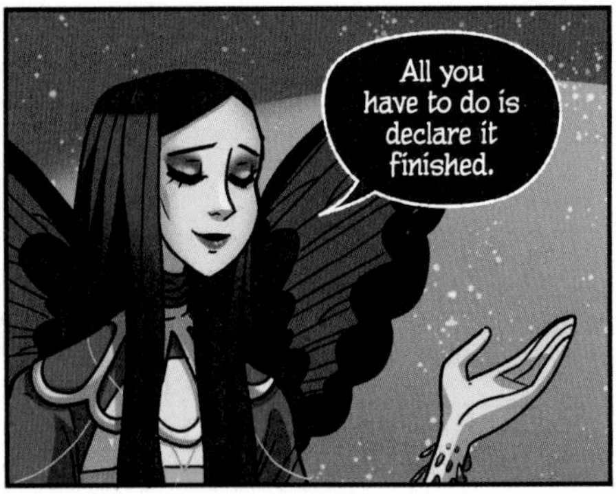
All you
have to do is
declare it
finished.

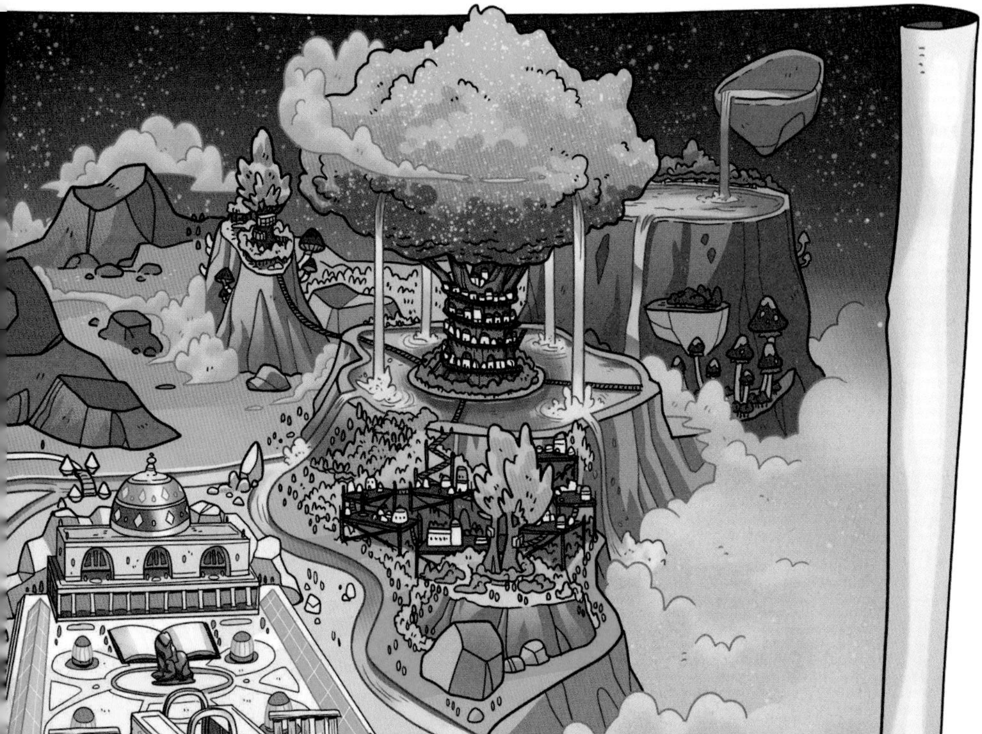
K
X
I
O

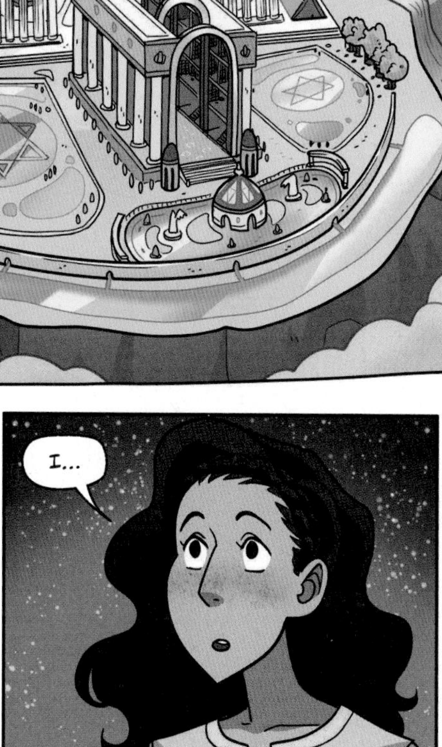
I...

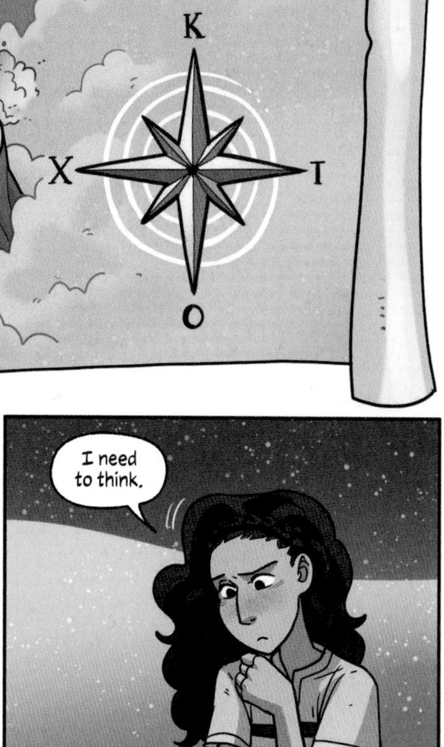
I need to think.

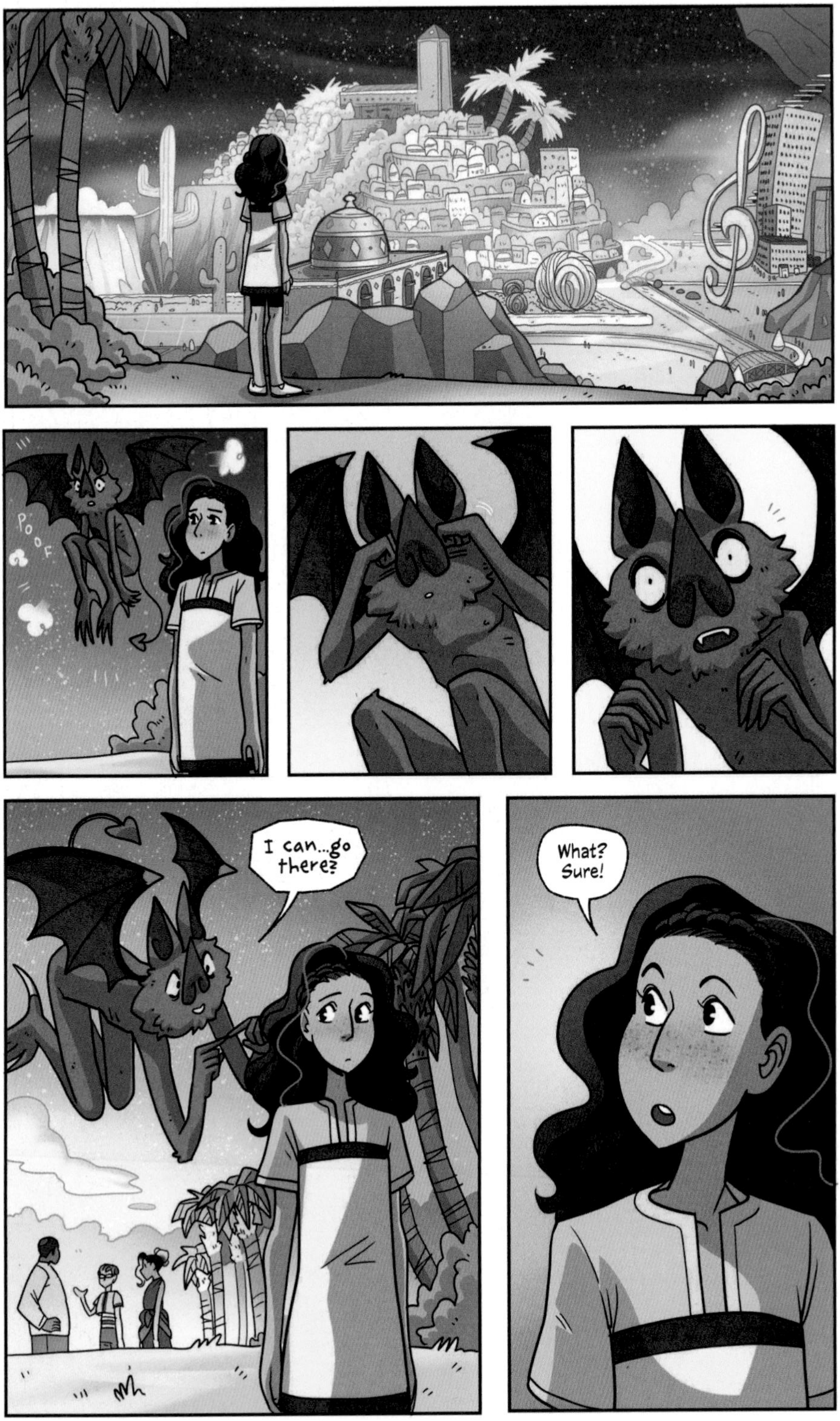
POOF
I can...go there?
What? Sure!

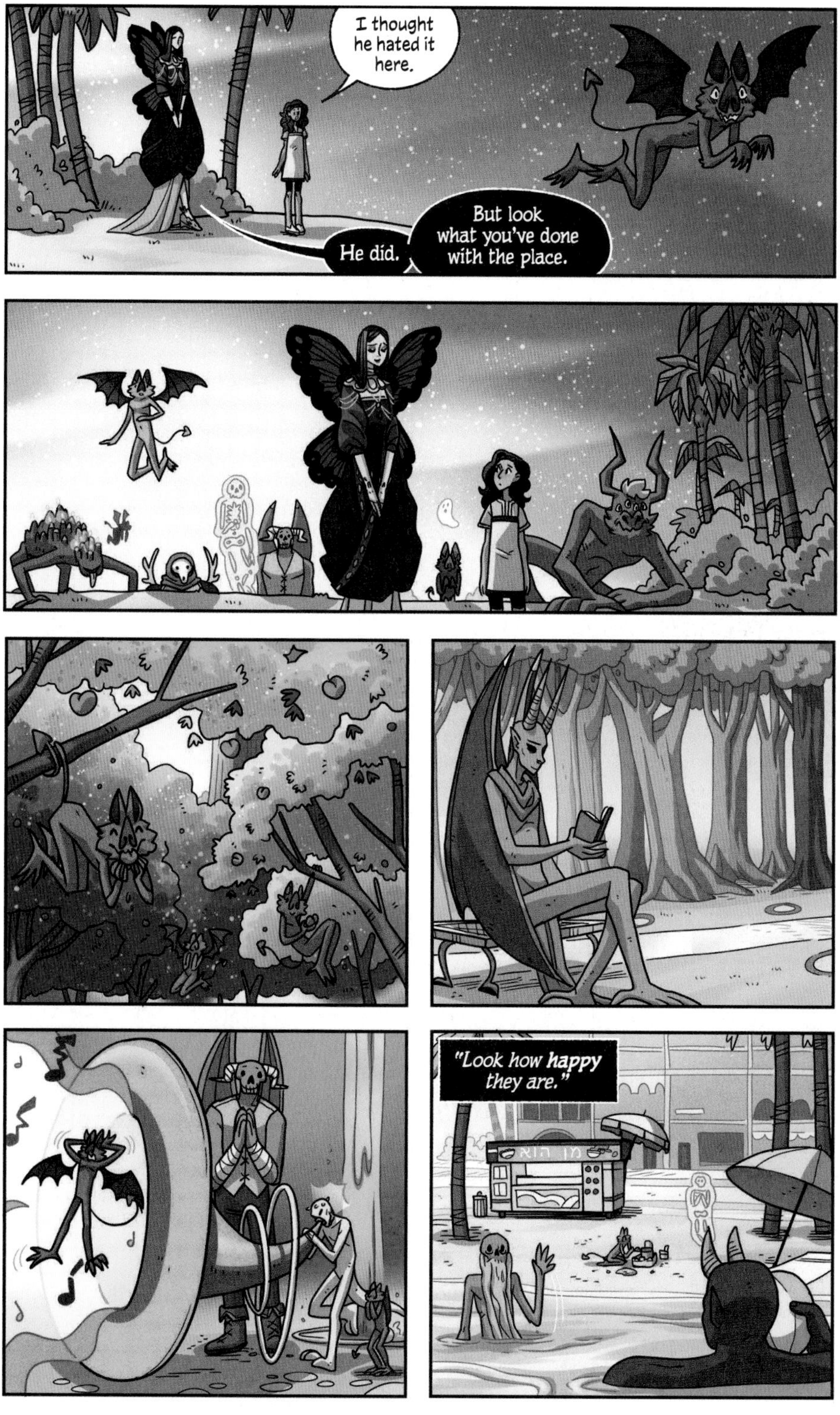

I thought he hated it here.
He did.
But look what you've done with the place.
"Look how **happy** they are."
מן הוא

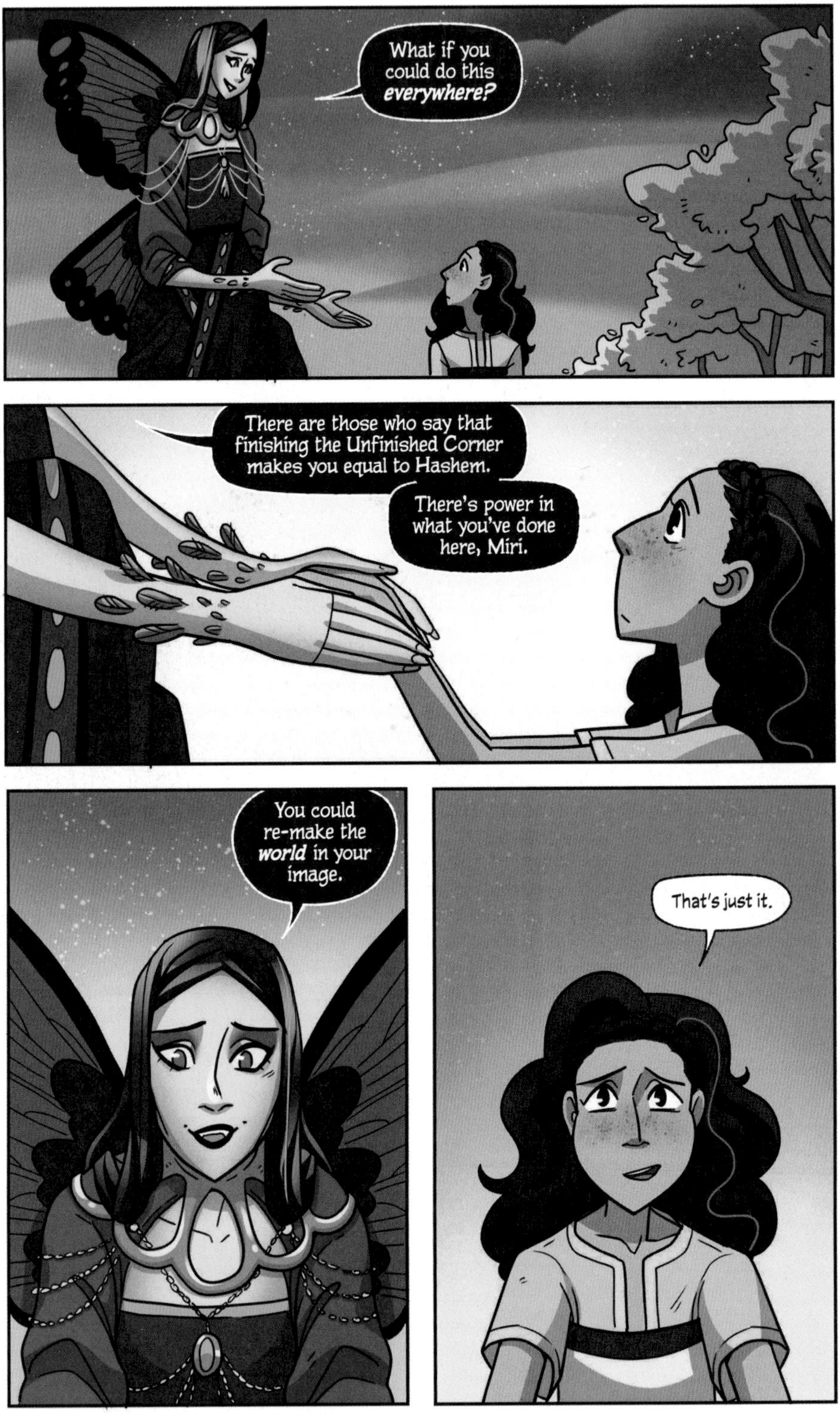
What if you could do this *everywhere?*
There are those who say that finishing the Unfinished Corner makes you equal to Hashem.
There's power in what you've done here, Miri.
You could re-make the *world* in your image.
That's just it.

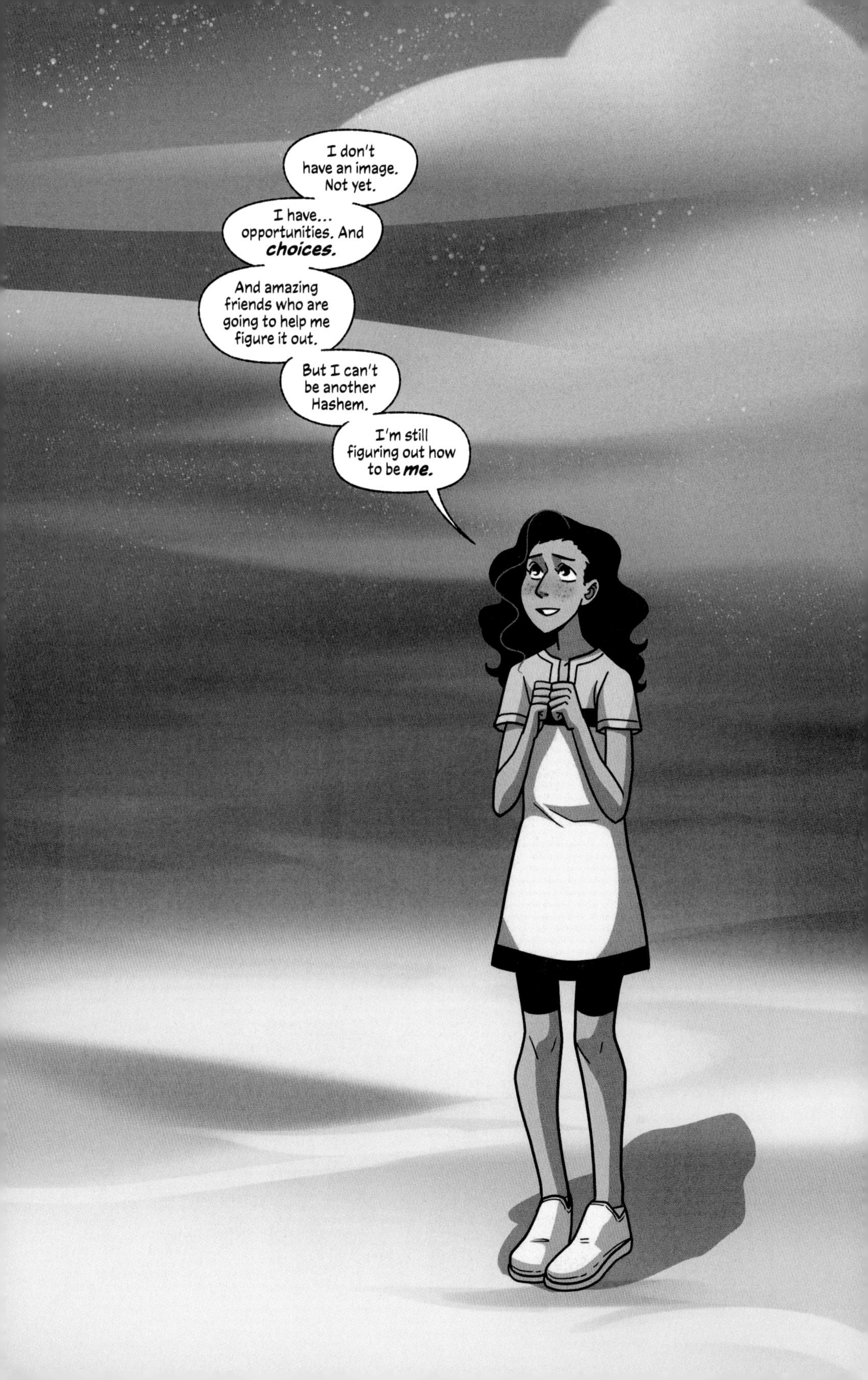
I don't have an image. Not yet.
I have... opportunities. And *choices.*
And amazing friends who are going to help me figure it out.
But I can't be another Hashem.
I'm still figuring out how to be *me.*

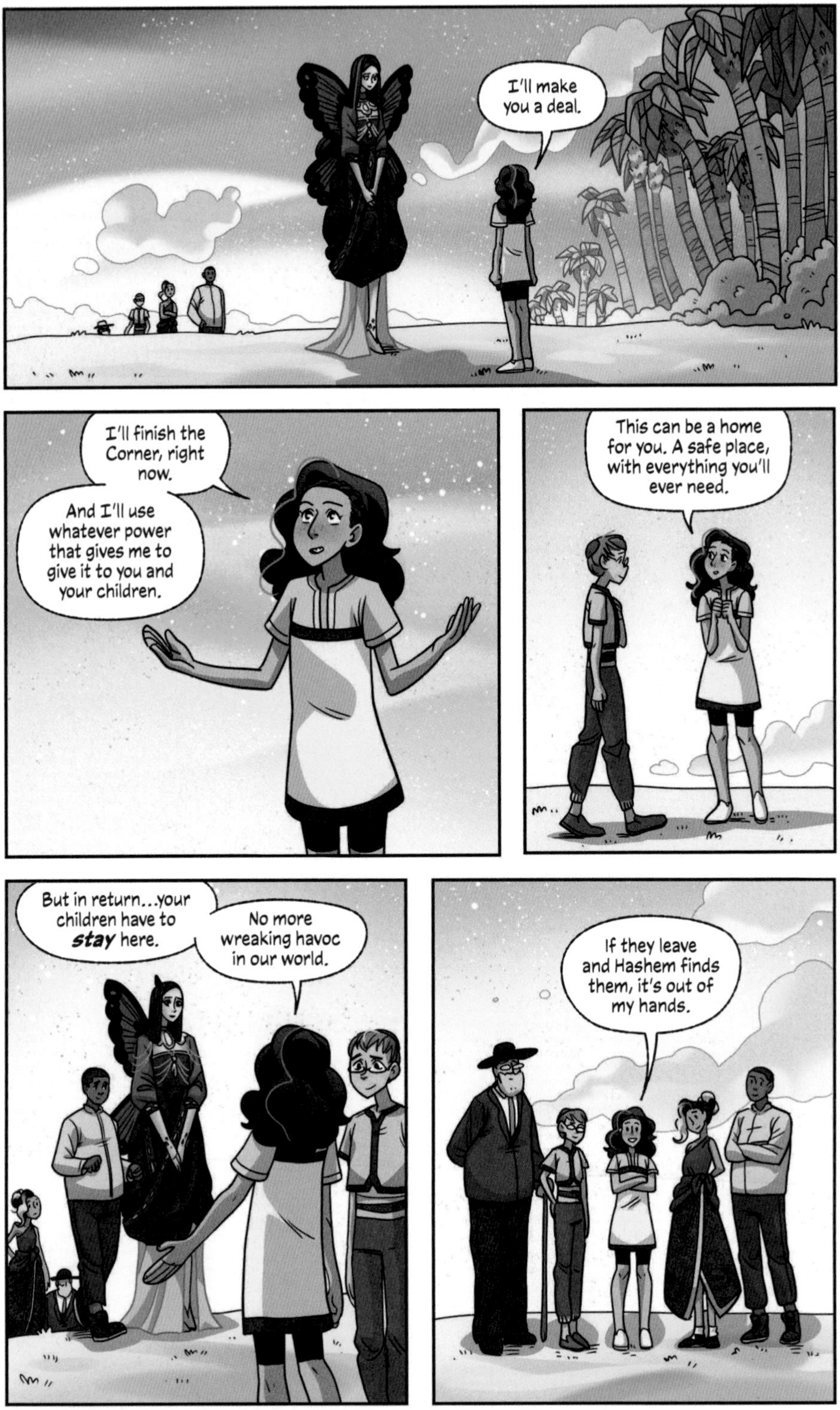
I'll make you a deal.
I'll finish the Corner, right now.
And I'll use whatever power that gives me to give it to you and your children.
This can be a home for you. A safe place, with everything you'll ever need.
But in return...your children have to stay here.
No more wreaking havoc in our world.
If they leave and Hashem finds them, it's out of my hands.

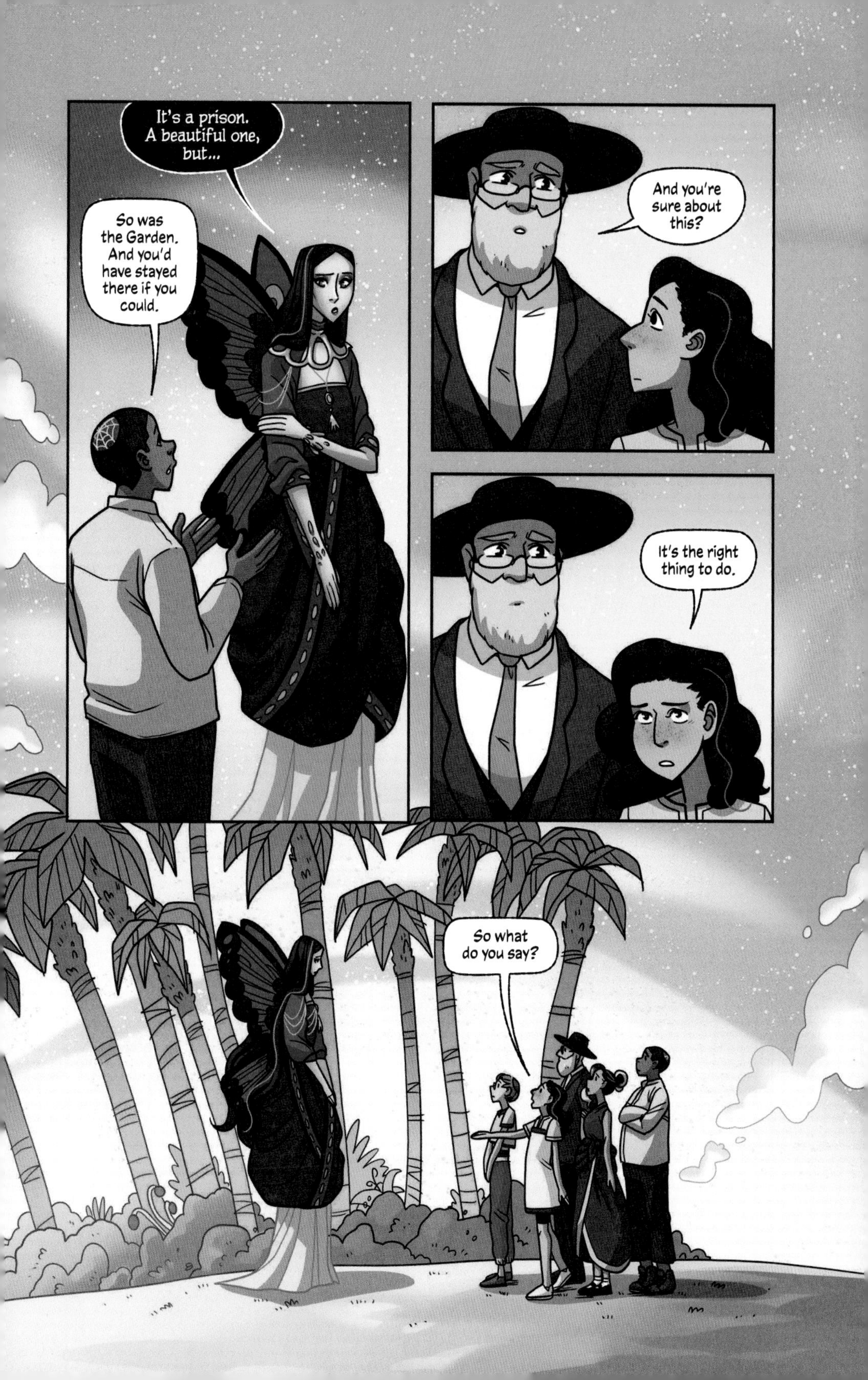
It's a prison. A beautiful one, but...
So was the Garden. And you'd have stayed there if you could.
And you're sure about this?
It's the right thing to do.
So what do you say?

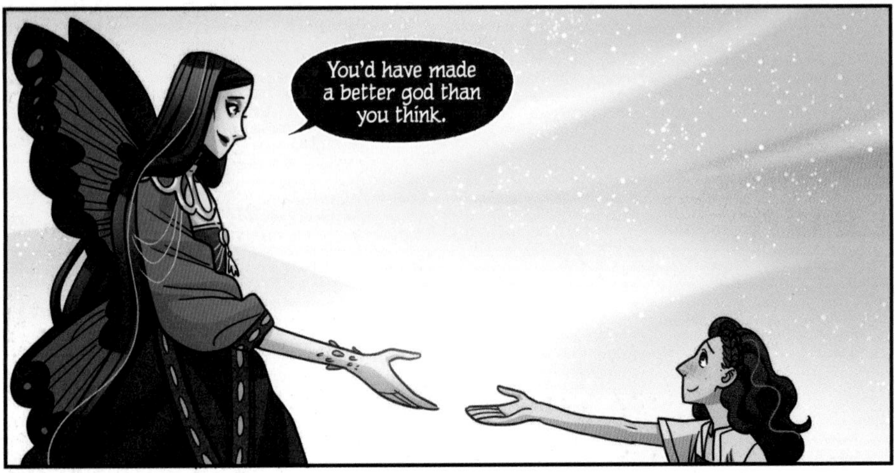
You'd have made a better god than you think.

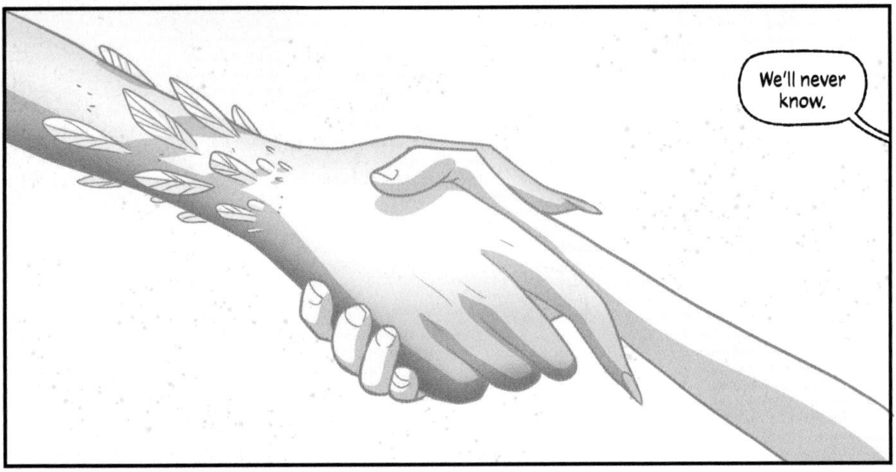
We'll never know.

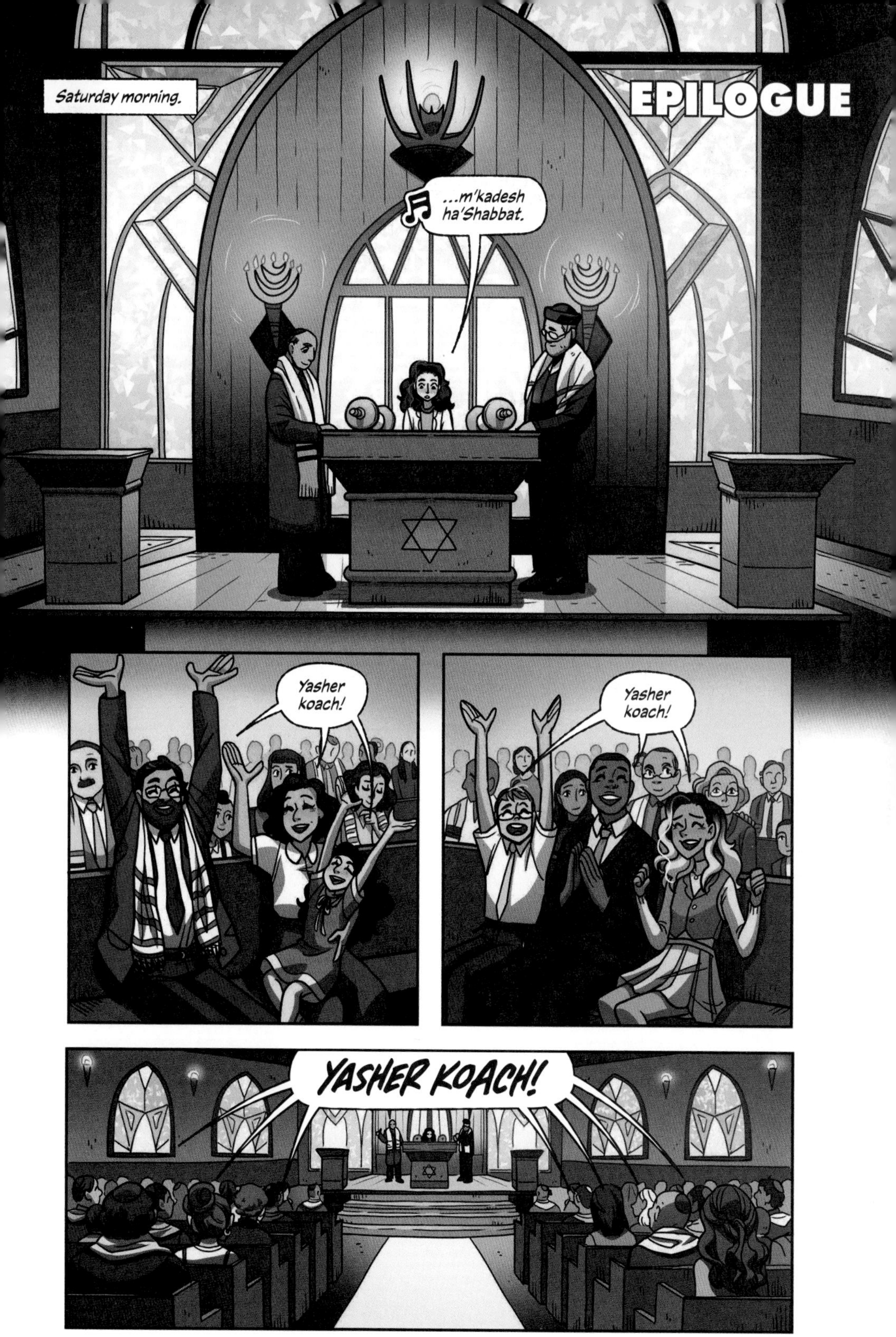

Saturday morning.
EPILOGUE
...m'kadesh ha'Shabbat.
Yasher koach!
Yasher koach!
YASHER KOACH!

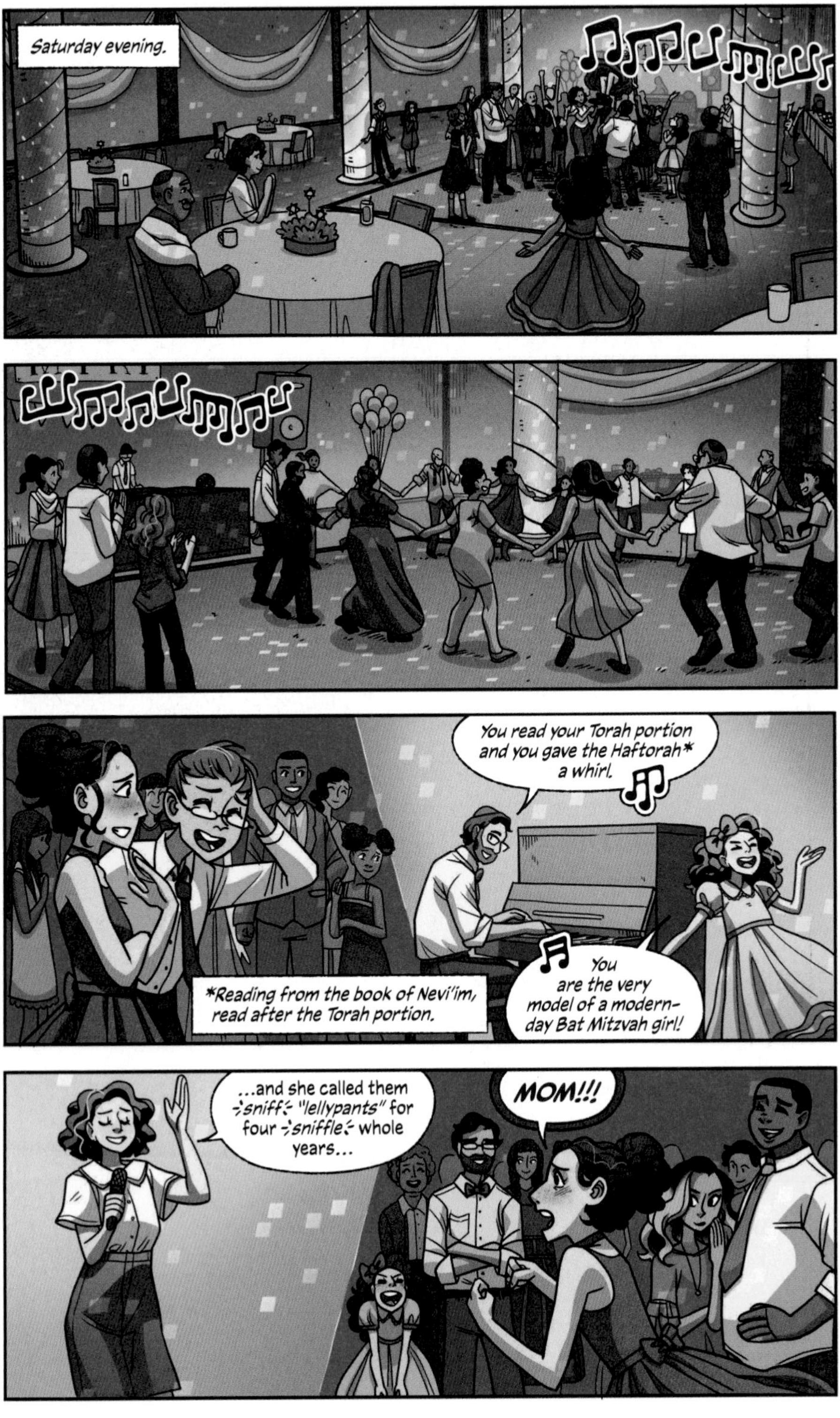

Saturday evening.
You read your Torah portion and you gave the Haftorah* a whirl.
You are the very model of a modern-day Bat Mitzvah girl!
*Reading from the book of Nevi'im, read after the Torah portion.
...and she called them -sniff- "lellypants" for four -sniffle- whole years...
MOM!!!

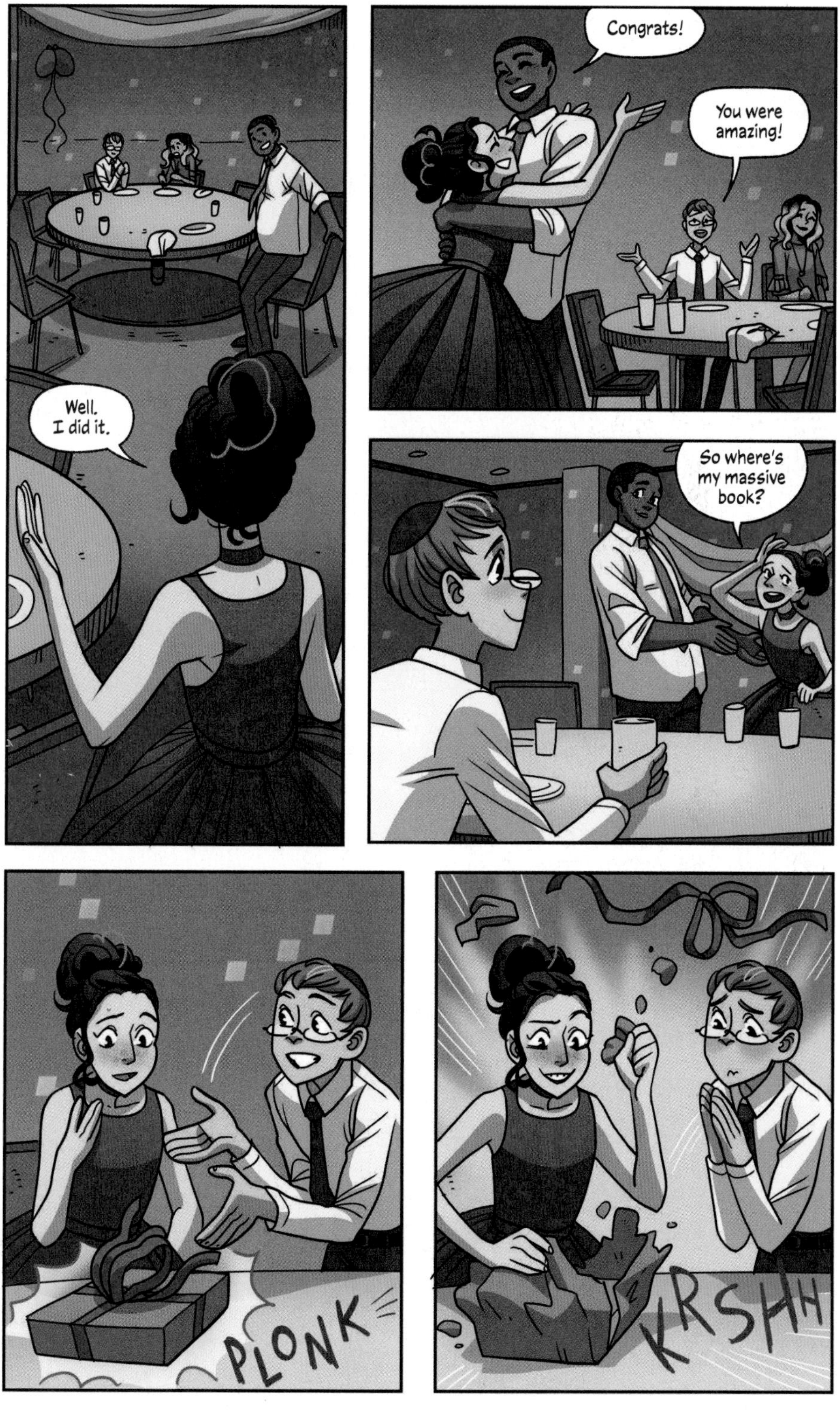

Well.
I did it.
Congrats!
You were amazing!
So where's my massive book?
PLONK
KRSHH

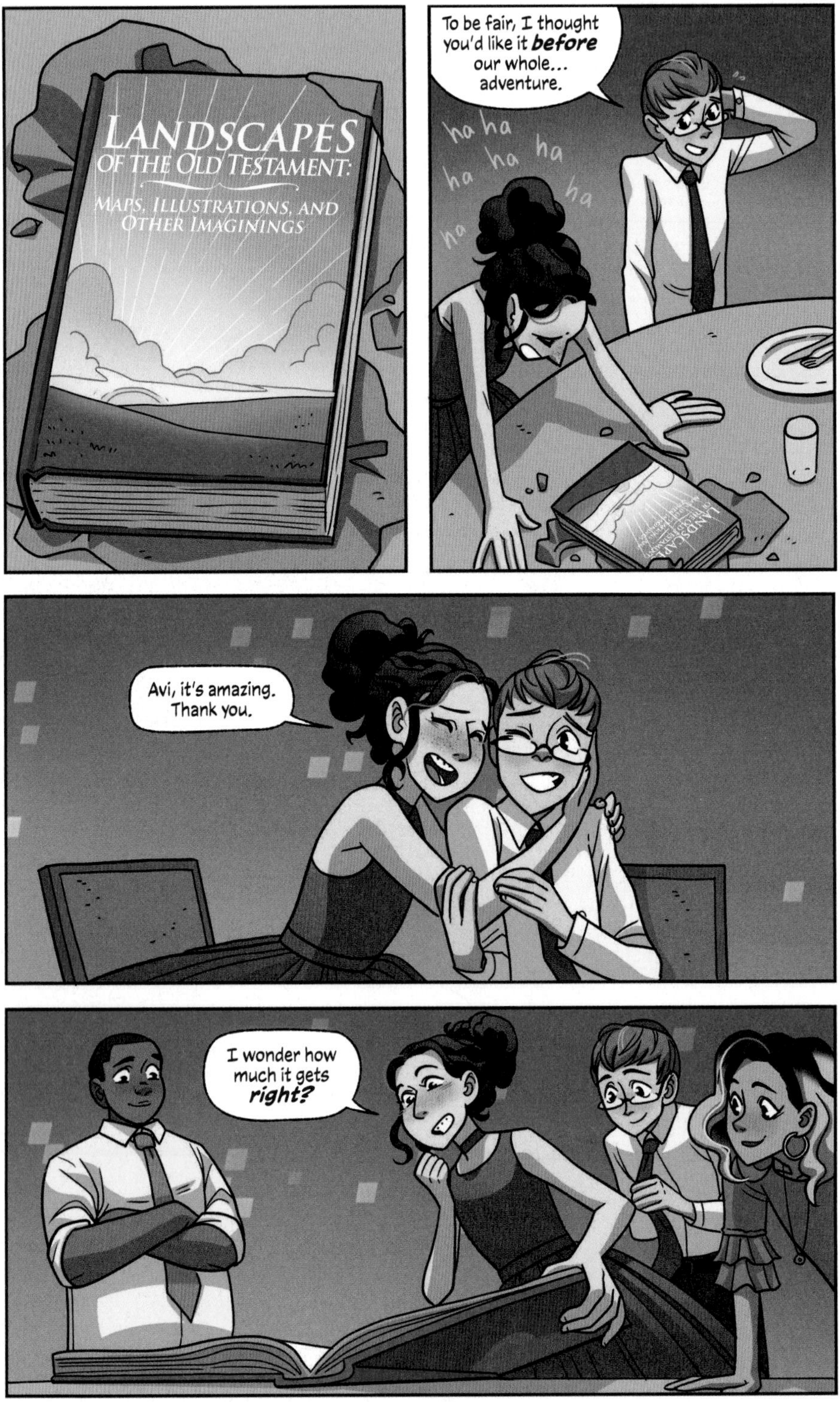
LANDSCAPES OF THE OLD TESTAMENT:
MAPS, ILLUSTRATIONS, AND OTHER IMAGININGS
To be fair, I thought you'd like it ***before*** our whole... adventure.
ha ha ha ha ha ha ha
Avi, it's amazing. Thank you.
I wonder how much it gets ***right?***

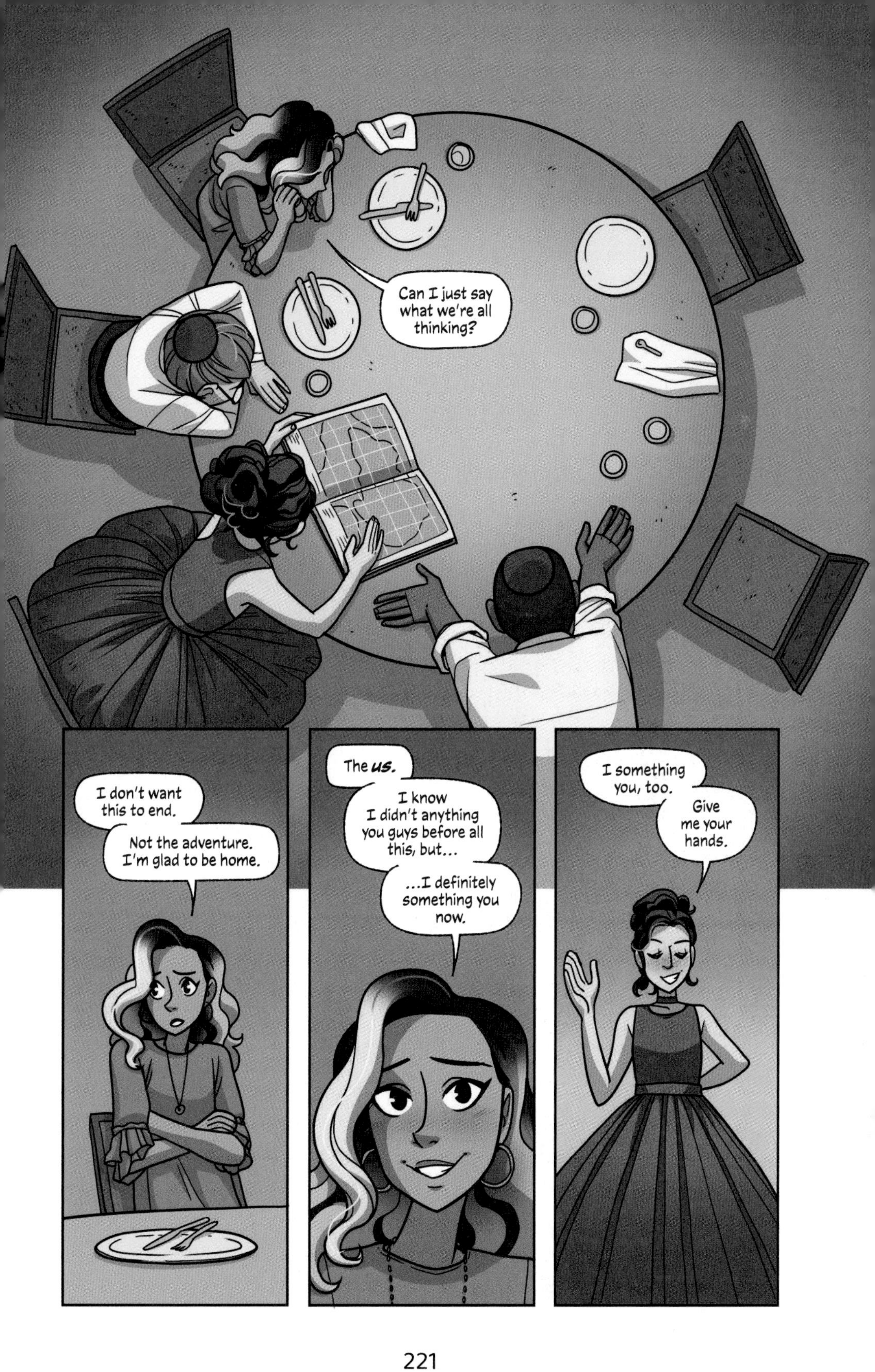
Can I just say what we're all thinking?
I don't want this to end.
Not the adventure. I'm glad to be home.
The *us.*
I know I didn't anything you guys before all this, but...
...I definitely something you now.
I something you, too.
Give me your hands.

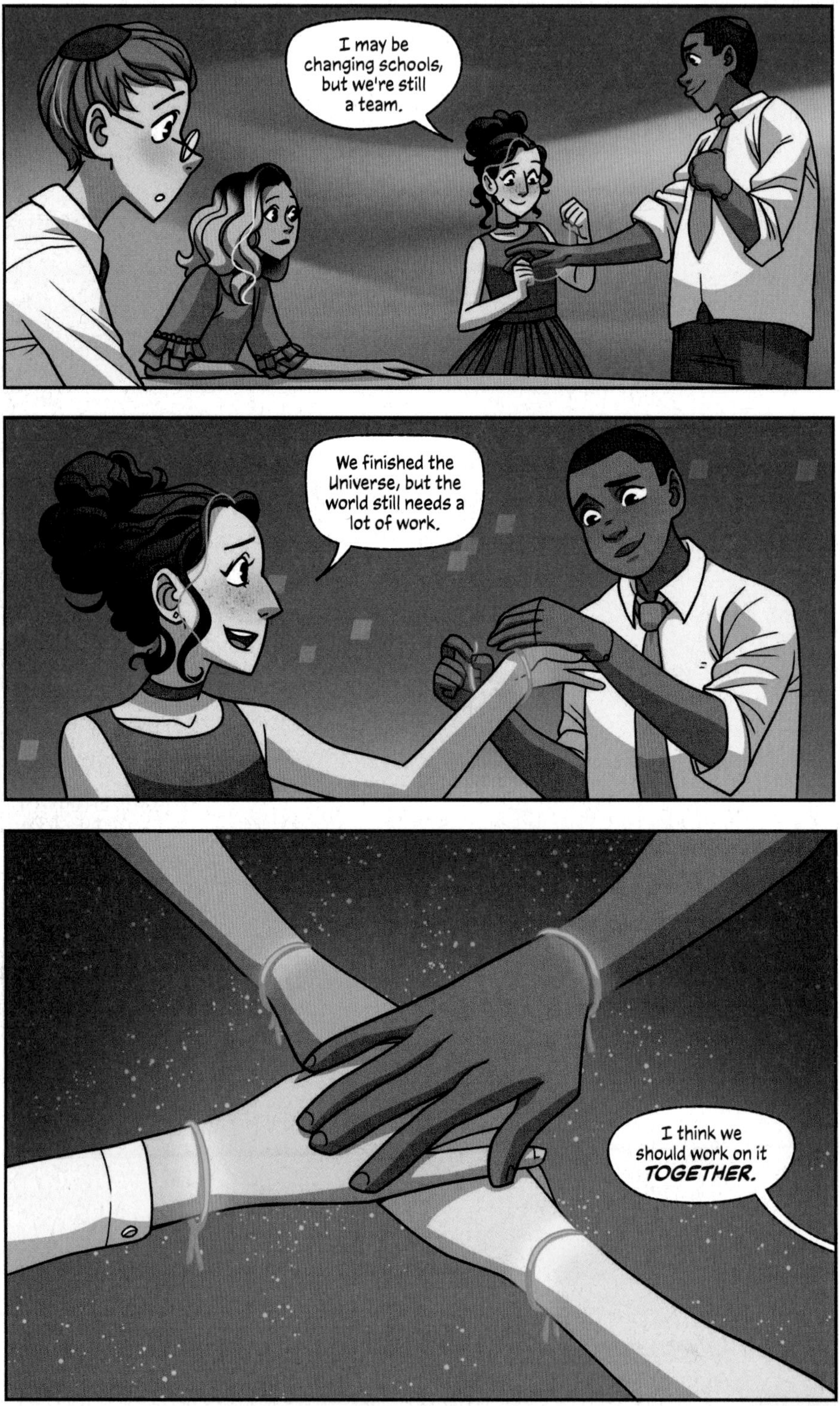
I may be changing schools, but we're still a team.
We finished the Universe, but the world still needs a lot of work.
I think we should work on it *TOGETHER.*

הסוף

Author Bios

Dani Colman is a writer and educator from London, England. She plays the violin, dabbles in standup comedy, and is absolutely terrible at videogames. When she isn't writing comic books and novels, she teaches aspiring writers how not to annoy their editors. She currently lives in San Francisco with her husband (creator of many comic books), and two cats (creators of many hairballs).

Rachel 'Tuna' Petrovicz is an illustrator and comicker hailing from Vancouver, Canada, with a lifelong goal of befriending all the cats she sees. She may not be able to hug EVERY cat, but she'll certainly try.

Whitney Cogar is a comic colorist and illustrator from Savannah, GA. She contributed colors to the two-time Eisner Award-winning *Giant Days* (BOOM! Studios), the *Steven Universe* comic series (BOOM! Studios), and Lucy Knisley's *Peapod Farm* series (Random House). She enjoys building punchy, rich enviroments in her work, and designing enamel pins.

Jim Campbell is a twice-Eisner-nominated letterer who lives and works in a small English market town that has a lovely pub at the end of his street. Mostly, he works from home and not in the pub. Mostly. As well as books from Wonderbound, his work can regularly be found in 2000AD, and in titles from Aftershock, BOOM!, Dark Horse, Image, Oni, Titan and Vault.

WONDERBOUND

YEAR ONE – 2021

Wonderbound publishes science fiction, fantasy, and spooky graphic novels for the young and the young at heart.

Grab a ticket to Wonder!

🐦 📘 📷 ▶️ @readwonderbound

WRASSLE CASTLE BOOK 1: LEARNING THE ROPES
Written by Paul Tobin & Colleen Coover
Illustrated by Galaad
Letters by Jeff Powell
Price: $9.99
ISBN: 978-1-638-490-098

In Stores: 9/21/2021

VERSE BOOK 1: THE BROKEN HALF
Written & Illustrated by Sam Beck
Price: $12.99
ISBN: 978-1-638-490-104

In Stores: 9/28/2021

SEPTEMBER

THE UNFINISHED CORNER
Written by Dani Colman
Illustrated by Rachel "Tuna" Petrovicz
Colors by Whitney Cogar
Letters by Jim Campbell
Price: $12.99
ISBN: 978-1-638-490-111

In Stores: 10/19/2021

HELLO, MY NAME IS POOP
Written by Ben Katzner
Illustrated by Ian McGinty
Colors by Fred C. Stresing
Letters by AndWorld Design
Price: $9.99
ISBN: 978-1-638-490-128

In Stores: 10/26/2021

OCTOBER